PASSION'S SURRENDER

Their lips were only inches apart. Kristina knew instinctively that Danton was going to kiss her. No sooner did that thought rush through her pretty head than his sensuous mouth met her lips. The sensation that contact stirred was like none Kristina had known.

Her head whirled giddily, and she clung to him. Her sweet surrender had a wild effect on Danton; he felt intoxicated by the flowery fragrance of her auburn hair.

When his lips finally released hers, he moaned in sweet agony, "Oh, Kristina—I shouldn't!"

Breathlessly she stopped him. "But I wanted you to, Danton."

Her beautiful eyes glazed with desire, she whispered against his cheek, "Please, kiss me . . . kiss me again, Danton."

Every fiber in his body was alive, wanting to love her endlessly. His hand moved to caress the tantalizing flesh pressing against his chest and she gave out a soft moan of pleasure.

Whoever she'd been, whatever she'd known before, could surely not have prepared her for this ecstasy. Danton's powerful essence was demanding to conquer and possess her, and she had no fear of being taken by this handsome man—for she wanted, more than anything in the world, to be his. . . .

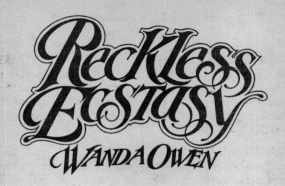

Reckless Ecstasy

WANDA OWEN

ZEBRA BOOKS
KENSINGTON PUBLISHING CORP.

ZEBRA BOOKS

are published by

Kensington Publishing Corp.
475 Park Avenue South
New York, NY 10016

First printing: May 1986

Printed in the United States of America

I dedicate this book to you, Steve Stephenson. My heartfelt thanks for the support you and your book store, Steve's Books, have so generously given to me since my first book was published.

Prologue

The fancy upholstered carriage drawn by feisty, prancing bays rolled down the street of El Paso. The elegance of the plush carriage and of the lady inside provided an impressive sight for the staring passers-by milling along the street. The hair of the woman within glowed like the flames of a fire, and her eyes were as brilliantly green as emeralds. There was an air of cool haughtiness about her. Indeed she held her head as highly and arrogantly as did the bays drawing her carriage. Only when she glanced over at the girl sitting beside her did she mellow with warm adoration. Whatever the busybodies and gossipmongers said about Florine Whelan, none could say she wasn't a good mother to her daughter, Kristina.

As for pretty little Kristina, she was too young and too sheltered to know that her mother was considered a brazen hussy and wanton woman because she was a lady gambler and the owner of the notorious Crystal Castle.

On the second floor of the spacious building housing the Crystal Castle, behind heavy, carved-oak doors, Kristina existed. A guard was posted outside during the evening hours to prevent any invasion of that sacred domain. Cara, a devoted governess, was

Kristina's constant companion while Florine was downstairs attending to her business. Few were allowed in this private haven, Florine's little castle. She had taken great pride in acquiring lavish furnishings to create the luxurious surroundings for her little "princess."

Florine Whelan had not enjoyed such comforts as a child. In fact, when she had been only four years older than Kristina was now, she had appeared on the El Paso scene. The town had just become the gambling center, so her first few years there had been spent as a dealer for another gaming establishment that had since gone out of business.

She was a bold, daring lady with great confidence in her skill at faro and monte. The famous Spanish gambler, Lolita, had taught her how to play monte back in San Antonio, and she had taught her quite well.

Some concluded Lady Luck was with her, but Florine declared that her expertise had won her the Crystal Castle. Whichever it was, she'd proved to be a successful business woman for her enterprise had prospered, while other gambling establishments had folded and sold out.

Gamblers from Natchez and New Orleans, from Dodge City and San Francisco, knew of the Crystal Castle and they had heard of its voluptuous proprietress, Florine Whelan. Yet the only person who knew anything of her past was her mulatto maid, Solitaire. Although there was much speculation Solitaire, who'd arrived in El Paso with Florine, had revealed nothing. The maid and the governess, Cara, were quartered on the second floor with their mistress and her daughter.

Kristina's infancy and childhood had gone so smoothly that Florine finally realized she'd been silly to worry about raising her daughter right there in the gambling hall. Swiftly, the years had passed, and being

8

a gambler, Florine Whelan could certainly boast that Lady Luck was riding on her gardenia-white shoulders. Life had been kind to her since Kristina's arrival.

Her lovely reflection in the mirror revealed no wrinkles, and having a baby had only enhanced her curvaceous figure. Her green eyes could still sparkle with excitement even though they'd seen the sordid side of life, and that tempting, tantalizing glint lured men to her like bees to honey. So the thirty-three-year-old lady gambler had no complaints, not until that all-knowing, prissy maid of hers had posed a problem she'd not taken notice of until Solitaire pointed it out.

It had been an innocent comment the maid had made when she'd been styling Florine's flaming red hair.

"Lord, couldn't believe my eyes yesterday, *mam'selle!* Like it happened overnight!" Solitaire had declared. "The child's just blossoming out."

Florine's fine-arched brow had raised, questioning her maid. "You aren't saying what I think you're saying, are you, Solitaire?"

"That's what I'm sayin', *mam'selle.*" The mulatto's dark eyes gleamed, and she nodded her head, a smug look on her face.

The spark Solitaire had lit was fanned to flame the following evening when Florine's current paramour was a dinner guest in her lavish quarters before going downstairs to join his cohorts in a game of cards.

Jason Hamilton and Florine had been friends a long time. He had been her business adviser and counsel, as well as her banker, and only recently had they become lovers. Jason was one of the few men Florine trusted, but not completely. She would never allow herself that costly luxury again.

Like a young, long-legged colt, Kristina had bounced into the room, unaware that her mother was entertaining. To the eyes of the forty-five-year-old banker, she presented a breathtaking vision, with the

9

silk robe clinging to her youthful curving body. Her hips were firm and rounded, her waistline so tiny his two hands could have encircled it, and her blossoming breasts thrust against the thin robe. Her gorgeous mass of dark, glossy auburn hair framed the loveliness of her delicately featured face, then flowed over her shoulders and extended halfway down her back. Her eyes, so like Florine's, yet enhanced by a thick outline of dark lashes, flashed like green fire when she stopped short in wide-eyed surprise at seeing Jason sitting beside her mother.

"Oh, hello Mister Hamilton! I . . . I didn't know you had company, Mother," she apologized, retreating meanwhile from the room.

An amused smile appeared on Jason's face as Florine gave a soft laugh and assured her startled daughter that she was not intruding. Kristina quickly picked up the book she'd sought and rushed back into her room, giving them a sweet, hasty smile before shutting her door. But noting Jason's expression Florine realized she'd been blind to Kristina's burgeoning womanhood. His comment further disturbed her.

"Dear God, Flo, what a beauty she's suddenly become!" Jason exclaimed.

"Yes . . . yes, she is," Florine drawled slowly. The words seemed to stick in her throat. Florine knew men well enough to be aware that Jason, devoted as he was, had been affected by the desirable vision that had invaded their privacy, and she could well imagine how the young, randy stallions, driven by desire, would seek to have their way with Kristina.

Ah yes, Florine Whelan mused, she had some thinking to do. She was not fool enough to think she could keep her daughter a prisoner within the walls of these lavish quarters. Kristina was just maturing sooner than Florine had anticipated.

10

On the days that followed Jason's visit to her rooms, Florine spent more hours with Kristina, and her observant eyes detected many things she'd overlooked. She left the business of the gambling hall in the capable hands of Sid Layman, one of her dealers.

And so it was that on this hot, sultry day in El Paso she was spending the entire afternoon in the company of her daughter. The pair had just left Florine's dressmaker, Señora Lopez. The visit to the shop was a special occasion for Kristina, for she had been measured for a fancy gown, a very grown-up one, that would be made for her approaching birthday.

She'd liked being fawned over by the dressmaker, who'd kept raving about her beautiful hair and pretty face, while her mother's smile, so obviously approving, had confirmed the *señora*'s appraisal. Kristina felt exalted, as if she were soaring high in the sky.

The miserable steamy heat, created by a torrid sun beating down on streets soaked by rains the previous day, did not wilt her spirit although it seemed to bother her mother, who moved her fan vigorously to ease her discomfort.

It was a special treat for Kristina when they stopped at the mercantile store to purchase several yards of ribbon for her mother also bought her a lovely wide-brimmed Leghorn hat. "You are of an age now, Kristina my pet, when you'll need to wear this when you and Cara go for your rides." Florine smiled at her pretty daughter, surveying her complexion, darker than her own. The girl had her father's coloring, and the blending of his black hair with Florine's flaming auburn had produced Kristina's deeper, richer auburn shade.

Kristina was too overjoyed to notice, but Florine did observe the smirking looks of two ladies in the store. The pair twittered, one to the other, about Florine and her daughter. Knowledge of the harm and the pain such people could cause Kristina stabbed Florine.

11

Dear God, she didn't know whether she could stand to send her daughter to some boarding school! But what else could she do—move to another place and take employment? As what? she asked herself. She knew only gambling, and although she had managed to amass a fair amount of money, it was hardly enough to last a lifetime.

She could become Mrs. Jason Hamilton but how long would that last? Florine knew Jason was sincere, but she did not think their marriage could endure the pressures brought to bear by his prudish, conventional friends. They lived in two separate worlds most of the time . . . she and Jason Hamilton, and Florine cared too much for him to allow his heart to cloud his judgment. As for her, God knows, she'd labored too hard and too long on El Paso's gambling scene to throw away what she'd built. No one had to tell Flo that the years were adding up on her!

Kristina, excitedly chattering away, had no idea of the disconcerting thoughts tormenting her mother. She was unaware that the dominating concern in Florine Whelan's life was ensuring that she might have a wonderful life.

When the carriage came to a halt and the black driver, Rollo, opened the door and helped the pair alight, Florine forced a smile as she turned toward her giggling, carefree daughter. At that moment stark reality hit her: money couldn't buy some things for Kristina and that impetuous miss would soon be wanting to explore what lay beyond those heavy oak-carved doors. Her childhood days were gone forever!

The sparkling-eyed Kristina was even more aware of that than her auburn-haired mother. Had Florine been able to know what her daughter was plotting, she would have been more disturbed than she was, for Kristina had decided she would wait no longer to see the magical, exciting world below her, in the Crystal Castle.

12

Part I

The Flame

Chapter 1

There would never be another night like this one, Kristina knew it as she sat surrounded by gifts, her friends looking on. Florine was exquisite in a gown of emerald-green satin, an emerald pendant at her throat and a bracelet set with emeralds on her wrist. Solitaire and Cara looked on as their little princess opened her gifts. Uncle Sid, Kristina's name for Sid Layman, was there, puffing on his long cheroot, and Jason Hamilton sat beside Florine. Kristina had insisted that her friend, Rollo, be present and her mother could not refuse her request. These people were Kristina Whelan's only friends. She was now fifteen, but she was more naïve than most girls that age.

The occasion was festive, and the laughter resounding within the walls of Florine's living quarters that evening rivaled the more boisterous sounds emanating from the gaming rooms. When the gifts had been opened and a fruity punch and a generously iced chocolate cake had been enjoyed by Kristina's guests, Rollo politely excused himself.

With a broad grin on his black face and bowing low to her as though she was, indeed, a princess, he expressed his gratitude at being included in the event.

15

"You're my friend, Rollo—one of my very best," she declared quite sincerely.

Rollo's gift had been a tiny rosette of velvet flowers for her hair. Uncle Sid had brought her a basket filled with colorful ribbons and had told her, "Thought you might use the ribbons for your hair, and the basket will serve to hold all those pretty wildflowers you pick when you and Cara go for your rides out in the country, honey."

A dainty little fan with lace edging was Cara's present, lace-trimmed handkerchiefs were Solitaire's. An imported music box of teakwood inlaid with mother-of-pearl was the gift Jason Hamilton chose for the young miss, and Florine, having decided it was time her daughter had a nice piece of jewelry, had given Kristina a ring in which a pale green peridot was set, a small diamond on either side of it.

It was certainly an exciting night for Kristina—a special night! She kept holding her dainty hand out to admire her new ring, marveling at how well it matched her new, green silk gown. The peridot was the same color. Then she played the coquette, flipping her fan out, her eyes gleaming teasingly. Noticing, Solitaire thought to herself that the taunting look would have an effect on any man she was around. The mistress was not going to be the only breath-taking beauty in Crystal Castle.

At eleven when the party ended, only Florine and Jason were left. Jason was more than ready to go downstairs to the private alcove he and Florine reserved for their own. He was eager to sip the champagne he'd ordered earlier. Fruit punch was not really satisfying at this time of the evening.

Florine bid her daughter good night, again wishing her happy birthday before leaving with Jason. Kristina was still flushed with excitement, but it was Florine's

16

gardenia-white face that turned a rosy shade when her daughter innocently inquired, "Now that I'm fifteen, Mother, how much older do I have to be to go downstairs?"

Florine delayed her response a moment, seeking to regain her composure. She realized she'd been naïve to think her daughter hadn't known what went on downstairs. With a forced smile on her face, she replied, "We'll see, darling. We'll talk about it soon."

But Kristina was feeling a new independence. Why, none of her friends had given her a toy this year, she'd noticed proudly! Her gifts were a grown-up's gifts and this pleased her immensely.

She prodded. "Tomorrow, maybe?"

Florine merely nodded her head and then hurried on out the door with Jason. Her jeweled fingers clasped Jason's firm arm, and for the first time in her life Florine was indignant because her daughter had dared to put her on the spot. As she walked quietly down the hallway, her high heels sinking down into the thick carpet, she realized that on this evening she and Kristina had entered a new cycle.

Jason sensed her tenseness, and he could not resist pressing her. Being a shrewd businessman, he knew she was more vulnerable at that moment. Bending his head close to hers, he murmured softly, "I could help you more than you realize, Flo, my darling. You've got a lot ahead of you in the next few years. I yearn so to share it with you . . . if you'd let me."

Her green eyes looked up at him, glowing with a warmth that made Jason swell with hope. "Oh, God, Jason . . . I guess I've allowed myself to dwell in a fool's paradise, thinking that Kristina was just a little girl. I have been a fool, haven't I?"

"You're no fool, Flo Whelan! You're a beautiful woman who has been working very hard at being both

17

mother and father to Kristina, and at running a business. Few could have managed both so well, my darling. Why do you think so many men admire you so, eh?" He flashed her a warm smile. Florine stood still, absorbing the handsome dignity of Jason Hamilton, pondering why she'd hesitated so long before she'd allowed him to become her lover.

"Thank you, Jason. I don't know what I'd do without you." She sighed, squeezing his arm tighter.

"That, my darling, pleases me more than you know. Come on . . . let's toast our future together!"

Florine didn't discourage Jason's hopes. She wanted to relax and she, too, needed a champagne.

Solitaire, having observed the scene created by Kristina, knew it had disturbed her mistress. She'd like to wallop that young miss! But she had seen the stubborn determination in that Tina's green eyes, like her mama's. No fence was going to hold the girl in now!

Kristina was a smart one, but then Solitaire had always known that. Now, she knew what had been going on in Miss Tina's head when she'd looked out the window in the evening, observing the carriages and the patrons of the Crystal Castle come and go. That minx of a miss had come to some conclusions.

Solitaire watched Kristina, who sat on her bed, carefully examining the bounty of her birthday. Solitaire didn't have to be told how delighted the girl was with the beautiful ring her mother had given her, nor with the music box which played a pretty ballad over and over again. Kristina swayed her body in tempo to the music. Without realizing it, Solitaire found she was doing the same.

Kristina turned to see Solitaire swaying to the beat of the music, and she jumped off the bed to clasp the maid's hands in hers. "Come on, Solitaire. We'll dance like they do downstairs!" Kristina's body moved in graceful motion along with the mulatto's. As they whirled, Kristina's radiant face looked up, and she asked curiously, "How'd you get the name Solitaire?"

"Mercy, you a nosey one this night! One year older sure done a spell on you!"

"Seriously, Solitaire! Did your mother name you that?"

"No, Miss Tina . . . your mother. She say it's perfect for me cause I like to play the game so much."

"You two have been together a long time, haven't you?"

"A very long time, Miss Tina," Solitaire remarked as she gave Kristina a wide swing. Kristina gaily laughed, enjoying herself immensely, but something she spied as she whirled past the window made her halt abruptly. She stood, staring down into the street below like one entranced, as Solitaire, curious, moved to see what held the girl's attention.

A handsome young man was sauntering down the street. His tailored black outfit was perfectly molded to his broad-shouldered, well muscled body. Solitaire released a sigh of admiration. His wavy, jet-black mane of hair vividly reminded Solitaire of the handsome devil who was Kristina's father. Of course this young gent was much younger than Kristina's father had been when he was at the Crystal Castle, when Florine Whelan had loved him.

"Isn't he absolutely gorgeous, Solitaire? Look how proudly he walks, as if he owns the world," Kristina declared.

"Maybe he thinks he does, Miss Tina," Solitaire remarked, thinking of the years gone by, of another man and another time.

As Kristina stood at the window, the sheer curtains pushed aside, she swore to Solitaire that the young man glanced up and smiled. "Oh, child . . . I doubt that," Solitaire muttered.

"Well, he did! I guess I know what I saw," Kristina responded. She tossed her dark auburn hair to the side and shrugged her dainty shoulders as she turned away from the window. "I'm not a child anymore, Solitaire, and you might just as well get used to the idea."

"Guess I might as well," Solitaire answered. As she turned to leave the room, however, she thought that it was really Mlle. Whelan who was going to have to be convinced of that. Solitaire wondered how she and Cara could stop this impetuous miss should she decide to go through those double doors and descend the stairs that led to the Crystal Castle.

Solitaire's private musings and concerns were warranted, for if the mulatto maid had been able to read her little Tina's mind, she'd have remained with the girl longer to see that she did go to bed. Excited, Kristina was not about to retire. Tonight she was determined to see that magical place below!

A strange spell which she could not understand seemed to have been cast on Kristina that night. She knew that everything had changed for her, as if a fairy godmother had swept a magic wand over her head transforming her from a sweet, docile child into a curious young lady who was capriciously eager to explore everything.

So it was that a half-hour after Solitaire had made her exit, Kristina sat with her fancy gown still on. She had removed only her pretty satin slippers, and she had tucked her feet under her as she sat staring out the window. People were still milling about on the street. How elegant some of them looked!

She was thoughtful and quiet, but she was shrewdly calculating her next move. Before she ventured out those double doors, she wanted to be absolutely certain that Cara was deep in sleep and Solitaire was settled in down the hall. She was certain that old Isaac would be napping off and on.

On her pert face appeared a look of cocky smugness. She was going to outsmart all of them. Did they think she didn't remember how they'd spoken of the past time and time again? She knew that Solitaire had been only sixteen, and her mother barely eighteen, when they'd come to El Paso. Well, that wasn't much older than she was this night, Kristina reasoned, resenting her guarded existence. She was no longer going to be confined.

Why was she not free to go through those double doors just as her mother and Jason had done? That she was not allowed to do so seemed ridiculous to Kristina. For more than two years now, she'd known what went on downstairs. She'd heard the music and the laughter, and she knew about the gambling. She wanted to see the exciting world below!

On more than one occasion, she'd quickly retreated from the living room upon discovering her beautiful mother in Jason Hamilton's embrace. The couple had no inkling that she'd observed them indulging their passions, but their intimacy had whetted Kristina's girlish curiosity. It must be a pleasurable experience, Kristina now thought, remembering the looks on their faces.

She suddenly recalled the strange, exhilarating effect the good-looking young man had elicited a short time ago. In her innocence, she could only imagine what these unknown feelings of lovers were like.

Patience was not one of Kristina's strong points, so, leaving her slippers there on the floor, she soon rose from the chair, hoisting her flowing skirt and petticoats so the rustling materials would not make a noise as she scurried out of her bedroom and through the parlor.

Every fiber in her young body sparked with excitement!

For only a second, she stood at the carved double doors before proceeding to cross the threshold and go beyond the boundary of a lifetime. For one fleeting moment, she felt a strange qualm about her own recklessness. Kristina had never questioned the devoted love of her mother, but what she was about to do would result in a harsh reprimand. She was defying Florine.

But there was no turning back now, she realized solemnly. She was driven forward by insatiable curiosity. It had been gnawing at her for months, urging her to see her mother's world, the world she'd been forbidden to enter.

When she did slip through the doors and step quietly into the carpeted hallway, she was amazed at how simple and easy it was to do. As she'd hoped, old Isaac sat in his chair, snoring away. Sounds of laughter and conversation wafted up the stairway as she made her way noiselessly past Isaac and headed for a turning in the hallway that would shield her from the old man's sight while giving her a perfect view of the ground floor.

When she reached her destination, a delighted smile lit her face. She leaned over the railing to get a better view. Already her right foot was beating out the rhythm of the lively music being played below. Soon her shoulders and body swayed to the tempo as her eyes danced over the moving crowd of people below. Such a glorious array of brilliantly colored gowns! And the ladies were accompanied by finely attired gentlemen of all ages. How gay they all seemed!

She strained to find a brilliant emerald green in the sea of blues, pinks, and purples below, but she could not see her mother's bright gown, nor could she see Jason.

She covered her mouth hastily when she noticed a heavyset man playfully pat the rear of a woman in a scarlet gown trimmed in black lace. Kristina stared as the woman teasingly reprimanded him, noting that he merely snaked his arm around her waist, pulling her closer and planting a kiss on her rosy lips.

It was obvious to Kristina that the lady was enjoying his embrace for she lingered willingly in his arms.

So, this is the grown-up world, she mused. This strange, opulent world would be hers before long. Suddenly, a cloud of gloom washed over her and she peered down to survey the front of her bodice. She did not fill out the front of her gown like the pretty ladies below. She had no rounded mounds of flesh to expose by wearing a low-cut style. Dejectedly, she slumped to the floor, crushing her petticoats. She heaved a desolate sigh, thinking to herself that it might be years before she really blossomed.

Her preoccupation with her feminine inadequacy was disrupted by the gust of light-hearted laughter that rose from below, and she saw a beautiful, blonde young woman being held in the arms of the handsome man she'd spotted earlier on the street. Envying the golden-haired lovely, Kristina told herself that she was almost as old as that woman.

She watched with interest as the man's tanned hand played on the woman's back, observing that the blonde responded with a lazy wiggle and then voiced a weak protest. It was clear to Kristina that the woman was not really trying to remove herself from his arms so why was she acting that way? Why the pretense?

Suddenly, Kristina realized that the young man's eyes were no longer on the golden-haired miss, but were staring upward at her although he still held the young woman. When he smiled and winked at her, Kristina thought she would surely faint. She pushed herself back away from the railing, wanting to hide from the sight of those wicked, dark eyes that made her tingle from head to toe.

Dear Lord, she'd never known a mere look could cause such a quiver in the pit of one's stomach!

In Kristina's cloistered existence she'd not been exposed to young girls' chatter about boys. For all of Florine Whelan's determined effort to give her daughter a protected existence, she'd overlooked the simple things denied Kristina. Her daughter had never had a playmate, never had friends of her own age.

Nonetheless, when Kristina quietly and thoughtfully slipped back down the hallway to where old Isaac sat napping, she knew instinctively that she was now not thinking a child's thoughts. The unfamiliar elation aroused in her by the handsome man downstairs was making her heart pound erratically. She breathed in deeply, as if she might faint, and she wished she were the one his lips had kissed.

As she was about to go through the doors, a shrill voice stopped her. "Where you been, Miss Tina?" Solitaire stood there looking like a thunderhead.

Kristina whirled around, her green eyes flashing brightly and her long lashes fluttering. Resentment flared in her and in an impertinent voice, she snapped, "Watching the crowd below!"

"Oh, you were, were you?" Solitaire smirked, not caring whether her inquiry sat well with the spunky young lady or not. Her hands were clasped firmly at her waist as she continued to glare at the fuming little beauty.

"I did! In fact that good-looking young man I saw from the window winked at me." As if she hoped to shock Solitaire, she haughtily added, "Yes, I think he's the man I'll marry someday."

Solitaire's dark doelike eyes gleamed with amusement. Mockingly, she mumbled casually, "That's nice,

Miss Tina."

"Well, I will, Solitaire. I'll show you!" Kristina sensed the doubt in the mulatto's tone.

A warm smile lit Solitaire's face and she drawled, "You just probably will, *mademoiselle*. Well, sweet dreams *ma petite*."

Disgruntled, Kristina said good night and then marched through the door. As Solitaire sauntered back down the hall, she sighed under her breath. Those silver-tongued gents were going to whisper sweet talk in little Tina's ears just like they had with her mama.

Dream on, sweet Tina. Dream your dreams like we all do, Solitaire thought to herself.

Chapter 2

The music, the laughter, and the silly blonde hanging on Danton Navarro's arm aggravated his irascible state of mind. He had been irritated when he'd arrived in El Paso, and weary from the hours of traveling. More to the point, he was tired of rescuing his twin brother, Damien. There was a limit as to how far he would go, even for his mother's sake, Danton reflected.

This frivolous little blonde had called him Damien so he knew he was on the right track. Damien had been there long enough to get himself known. But then it never took too long for Damien to make himself known, usually by the wrong people. Danton had to admit that this gambling establishment was the classiest one he'd been in. Still, he could not understand the presence of the sweet-faced young girl who'd peered over the staircase railing, not in a place like this.

She didn't belong in the Crystal Castle, he knew that! Danton recognized innocence when it stared him in the face. He figured she had yet to receive her first real kiss, for he knew that his teasing wink frightened her.

Perhaps, he should not have been so bold, but he had been unable to resist winking and smiling at the delightful young girl. Something about her wide-eyed, curious little face reminded him of his younger sister. Delores was shy too.

Danton Navarro would have found it preposterous, but amusing, had he heard the green-eyed minx predicting his future. Long ago, he had sworn to allow no woman to hogtie him or to distract him from his goals. He'd vowed to remain a bachelor until his thirtieth birthday, at least. Marriage was not in the cards for him yet.

The Navarro name and the family's vast wealth made it difficult to remain a bachelor. Danton realized that. On the other hand, his twin brother, Damien, recklessly exploited the situation. He loved to have women fawning over him.

Damien had always been the happy-go-lucky, friendly Navarro twin, Danton the aloof and reserved one.

Their temperaments were as different as day and night but their dark handsomeness was almost identical. Only the faded scar on Danton's face distinguised him from Damien. The years had made the scar less obvious, but Danton's memory of how he got it remained fresh.

As far as Danton was concerned, the notion that twins were sensitive to the other's thoughts was a fallacy. All his life he'd never been able to figure Damien out. Had he been able to do so, he would have been on guard long ago when Damien had lashed out at him with a knife. They had been boys. How could he have suspected Damien's ire when his brother had been smiling? But then, was not that charming smile of Damien's full of the devil's trickery?

When Danton left the Crystal Castle, he sauntered toward his hotel, satisfied that Damien would not appear at the gambling establishment that night. But the blonde named Trixie was not the only one who'd assumed he was Damien. Danton was certain the gorgeous redhead with the fiery green eyes was the notorious Mademoiselle Whelan he'd heard so much about.

Their eyes had locked for one fleeting second and Danton could not help pondering what would have happened had he stayed longer or chosen to sit down at one of the gaming tables. An arrogant part of him yearned to challenge the lady's skill. Danton's cool, calculating nature was an asset when he chose to sit at a gaming table, and although other pursuits occupied his time, he was a superb player of three-card monte or faro. His mother, Señora Lucía Navarro, had taught him to play, as astonishing as that might seem to most people.

Danton had been correct when he'd perceived that Florine Whelan was seething over his presence at the Crystal Castle. Indeed, she'd forbidden him—forbidden Damien, who she thought he was—to ever enter her establishment again.

Jason nervously observed Florine's temper rise to the boiling point. She was not heeding admonitions to calm down.

"I don't give a holy damn who he is or who his family is. They can own all of Texas, but this is my territory. I'm the boss!"

It was unusual for anyone to be evicted from the gambling house; Florine Whelan ran her business too well. In the spacious room with the roulette table, two monte tables, and three faro tables, there were the expensive glass chandeliers, a long mahogany bar, and cut-glass mirrors. No chair swinging or bottle throwing was permitted at Florine's place.

Jason, too, thought Danton was Damien, and he was glad that no encounter took place before the man took his leave. He quickly poured two glasses of champagne and then smiled broadly. "Now, darling, let's turn our thoughts to more pleasant things."

Florine managed a strained smile but her temper would not calm down quickly.

Jason sought to caution her. "Florine, don't rile that young Latin too much. I've heard some things about Damien Navarro—he's got a vicious streak in him. You don't need that!"

"No, I don't need it, Jason, but I won't tuck my tail and run just because of the Navarro name. A Navarro can be scum too, Jason."

Jason broke into a gale of laughter, knowing that she meant the upper classes have sullied members too.

"Believe me, Flo, I know. I rub elbows with them daily. I just don't want you to get hurt. Please, watch your step where young Navarro is concerned. He's not going to take what you did last night lightly. That is why he came back tonight to taunt you. You must know he resented it when you ordered him out of your place last night in front of his companions."

"Well, I should hope so. That's why I couldn't believe his audacity in showing up here this evening," Florine declared angrily.

"That's exactly the point, Flo. He did dare to come back here tonight. Don't you see?" The suave, dignified banker had spent half his life dealing with men from all walks of life—shrewd politicians up in Austin or the rugged ranchers from Dallas or Fort Worth. He felt he knew men. He'd seen the gamblers who flowed into Florine's gambling hall. They possessed varied personalities, but Damien Navarro was the troublesome sort. Jason had sensed that immediately.

Florine patted Jason's hand, for she noticed the lines of concern on his fine-chiseled face. "I see, Jason, I'll play him cool—I promise."

Despite the sophistication she'd acquired from her years in the gamblers' world, Florine could not know that the odds were already stacked against her, that the name Navarro would haunt her in the future. But few people did realize Damien Navarro's capacity to hate. Perhaps, the only person who could thoroughly appraise it was his twin, Danton. Most of his life he'd been aware of the volatile nature of his brother.

A short distance away from the Crystal Castle where the music still blared and the laughter continued to ring out, Danton Navarro had submitted to the weariness of his body and had retired for the night.

He'd had a glass of brandy, putting any thoughts of Damien aside, then he'd undressed. To hell with him and his shenanigans, Danton had told himself. There were other places he could have checked, but by the time he'd left the Crystal Castle it had dawned on him that this whole damned journey was a foolhardy waste of time. Because of it, he'd missed the cattlemen's convention in Dallas. He was always giving up something to track down his brother. Hell, with Damien, it was always some new escapade.

The truth was, Damien could be in Dallas right now or over in Fort Worth at one of his favorite haunts, maybe the White Elephant Saloon where they gambled upstairs. Danton had found him there once before. That time it had taken a man's life to save his brother! Danton Navarro felt no satisfaction from admitting he'd killed a man for his brother. He could not honestly say he'd been justified. The law had said so, though.

What he did for Damien wasn't, it never had been for him, but for the lady he adored more than anyone in the world—his mother. But despite the lovely Señora Lucía Navarro, Danton decided, his own life could no longer be ruled by Damien's whims. Nor would another man be killed because of Damien. A strange transformation had just come over Danton Navarro.

*　　　*　　　*

As Kristina's pretty head lay on her pillow, all sorts of romantic notions paraded through her thoughts. In those brief moments during which her eyes had met his, Kristina had memorized every single feature of his dark handsome face.

She didn't even know his name, but one day she would. Oh yes, she'd know him and she'd know what it was like to feel his long, slender fingers caress her as they'd caressed the golden-haired woman.

She shut her long-lashed eyes and released a soft sighing moan as her imagination soared. At that moment his sensuous mouth, his roaming hands, and his magnificent male body were hers in the private solitude of her room.

Chapter 3

The hot, sultry days of summer were no more torrid than the heated arguments Florine Whelan had with her daughter. As they persisted, a perplexing feeling of frustration engulfed the usually cheerful Florine, while Solitaire found herself in the middle of the fusses.

The maid found herself in Tina's corner part of the time for she knew the girl was struggling with growing pains and she realized that Kristina had been over-protected by Mlle. Whelan. Lord knows, Solitaire had shielded the child herself. Yet she also sympathized with Florine. For the first time Solitaire noted hints of aging on her beautiful mistress' fair face, especially after Florine had gone through a disturbing scene with her daughter.

On such occasions the determined redhead would scream, "Dear God, I didn't bargain for this, Solitaire! How dare she throw such things up to me!" Hurt and pain showed on her face.

"She wants to get her way, *mam'selle*. She's no baby anymore." Solitaire would say to soothe the mistress.

"I know that, but I can't let her roam around here like Sally or the rest. Does she hate me, Solitaire for the way I earn our living? Do you think she looks down her nose at me after I've worked so hard to give her all this?"

Although Solitaire's heart ached, she would quickly assure Florine that such was not the case. "She's just feeling her oats, *mam'selle*. That's all it is. It will pass."

"God, I wonder! Remember how we clawed and scratched our way clear across the country, Solitaire. Remember the things we put up with along the way? Oh, I don't know, Solitaire, perhaps . . . perhaps, I should just marry Jason and let the chips fall where they may."

"It's a thought, *mam'selle*. It's a thought!" Solitaire could certainly see a multitude of advantages for her mistress in such a marriage. After all, she was thirty-three, and beautiful as she was, there would come a time when she could not go on like this. In the whole country there were only a few lady gamblers in Mlle. Whelan's class. Marrying Jason Hamilton was about the only way Florine Whelan would be accepted by society, the only way she might achieve respectability.

"You going to take Miss Tina and go to Mister Hamilton's barbecue, *mam'selle?*"

"I'm thinking about it, Solitaire," Florine replied.

Solitaire's big dark eyes met her mistress' glance boldly as she offered her opinion. "Think it could be a wise idea. Might just let the little miss blow off some of that steam boiling in her."

Florine gave her maid a weak smile. "Yes, Solitaire. You and I know about the steam that can boil, don't we?"

Solitaire giggled impishly, "Yes, *mam'selle*. Only thing is I haven't reached my boiling points lately. My kettle has had lukewarm water for a long time."

Her comments brought a gale of laughter from Florine Whelan, and she embraced Solitaire, sighing, "Oh, Solitaire, what would I have done without you all these years? Dear God, haven't we done it all?"

"Yes, *mam'selle*. But it's me that sure needed you. I've never forgot what you did for this poor nigger girl." Solitaire did not try to stop the tears that crept down her cheeks. She loved her mistress with all her heart.

Florine broke their embrace to look at Solitaire. "You were a girl, Solitaire, and I was a girl, only a few years older. That's all. I had as much need as you, and with our strength and determination we survived. Most young girls couldn't do what we did," Florine declared. "Always look at yourself with pride, for you have the right."

"Yes, Mlle. Whelan. I do, and I thank you for that too." With a lighter air, the mulatto grinned. "Always said that riding all those railroad cars when we made the circuit caused these hips of mine to get this broad."

"Well, we took them, didn't we? My winnings from all those traveling gamblers provided us with the money to get us here. Lord, we went all the way—Silver City, Dodge City, Kansas City, Tascosa, Santa Fe, and good old Tucson." The two women sat, smiling and remembering the past that only they shared. It was their own private interlude; it always would be.

"Reckon that Miss Tina will ever have the wild, crazy fun we had?" Solitaire asked.

"Who can say, Solitaire?" Florine silently prayed her daughter wouldn't have the heartaches she'd known, but thinking of the young girl's loveliness, she was uneasy. In another year or two, she knew that Kristina's beauty would become all the more breathtaking. Kristina's nature, Florine knew, was a combination of her father's impulsive recklessness and her mother's bold determination. That was a treacherous mixture for a pretty young lady.

Solitaire had her own qualms. She knew Florine was unaware that Kristina was now expert at the art of sweet persuasion. Florine had no idea that her daughter had cleverly concealed from her the occasions when she'd slipped down the steps to sing a couple of songs with Charlie, the piano player. Kristina had waited until Florine had gone out with Jason and Uncle Sid had been left in charge. Sid Layman was powerless to forbid her.

Usually, Kristina would choose a late hour when the majority of the crowd had left and only two or three customers remained. She would play the coquette with these customers as she did with Charlie and Sid.

However, the piano player did question Sid's wisdom in allowing her to continue these little escapades. Even though he enjoyed playing a pretty ballad and listening to her sing, Charlie noticed something else in the young lady when he livened up the tempo. A provocative look came into her green eyes and her young body swayed temptingly. The lusty looks of the customers were also obvious to Charlie. He felt that Sid was flirting with big trouble!

Kristina was an innocent maiden now, Charlie figured, but it wouldn't take much to make all that sensuousness come alive. When that time came there would be a new queen in this castle!

Yet the girl was irresistible when she purred sweetly, "Oh, I just love to sing when Mama's away." Then, with a look of utter helplessness, she'd plead. "You won't betray me, will you?"

The quick response of the staff was always the same: no or never. They'd be rewarded with one of Kristina's warm, sweet smiles.

"Oh, thank you. You're darlings!" she'd say.

Sid's and Charlie's chests usually swelled when the youthful little goddess with lustrous, auburn hair and golden skin told them how grateful she was, then let her thick black lashes drop slightly over her brilliant green

35

eyes. Oh, she was a tempting coquette!

When Kristina became truly involved in the song she was singing, she would rise from her stool and glide across the floor, giving vent to the emotions she was feeling. Her movements were graceful, like a dancer's, although for her, such coordination was instinctive.

Florine had no idea that Kristina had such a gift. Cara had only informed her employer of Kristina's abilities as a student. In her candid way, she had not minced words about Kristina's lazy attitude toward subjects that did not interest her. It perplexed the conscientious Cara that she could not instill a desire for learning in Kristina, but her little charge was stubborn.

Florine had made it clear to the governess that she did not consider her remiss in her duties. She knew her headstrong daughter could be frustrating.

By the time the new year of 1881 was ushered in, Florine had made up her mind to accept Jason's proposal of marriage. Kristina seemed to respect and admire him; perhaps his manly influence was the answer to her dilemma.

Solitaire could conceal Miss Tina's mischief no longer. In doing so, she felt disloyal to her beloved mistress. That feeling she could not live with, so she gambled on losing Kristina's favor.

Solitaire's disclosure clinched any doubts Florine had about removing her daughter from these surroundings. It had to be done, and at once, yet the thought of selling the Crystal Castle devastated her.

Why did she have to sell it? she asked herself. She could always become a silent partner, offer the ambitious Sally O'Neal a share to manage the establishment. Sally had been with her longer than anyone except Solitaire. If she knew the feisty blonde as well as she thought she did, Sally would jump at the opportunity.

It wasn't Florine's way to prolong agony so the practical gambling lady sized up the cards she was holding. She had two choices: she could send Kristina away, be unable to see her for months, but continue to operate the Crystal Castle, or she could marry Jason and leave the Crystal Castle to live with him and Kristina at his ranch on the outskirts of El Paso.

For Kristina's sake, Florine knew what she must do.

The red-haired lady tightened the belt of her gold brocade robe and summoned her maid.

"Solitaire, please ask Sally to come up here. I want to talk to her."

"Yes, *mam'selle*," Solitaire answered. She wasted no time in carrying out the order for there was the tone of impatience in her mistress' voice.

Within moments, Sally O'Neal was being ushered into the living quarters of her boss. She was obviously curious about this summons to Mlle. Whelan's sanctum. She did not think she'd done anything to displease her boss, but as she'd mounted the steps and walked down the long hallway, an uneasy feeling had rushed over her.

Florine's face did not indicate any displeasure, however, and her tone was cordial when she said, "Have a seat, Sally. I have a business proposition to discuss with you. I intend to make you an offer I hope you'll accept." Whenever an advantageous idea occurred to Florine, she acted on it. She felt they were omens, and she'd be wrong if she didn't listen to them. This was how she felt about offering Sally, the employee who'd been with her the longest, a partnership in the Crystal Castle. She would split the profits right down the middle. That seemed, to Florine, the perfect solution.

When she told Sally of her idea and of her decision to marry Jason Hamilton, she knew the young woman was stunned. "Well, what do you say, Sally?" she asked.

"I say I'm flabbergasted! I—I can't believe it!"

"Well, believe it, honey. Aside from Solitaire, you've been with me longer than anyone, and I think we've done pretty well together. You'll make money and so will I."

Sally's fair face brightened. "Christ, Florine, I think I'm numb! Honest to God, I don't think I can move!" The two women broke into laughter.

"We got a deal?"

Sally nodded her head, smiling. "You've given me one hell of a birthday present, Florine."

"What's this one, Sally?"

"Twenty-six, Florine."

A sly grin appeared on Florine Whelan's face and she remarked, "You little imp, after all this time I learn you were only fifteen when you started here. You told me you were eighteen."

Sally's head dropped and her blue eyes darted down to her lap.

"I know, Florine, but I needed a job so desperately I'd have said anything to get a roof over my head."

Florine reached over and patted Sally's hand. "I know the feeling, Sally. I've been in the same position. Our arrangement will give you a roof over your head for a long time, partner."

So the deal was made. Florine had no qualms about her impulsive decision, and Sally O'Neal was delighted with the arrangement.

As Florine sat, deep in thought, a slow smile came to her face. Then she mumbled to the quiet, empty room, "Well, old girl, you've dealt the cards. Now let's see you play them!" She knew the gamble she was taking, but Kristina's future was at stake. She just prayed that old Lady Luck was still on her dainty shoulders.

As she often did when plagued by problems, Florine played a game of solitaire, which seemed to soothe her nerves.

Dear Lord, it seemed like only yesterday when a pert little blonde named Sally O'Neal had bounced into her establishment and asked for a job. At that time she'd been no older than Kristina was now.

Chapter 4

Over a hundred miles from El Paso, on the Silvercreek Ranch owned by the Navarro family for three generations, another lady sat playing a game of solitaire. Like Florine Whelan, Señora Lucía Navarro indulged in private musings as her nimble fingers placed the cards on the small, square teakwood table. Her daughter, Delores, was nearby, curled up in a chair, reading a book. It was a lazy, slow-moving winter day at the ranch. Lucía's sons, Damien and Danton, were absent from the house.

It was a day for reflection, and Lucía was thinking about her deceased husband, Victor. Such a powerful, masterful man he was! Although of Spanish descent, Victor had never been the object of the wrath or resentment of the Anglo-American ranchers. Fondly, she recalled the birth of her twins. Victor had been so filled with joy he was like a young boy. Having married late in life, he could not believe it when fortune smiled on him again a few years later and little Delores was born. Life with Victor had been wonderful!

After his death, she knew there were those who doubted she would be able to run Silvercreek Ranch without Victor's firm hand to guide her. However, few realized or appreciated the determination of the demure, soft-spoken lady Victor had so respected.

In the last seven years since his death Lucía had never relinquished the reins completely to her sons. Being a clever woman and a just one, Lucía knew her sons for what they were. Fortunately she had a foreman, Santiago, who had earned Victor's trust and admiration, so the ranch had managed to survive without Señor Navarro.

It was her son, Danton, Lucía relied upon where family matters were concerned, especially difficulties created by the irresponsible Damien. She knew a time would come when Damien's guardian angel would not be on his shoulder—or Danton would not be around to save him. But the strong-willed Lucía would not let herself brood about that possibility.

Oh, she'd seen Damien's restlessness the last few weeks. Of course, it was the winter season at the ranch and things were moving at such a slow pace. Danton was away in the city pursuing his law practice so he only came out to the ranch on the weekends. Danton was a busy, ambitious young man.

Lucía knew that she wasn't the only one missing Danton. Pretty Molly Langford from the neighboring ranch was anxious for him to come back to Silvercreek. When she and her father had stopped by on their way into town, Molly had inquired about Danton.

Lucía sometimes wondered if Danton's cool indifference toward young ladies was not more devastating than Damien's charming ways. The two of them never ceased to amaze her. They were so different.

Santiago swore Damien could charm the horns off old Emil Cruz's billygoats, and so he could. Lucía had seen how the young ladies eagerly fawned over her son. She prayed that he'd have the good sense not to trifle with the young married ladies, at least, but she did not

41

fool herself into thinking that a boundary° like that would stop him. Damien was a rascal!

She had been the target of his devious charm at times. On such occasions, she'd allowed Damien to think he was fooling her. Afterward, she'd smile that lovely smile of hers, knowing he'd left her presence feeling cocksure of himself although she was wise to his manipulativeness.

Finishing her game of solitaire, Lucía stole a glance at her daughter drowsing in the leather chair by the massive stone fireplace. The book lay on the floor, having slipped from Delores's limp hands. Lucía was not surprised when Damien suddenly came bursting through the grilled archway, his dark eyes sparkling with anticipation and she knew he was about to spring another "marvelous idea" on her. He swaggered over to hug her and plant a kiss on her forehead. "Mama, can you do without me for a few days? Think I'll go up to Mack's place while things are so slow. Good time to get a little hunting in and Mack will welcome my company."

Lucía laid the cards down on the teakwood table, and the expression on her face did not change as she turned to stare up at Damien's face. It could have been a boyish grin he displayed, his dark eyes so bright and eager. She knew he awaited her approval of his stated plan.

"Oh, I'm sure Mack would enjoy your visit, Damien. Who would not enjoy your company, my son?" She smiled. "You must invite this Mack you always talk about to your home sometime, Damien. He'll question your manners." Her dark eyes observed his reaction. Lucía Navarro was playing her own type of trickery.

The last thing I'd ever do is invite Mack into this house, Damien silently thought to himself, but he mumbled some lame excuse, saying Mack was a rather shy individual . . . a loner.

"I see. Then he is lucky to have a friend like you. You know, Damien, it would be nice if your brother went hunting with you. Danton needs a relaxing hunting trip. He works too hard at his law practice and at the ranch."

Lucía put Damien in a quandary by suggesting this, for Danton was enough of a thorn in his side right here at Silvercreek. Damien decided to make a hasty exit before he found himself swimming in deep water. While he could not detect it from her sweet, pleasant face, Lucía was amused by the fidgeting Damien. She already anticipated his hasty departure.

As soon as he'd left the room, Lucía heard her daughter's hurt little voice.

"Damien didn't even tell me goodbye."

Lucía sometimes wished Delores didn't worship her older brother so much. She was like a doting puppy where he was concerned. How often her mother had observed the effect Damien's attentions had on her when it pleased his fancy to bestow them on the girls. At other times he completely ignored Delores as he had just done and his younger sister was devastated. Lucía wished her daughter didn't idolize him so.

It would be far better for a sensitive young girl like Delores to worship Danton. Yet her feelings for him weren't so intense, although she loved him. Danton was more of a father to Delores.

To soothe Delores' hurt feelings, Lucía shrugged and light-heartedly remarked, "You know our Damien when he's all enthused about something. It consumes him. Perhaps, he is the baby in this family, eh?" Lucía laughed so gustily that Delores laughed too.

Is there anything on earth more complex or complicated than being a mother? Lucía wondered. The cares of a mother only increase as her children grow older.

She and Florine Whelan would have agreed. Florine was finding it difficult to interpret Kristina's changing moods. In part she blamed them on Kristina's reaction to her announcement that she was going to marry Jason Hamilton even though, at first, her daughter had seemed delighted.

Kristina did have some qualms about her mother marrying, about having to share her with Jason Hamilton. She'd never had a father around to tell her what to do, and she was already imagining that she wasn't going to take well to Jason Hamilton, or any other man, giving her orders and lording it over her. She had always lived with Florine in their little "castle."

But her mercurial moods were not only directed at just her mother; the mulatto maid, Solitaire was in disfavor too. That nosey blabbermouth had obviously found out about her slipping downstairs when Florine and Jason went out in the evening, and she had run to tell Florine. Kristina felt that Solitaire had betrayed her, so she took great delight in being rude and disrespectful to the mulatto who adored her. Although Kristina knew she was hurting Solitaire, she could not seem to bridle her youthful resentments of the ones she loved so dearly.

Her querulous moods perplexed her even more than they did those being punished by them. It seemed only Sid Layman and old Rollo escaped her venom.

Kristina was convinced Florine was postponing her wedding to Jason because she was awaiting her daughter's final approval. But the naïve Kristina had much to learn about her mother. She knew only the doting, indulging woman Florine was in their living quarters at the Crystal Castle. Kristina knew nothing of the calculating, determined business woman who ran the Crystal Castle.

Florine really was delaying her wedding to Jason in order to assure herself that Sally O'Neal could run the establishment successfully. Florine was no fool, and she knew no one was going to put into the Crystal Castle the blood, sweat, and tears she had. She could trust Sally, though, and she'd found out a long time ago she had to put her employees on their honor to a certain degree.

She'd vowed to Jason that another two weeks would be all she'd need to get her affairs in order so the marriage could take place. Then, in that very firm, candid way of hers, she'd told Jason, "Now, honey, you know I'm not going to be content to sit by the hearth and knit, don't you? I'm going to be wanting to come in once in a while to check on things." As she'd thought, Jason had willingly complied with her wishes. He wasn't petty or narrowminded.

When she'd returned to her quarters at the Crystal Castle to find Kristina in one of her good moods, she had been pleased. Their evening repast went pleasantly. Cara and Solitaire had sensed that this was an evening when the mistress and her daughter should be left alone.

Florine considered this the proper time to invite Kristina to join her in a glass of wine. It was Mlle. Whelan's way of saying Kristina was a grown-up young lady, no longer a child, and Kristina was delighted by the gesture.

She exclaimed gleefully, "I can have a glass of wine with you, Mother? You mean it?"

"Why not! You're almost sixteen. Just one though." Florine grinned slyly.

"I . . . I think it's fantastic!" Kristina straightened up in her chair. What an exceptional night this was proving to be. Her mother's declaration that she was officially grown-up meant everything to Kristina. She could not wait to tell Solitaire later.

While they dined, Florine spoke to her daughter about her plans for the future, after she married Jason Hamilton. "Oh, honey, we'll have more time together and there will be Jason to take care of us. You'll see, Kristina, we'll have a good life."

Florine painted a wonderful picture of the exciting times they'd have and of the places they'd visit. Kristina was influenced by her mother's enthusiasm, and the evening went by so swiftly that they were shocked at the lateness of the hour. When their conversation finally slowed and there was a moment of quiet, both realized that the noise had ceased in the gambling hall below.

While Florine went to her bedroom to change into her nightgown and negligee, Kristina looked out the window at the street below. She had done that often since the night she'd first spied that devilishly handsome man ambling into the Crystal Castle.

She still blamed Solitaire for blabbing to her mother about her surreptitious escapades, and despite the mulatto's attitude she knew that she was no child. Only a young lady would be having the wild, stimulating dreams she'd had almost nightly. In her childhood dreams no handsome young man with hair as black as coal and eyes to match had galloped up to her and swept her off her feet. Together, they rode to some faraway place, and when he finally lifted her off his huge stallion and held her close in his arms, she burned with liquid fire. No, that was not the dream of a child!

She was amazed herself by the bold, reckless things she did in those dreams. She'd let her hand brush the falling wisp of hair from his forehead or she'd let her finger explore the sensuous outline of his lips. Then he'd flash a broad grin at her, showing off a magnificent set of pearly white teeth, before his mouth took hers, and she yielded to him, returning his ardent kisses.

Now she felt flushed as she recalled the dream, the giddy effect of whirling and spinning as if she were soaring to the peak of some mountain top. Would it be like that?

As if driven to seek this man of her dreams, Kristina searched the dark El Paso street, finding it deserted. There was not even one late night roamer about.

Out of her sight, however, lurking at the back of the Crystal Castle four masked men waited and watched as Sally O'Neal and Sid Layman meandered down the street and out of sight.

One masked man grumbled, "When the hell is that ole nigger going to move his butt?"

"Shut up, Dake. He'll go in a minute," the tall masked man admonished his cohort sternly.

Soon Rollo shuffled off, and the five moved to the door, finding its lock no obstacle. Once in the darkened downstairs area, the tall one gave the others a gesture that meant they should move cautiously and quietly.

The tall man's heart pounded with the reckless excitement at the punishment he was about to execute on the woman upstairs. A broad, sinister grin broke out on his face when he thought about the scion of the esteemed Navarro family being a masked robber of a gambling hall!

The strait-laced Victor Navarro would be mortified. He would turn over in his grave if he could see his son masked and with a gun in his hand. Dios, he'd turn over in his grave, Damien thought as he ventured on toward the stairs that led to his prey.

The carpet made their approach noiseless as the men climbed upward and then stalked on down the hallway until they reached the huge double doors of the living quarters. Damien halted his cohorts there, directing two of them to tie up the women in the two rooms down the hallway to prevent Solitaire and Cara from rushing out. He waited until that was done; then he reached for the matching brass doorknobs to check them, prepared to blast the lock open as the other masked men stood behind him.

Surprised, he turned to his companions. The lock was conveniently not secured. Inside the quarters, Kristina detected the noise made when Damien had turned the knobs, but she shrugged it aside when Florine, in the process of removing her gown without Solitaire's assistance, called out to her for assistance. Hastily, she went to oblige her mother.

She was just entering Florine's boudoir when the massive carved oak doors seemed to explode. Frozen by shock, she stood like a statue.

Then, recovering, Kristina gave out a frightened shriek and Florine cried, "Dear God!" With the instinct of a mother lion, she rushed to her daughter's side putting her arms protectively around Kristina's shoulders. "What is the meaning of this?" she demanded, not daring to show the fear churning within her.

One of the masked men lunged toward them and his rough hands yanked Florine from her daughter while another encircled Kristina in his arms. The tallest man just stood, glaring at the furious woman struggling to free herself. Florine was enraged at seeing the hands of the man clutching Kristina lustily creeping over her ripening breasts. Oh, she wanted to kill him!

"Mother? . . ." Kristina screamed out, trembling with a panic she'd never known before.

The tall man took a step forward then, directing his remark to Florine, "The meaning is, *puta,* that you're being robbed!"

"Don't call me a whore, you cowardly bastard!" Florine sternly rebuked the foul-mouthed man.

In response, she received a sharp slap across the face. Damien had yearned to do that since she'd so arrogantly ordered him out of the Crystal Castle many

48

months ago. He felt good when he struck her, but Florine's eyes sparkled, not with tears but hate.

Admiration for her mother blossomed in Kristina as she watched her beautiful face take his cruel blow. When Florine's hair fell over her face from the jarring slap she'd received, Kristina's own fury mounted, and she tried desperately to free herself. Finding it impossible, she bit the hand of the man who held her prisoner. He screamed out in pain, but his hold on her only tightened until Kristina felt she could not get her breath. I can be brave like my mother, she told herself.

Giving a deep throaty laugh, Damien said to Florine, "Your safe, *señora*. Shall we get on with our business?"

Through clenched teeth, Florine hissed, "Yes, by all means and then take your filth out of my sight!"

Mockingly, Damien taunted the irate woman whose main concern, he knew, was for her daughter. He looked at the young girl. Her exquisite gown was rumpled from struggling, and the neckline, pulled sideways, displayed her blossoming cleavage. Young, she was. Excitingly so, Damien noticed. All fresh and virginal, he'd wager!

"Ah, you want us gone . . . *sí?*" Damien teased. Florine did not answer him, knowing he already had a weapon to use against her. She walked to her safe and opened it, reaching for the stacks of money inside. Damien's dark eyes were not concealed by the bandanna mask, and Florine's green ones locked with his. She'd caught the accent in his last remark, and Jason's admonitions came to haunt her. Navarro . . . Damien Navarro. Dear God, that had happened months ago. She'd almost forgotten the incident and the man!

"There . . . you have it. That's everything I have."

Damien took her offering. He was feeling giddy, elated. In fact, he was like a man intoxicated, and so he became reckless. Not satisfied by having more than he'd lost at Florine's tables that night, he wanted her to know who was causing her this agony.

"Take the girl away!" he ordered. As the man holding Kristina dragged her from the room, the girl cried out. Her daughter's helpless screams were more than Florine could endure. She remembered the derringer in the safe, and since she was still squatting by the safe's door, her hand reached for the gun. The explosion and the pain registered with Florine at the same second.

"You stupid son of a bitch! Now, you've gone and done it." Damien had already removed his mask and the woman's eyes were piercing his face, stunned as she was. His eyes had darted away from her as he'd sought to untie the kerchief, and his masked cohort had seen what Florine was reaching for and had pulled the trigger of his pistol. Now Damien stood before her and he knew those green eyes recognized him.

"Let's get the hell out of here fast!" Damien turned swiftly, angrily pushing the man who had shot her. This was more than he'd bargained for. *Madre de Dios,* much more!

The shot and the heavy shuffling of their booted heels were heard by Solitaire and Cara. They knew the marauders were leaving but neither could rush to the rescue of their mistress and Kristina for they were both bound to bedposts in their separate bedrooms.

Florine lay in a pool of her own blood, but the pain in her body hurt less than the one in her heart. Never had she known such panic! Never had she felt such hatred for a man!

Chapter 5

Clouds moved up from the south to block out the bright moonlight which had been lighting the winding trail the four nightriders traveled as they rode from El Paso. For the first hour they followed the Rio Grande River.

Damien spurred the roan mare mercilessly to put as much distance as he possibly could between him and the town of El Paso. His finger still itched to put a bullet in Jesse for his stupidity at the Crystal Castle. Hell, he hadn't wanted Florine Whelan to be shot!

So upset was Damien by that unplanned event, he had not noticed that he had another problem on his hands; this one was not planned either.

Dake Davenport and his pal, Wes, rode about a quarter of a mile ahead of Damien and Jesse. In the saddle with Dake was Kristina, her auburn hair blowing wildly as they galloped swiftly through the night.

Dake's lusty passion had been so aroused when he'd held the girl back at the gambling hall that he'd given way to the impulse to take her with him, intending to enjoy himself once they made camp.

Kristina could not possibly know the foul thoughts

going through her captor's mind as they rode through the countryside. She was numbed by fright and the chill of the late night air, and the man's arms, enclosing her and holding the reins of his horse as they galloped over the trail, were her only source of warmth.

The scent of his hot breath was obnoxious, and the feel of his body pressed against her back made her rigid and tense. He kept telling her what a pretty little thing she was, but she spoke not a word to him.

Finally, so weary she could no longer control her limp body, she leaned against Dake's big chest. Noticing her surrender, he was flooded with gnawing impatience to make camp.

"Hell, I'm stopping up there, Wes. What do you say?"

"Fine with me, Dake. We'll be safe enough now," Wes said, already slowing his horse. He yearned for a hefty shot of the whiskey in the flask in his saddlebag. Wes's weakness was liquor, not women.

When Damien and Jesse caught up with the others, reined their horses, and dismounted, only then did Damien see the girl's shadowed image. She was still perched on Dake's horse. He'd lined himself up with a bunch of idiots, he decided.

A stream of curse words flowed from his mouth and he marched over to the lanky Dake, grabbing the collar of the man's shirt and backhanding his face three times. "You crazy sonofabitch! Why did you bring that damned girl?"

But Dake was a man possessed by desire. At that moment, what Damien Navarro thought meant nothing to him.

"It suited me to, Navarro!" Dake barked out in an insolent tone.

Although the night was dark and the moon was hidden by low-flying clouds, Damien detected a wild look in Dake's eyes.

Damien's hand caressed the pistol in his holster. He would use it if Dake pushed him too far. "Doesn't suit the rest of us, Dake. The girl means trouble and we don't want a noose around our necks cause you're hurting for a woman. Besides, think about it. Tomorrow, you'll have your split of the money and you can have yourself a real woman in Pecos."

Jesse stood behind Damien. He knew Damien Navarro was angry because he'd shot Florine Whelan back at the Crystal Castle, and he hoped he might reinstate himself in Damien's good graces by cajoling the hot-blooded Dake.

"Hey, virgins are a pain in the ass anyway. You know that, Dake. You need more than a skinny little kid."

Jesse flung an arm around Dake in a comradely manner and guided him away from Damien. Dake was still grumbling, but Damien's hand eased away from his pistol.

Wanting to keep his distance from the daughter of Florine Whelan until he could decide what to do with her, he sent Wes over to help the girl off the horse and to give her a couple of blankets.

Swathed in the blankets, Kristina sat in the shadows, her teeth chattering and her body trembling, as the four men gathered around the campfire. They took turns at sipping from a bottle of whiskey, all except the tall, lean man who seemed to be their leader. He towered over the others, like a general giving out orders. For one fleeting moment back at the Crystal Castle Kristina had mistakenly thought he was her handsome prince.

A finely attired gentleman like the one she'd admired that night would be gallant and genteel, however, she told herself. He certainly would not associate with the likes of these scoundrels—not the man of my dreams.

53

She could not hear their deep, mumbling voices clearly enough for her to distinguish everything they said as they huddled together, but bits and pieces of their conversation echoed in her ears and occasionally she could see their heads turn in her direction.

As the night breeze whistled through the tall pines, a voice seemed to warn her of impending danger. She could have sworn it was her mother's voice she heard. Go just as fast as you can, it seemed to say. While the men are busy and at a distance, slip through the thick underbrush. Now or never, the voice insisted.

Raw instinct took over and Kristina could lie there no longer. She secured the blankets more tightly around her shoulders and then began to crawl over the ground through the bushes. When the bushes thinned and she had room to turn from side to side, she estimated that she'd crawled about one hundred feet from where she'd been sitting. She slowly stood up to get her bearings.

Her view of the men was blotted out by the shrubbery so she was satisfied that they could not see her either. Fearful that she would make a noise, she began to walk very cautiously. Dear God, she'd never known what it was to be so scared and so helplessly alone! Her soul cried out for the comforting arms of her mother, of Solitaire and Cara. For the first time in her life she found the world more frightening than the worst nightmare she'd ever had.

Without being aware of it, she broke into a run as her panic had mounted. How long she ran she did not know, but it seemed like forever. Finally, she was forced to stop when her long hair became caught in the low branch of a tree. She was breathless, gasping.

She strained to hear the sounds of the men's heavily booted feet coming after her, the sound of deep voices. She stood still, taking deep gulps of the cold night air. In which direction should she go? she wondered.

Her head hurt where wisps of hair had been pulled from her scalp by the tentacles of branches, and she swept her tresses back behind her ears before starting to walk on. She chose to go where the bushes weren't as thick, but her brief moment of rest had caused extreme weariness to set in. Her legs were now very weak. She listened as she walked determinedly on, wondering if she could run now if she had to.

Her courage gathered as she moved in and out through the trees for she seemed to be the only soul in the woods. All the creatures of the forest slept. Oh, how she longed to be in her bed with the soft silk pillows and the warm coverlet of satin. It would be sheer heaven to be nestled there. The luxury of her surroundings had never dawned on her before. In her pampered life, she'd always taken so many things for granted. She'd never imagined life to be otherwise.

When a sudden noise came to her ears, she froze in her tracks, her bravery swept away. They'd discovered her gone! Oh, God, she could not let them catch up to her! She broke into a wild run plowing wildly through the thick undergrowth despite the way the ragged branches scratched her flesh.

Having no idea where she was and no familiarity with the area, she could not know she was heading directly toward the edge of a high bluff. With an abruptness that allowed her no time for fear, she found there was nothing under her feet. She was falling into empty space, whirling into an endless series of tumbles. Momentarily blackness engulfed her!

Then pebbles stabbed her flesh; briars tore at her gown and yanked at her hair. Finally, as her battered body came to rest, her head struck a boulder, and Kristina had lost consciousness.

There was no way to measure the time she'd lain on the ground. Miraculously, the blanket had clung to her small shoulders, but she had lost her slippers in the tumble down the cliff. Her thick lashes fluttered open slowly to see the new day dawning. She attempted to raise up her head, but it throbbed painfully. She desisted.

Lying on the ground, she surveyed the jagged cuts and scratches on each of her arms, the torn silk sleeve of her gown. Her hand trailed up to the side of her head to feel the dried blood where her head had hit the boulder on the ground beside her.

Determined to try again to get up off the ground, she rolled onto her side and pushed with all her might. With an extreme effort she managed to get herself to a sitting position!

A golden haze surrounded her. A towering wall of trees rose above this mist. Listlessly, she sat, staring around her and then at herself. What once had been a beautiful gown was now a shambles. She held out her soiled hand. Her fingernails were broken, but the exquisite ring with the peridot stone sparkled back at her.

She swept her mass of hair away from her face, and a wave of loneliness engulfed her. At that moment she felt that she did not belong here or anywhere else. The question that came to her mind she could not answer. She did not know who she was!

Disturbed, she rose from the ground and started to walk, not knowing where she was going or who she was seeking. She knew of no Kristina Whelan, nor did she walk in fear of the men she'd fled last night.

Like an innocent, newborn babe she wandered slowly along the wooded path which followed the bluff she'd tumbled down the night before. No fear churned in her now, but she limped because of the pain in her ankle. She was very aware of the pain.

Such innocence was hers that the pounding hooves of the dapple-gray horse stirred no disturbing emotions within Kristina. But the man astride jerked the reins sharply at the unlikely sight he'd suddenly come upon deep in the woods at a short distance from Emil Cruz's cabin.

The young woman stood under the trees, her rumpled hair flowing around her tiny shoulders, and to Danton, her locks looked like liquid copper. The morning sun's rays were bringing out the rich, glossy luster of her tresses, and she possessed the face of an angel if ever he'd seen one. Her eyes were such a brilliant shade of green. No emerald sparkled any brighter, he thought to himself. Danton Navarro was entranced by the sight of Kristina.

He sat his horse for a brief moment, letting his dark eyes dance slowly from the top of her head to her toes. He noted that she was without shoes and his heart went out to her. She suddenly reminded him of a kitten, the one he'd found along the road a few weeks ago and had taken back to the ranch.

"Good morning, miss. Are you lost?" Danton inquired, feeling that might be the answer to her unusual situation.

She smiled at him and Danton was stunned by her breathtaking loveliness. "I . . . I guess I am," she mumbled. Danton's black eyebrows arched. He dismounted from his horse and walked over to where Kristina stood looking up at him with such wide-eyed innocence that Danton knew she was not playing some game. She was being quite honest.

"Who are you? Can you tell me that, little kitten?"

She had a blank look on her face as she shook her head. "I don't know."

Danton felt compassion for the beautiful slip of a girl who looked so battered and disheveled. His dark soulful eyes danced over her face. "So I guess it would

57

be useless to ask if you could tell me where you've come from or how you happened to be here?"

With a helpless shrug of her blanket-covered shoulders she sighed, "No, I can tell you nothing."

Danton placed his hands on her shoulders. "It's all right, little one. One thing is certain: you need something done about those cuts." He gave her a warm smile, and Kristina smiled back at the nice man whose arm was so comforting. His closeness was reassuring, but she did not recall that this was the handsome man who'd captured her heart many months ago. At this moment, he was just someone kind.

However, as his strong arm encircled her, he won her heart again.

She obeyed his guiding arm which urged her toward his horse. "We'll take you to the Cruz's house, and if I know Ramona she'll fix you up fine. You're chilled, aren't you, poor little kitten?" The heat from him permeated her, and she made no protest as he hugged her closer to his side. Once he'd hoisted her atop the dapple-gray animal and leaped up behind her, he clutched her so tightly that she could feel the strong pounding of his heart.

As Danton Navarro held her possessively, yearning to stop the trembling of her body, a strange feeling consumed him. He wanted her to be forever in the circle of his arms. He did not know what had happened to this sweet girl, but he could see that some havoc had taken its toll on this fragile flower. Beauty such as hers should be pampered and cherished. Most assuredly, such a glorious creature was made for loving, and he could not deny that he ached desperately to make love to her.

He was very aware of the curves of her tiny waistline and her rounded breasts which occasionally brushed against his extended arms as they jogged along the trail

58

leading up to the mountain cabin of Emil Cruz. His muscled thighs pressed against her legs, partially exposed because of her rumpled and torn skirt. Her dress had been no simple frock, Danton realized. He noticed the dress because his mother and sister had expensive taste in fashionable gowns.

He could not deny that the way she so trustingly nestled in his arms pleased him. She was so guileless. Danton shuddered to think what could have happened to her if some roving scoundrel had chanced upon her in the woods.

He could not resist letting his cheek lean against her face as they rode along. In a soft, deep voice he asked, "Are you feeling warmer, little one?"

"Oh, yes. Thanks to you," she replied. Somehow, it never dawned on her not to trust him. To be at the gentle mercy of this man seemed natural and right to Kristina. When she turned her head slightly, his lips touched her cheek. They were warm and tender. She sought not to move away or separate herself from them.

Strangers, they might be, but it already seemed that their hearts and souls were fusing, binding them one to the other. Young and unknowing as she was, Kristina sensed this. Danton Navarro, despite his sophistication was baffled, but the sweet exhilaration she instilled in him was enough for now.

Later, he knew, the tantalizing temptation she presented might enflame his desire. This was a new experience for the handsome Danton Navarro!

His usually hot-blooded Latin nature could think only of being very protective of her. He put his own desires aside, for difficult as it was for him to admit it to himself, he knew she was going to be more to him than just a chance encounter on a mountain trail.

Chapter 6

The kitchen of the Cruz's cabin was the largest room of their humble dwelling. Rays of bright sunshine flowed through the window between the bright, floral curtains. The view from that window was a glorious one of the mountainside. Tall trees dotted its slopes, and a purple haze hung over the peak on this winter morning.

Ramona Cruz's diligent dusting, waxing, and mopping had made the room sparkle with a clean freshness. The aroma of brewing coffee mingled with the fragrance of the *ristras,* the long strings of dried chiles. The dried peppers had turned from bright red to a deep, rich burgundy shade. When Ramona cooked, she plucked one from the handily clustered bunch to put in her pots of food.

Emil, Ramona's huge husband, was a fierce, ugly-looking man, but he possessed a gentle nature and kind heart. Those who knew him, like Danton Navarro, were aware of this, but to a stranger, he could be awesome and frightening. Since his boyhood, Danton had known Emil, for he'd accompanied his father to the Cruz's to purchase some of the Mexican's fine goats.

"You don't worry, Señor Danton. My Ramona will take care of the girl," Emil said, a broad reassuring grin on his swarthy face.

"Oh, I know the miracles Ramona can perform, Emil," Danton told him.

"How can something like that be, *señor?* How could that wee little one have wandered up on the mountains? She . . . she's not from around here, I know. Where has she come from?" Emil seated himself on the wooden chair across from Danton.

"I can't imagine, Emil. She cannot tell me either. But obviously she was brought to the area by someone, and it is evident that she's no neighboring rancher's daughter. Her clothing is expensive, as is the piece of jewelry on her hand. I noticed that at once."

"I never took notice of that. That is why you are such a fine lawyer, Señor Danton," Emil exclaimed proudly. "Whoever this little lady is, she is lucky that such a fine man found her. What will we do, *señor?"*

"I've been thinking about that, Emil." Danton knew the Cruz's situation and the cabin's limited space. Besides, Emil had no resources with which to help the girl. There was only one solution to the dilemma facing them: he'd just have to take her back to Silvercreek with him. From where he sat, he could look through the doorway and observe Ramona attending to the cuts on the girl's arm.

Swallowed up in one of Ramona's smocklike garments, the copper-haired waif looked like an appealing ragamuffin. She was submitting herself to the chummy Mexican woman's gentle touch, but a couple of times she'd turned to look at him as though she needed to reassure herself he was there. That gesture had an effect on Danton which he couldn't have put into words.

By the time he'd finished his second cup of coffee,

there was no question in Danton's mind about his plans for the girl. He was taking her to Silvercreek. While his mother would certainly be astounded by this unexpected houseguest, he knew her well enough to be certain she'd be her usual gracious self once he'd explained the situation. He simply would remain at the ranch for a few days. Since he had no pressing business, a few days away from his office wouldn't hurt.

The hefty Ramona waddled away from Kristina and entered the kitchen where the men sat conversing. She addressed Danton as she approached the table, "I'm slowly getting the poor little dear cleaned up, but I think I'll get her some warm milk and a little food before trying to untangle her hair. That is going to take some doing, Señor Danton."

"You're the boss, Ramona! Right, Emil?"

Emil chuckled, "Oh, *sí* . . . always Ramona is the boss."

The large woman playfully rumpled her bear of a husband's head before she moved on to her cupboard. "With food and some rest, I think she'll be just fine."

Danton suggested that they leave the ladies to their business, so he and Emil went out to look at the goats he wished to buy. "I've . . . I've decided I should take the girl to Silvercreek, Emil," he said.

Danton had not planned on spending the night with the Cruz family, but when he and Emil closed their deal and returned to the cabin, Ramona informed them that the girl was sleeping peacefully. "She could use the rest, *señor,* I think. This young one has had a most trying experience, I am certain."

Emil hastily spoke up, "We have not much to offer you . . . but if you could spend the night here, it would be better for the girl, would it not?"

Danton knew Emil spoke the truth. The sun would be sinking before long and it was quite a ride to Silvercreek. Furthermore, the air would have a chill to it after the sun went down. "Are you sure it wouldn't be too much trouble?"

"Trouble? No, it would be an honor, *Señor* Danton. Wouldn't it, Ramona?" His wife quickly declared her agreement. So it was decided that Danton would remain at the Cruz's overnight, and the next morning he and the girl would start for the Navarro ranch at the first dawn of light.

When morning came and Ramona prepared a hearty breakfast for them all, Danton had to admit to himself that he'd enjoyed the evening in the Cruz's humble home. He'd slept just as soundly on his makeshift bed as he would have in his sumptuously furnished room at Silvercreek.

By the time the hands of the clock were indicating the hour of seven, Danton and Kristina were atop the dapple-gray horse, waving farewell to the Mexican couple. Kristina's long hair, now free of tangles, was plaited into two long braids, and she was wearing an outfit Ramona had assembled. The kindly woman had made a small bundle of Kristina's torn, soiled garments. The girl looked even more fragile and helpless in the baggy pants and the oversized tunic, Danton thought as he gazed at her. An old plaid blanket with a hole cut in the center served as a poncho, for Ramona had wanted the girl to be warm on the long jaunt to Silvercreek. On her feet Kristina wore oversized woolen socks and leather moccasins. She didn't mind the shabby attire for she was scrubbed clean and her stomach had been filled with Ramona's good food. As they trotted down the lane, Danton's encircling arms warmed and comforted her, and she felt serene and happy.

"I can never forget them. They were so kind to me," she said suddenly.

His arms clasped her closer as he replied, "Ah, but it is so easy to be kind to you, *chiquita.*"

"This name you call me . . . what is that?" she wanted to know.

Danton laughed. "It means you're a little one. Now that brings up another subject. Please call me Danton or you'll make me feel like an old man. My imp of a sister will laugh her head off if you call me Señor Navarro."

Kristina turned her head slightly. "You have a sister? What is she called?"

"Her name is Delores. At Silvercreek—that is our ranch and where I am taking you, little kitten—my mother and my sister live, and I also have a brother, Damien."

"How nice." Kristina suddenly became so quiet that Danton wondered what was going on in her pretty head. He knew it must be filled with apprehensions, about him and about the strange place he was taking her.

"Since we've settled what you must call me I guess I must christen you, eh?"

"I . . . I suppose," she mumbled, a rather forlorn tone to her soft voice.

"All right . . . I shall name you Kit. How do you like that, little one?"

"Guess it's as good as anything."

Instinct suddenly ruled the usually controlled Danton Navarro, and he gave way to the impulse to plant a featherlike kiss on her silken cheek. "It will be all right, little Kit. I'll see to it . . . trust me. No more harm will come to you. Silvercreek will welcome you with open arms. It can be your home for as long as it takes to find out who you are and how you happened to be up in the Parrilla Mountains."

She gave him a weak smile and replied, "I do trust you, Danton. I may not know who I am, but I know you're a good man."

"I'm glad you feel that way, Kit. I promise to take care of you," Danton said. Actually her response delighted him, and he found himself in the grip of feelings that went beyond the bounds of the usual feelings a man has for an attractive lady he'd like to seduce. His chest swelled with the intensity of his emotions.

As they traveled eastward toward Silvercreek, Kristina questioned him about his sister, his mother and brother, and Danton described them to her. Only when he spoke of Damien did he have some qualms about her staying at Silvercreek.

Perhaps, for this innocent young lady's sake, he would delay his return to the city even longer than he'd planned. He had only to envision her in one of Delores' frocks, instead of the hastily concocted garb provided by Ramona Cruz, to know that she'd capture Damien's roving eyes. No beautiful female escaped the randy Damien's attention. His brother had stalked such women since he'd been sixteen years old, Danton recalled.

Since this little beauty was the loveliest creature Danton had ever seen and refreshingly naïve, he knew Damien would seek to conquer her. Danton vowed to himself that he'd not let that happen.

Kristina did not know Danton had appointed himself her protector, but she did know he was the most handsome man she'd ever seen. His deep voice impressed her, and his breath, when he murmured softly, touched her cheek like a warm caress. She wanted to remain close to him. When his black eyes gazed into hers, she felt he was seeking the depth of her, the very essence of her being. No man could possibly be more magnificent than this Danton Navarro, she assured herself.

She had not realized that they'd accomplished the descent from the mountains where Emil and Ramona lived until she turned to the right and noticed that the dense growth of trees had thinned out. Now, in the distance she could see a winding, weaving river.

The misty purplish haze which had surrounded them as they rode through the mountain trail had suddenly lifted, and below was a bright scenic valley. A river ran through it and groves of trees dotted the countryside. Did she only imagine it or did the dapple-gray horse sense that they were nearing his home? The stallion's pace had quickened, it seemed.

Home . . . where was her home? She suddenly envied Danton Navarro for he knew exactly where he was going and where he belonged. Someday she would too!

Before a cloak of melancholy could wash over her, Danton's deep voice distracted her. "Look, Kit . . . over there! See where the river bends to the north. In the springtime nothing is as beautifully green as that valley over there." He stopped himself just in time before he compared it to the glorious beauty of her green eyes.

"I'll bet it is." Since she had no memory of her past, Kristina could not know that the assurance Danton had instilled in her during their brief time together was growing, but there was confidence in her voice when she remarked, "I probably won't be here to see it come the spring, Danton."

Her remark brought a frown to Danton Navarro's brow. It was true that when he found out who she was she would leave Silvercreek—and him. The thought of saying farewell to her when that time came did not sit well with him.

When they galloped through a gateway in a fence which seemed to extend for miles, Kristina noticed a massive boulder. Across the width of it, the name SILVERCREEK had been chiseled.

"How did your ranch come by its name, Danton?" she inquired, as they cantered down the long drive that led to the sprawling ranch house almost a mile away.

"I should make you wait until we get to the house and let my mother tell you that. You see, she tells that story with such feeling. Silvercreek and what it stands for are very dear to her. However, Kit, I'll tell you."

"Go ahead," Kristina urged. "You've made me most curious!"

"Well, when they were first married and came here to live—my father and mother—they were walking in the moonlight down by the little creek that runs behind the original house on the ranch. As the moonlight played on the waters of the creek, my mother remarked that it made the creek look like silver. My father decided that night to call their ranch Silvercreek and so they did."

"Oh, Danton, that's a wonderful story. I'm sure you have a very nice mother. Your father is dead, you said?"

"Yes. He died when Damien and I were twenty. We've tried to take over for him, but it is a tall order."

"Oh, Danton, I think you could do anything you wished to do," Kristina declared.

Once again, she ignited a strange prideful feeling in the man sitting behind her. He basked in her overwhelming faith and trust for a moment, then he became realistic.

"Ah, little one," he sighed, "I'm just a man. I would not want you to become disillusioned about me." He could not reveal to this sweet, innocent girl how sorely he'd been tested while riding so close to her all the way from Emil's cabin. He could so easily have given way to the urge to stop the dapple gray, lift her off the beast, and make love to her. God knows, he'd wanted to!

Madre de Dios, she could not know the tantalizing temptation he'd fought.

Chapter 7

Santiago Lopez watched the dapple-gray thorough-bred prance up the long winding road toward the house. All the while, he continued to wrap the rope over his one arm with even, equal loops, in his usual, precise way. Santiago was busily putting the barn in order on this winter afternoon for he had free time on his hands and the Mexican foreman could not abide idleness.

He'd spent over twenty years of his life at Silvercreek, and he loved the ranch and the land. If he'd worshiped any mortal man, it would have been Victor Navarro, and his admiration for Señora Lucía was boundless.

He watched Señor Danton approach, wondering about the little vagabond accompanying him. What stray has he rescued now? Santiago wondered, shaking his head. Santiago couldn't recall how many times he'd witnessed Danton bringing some helpless stray back to the ranch. The young man's heart was as big and vast as the sprawling acres of Silvercreek. A pity some of it hadn't rubbed off on his twin brother, the foreman mused thoughtfully.

Danton saw the foreman standing by the barn and he waved to him. "That is Santiago," he told Kristina.

"You'll soon learn that he is the real boss at Silvercreek." Giving a light-hearted laugh, he confessed to Kristina that Santiago was the most trusted friend he had in the whole world.

Danton could almost read the Mexican's thoughts as they rode nearer and Santiago pushed his wide-brimmed hat back on his head. Santiago had noticed that the little "stray" with Danton had long, lustrous plaits of copper-colored hair. Danton had a girl with him! Now, what in the world is he doing with her? Santiago wondered.

A quizzical frown creased his bushy brows by the time Danton reined in the horse and tossed the reins to Santiago. A broad grin on his face, Danton quickly introduced the young girl as Kit. Then, unceremoniously, the young man took Kit's hand and rushed her away, leaving the gaping Santiago to flounder in befuddled curiosity. Danton smiled with amusement.

Danton stole a couple of glances at the tiny miss walking by his side as they walked through the garden area of the courtyard and up the stone path to the front entrance. She gave no indication that she was feeling apprehensive and he was happy about that. He certainly could not have blamed her had she been upset, though. In fact, she kept pace with his long strides and her head was held high. Her bearing was almost arrogant.

What a pert little nose she has, Danton suddenly thought. He'd wager she might weigh a hundred and five pounds dripping wet.

Kristina felt his eyes measuring her, and when he gave her a big smile she eagerly responded with a smile of her own.

He opened the door and invited her to enter the long black- and white-tiled entranceway. A cozy warmth greeted her once Danton had closed the front door, but there seemed to be no one in the house as they moved down the hallway. As they moved past the arch leading into the parlor, however, a voice called to Danton. The voice belonged to a most impressive lady.

Kristina was having her first glimpse of Señora Lucía Navarro. She stared openly at the lady, admiring her beauty, and a moment later, she was relieved by Lucía's gracious warm greeting. Noting the woman's lovely gown, Kristina was embarrassed by her baggy attire.

"Mother, this is Kit, and let me add quickly, for her sake, that this is my name for her. Kit, this is my mother."

"Welcome to our home, Kit," Lucía said, extending her hand to the girl and knowing instinctively that Danton would enlighten her as soon as they sought the refuge of her sitting room. "Emil and Ramona are all right?" she inquired.

"Just fine, Mother." Danton did not have to ask where she was guiding them, nor did he have to request that some refreshments be served. He knew they were going to the sitting room.

When they were comfortably settled on Señora Lucía's brightly colored settee and her housekeeper had set out a tray bearing a carafe of freshly brewed coffee and some cinnamon cakes, the *señora* poured the coffee and looked at Danton, signaling to him that she was ready to hear about this delightful, bright-eyed girl who'd accompanied him from Emil Cruz's cabin.

She was not of Mexican descent, Lucía was certain of that. At first, she'd felt this might be a relative of Emil and Ramona Cruz, that Danton had offered the girl a job at Silvercreek. But on more careful scrutiny, Lucía swept that fleeting idea aside. She noted the green eyes darting back and forth between Danton and herself. Such divine eyes they were, and they reflected such honest adoration for her handsome son. She wondered if Danton was aware of that adoration. Lucía rather doubted it, knowing him as she did. Now, Damien would be, she thought with amusement.

"I've offered little Kit the hospitality and shelter of our home, Mother. She was wandering along the trail when I came upon her on my way to Emil's. Ramona tended to all her cuts and bruises but she couldn't tell me how she got them, nor could she tell me what her name is." His eyes turned to Kristina who gazed back at him. Lucía studied the two of them.

"Of course, our home is your home . . . Kit, is it?"

Danton chuckled. "That's what I named her, Mother, for she reminded me of that little lost kitten I brought home, remember?"

"Yes, Danton," Lucía softly laughed. "My dear, my son means that in the kindest way, I assure you. He adored that little kitten."

Lucía wondered if she'd embarrassed her handsome son for she could have sworn he was blushing slightly.

"Do you still have the kitten, *señora?*" Kristina inquired.

"Oh, we certainly do and we stay rid of mice, I can tell you," Lucía confessed. "She earns her keep, but she's hardly the little kitten he brought home that day."

Kristina decided that if the rest of Danton's family was half as nice as he and Señora Lucía, she had been very fortunate to be found by him.

A short time later she was put in the capable care of the housekeeper to be shown to her room, which the *señora* said was right across the hallway from her daughter's room. "Delores will be so happy to have someone her age for company. After all, older brothers tend to be bossy," Lucía light-heartedly jested.

After Kristina had left the room with Drusilla, the housekeeper, Danton and his mother spoke further about the girl and her situation. Danton asked his mother, "Hasn't Damien got back from his hunting trip yet?"

"No, he hasn't, Danton," Lucía replied. Hastily, she sought to assure him that he should not let Damien's absence delay his return to his office in town. "We'll be just fine, dear, and you know I'll take care of our little guest. What will you do, Danton—about finding out who she is, I mean?"

"Oh, I've got a couple of ideas I'll pursue when I get back to town. I'll be able to stay around for a day or two though," Danton told his mother, shrugging his broad shoulders offhandedly.

"Well, how marvelous!" Lucía exclaimed with delight. Somehow, she'e already decided that Danton might linger a little longer than he'd originally planned, but just as she let Damien think she didn't see right through him, she let Danton believe she was unaware of his intentions. Whatever the reason for his extra time at Silvercreek, she welcomed his presence. It gave Lucía a feeling of security since the death of her husband.

"Delores must be visiting her friend, Della, or we would not have had such a long period of quiet." Danton grinned impishly.

Lucía broke into laughter. "You're right. But it is your friend she's visiting. In fact, Molly will be delighted to know you're to be here a little longer. She was most disappointed yesterday when she picked up Delores to find you had gone to Emil's."

Molly Langford was a sweet young lady and a very pretty one, but Danton had begun to realize that she was far too serious about him. Jack Langford, Molly's father had already let it be known that the union of his Molly and Danton Navarro would meet with his overwhelming approval.

Old man Langford's eagerness would have dampened Danton's ardor had he found Molly irresistible, but to him she was just a nice girl he had escorted to several social functions.

"Molly, eh? What was the occasion?" Danton wanted to know.

"Oh, girl stuff. I think they are going to work on a new frock for Molly. Ranch life can be lonely for young girls, Danton. I want to talk to you about sending Delores to the school in Austin next year. Miss Brewster's is reputed to be a fine school and with you in Austin most of the time—well, it might be good for Delores."

Danton's thoughts were on another girl, however. He wondered how old Kit was. She could not be as young as Delores, he was certain of that, and certainly she was not as shy!

"I think Miss Brewster's School for Young Ladies could be the answer for Delores," he replied. "I would suggest that you take her on a tour of the school in the spring—that is, if you can talk Delores into going that far from home."

"Thank you, Danton. I felt you'd say that. Now, I must go talk with Drusilla about dinner. We have a guest . . . yes?" She reached up and gave his cheek an affectionate pat before turning to leave the room.

Danton watched her move gracefully through the doorway. What is that glint in her dark eyes all about? he asked himself.

Like most of the people around Silvercreek, Danton knew Lucía Navarro was no simple-minded, frivolous lady. He could have sworn she could read their minds when he and Damien were growing up and bubbling over with mischief. As he'd matured he'd come to realize that her abundance of common sense made her wise. Her judgment was sounder than that of most

73

people he knew. It was little wonder Victor Navarro had held her opinions in such high esteem.

Kristina felt very contented when Drusilla ushered her into the bedroom which was to be hers. She did not know it was done in the same colors as her beautiful bedroom at the Crystal Castle, but a feeling of serenity rushed over her and she sank down on the canopied bed and sighed. "Oh, Drusilla this is a lovely room," she said.

"Yes, miss. Nothing is prettier than pink." The middle-aged housekeeper could not help ogling the strange mixture of garments on the young lady for it was odd to see such a beauty draped in such coarse clothing. The *señora* would tend to that though, for there were many gowns hanging in the closet of Señorita Delores' bedroom.

"I'll prepare a bath for you, miss, if you'd like?" Drusilla offered.

"That would be nice, Drusilla," Kristina replied. After meeting Danton's attractive and tastefully dressed mother, Kristina felt self-conscious about her own appearance. She yearned to have a frock to slip into after the refreshing bath Drusilla had proposed. The remainder of the gowns in her bundle had been lovely once, she thought to herself.

Drusilla excused herself, only to return to the room in a few minutes. As if she'd read Kristina's mind, she had on her arm a lovely rose-colored gown and an assortment of white lacy garments. She also had brought a pair of soft leather slippers in a fawn color.

"*Señora* thought you might like to wear these after your bath, miss," Drusilla said, her face showing compassion for the girl now that the *señora* had enlightened her about the little guest's dilemma.

74

"Oh, how thoughtful of the *señora*," Kristina exclaimed, fingering the soft, luxurious material of the pale rose gown.

"Ah, yes . . . that is the way of Señora Navarro. I brought this ribbon for a sash. You are such a wee one that Miss Delores' waist is probably larger." Drusilla spread the gown and the undergarments on the bed, and she set the toilet articles and towels in their place.

She left Kristina alone then, reminding her that if she needed anything at all she could just request it.

While his mother and Drusilla had been engaged in conversation, Danton had left the sitting room, bidding his mother a hasty farewell and telling her he'd see her at dinner. He was off to talk to Santiago about his transaction with Emil Cruz for the goats.

Little had he known that his impulsive offer to go to the Cruz's for Santiago would turn out as it had. But the old Mexican hadn't been feeling too well the day before so Danton had suggested that he ride over to Emil's in his stead. It was a long ride and certainly too taxing for a man of Santiago's age, especially when he was battling a chest cold.

As Danton walked jauntily out to the barn to find his old friend, he was secretly glad he'd given way to an impulse to gaze upward at the window of Kristina's room. Her pretty face had stared down at him, and she had watched, fascinated, as his magnificent, male body moved gracefully away from the house. Her green eyes had measured and absorbed the whole of him, from the top of his black wavy hair down to the expensive leather boots on his feet. He wore no coat, only a rich brown, leather vest. Kristina had recalled how she'd leaned back against his broad chest as they'd ridden along the trail coming to Silvercreek. The heat of his body had felt good. It had permeated her back.

His muscled arms, when they encircled her waist, had a masterful, powerful touch. Now as she watched him, she did not doubt the strength in those arms or that they could urge a woman to surrender in his embrace.

Her eyes flashed brighter and her long lashes fluttered with a rush of excitement. What was it, this queer feeling washing over her?

Something seemed so familiar about this scene. She struggled to recall what it was as she stood by the window looking down at the handsome Danton. Have I watched you before, Danton Navarro? her heart cried out. But she felt she was indulging in whimsy. How could she forget someone like Danton Navarro?

If she had seen him before, it must have been in her girlish fantasies. Yes, that must be it.

Chapter 8

It had taken Drusilla only a few minutes of stitching to take in the waistline of the pale rose gown so the frock fit Kristina to perfection. Then she'd held the folds of material while Kristina had slipped her arms into the fitted long sleeves and her head through the squared lace-edged neckline. Finally, Drusilla tugged the gathered skirt until it fell the way it should.

"There, Miss Kit. We got you fixed up mighty pretty. Sure is a nice color to go with that hair of yours," Drusilla told her.

Kristina looked at herself in the mirror. As a result of pulling the gown over her head, long strands of hair streamed over her face. "Now, if I can just get some order to all this hair." She laughed.

"I brought you a pretty ribbon or a couple of haircombs, should you wish to use them," the housekeeper offered.

"Well, we'll see which works, Drusilla. I . . . I hope Señora Lucía's daughter doesn't mind my wearing her clothes."

"Oh no, miss. I can tell you that little Delores is a sweet child. In fact, I just happened to hear her and the *señora* talking awhile ago downstairs and she's eager to see you. Fact is, Señora Lucía was having to restrain her from rushing up here to meet you before dinner."

Kristina smiled, "Really?"

"Really. The *señora* was telling her that she shouldn't bother you."

Kristina whirled around from the full-length mirror in which she'd been surveying herself, and with a flip of her head, she swung the hair out of her eyes. A serious look on her lovely face, she murmured falteringly, "I . . . I guess you've been told about me, Drusilla . . . about my memory?"

After hesitating for a second, Drusilla answered candidly. "Yes, ma'am, I was told. It's nothing you can help. Any of us could have that happen. Most likely you got a hard blow on your pretty head. I've heard that can happen."

Kristina gazed down at the floor for a moment before letting her eyes dart back up to the housekeeper who had a friendly look on her face. "I suppose that's possible," Kristina said, shrugging her shoulders.

"Well, you will just have to give yourself time, dear. Everything will be all right. Can't think of nicer people to be with than the Navarros in the meanwhile."

"And you are nice too, Drusilla," Kristina said, taking a seat at the dressing table.

Placing her hands firmly on her broad waistline and tilting her head at an angle, Drusilla gave the young girl a pleased smile. "Thank you, miss! You need me to help you with your hair?"

"No, I can manage, Drusilla. Shall I go downstairs when I finish? Is that what the *señora* wishes?"

"Oh yes, ma'am. Whenever you wish. You will soon find out that Señora Lucía wishes you to do as you'd like. Gracious hospitality abides in this house—always has." Drusilla winked and pointed a finger at Kristina, saying, "You'll know what I mean before the evening

78

is over."

As Kristina descended the stairway to join the family for dinner, she realized that she should have felt apprehensive, but she didn't.

After the refreshing, perfumed bath, in the lovely freshly pressed gown with her hair brushed to a coppery luster, she looked ravishingly radiant and glowing. She had no need of jewelry to make her sparkle but she did notice the lovely, twinkling peridot ring on her finger. Curiosity rose about who had presented the exquisite piece of jewelry.

Before getting her first glimpse of Danton's younger sister, Kristina heard the girl's soft voice and then Lucía's melodious laughter as she turned to go into the parlor.

Delores, who was dressed in a pretty frock of jonquil yellow, immediately shot her eyes in Kristina's direction and smiled at her, thinking as she did so how that shade of yellow accented the girl's dark good looks. Kristina noted that Delores let her long, black hair hang free and that it was unadorned as her own was.

Señora Lucía Navarro rose from an upholstered chair and rushed to greet her. As though to reassure Kristina, she clasped her hands in hers and led her to her daughter. "My dear, I wish you to meet my daughter, Delores. Delores, this is our dear little Kit."

Unbridled admiration in her voice, Delores declared, "Lordy, you're beautiful! Isn't she beautiful, Mother?"

Lucía laughed and hugged her daughter. "Can you believe, Kit, there are those who think my little Delores here is shy?"

"Well, I think you're beautiful too, Delores," Kristina told the black-haired girl standing beside her. Their heights were almost the same. Delores was a bit taller than Kristina, but her figure was more boyish, without the curving waistline, and her bosom had not yet developed.

"Dinner will be served shortly, Kit. I hope you like Drusilla's special recipe for roast chicken." Lucía motioned Kristina to a seat. Danton had not yet appeared, and Kristina wondered if he would be absent from the gathering that night.

But as she took a seat on the settee and Delores sat down beside her, she suddenly knew without turning her head that he was standing in the archway. He looked so devastatingly handsome that she could not restrain a deep intake of breath.

He wore no coat, only a frosty-clean white shirt, open at the neck where a silk scarf was tied. His dark blue pants seemed molded to his firm masculine body, and although he had obviously brushed his blue-black hair, one stubborn wisp seemed determined to fall over his forehead. He ambled slowly into the room, thinking it contained a marvelous array of gorgeous ladies. Immediately recognizing Delores' gown on Kristina, he decided it was much more flattering on Kit whose fuller figure made it more seductive. His dark eyes danced over the lovely curves accented by the rose material, coming to rest at the neckline trimmed with lace. He was very aware of Kit's beauty. Suddenly he was glad Damien was not with them.

"Good evening, ladies," he said.

Did he detect an impish look in his sister's eyes? Was the little minx starting to matchmake for him? Probably so. She often did.

"Danton dear, it would appear the ladies are going to outnumber you tonight," Lucía commented light-heartedly.

"A situation, Mother, I do not mind at all." He strolled over to lean against the massive stone fireplace. "Good evening, Kit. May I say you look very fetching in that rose gown?"

"Thank you, Danton," Kristina said, giving him a warm smile. His black liquid eyes did more than warm her; they seemed to set her aflame. She felt flushed, as if burned by the summer sun.

Delores giggled. "I shall never wear that gown again, I swear it! Not after I've seen it on Kit. It looks much better on her than it did on me."

"Oh, Delores!" Kristina sighed, and her eyes darted from Delores to Lucía before finally lighting on Danton's handsome, tanned face. "You have a very sweet sister, Danton."

Shrugging his broad shoulders, he smirked playfully. "Well, I guess so. Most of the time, she's pretty nice."

"Now, Danton!" Delores protested weakly. She hoped he wasn't going to start teasing her unmercifully as Damien sometimes did.

Lucía Navarro threw her hands up in a gesture of surrender. "You see, Kit, what I put up with and when Danton's twin is added to this crowd it's even more hectic."

"Oh, Señora Navarro, you have a beautiful family," Kristina declared.

Lucía Navarro was about to say that she was sure the auburn-haired girl had a nice family somewhere too, but Drusilla appeared at the door to announce that dinner was ready. Delores hastily took Kristina's arm to guide her into the formal dining room, leaving Danton to walk with their mother.

Lucía clasped her son's arm, suppressing a smile as she watched Danton frown. So that is the way it is, Lucía mused. Danton's emotions were obviously already involved. It could not be otherwise, or he would not have reacted so, not her aloof, elusive son.

Lucía Navarro was a woman with an inquisitive

nature. Most people would not suspect it—her own children were not aware of it—but her beloved Victor had known. Tonight, her curiosity was whetted.

As they sat around the long dining table illuminated by candlelight that accented the white linen tablecloth, the cut-crystal glasses, and Lucía's fine china and silverware, she thought about Victor as she ate and observed those around her.

Yes, she could see his face. With great dignity, he would have measured her, and he'd have given her just a slight hint of a smile. For Victor was not a man without humor. Who knew that better than Lucía Navarro!

She noticed that Danton was drinking his white wine but that he ate little of the roast chicken which she knew he usually devoured with relish. The two girls, however, certainly appeared to be making up for Danton's diminished appetite, and they giggled and chatted like two friends of longstanding.

The lovely little Kit was certainly a well-mannered young lady. She had obviously been brought up as a proper young lady should be. Her parents had to be people of quality for her to have such grace and charm, Lucía concluded.

Drusilla busily moved around the table, clearing away their plates so she could serve the dessert, a bread pudding with a special lemon sauce.

"That was the most delicious meal I've eaten since . . ." Kristina stopped speaking and a look of despair blanketed her face. She laughed, feeling slightly embarrassed. "Well, I guess I can't say . . . I don't remember."

"Well, Drusilla will be pleased to know you enjoyed it, Kit," Lucía told her. "That is the main thing."

"Serves Damien right that he didn't make it home to get some of Dru's good bread pudding," Delores said.

82

A deep voice resounded through the room, causing everyone at the long dining table to turn around. "But Damien isn't going to miss getting his share, sweetie."

"Damien!" Delores exclaimed, as she looked up to see her other brother standing in the doorway.

Lucía turned in her chair, pleased to see that her wandering son had returned to Silvercreek. Kristina's back was toward the doorway but she, too, swung around to gaze upon the towering figure standing in the shadowy entrance.

The spacious room was lit only by the three candles, one at each end of the table and another on the long sideboard across the room.

Damien had already spotted the young lady sitting with his mother, Delores, and Danton. From where he stood her long flowing hair appeared to be chocolate brown, and even when Kristina turned her emerald eyes upon him, he saw no resemblance to the young lady from El Paso. Quite the contrary, he was intrigued by the enchanting sight Kristina presented and he wondered if she was a new arrival in the area.

He moved with that elegant grace of a dancer as he went around the table to give Lucía Navarro a kiss on the forehead and then greeted his sister in the same fashion. "Nice to see you, Danton. Didn't know you were going to be here at Silvercreek," Damien declared, his eyes on Kristina as he spoke.

Danton didn't get a chance to reply for the exuberant Delores interrupted. "This is Kit, Damien—Danton's friend." Before anyone could stop her and much to the *señora*'s chagrin, Delores was giving Damien explicit details about why Kit was at Silvercreek.

Danton was seething at the thoughtlessness of his young, impetuous sister and Señora Navarro was sorely tempted to ram her linen napkin into Delores' busy mouth. Kristina, however, found the situation

83

amusing because she already felt quite fond of Danton's sister. She pictured her as her own younger sister although she felt that it was a relationship she'd never known in her past life.

By the time Delores had ceased to talk, Kristina wore a smile on her face and Lucía calmed down. None of those seated at the table noticed Damien's tense reaction, and his turbulent feelings were hidden when he played his charming self and directed his words toward Kristina, "Nice to meet you, Señorita Kit . . . isn't it?"

"Yes, Kit. That is what Danton has christened me," Kristina smiled up at the towering figure standing beside her. Appraising his dark handsomeness, she found his resemblance to Danton amazing. How could someone tell them apart? It had a startling effect on her when he took her hand. His dark black eyes seemed to be boring into hers, and she felt the heat of him penetrating her hand as he held it.

Why she did it, she could not say, but something urged her to glance across the table in Danton's direction. When she did, something about his demeanor chilled her to the core.

To Danton, the scene he was witnessing was an old one. It had been repeated many times with various young ladies since he and Damien had discovered the difference between boys and girls. Only this time, an overwhelming river of jealousy flooded Danton and he had an insatiable desire to sock Damien's smiling face. His fists clenched, and his mouth and jaw tightened. He wanted to warn Kit not to be taken in by Damien's shallow charms as so many pretty girls had been.

To prevent the black fire of his eyes from searing into her when she glanced his way, Danton glanced away from Kit, fearing his anger would show and she'd think it was directed at her.

84

Damien was experiencing a different kind of agony. The minute Delores had started her tale about the girl sitting at their table Damien had felt as though a sharp bolt of lightning had struck him in the gut. Impossible as it seemed, this auburn-haired enchantress was none other than Kristina Whelan, Florine Whelan's daughter.

He should have known it would be Danton that dealt him this hand. Danton was his nemesis, Damien had decided long ago. He was a fatalist, and had also decided that the time would come when he and Danton would engage in a life or death battle. Was this slip of a girl to be the spark that would enflame their fury?

If so, Damien mused, I will certainly take this sweet nectar as my bounty. Wild desire shot through him as he gazed at Kit, and he was determined not to deny himself the sensuous pleasure he craved even if he was to pay a price for the sins he'd committed already.

As long as little Kit didn't regain her memory he was safe, but should those gorgeous green eyes ever flash wide with recognition, he could be a dead man.

Damien knew his twin brother resented the attention he was paying the girl. That was not like Danton at all. Could it possibly be that the girl had captured old Danton's heart? Seeking to goad his brother, Damien quipped, "How'd you happen to come up with the name of Kit, Danton old boy?"

Damn him, Danton thought. Nonetheless he forced a smile. It would not do for Damien to suspect the truth, that he was infuriated by the attention Damien had showered on Kit. Pushing back his chair, he ignored Damien, addressing himself to his mother and the young ladies.

"If you will excuse me, ladies, I'll go have a cheroot."

Nonchalantly, he turned to leave the table. With a roguish twinkle in his eyes, he challenged Damien, "I'll let you try to figure the name out. Until you can, it will be a little secret between me and Kit. Isn't that right, Kit?" He winked at her.

As Kristina smiled at him, the strangest sensation washed over her. She had butterflies in her stomach as she'd had that night at the Crystal Castle when he'd winked at her, but she didn't remember that. Kristina had no memory of that night.

Danton strolled out of the room, unaware of the quandary he'd left her in. His young, male body was stirred by her radiant smile as he stepped onto the long veranda to puff on his cheroot.

Kristina, left with the rest of Danton's family, floundered in a mental maze, trying to discover why Danton's winking at her should have such a disturbing effect on her. He had winked and smiled at her, and she had responded with a smile for she was pleased that he was not irritated with her.

What Danton Navarro thought about her was very important to her. His smile made her heart surrender, and she knew that his lips could captivate her and she would be powerless to deny him anything!

Chapter 9

Accustomed now to being addressed as Kit, Kristina Whelan responded as readily as though it had always been her name. After several weeks of living at Silvercreek, she found herself feeling that it was, indeed, her home and that the Navarros were her family. Damien was the only exception, for no brother would look at his sister as Damien looked at her.

She adored and was adored by old Santiago who definitely played the watchdog when Danton had to leave Silvercreek to go back to Austin. More than once, Santiago had discreetly stalked the young couple when Damien had taken Kristina for a horseback ride across the countryside. Santiago knew young Damien would have been furious if he spied him, but luck had been with the old Mexican so far.

Lucía was just as protective of her young charge, for she knew Damien's penchant for beautiful young ladies. Her son or not, she would not allow him to take liberties with Kit. Lucía couldn't explain why she was so drawn to the auburn-haired little stranger living in her home, but the bond was there.

She had become so much a part of their lives that Lucía Navarro wondered if their meeting had been destined. It was almost uncanny. The servants in the house and on the ranch had taken to the girl as though she'd lived there all her life, and she was truly Delores' sister.

Kit's spontaneous warmth and her outgoing personality had been a good influence on Delores. Lucía had noticed a decided difference in Delores, particularly in her devoted worship of Damien. Now, she spent time with Kit, and her feelings were not hurt when Damien shrugged her aside. If he wanted to be in Kit's company, he must include his sister at Kit's insistence. Lucía knew Damien often gritted his teeth and restrained a loud complaint.

Oh, there was tension too. When Danton returned for the weekend Lucía noticed the signs of an explosive situation developing. So far, it had not gotten to the point where a confrontation was inevitable.

Each time Danton returned to Silvercreek Lucía had prodded him, asking if he'd gleaned any information about the young girl, but he always shook his head and answered, "Not a thing, Mother." Privately Danton chided himself for practicing such a deception, for it wasn't in his nature to do so. Yet he knew why he was not earnestly seeking to find out who Kit really was and where she'd come from. He'd confessed that to himself. When he was in Austin at his law office, his thoughts were back at Silvercreek with the beautiful girl with the flaming hair and the flashing green eyes. Her tantalizing image haunted his sleep, and the devious antics Damien might indulge in while Danton was not around were the cause of tormenting nightmares.

It was hard for him to lie to Lucía Navarro, and guilt hung heavily on his broad shoulders. He had made no inquiries about a missing girl when Sheriff Gorman had visited his office a week ago. What had caught Danton's attention, however, was Gorman's conversation about the four masked men who'd robbed the Crystal Castle, shooting the proprietress, Florine Whelan. He recalled his trip to El Paso and his fleeting glimpse of the attractive lady gambler some six or seven months ago.

A suspicion grew in him, and it didn't fade as the days had passed. Regardless of how it repulsed and sickened him, that robbery could be Damien's handiwork. His brother had some unsavory pals. The ridiculous notion kept cropping up in his mind.

In part, that was the reason he had come to Silvercreek this weekend. He wanted to have a talk with his twin brother. His arrival at Silvercreek had started on a sour note. He'd seen Damien atop his huge black stallion, with Kit riding the little roan mare alongside him. Damn, this was just what he had been afraid of!

What a glorious sight she was atop the mare though, her long tresses flowing so wild and free; only a glossy black ribbon keeping her hair from obscuring the full impact of her beautiful face. The big smile on her face made Danton's heart pound with a rapid, erratic beat for she was obviously delighted to see him.

She looked more beautiful now than when he'd last seen her, and that was only a week ago. She wore one of Delores' soft, silky blouses over a black twill, divided skirt. The tantalizing sight of her jutting breasts, outlined so perfectly in the sheer blouse, fired Danton's desire. He wanted to rush to her, take her in his arms, and capture those rosebud lips in a long, lingering kiss.

Suddenly Damien swung his hat into the air and called out a greeting, and Kristina gave an excited, eager wave of her hand. Although the three young people were unaware of it, back in a grove of trees, Santiago quietly sat his horse, watching the scene as the young *señor* returned to Silvercreek. He smiled sadly as he observed the trio, for he felt that trouble lay ahead for them. So young they were and so full of spirit! He was not fooled for a minute as to why Señor Danton's trips from the city were more frequent, and he was certain even though the *señora* had not confided in him that she knew.

He watched until Danton's mount was beside the roan and the huge black stallion, then he urged his horse onto the trail back to the corral. Santiago knew his obligation was over for this day. Señor Danton was home.

Together, the three cantered up the long drive toward the house. There was little conversation, but Kristina could not keep from noticing that Danton's eyes were on her each time her glance darted in his direction.

"I'm glad you're home, Danton," she said, smiling.

"Are you now, little one?" He tried to sound casual and light-hearted.

"Of course, I am!" She laughed softly and her eyes flashed brightly.

"Well, I'm glad to be here. Tomorrow morning, I'd enjoy your company on a ride before breakfast, eh? You are much better than you were, I see."

"Oh, I am, and you'll see for yourself. Damien has been taking me out often," she confessed. "I have improved, haven't I, Damien?"

"Tremendously!" Damien declared. With a teasing smirk on his face, Damien sought to taunt his brother by saying, "I've been trying to stand in for you while you've been busy, Danton. Our little Kit here is a vivacious bundle of energy and vitality." His hat was set at a cocky angle, and his black eyes sparked with the same boyish mischief Danton Navarro knew quite well.

Danton gave him a slow, easy grin because he knew

exactly what Damien was doing. As he knew Damien, Damien knew him. Each possessed a hot-blooded Latin temper but Danton liked to think he had more control. Lately, though, he couldn't be too sure.

While he would have preferred to stay at Kit's side, Danton excused himself when they reached the stable, saying he had to speak to Santiago. "Tell Mother I'll be up to the house shortly, Damien," he requested before turning away from them.

Kristina sensed the coolness in his tone, and she felt disappointed as Damien clasped her hand and they jauntily strolled toward the house. She paid no attention to Damien's chatter, but twice she turned back to look at his brother's towering figure. Danton's back was turned to them. He would have been pleased to know of her disappointment and of her yearning to be beside him.

Mumbling as if she were talking to herself, Kristina grumbled. "Is he always so serious, Damien?"

"Most of the time. Not me, *chiquita!* Not me or you either, I'd wager," he said as he gave her a tickle under her chin.

She looked up at him and giggled. "You're never serious, Damien Navarro!"

"Bet you never were, little Kit," Damien prodded. He had often done so over the last few weeks, attempting to check on her memory, for he found it harder and harder to relax with Kristina Whelan living at the ranch.

He cursed the always gallant Danton, blaming him for his sleepless nights. But had it not been that way as long as he could remember?

It was a pleasant family gathering that evening at Silvercreek. The dinner was superb and the conversation at the dining table was casual and pleasant. Lucía wore an elegant black frock, and she indulged in a third glass of wine. There was no verbal sparring between her handsome sons. The dinner hour had been pleasant.

Santiago's report to Danton had lightened his mood, and when they strolled out of the dining room, Kristina leaned close to whisper in his ear, "Could we go for a stroll, Danton? I've something to talk to you about."

His heart leaped with joy at the thought of being alone with her, but in the next moment, he wondered what was troubling her.

"Of course, Kit. Should you get a shawl?"

"I brought it down when I came to dinner." She smiled impishly.

"So you were planning this, were you?" he teased.

"Yes."

She took his arm and they politely excused themselves. Lucía remained unruffled, but Delores and Damien exchanged glances as they followed their mother into the parlor, their curiosity about Danton and Kit whetted.

Calling Damien's attention to her, Lucía invited her son to join her in a brandy. "Perhaps, a game of gin?" she added.

Silvery moonlight showered the courtyard gardens as Danton guided Kristina down the flagstone path. Her tiny hand was on his arm, and its light touch made a liquid flame surge through his body!

Whether it was the magic of the moonlight or whether he merely gave in to an impulsive desire, Danton slipped his arm around her back, encircling her waist. "What is it, Kit? Nothing is wrong, is it?"

She dared not be so bold as to say that nothing could be wrong with his arm around her, but she thought it. To her, Danton Navarro was everything a man should be—powerful and strong!

"I guess you'll probably think me childish and silly, but I've been bothered ever since your mother mentioned the party she's going to give in a few weeks. Now, don't laugh at me, Danton, but how am I going to be explained?"

"Why, you are our guest, Kit," he said quite simply.

She froze. "No, that's not what I mean. How will I be introduced to people, as Kit or Miss Kit. Miss Kit what?"

She was serious, and Danton now understood. Noting how adorable and childlike she looked, he gave way to another impulse. He picked her up in his arms and strode to one of the garden benches to sit down. There she sat on his lap as he began to speak. "I see what you mean, little one."

"You gave me a name, Danton. You gave me the name of Kit, so Kit what?"

As he gazed at her face, lovely with the moonlight gleaming on it, he knew he never wanted to be parted from her. That was the reason he hadn't tried to find out who she was. A voice within him cried out that the name he wanted to give her was his own: Navarro. But that was not possible just yet!

"What about Kit Winters? How does that sound to you? I found you on that mountain in the winter. I'll never forget the sight of you hobbling along that wooded trail as long as I live." His intense, black eyes danced over her. Their lips were only inches apart. Experienced she might not have been, but Kristina knew instinctively that Danton was going to kiss her. No sooner did that thought rush through her pretty head than his sensuous mouth met her lips. The sensation that contact stirred was like none Kristina had ever known, much more overpowering than she'd imagined.

Her head whirled giddily, and she clung to him. Her

sweet surrender had a wild effect on Danton. His head whirled, and intoxicated by the flowery fragrance of her, he nuzzled her auburn hair.

He felt the slight motion of her body pressing on his lap and her breasts brushed against his chest as he held her head with his hands. When his lips finally released hers, he moaned. "Oh, God . . . God, Kit! I shouldn't—"

Somewhat breathless, she stopped him, "But I wanted you to, Danton." Her beautiful eyes were now glazed with passion. With her lips against his cheek, she whispered, "Please, kiss me . . . kiss me again, Danton."

He would have had to be dead to deny her plea, and Danton Navarro was anything but dead. Every fiber in his male body was alive and wanting, wanting to love her endlessly. His hand moved to caress the tantalizing flesh pressing against his chest, and she gave out a soft moan of pleasure, then crying out his name.

Whoever she'd been or whatever she'd known before, surely she had not known such ecstasy, Kristina was certain of that. Could she possibly have forgotten such a thing? She couldn't have!

The powerful essence of the man was demanding to conquer and possess her, yet she had no fear of being possesed by Danton. She wanted to be his. Willingly her enflaming body sought his, and Kristina felt that she was soaring to the heavens.

The strumming of a guitar brought Danton down from the lofty height of rapture. With lightning suddenness, his sanity returned. His behavior was despicable! Danton had had his share of women, and he knew he wouldn't have behaved this way with anyone, only with the girl named Kit. With her, everything was different. What was it about this enchanting little waif that elicited such intense feelings from him? God, if he only knew!

His sophistication and intelligence could not help him now. He was a man with a weakness he couldn't control. At least, he almost hadn't!

He knew who was strumming the guitar, and he wondered if that sly old fox, Santiago, had done it on purpose.

Kristina was stunned by Danton's abrupt release of her, and she stared up at him, her eyes full of perplexing questions he was not about to answer.

Taking a deep breath, he muttered, "I shouldn't have done that. Forgive me . . . please!"

Falteringly, she replied, "Forgive you? What should I forgive—the fact that you wanted to kiss me and I wanted you to?" She made it seem so simple and uncomplicated, and her honesty endeared her to Danton all the more.

"No, my sweet, innocent Kit. Not the kiss, but what kissing you could lead to." Danton almost wished she'd slapped his face or cursed him. That would have been easier to deal with.

Kristina's own frustrations were now making her angry. "Are you saying you don't like me or like kissing me?" There was a pout to her lovely mouth, and hurt showed in her eyes.

Christ, he couldn't allow her to think that, not for a moment! Dear God, she obviously knew nothing about men and women! Danton scratched his head as he tried to decide whether he should explain that he cared very deeply for her and wanted to protect her.

Blunt honesty, he supposed. He took her hands in his and his black eyes were mellow and warm with emotion as he spoke, "I like you very much, Kit, and yes, God knows, I want to kiss you, again and again. But I am a man, Kit, and I want to love you like no man has the right to love you unless he's your husband. Do you understand, *querida?* Do you know what I'm trying to tell you?" Damn! He felt like a stupid idiot. He was stammering, seeking the right words, doing a miserable job of it.

She sat quietly for a moment, staring at their joined hands. "I see. I understand . . . I think." Her green eyes turned to look into his. "What does *querida* mean, Danton?"

Only then did he realize what he'd called her, and he reluctantly answered her. "Many things. Darling . . . dearest . . . the woman I love."

The most radiant smile came to her lips, and her soft voice was etched with smug assurance when she tilted her head to one side and remarked, "Well, I can be very patient, but you might as well know, Danton Navarro, I think I love you too."

Danton set her on her feet, and in his deep, firm voice, he said, "Come on, you little witch! You've cast enough spells on me for one night! I'm getting you back to the house before we do something we'll both regret!"

Kristina smiled as she followed him. His eyes were still warm with desire so she knew he wasn't as angry as he pretended to be.

Chapter 10

The same moon that showered its silvery beams on Kristina and Danton earlier filtered through her bedroom window now. Kristina lay, quiet and thoughtful, on the canopied bed. A multitude of thoughts rushed through her head. It had been a strange but wonderful evening. Was it the magic of springtime? The *señora* had mentioned that morning that the spring was coming to the countryside because she'd seen a little purple crocus in full bloom.

Kristina knew some kind of magical spell had been cast on her. She'd never felt so enchanted, so transformed. Even though Danton was no longer near her, his essence lingered on. It was sweet and wonderful to just lie there and think about him as she stared out the window into the night's quietness.

Random thoughts mingled with her musings on Danton. She thought of Damien, of the quizzical look on his face when she and Danton had returned to the house from the courtyard. It was amazing that, having shared the intimate interlude with Danton, she could never confuse the Navarro brothers again. Yes, they had the same black eyes and the same handsome features, identically arched black brows and the same sensuous-looking mouths . . . but now she could see the difference in them. She would swear that she'd never mistake Damien for Danton. She could not put it into words, but she was aware of a marked difference.

Señora Navarro had smiled softly when they'd returned to the house, as though she knew exactly what the two of them had been about in the courtyard garden. Kristina wondered if she'd had a telltale blush on her face when they'd strolled in to join the *señora* and Delores. Oh, she had no doubt Delores would enlighten her about that tomorrow.

Tomorrow . . . how would she feel upon coming face to face with Danton? Would she be embarrassed about what had happened between them?

She vividly recalled his strong hand cupping her breast with such a tender touch, a touch that made her shiver. While she could have sworn this feeling was new and wonderful, in a disturbing, veiled mist she had visions of a man like Danton and another woman. Because the woman with him was not her, she decided to think on that no more. The blonde-haired woman clinging to the man she loved was an unpleasant mental picture.

Sleep conquered her shortly and she slept deeply until late the next morning. It was just as well she enjoyed the extra few hours of rest because if she had awakened in time to keep her riding date with Danton, the weather outside would have changed those plans. An April shower dampened the countryside around Silvercreek, and even Danton had been tempted to ignore the hands of the clock and roll back into the bed.

Instead he'd reluctantly sat up and swung his feet onto the floor. Rain or not, he had some urgent matters to settle with his brother. It wasn't hard to read Damien's thoughts about Kit. Last night, he'd known that he'd not tolerate one false move from his twin brother where she was concerned. Damien was going to know what to expect from him should he be foolhardy enough to try one of his shenanigans.

Danton dressed in the casual clothes he always wore at the ranch, forsaking the finely tailored coats and pants he ordered from London and wore in the city of Austin. It was rare for him to prefer solitude to his mother's gracious company on mornings like this but on this day he was glad he was enjoying Drusilla's strong black coffee alone.

Having been in the Navarro household for many years, Drusilla sensed the young *señor*'s mood and obliged him by not chattering as she served him. She puttered about silently, allowing Danton the quiet comfort of the early morning hour. The only sounds in the spacious house seemed to be the pitter-patter of the rain drops pelting the window panes. It wasn't a hard rain, just one of the light spring showers which always seemed to enhance the green of the grass and trees.

In the stillness Danton reflected on the preceding night. Could his family see how infatuated he was with the lovely girl he'd brought home? He had noticed his younger sister staring curiously at the two of them, and he knew Lucía Navarro's amazing talent for seeing through any deception; but it was the apprehensive look on his brother's face which whetted his interest.

"Well, Danton, I thought I was the only one up around here." The voice broke into the quiet solitude. Danton turned to see his brother posed in the doorway. Damien sauntered into the room and sank into the chair across from Danton. "Good morning to sleep. Mother's extra glass of wine must be the reason she's not down yet." He laughed.

Danton merely mumbled in response. This particular demeanor of Danton's always left Damien a little apprehensive for he could not interpret his twin's mood at times like this.

"You going to get back for mother's shindig?" Damien let his dark eyes dart over to his brother as Drusilla placed his usual plate of ham and eggs in front of him, greeting him briefly, and instantly returned to her kitchen. It seemed the Navarro family was going to eat in shifts this rainy morning, and Drusilla detested that for it dragged out her chores.

Danton stared off in space at nothing in particular. "Probably and what fair little *señorita* are you planning to escort this time, Damien?"

Damien chuckled, "Haven't made up my mind just yet, Dant!" Caution, Damien told himself, for something about Danton's look urged it. "Might just give that cute little Carmella the pleasure of my company. What do you think?"

"Carmella Morilla is a beautiful girl. Has her family recovered from the shock of Miguel's death?" Danton asked. He knew the Morilla family had been stunned by the death of their only son who had been thrown from his horse. The young Miguel's neck had been broken.

"Mother paid a visit to them last week. According to her, an air of great sorrow lingers at Los Palacios, but Roberto Morilla told her he plans to come because he feels he must make Antonia get out and join the living."

One is never prepared for the death of a loved one, Danton mused. He thought about the death of his father. Victor's death had affected him far more drastically than any of his family had realized, for he was the only hero Danton had ever had. How often Danton thought of their last conversation, when they'd taken one of their walks around the grounds of Silvercreek.

It was evident from the tall impressive figure of

Victor Navarro that he was a strong, dignified gentleman. Family and tradition had played a most important role in Victor's life. Danton's chest had never expanded with such pride as it had when Victor had voiced his delight about Danton's becoming a lawyer.

"I will confess to you, my son, that I wanted always to be a lawyer, but I became involved in ranching and I never got around to it," Victor had said.

Danton knew he would never forget that moment or that day as long as he lived. On that day he'd felt that he was a man . . . he'd known it!

And it was on that day that his father had told him, in a confidential way, that he knew Danton's twin brother had a weakness in him. Danton had since wondered if Victor had some forewarning of his death and had intended to prepare Danton with a warning.

As they sat together now, he and Damien, he found it hard to imagine this handsome, engaging brother was guilty of any wrongdoing. Yet he knew better. He'd witnessed the evil in Damien.

In homage to the man he so greatly respected, since his father's death Danton had done all he could to ease Lucía Navarro's concerns. That was what his father would have wished him to do. After six years, however, Danton wondered if he'd really done the right thing. While he'd been trying to make things easier for his mother, hadn't he also made it easier for Damien to get into more trouble?

Danton had never been able to ease his own conscience about killing that man in the White Elephant Saloon up in Fort Worth over a year ago. Perhaps, he should have allowed his twin brother to pay the price for his irresponsible ways. Perhaps, he'd been prejudiced to blame the whole fiasco on Damien's buddy, Wes Clarke. Hell, Damien was a man now!

101

"Want to go out to the barn with me, Damien?" Danton asked, pushing back on his chair. If he tarried any longer at the table, their mother would be joining them, or Delores or Kit. He wanted no interruptions once he started to talk to Damien.

"Sure. I'm not busy, not with the rain coming down," Damien remarked. He rose from his chair. "Might just be the right time for a good poker game in the bunkhouse with the guys. What do you say?"

"Later . . . maybe."

Danton shrugged Damien's suggestion aside. More important matters occupied him. He informed his brother that he'd run upstairs for his slicker and then meet him in the hall. However, Danton wasn't there when Damien came out of the dining room.

Damien fidgeted at the unexpected delay, but upstairs Danton had not anticipated what he would encounter as he dashed down the hallway which was darker than usual due to the cloudy skies.

Still drowsy with sleep, Kit had emerged from her doorway to amble across the hall to Delores' room, a habit both girls had gotten into since Kit's arrival at Silvercreek. Usually the two young ladies went down for breakfast together. This morning Kit had found herself in need of a needle with which to sew a loose button on the blouse she intended to wear with the light-weight wool skirt. The rain had put a chill in the air. It hardly feels like springtime this morning, Kit thought.

As Danton's booted heel lifted off the top step to make a bold, lunging stride down the hall the two of them collided. His huge body plowed into hers though he tried desperately to break his momentum.

"Lord!" Kit gasped, feeling jarred as he slammed into her. Instinctively, his arms reached out to her, and once again, her petiteness struck him. Danton had a startled look on his face when Kit tilted her head up to look at him. His black eyes were wide and alive, for the sight of her was enough to spark all of Danton's senses.

Had Kristina been a worldly woman wanting to use her feminine wiles to entice a man, she could not have been more successful. But she was not, so she just stood there, staring up at Danton.

In the pale green robe which was trimmed lavishly with ecru lace, she was a breath-taking sight to Danton. The stand-up lace ruffle at her neck and throat descended sharply to display the cleavage of her blossoming breasts. Those soft mounds of satiny flesh drew Danton's dancing eyes, and they aroused his desire. He wanted her. Damned if he didn't! Right now . . . this minute!

He guided her slowly toward the wall, his arms encasing her. "Are you hurt, *querida?* God, I'm . . . I'm so sorry." Danton's voice was husky due to the emotional state he found himself in.

"I'm . . . I'm all right, Danton." Kristina's dainty hand went up to his cheek, for he seemed to be unduly concerned over her. "Are you all right?"

A weak smile came to his lips as he mumbled, "You could hardly do me any harm, little Kit." He stood motionless, his huge body pressed against hers as he let himself drown in the beautiful green eyes staring up at him. Kit was entranced too, consumed by the sensations she was feeling. She felt the power in him build and mount as his intense craving grew. It excited Kristina that he should feel this way, that she could do this to him. This wild, wonderful attraction between a man and a woman was still new to her, but she could not deny that she wanted to know more of it. Once again, she told herself she could not possibly have known this feeling before. Once again, she was dismayed because she could not remember! When would she be normal like Delores or Lucía Navarro? Why had such a curse been put on her?

As her half-parted lips started to move, Danton could no longer deny himself their sweet nectar. He bent to kiss her. The right or wrong of it was of no importance at that moment. He was aware only of his desire. It was an unhurried, lingering kiss that left both of them breathless when Danton finally released her.

He muttered in a low voice, almost like a moan of anguish, "Dear God, Kit, you make it hard on a man!"

Stunned to find him deserting her and puzzled by his remark, for a second Kristina was bedazzled. Then she marched back to her room, her need of a needle entirely forgotten. As she slammed the door, she muttered angrily to the now empty hallway, "Well, Danton Navarro, you don't make it very easy for a lady!"

Men were devilishly hard to understand, she was beginning to think. Danton Navarro had had her in a state of confusion since he'd last returned from Austin.

She flung herself down on the bed and stretched her body lazily. Then a slow smile came to her face as she thought about what had just happened between them. He had called her *querida* again, and she'd liked the way his deep voice murmured it. She wondered if it was the handsome Danton Navarro who was naïve.

Across the hallway sitting back down on her bed, Delores was thoughtful too. She had heard the noise in the hallway and had opened her door just in time to see her brother kiss Kit. She'd muzzled her mouth to stifle a giggle and had quietly shut the door. But now she was smiling about what she'd seen. Danton and Kit! The idea pleased her tremendously!

Anger gnawed at Danton Navarro. He was annoyed by his utter lack of control where Kit was concerned. He'd never been faced with this dilemma before. It was rather lucidrous that he, the astute young lawyer, could be manipulated by this naïve girl. Yet, she had a far more devastating effect on him than the sophisticated Estellita Valero for whom he'd played the role of escort in Austin for a couple of years. With Estellita, he was always in control!

The oppressive gloom that had settled in over the Crystal Castle since that horrible night so many weeks ago would have lifted if those who loved her could have seen Kristina sitting in the bedroom of the Navarro ranch house. But her mother and her friends in El Paso feared that their beautiful auburn-haired "princess" had come to a disastrous end.

For the first few weeks after that ill-fated night Florine Whelan had been unable to feel much of anything for her own life hung in the balance. Her devoted Solitaire spent endless hours by her *mam'selle*'s bedside, as did Jason Hamilton.

What little information Jason could tell the sheriff was of no significance, nor could Solitaire provide any leads. The sheriff's posse had searched the surrounding countryside for a number of days afterward without turning up a clue that might reveal the girl's whereabouts.

But slowly and tediously Florine Whelan was brought back to health, and it was a glorious day for Jason and Solitaire when she was finally able to sit up, propped by pillows.

For Jason Hamilton, his dreams had come true when he'd again convinced Florine to become his wife so he might take care of her as he yearned to do. When Florine had accepted his proposal, they had celebrated by trying out her new wheelchair for the first time. On that day champagne and tears mingled with new hope. Florine was determined that as long as she was alive she had to make herself believe there was hope of finding Kristina. Dear God, she had to hope!

Without Jason and Solitaire, Florine could never have survived those harrowing days and weeks.

Chapter 11

Damien's impatience mounted as he waited for Danton's return. He paced down the hall toward the front entrance. When he heard the beating hooves of a horse and its rider, he glanced out the front door to see who was arriving. At that moment he was damned glad he had been pacing up and down.

He couldn't believe that the addle-brained Jesse would dare to come to Silvercreek. But he was out there, ready to dismount from that pinto of his. Damien dashed out the door, intending to stop Jesse from getting one foot closer to the house. He cursed under his breath. *Madre de Dios,* it could not have been a worse time to have the likes of him arrive, not with Danton here at Silvercreek!

The little scum had openly defied Damien's direct order that he never show his face around the ranch or anywhere near Silvercreek. That made Damien's temper soar as he marched out to face Jesse.

As Danton watched the strange scene enacted by the hitching post, he wondered who the stranger was. Why had the man come out on such a morning as this? He looked like a river rat. Streaming rivulets of water dripped from his wide-brimmed hat. Danton certainly could not recall any of the neighboring ranchers having a pinto like that one; but it was obvious that Damien knew the man.

Rather than go on out the door to where his brother and the stranger stood by the hitching post, Danton stood and observed their animated conversation. His slicker was draped over his arm and his thoughts of Kit had been forgotten.

Knowing his twin so well, Danton knew he was furious when he dismissed the rider. Danton continued to stand at the door after the man rode back down the long drive to see what Damien would do.

It seemed to him that Damien was debating whether to return to the house or go out to the barn. In the end, he ambled slowly toward the barn, and only then did Danton venture out the door to follow his brother.

When he came face to face with his brother as he entered the barn, he wasted no time inquiring about the stranger. He noticed that Damien had had a peculiar look on his face even before he'd heard Damien approach.

"Who was that guy, Damien? Don't think I've seen him around here before."

"Ah, just some drifter riding through—looking for work with spring coming. I told him we had all the hands we needed." Damien answered him in an offhanded manner, and then he turned his back toward Danton and strolled on down by the stalls. Danton had always had an uncanny effect on him when they locked eyes and Damien sought to lie. It was the same with his mother. God, there was a lot of Lucía Navarro in his twin, but Danton had also been a constant reminder of their stern, strict father.

Damien had often wondered who it was he had taken after. From what black sheep in the Navarro family had he inherited his ways? He wasn't Danton's breed of man!

Danton's brow arched with a skepticism he didn't try to conceal. There was no doubt in his mind that his brother lied. For some reason Damien was covering up the fact that he knew the drifter. Perhaps he just didn't want it known that he was acquainted with the little weasel.

Damien, who was almost the identical image of Danton, mystified his brother. They had been born into comfort and privilege. As sons of a wealthy and respected family, neither of them had needed to struggle for a living or an education. Danton had striven to become a man who was the equal of Victor Navarro and to have Lucía look upon him with pride in her eyes. Damien, however, had seemed to have an insatiable need to sully the Navarro name. Why would he want to do that?

Damien had begun to associate with unsavory characters at the age of eighteen, and he'd made his proclivity known to Danton shortly after he'd returned from visiting a friend of his in San Antonio. Danton had always felt that if he ever figured out the answer to Damien's strange behavior it would go back to the trip he'd made to San Antonio almost eight years ago, for that was when the quirk in his twin's character first emerged.

"What do you want to talk about, Danton? Something you want me to get done around Silvercreek when you go back to Austin?" Damien had again assumed a casual, happy-go-lucky facade.

"See anything of that dude . . . I think you said his name was Wes? Wes Clarke." Danton decided he might as well come straight to the point because Damien had not hesitated to lie about the stranger who'd come to Silvercreek looking for him.

Swaggering around and kicking aimlessly at the

barn floor, Damien shrugged. "Can't recall, Danton. Not for months, it seems like."

"Well, that's good, Damien—for your sake at least. Word's out that a dude fitting his description is wanted in El Paso for a robbery and a shooting. The Crystal Castle should ring a bell with you. As I recall you lost a wad there over six months ago."

Danton credited Damien with one thing: he could lie smoothly. While he didn't admire this quality in Damien, he never ceased to be amazed by it. But as old Santiago always said, "Chickens do come home to roost." He felt that Damien would soon have to face more than even he could handle.

Damien laughed good-naturedly, "Guess Mother didn't do as good a job of teaching me how to play cards." In the secret abyss of his mind he fretted, however, because nothing he'd ever attempted had equalled Danton's accomplishments. Danton—the paragon of perfection.

Danton was a magnificent horseman by the time he was fifteen, according to their father's appraisal. Danton was the brain, the genius. When the two of them had been sent away to school, it was Danton's marks that impressed Victor Navarro. Then his brother's move to become a lawyer had deeply touched Victor. Damien would never forget the night—they were all seated in the parlor—when old Victor had heaped praise on Danton.

Danton lit up a cheroot and ambled toward the barn door, noting that the sun was breaking through the clouds. As far as he was concerned, it was hopeless to try to talk to Damien for his brother was a confirmed liar. Where Kit was concerned, he had decided to deal with that issue in another way.

He had warned his brother that Wes Clarke was being sought by the law, and the rest lay in Damien's

109

hand. Kit's well-being . . . he planned to see to that himself.

That decided, he declared, "Well, looks like it's going to be a nice day after all. Think I'll go fetch Kit so we can have that ride we talked about."

"Guess the rain stopping puts that poker game I was thinking about on the back burner," Damien smiled. The fellows in the bunkhouse were not like the high-stake players Damien encountered at places like the Lucky Lady or the Crystal Castle so he could hold his own. He had been foolish enough to try his luck against experts, and he had lost the inheritance he had been left by his paternal grandmother. Danton had invested his portion in his law practice, and in property in the city of Austin.

"Felt lucky today, Damien?" Danton teased his twin.

"Yeah, I did," Damien shot back. His smile masked the anger and upset he was feeling. Danton's revelation about Wes bothered him very much, especially so because Jesse had appeared that morning.

The brothers emerged from the barn together to be greeted by the sight of Kit coming toward the barn. From her attire, it was obvious that she was anticipating the ride she and Danton had planned earlier. She wore Delores' divided skirt and a blouse. On her pretty head rested one of Delores' flat-crowned felt hats, the narrow band tied beneath her pert chin.

As she jauntily strode along, her auburn curls bobbed up and down on her shoulders, and her face glowed, its radiance outshining the sun in Danton's opinion. Both young men stopped, awaiting her.

"Good morning, you two. I'm ready, Danton. Are you?" There was a hint of mischief in her question.

Recalling their brief, but blazing encounter of only an hour ago, Danton could have sworn he saw a challenge in those green blazing eyes. The little imp!

Was she boldly daring him?

A broad grin split his face, and he was suddenly light-hearted. Damien was forgotten, as were the other problems that had been bothering him. "What are you waiting for?" he shot back at her.

Damien watched the two of them, and the fire in his brother's eyes verified what he'd already begun to suspect. Danton looked like a lovesick calf. He found that very amusing, but at the same time, he suddenly realized he could use this unexpected turn of events as a weapon against Danton.

He could have been invisible. The two of them were so oblivious of his presence. A few moments later, Damien called out a farewell to the pair. As he walked toward the house, he could not help chuckling to himself. Danton, of all people! Danton had a weakness too. Luckily he'd stumbled on it.

Danton and Kit walked back into the barn to saddle their mounts for the ride over the countryside. Neither had anything unpleasant in mind.

Danton's dapple-gray stallion dwarfed the little red roan Kit usually rode. With her petite figure, she and the slender reddish brown mare were well matched. The little mare was feisty enough, but she obeyed Kit's command, showing the gentle side of her nature when the auburn-haired miss was atop her.

As Danton and Kit started off at an easy pace, he commented, "Seems you and Scarlett there have become great friends, Kit."

"I love her. I can't imagine why Delores doesn't like to ride her," Kit remarked.

Danton broke into a gale of laughter, "She didn't tell you why?"

"No," Kit said, an amused, questioning look on her face. Something had tickled his funnybone.

"Well, Delores didn't find it very funny one morning

111

when old Scarlett decided she liked the taste of my sister's brand-new bonnet. Delores had taken her straw bonnet off and hung it on a post and Scarlett helped herself to a nip of it. My sister was so mad she could have killed that little mare."

"Well, I'm sure glad she didn't." Kit giggled.

"Best you don't tell her I told you about Scarlett and her bonnet. Don't want to put the idea into her head again." He pulled his reins to the left to guide them into the open pastureland and away from the road.

Danton's eyes could detect hints of greening in the pastures. Droplets of moisture from the earlier rain clung to the blades of sprouting grass, glistening like crystals when the sunshine struck them.

Danton knew the scenic spot he wanted Kit to see. He wished it was a few weeks later so she could pluck herself a bouquet of the wildflowers that grew there, but he told himself he'd bring her back when they were in bloom.

Kit didn't really care where they rode. Just being at Danton's side, alone with him, made her happy. Lately, she'd told herself time and time again that she was being foolish to think anything would come of all this. One day, she'd leave Silvercreek and Danton Navarro just as suddenly as she'd arrived. Danton would arrive from Austin and announce that he'd discovered who she really was, and he would take her back to wherever she'd come from.

Tears always began to gather in her eyes at that thought, for she knew they'd never see one another again. That devastated her. Worse still, she had asked herself how she'd feel if Danton arrived at Silvercreek with an attractive woman on his arm. She knew he must have a lady friend in Austin. A handsome man like Danton, a prominent young lawyer and bachelor, would have a bevy of ladies vying for his attention.

112

Damien was always speaking about one girl or another, and Delores had told her what a ladies' man he was; so Kit had to conclude that Danton, with his striking good looks, had the same impact on the fair damsels in the city where he spent so much time.

What a faraway look she has on her face, Danton thought as he turned to gaze at her. She had not said a word for several minutes, and as they'd ridden along, he could not help wondering what occupied her thoughts.

Veering Sombra, his fine gray stallion, in the direction of the trees edging the pastureland, he urged, "Follow me, Kit, but be careful to duck your head or your hair will catch on the branches that hang a little low."

Kit reined Scarlett behind Sombra. "Where are we going?"

"I'll show you. Just follow me."

She obeyed his command and trailed after him, through the numerous willow oaks growing there. The wide-spread crowns of the tall trees blocked out the brilliant sunlight now. In the cool, quiet serenity of the wood, Kit felt that they were the only two people in the world. Wild ferns flourished on the ground, and as they rode along, she noticed that their leaves had such a delicate, lacy design that they looked fragile.

Then her ears heard a new sound that she couldn't quite associate with anything familiar. It was almost a soft rhythmic beat. Kit strained to take it in, wondering what in the world it was. She was not imagining it, for it became more distinct as they advanced along the trail.

When she could restrain her curiosity no longer, she asked Danton, "What is that sound I hear?"

"You'll see in just a second." He laughed, like a boy plotting some mischief, and he turned to look back at her, a broad grin on his face.

113

The next thing Kit knew she was beholding one of nature's extravaganzas. A rise of ground totally overgrown with wild ferns met her eyes, and in the center was a miniature waterfall that emptied into the small, narrow creek. Huge boulders jutted out, and the water tumbled over them to splash into the creek. A deep green growth of moss, like rich velvet, covered more boulders that caused the little creek to curve in a half-arc before it straightened out. It was such a glorious sight! Kit sat atop Scarlett, speechless, for she could not find the words to express the beauty of the scene they'd come upon. As Danton watched her, he didn't have to be told what she thought. He knew that she shared his feelings about this place.

It was in this spot that Victor and Lucía had stood in the moonlight years ago. Inspired by its beauty they had decided to name their ranch Silvercreek.

When they dismounted and stood by the creek, his arms enclosed Kit. He knew then that he was feeling the same enchantment and magic Victor Navarro must have felt when he'd placed his arms around his lovely Lucía so many years ago.

Before they left this spot of enchantment, Danton decided, he would make her his. No longer could he endure the torment, the ache, which had been mounting in him for weeks now.

Chapter 12

It was an idyllic setting in which to make love to a woman or to seduce a young innocent girl like Kristina. But the hot-blooded Danton was so consumed by the fire in his veins that he could think of nothing but kissing Kit's sweet lips. He yearned to caress the satiny body of the beautiful girl standing so tauntingly close to him.

As his body pulsed with a surge of wild desire, he turned her around and pressed her against him. She looked up at his face, warm with passion, and she seemed to understand what his eyes were telling her.

Her lips half-parted, but she uttered not a sound as her breasts pressed against his broad chest. Slowly and sensuously, his mouth captured hers in a kiss that cried out his need of her, and Kit did not seek to deny him for she loved the sensations he sparked within her.

Neither was aware that they sank to the carpeted grassy ground below. Danton's hands had bewitched her with their magical touch, each caress firing a searing flame on her silken flesh. Her head seemed to be whirling with a reckless giddiness she no longer could control, nor did she wish to. She did not care that her flesh was now bared to his touch and his lips. The ecstasy was far too pleasurable!

"Oh, *querida,* I never wanted anything so much in my life. Say it is so with you. Say it," he moaned huskily.

"I—I want you, Danton. Oh yes!" she breathlessly gasped.

With eager, anxious movements, he removed his pants. Then his lips aroused the nipple of one breast and then the other, making her body arch eagerly against him. It delighted him that he was exciting her so. Never in his life had Danton wanted to please a woman as he did now. For the first time he wanted to give of himself, not just take from a woman to satisfy his own hunger.

He felt her sweet surrender and he knew the moment had come when he must truly make her his, his one and only woman! So he moved to burrow himself between the satiny flesh of her thighs, but his lips never left hers as his hands roamed and explored.

Her soft, kittenish moans echoed in his ear as he whispered intimate words of love, soothing her before doing what had to be done.

"I'm going to be as easy as I can, *querida.* I promise you. Believe me."

He gave that sharp, necessary thrust, and Kit gasped.

"I know, my darling. But that will never be again."

Kit's moments of pain were brief, and she soon experienced an amazing surge of tantalizing pleasure as Danton began to slowly sway. As he stimulated her with sensuous, teasing motions, Danton felt her body begin to move in synchronization with his. He was thrilled by the new rapture they were sharing. Within moments a passion he'd never known before engulfed him and he soared to lofty heights.

He knew his beloved Kit was going with him for he felt her fingers dig into his back, clutching him closer

116

and closer. That knowledge increased his wild, untamed delight.

He would have wished to linger forever in the velvet folds of her silken flesh, but he was a mere mortal. He could no longer restrain the giant shudder of his male release. Kit gasped breathlessly, and her arms encircled his neck as though she wished never to release him.

Once again, he told her of his love; then he kissed her. As he gently pushed back the damp wisp of a curl falling over her face, she lay quietly in his arms.

When she continued to stare at the sky, he was filled with uncertainty. Was she disillusioned? Was he some kind of cad? Dear God, he'd made love to her with such fierce urgency. His hot-blooded desires had been selfish. But he had tried to be as gentle as possible, he reminded himself, and he was no marble statue.

Some devilish voice kept whispering in his ear, justifying what he had done, but his more mature self told him he should have been protective of her. He should not have ravaged her. Secretly, he pleaded with her to look at him, to reassure him with a sweet smile that she wasn't repulsed by him! God, he would be devastated to think that!

But Kristina's quiet mood was due to none of the things Danton was thinking. She was dwelling in an amazed limbo because of all that had happened between them. She felt no embarrassment though his naked body still lay next to hers—she was feeling too much love to be self-conscious—but she did wonder if Danton would think her wicked for her abandoned lovemaking. But their coming together had been more pleasurable than anything she'd ever imagined, and she had wanted to surrender to Danton Navarro. Now she wanted his love forever. She had known him in this most intimate way, and she loved him with a passion she'd never known before. There was one thing she did know about her past; she had never been with a man before.

Danton could endure her silence no longer. He had to know, so he murmured softly in her ear, "Are—are you all right, my little Kit?"

"Of course I am, Danton. Should I not be?" she drawled softly.

"I could say I'm sorry, but I'm not, Kit. I've wanted you since I first laid eyes on you."

Kit flung her arms around Danton's neck and pressed her body against his. She felt she would explode with happiness.

Navarro instantly responded to her display of affection. He was so relieved that she had no regrets about what had happened. He could not have endured it if she'd looked upon him with disgust or if hatred had flashed from those green eyes.

He clutched her, letting himself leisurely savor her soft, silken flesh. His lips caressed her face with featherlike kisses, and his huge hands played with her hair, tousling it. With pleasure he noted the look of passion on her face, and he was elated that he stirred her as she stirred him. His desire heightened, carrying them with it until they soared.

This time she gasped with pleasure as he buried himself in her and together they swayed to the beat of sensuous ecstasy. Danton had had many women, and he knew this sweet woman-child moved with him naturally. Guided by instinct, she was unashamed and willing. This pleased him exceedingly. She was that rare woman he'd always envisioned but had never hoped to find. Yet she was in his arms.

As his body quivered, he let out a deep, throaty gasp, *"Querida mía!* Mine—forever mine!" Kit released an ecstatic moan; then, too breathless to speak, she laid her head against his broad chest.

Not one hundred feet away from the spot where the two young lovers lay in their bower of rapture, lusty black eyes ogled them. He'd had no cause to concern himself because his fine leather boots had made a noise as they'd crushed some broken branches when he'd crept toward the spot where he could watch them. The lovers were in their own little world.

Damien had known where his brother was headed when Danton and the beautiful Kit had cantered down the side road as they left the ranch. The question that had gnawed at him for the last several weeks while the copper-haired stranger had been under their roof was now settled. Damien felt smug, knowing what he'd seen gave him power over his strong-willed brother. On the other hand, he now felt a vicious need to possess the girl too. The sadistic streak in him compelled him to have her. Anything belonging to Danton, Damien coveted. Even Damien himself didn't know when that had started, for it had been so since their early childhood.

Victor had unwittingly triggered Damien's behavior when he'd presented Danton with the young colt he'd helped Santiago deliver from a prized mare. Damien could never equate the magnificent guitar his father had given him with the colt, although his talent leaned more toward music than horses. No one else would have accused Victor Navarro of being unfair. He was a generous man—but not to his son, Damien.

Today, the cunning Damien had decided to trail the pair a few minutes after they'd ridden out of sight. Luck, he'd felt, was with him because that pest of a man, Santiago, wasn't around to dog his movements. Hastily, he'd flung a saddle onto the black stallion, and he'd galloped away from Silvercreek.

He rode swiftly if for no other reason than to blow

off steam. He was still furious because Jesse had dared to come to the ranch. Again, he questioned his own shrewdness in lining himself up with the likes of Jesse.

He realized there was nothing he could do about Jesse for the moment, but he was already pondering a solution to that problem. Who'd miss Jesse anyway? Damien laughed sardonically. He already knew the answer to that question.

That was quite a touching scene he'd witnessed . . . his twin and the lovely Kit. It had an effect on Damien, he couldn't deny that. So the gallant gentleman, Danton Navarro, had a few dents in his armor, Damien mused.

When there'd been no more to see, Damien had quietly slipped back to where he'd secured the stallion to a sapling. He found himself in dire need of the soothing balms of a gal named Fanny, so when he figured it was safe to mount his horse he headed for Pecos. Damien was in a hurry. An afternoon with Fanny seemed like the best solution at the moment.

They rode back to the barn at Silvercreek much as they'd cantered away from it a few hours earlier, but to Kit, it seemed that a whole lifetime had been lived in the interim. Long after she had parted from Danton to go up to her room, that strange feeling consumed her. While she sat in the tub of warm, scented water taking a leisurely bath before dressing for dinner, she felt detached, as though she were looking at someone other than herself.

She was a woman now, a woman with the look of love on her glowing face. The very essence of her being had been awakened and brought to life. She had loved and been loved by the handsome Danton Navarro. The romantic enchantment of that interlude had permeated her being. As she sat in the tub she relived every golden moment of their hours together.

She envisioned his black eyes adoring her, and she began to tremble with excitement. His hands, strong yet gentle, seemed to be caressing her. She sighed with pleasure. Mingled with the tender touch of him she felt his masterful presence.

Still in a trancelike state, Kit dressed in one of Delores' gowns. The calico print had tiny clusters of white flowers on a black background. The decorative blossoms brought their magical spot more vividly to mind. White wildflowers would bloom there soon, and she and Danton would return. She knew it.

Around her neck she tied a narrow black ribbon, centering the tiny cameo pin attached to it. She dabbed jasmine water behind her ears and at her throat.

Drusilla had treated her as though she were the very same girl she'd been before her tryst with Danton, but as Kit stood in front of the full-length cheval mirror, she knew that girl was forever gone. However, the qualms she'd had about facing Señora Lucía or Delores this evening were now gone. She was confident they would not notice the change in her either. But how could she meet Danton's eyes? Could she possibly hide the love she felt?

By the time she stepped out into the hallway, she asked herself why she should try to hide what she felt in her heart for Danton Navarro?

She could not remember Kristina Whelan, but Kristina's independence and her free spirit were making themselves known. No bump on the head could take them away from her!

Chapter 13

A gentle night breeze blew through the courtyard garden, and a full moon gleamed down on the area where the two girls strolled along the pathway. Kit couldn't help wishing it was Danton she was walking with instead of Delores. She could not help being slightly annoyed, as well as disappointed, when the *señora* casually announced that they had been deserted for the evening. Oh, Lucía's remark had been a casual one, but Kit felt deserted when Lucía Navarro had remarked that Danton had been invited to have dinner at the ranch of their old friends, the Camerons.

"Arthur Cameron feels Danton could make an impressive mark in politics, and he's invited some people he wants Danton to meet. More to the point, he wanted them to meet Danton." It was obvious that it pleased Lucía Navarro to think of her son in politics. Always the epitome of graciousness and charm, Lucía was nonetheless unpretentious and outspoken. "As far as Damien is concerned, I have no idea where he might be." She laughed light-heartedly.

"At one of his girl friend's houses, no doubt," Delores volunteered slyly.

After the meal Delores had suggested that she and

Kit take a walk in the garden. "It's a glorious night. So mild out that there's no need for a shawl, Kit."

As soon as they were outside, Kit suspected that Delores was interested in more than a night stroll. The excitement on her face made that evident. She decided Delores wanted to tell her something she didn't want her mother to hear.

"Do you know what Mother's planning, Kit?"

"The party, you mean?"

"No. It has nothing to do with the party! We're going to Austin to shop, and I can't wait!" Her usually soft voice was made shrill by excitement. "Oh, I hope I'll see that divine Fernando Valdez. Remember I told you about him."

Kit laughed at her little friend. "I remember. You've told me a dozen times how good-looking he is."

"Well, you'll get to see for yourself—I hope! You will be going with us, Kit."

"Me?"

"Of course, silly. Mother says she's intended for a long time to get you to her dressmaker's for some gowns, and with the party coming up, she says she just must. Oh, Kit, I can't wait!"

Kit cajoled her playfully. "I'm just afraid you'll have to, Delores. Will it be soon that we go to Austin?"

"Oh, yes. From the way Mother was talking we might accompany Danton back when he leaves Silvercreek." She giggled mischievously. "I don't know whether we should all go off though and leave Damien alone. He's such a lovable rascal . . . really!"

"You adore Damien, don't you?" Kit smiled, for Delores' adoration was evident on her pretty olive-complexioned face.

"Yes and the truth is he's impossible most of the time. Damien is one of those rare people—I don't know exactly what I'm trying to say . . . Old Santiago has

123

always said he could charm the devil himself, so I guess that is as good as anything I could come up with."

Kit was thinking about Danton as Delores chattered about Damien. On that score the two brothers did share something. She had been totally charmed by Danton.

Kit tilted her head to the side in a jesting manner, but her question was quite serious. "Now, how do you describe Danton?"

"How would I describe Danton?" Delores drawled thoughtfully. "I guess I've looked upon Danton as a father since Father died. Perhaps, I'm more in awe of him. You know what I mean by that, Kit. Danton isn't a cutup like Damien."

"No, Danton isn't," Kit wholeheartedly agreed.

"But shall I tell you something, Kit," Delores said, turning quite serious and as though she intended to relate some very confidential fact.

"Please do, Delores." Kit smiled, knowing she couldn't have stopped her anyway.

"You can't imagine how the ladies pursue Danton. There is a young widow, Señora Estellita Valero. She's from Austin, and she is absolutely gorgeous. She's had her lovely eyes on Danton for over a year. He does go out with her a lot, I think."

Delores had no idea of the pain she was causing. Kit felt as though a knife was stabbling mercilessly into her stomach. She wanted to scream out, to deny what Delores had said, to tell her to shut up. But she didn't dare.

"Wait until Mother's party and you'll see how all the ranchers' daughters flock around him—even a couple of the ranchers' wives." Delores rambled on and on.

Kit became more and more irritated as she listened to Delores' incessant chatter, but one remark struck her. Delores had casually declared that Danton's future wife would have to fit into his way of life.

"Danton's wife will have to be a special lady," she went on, "for he will have to be proud to present her. Do you know what I mean, Kit? She will have to come from a highly respected, prestigious Texas family. Of course, it goes without saying that Danton will choose a beauty." Kit could feel no anger toward Delores for she had been warm-hearted, but she could listen to no more. She felt she would dissolve into tears.

"It's getting a little chilly, Delores. Shall we go in?" Kit struggled to keep her voice even.

"Oh? Well, all right. I hadn't noticed," Delores replied.

She rose from the bench she'd been sitting on, and completely unaware of the torment she'd stirred up in Kit, she walked back down the pathway with her. Delores' camaraderie with Kit was truly the happiest experience she'd had for a long time. But she'd been so busy talking, she had not stopped to think about what she'd observed that very morning in the hallway. She had forgotten about seeing her brother kissing Kit or she wouldn't have mentioned his conquests.

Delores had readily accepted this strange girl with the copper-colored hair as her sister, and because of that Kit seemed an unlikely target for Cupid's bow where Danton was concerned. With Damien, any female could be the target.

When they entered the house, Kit hastily excused herself. She had no desire to return to the parlor or the sitting room. Señora Lucía was far too perceptive a lady. Tonight, Kit wanted to be alone with no eyes scrutinizing her.

She swiftly mounted the steps, and when she had closed the bedroom door, she heaved a sigh of relief. With fractious motions and a frown on her face, she roughly yanked at her clothing, then kicked her slippers off her dainty feet. A lot of good it had done her to take such care with her appearance this evening, for Danton had not been there to appreciate the effort. This vexed her!

Had she taken what had happened between them far too seriously? If Danton had so many ladies eager to do his bidding, perhaps this afternoon was not as special to him as it was to her. How naïve of her to have thought it was.

Suddenly curiosity gnawed at her. She wondered just how many times Danton Navarro had lain with a woman. With aggravating jerks she slipped the coral-colored gown over her head; then she reached for her peignoir. The knot in the ribbon around her neck irritated her, and she fumed as she undid it.

Dejected and miserable, she removed her petticoats and jumped on the bed. "If I'm good enough to be your lover, then I'm good enough to be your wife, Danton Navarro," she muttered in a low voice, needing to release her frustration somehow.

She reached over to the nightstand where the lamp sat, and beside it the peridot ring. Obviously she had not put it back on after she'd dressed to go down to dinner. Quickly she slipped it back on her finger, wishing that little ring could talk and tell her who she was and where she'd come from. If only . . .

She let her fingers gently touch and caress the stone, and with every fiber, she strained to jar some fragment of memory. Was her own mother someone like the grand lady downstairs? What about her father? Did he live, or was he dead like Danton's father? Was her heritage one Danton could point to with pride, the background he would desire for the woman he picked to be his wife?

Dear God, she had to know! It was essential that she know.

Call it a mother's instinct but Florine Whelan would not believe that her beautiful daughter was dead. She had always insisted that she would sense it if Kristina no longer lived. But the strange phenomenon she'd experienced this evening had removed any doubt that her daughter lived. Florine did not intend to tell Jason about it. She would tell only one person—the one who would believe her. The understanding Solitaire, with her own particular superstitions, she would relate to Kristina's voice calling to Florine from somewhere far away.

Why, she had even seen the exquisite pastel gown Kristina had worn, and her daughter's face seemed serene and happy. What was that shining gleam in her daughter's eyes, the special softness in her voice as she told Florine not to worry about her? It seemed that she wanted to ease her mother's mind so Florine's health would improve.

The greatest consolation Florine derived from the voice she'd heard was Kristina's statement that they would see each other again. Before the vision had faded and the voice had quieted, Kristina had promised that it would happen soon. Hope now lifted Florine's spirits.

Later when Solitaire joined her mistress, Florine dared to mention what was on her mind. It turned out that Solitaire, too, was filled with the same eerie feeling that her little Tina was reaching out to her.

"I know one thing, Solitaire—she's alive!" Florine declared. "My daughter is not dead. God, I'm glad you're here, Solitaire! Jason would think me insane if I confided in him. As dear as he is and as patient as he's been all these months, he'd find this hard to believe."

For her part, Solitaire found it hard to believe how the last months had aged the vivacious lady sitting before her in the wheelchair. However, Solitaire could believe that one day the wheelchair would be discarded and Florine Whelan would walk again. Those first weeks after she'd been shot, Florine's life had hung by a thin, delicate thread. But Solitaire's devoted care and Jason's constant love and attention had pulled her through.

Her recovery had been very slow. Indeed it had been a banner day when Jason had brought the wheelchair home so Florine could move around the house. No longer was she a prisoner in her boudoir. That was a giant stride for the new mistress of Hamilton Ranch, and on the first day of April, 1881, sitting in her wheelchair, Florine married Jason Hamilton. Nevermore would she doubt Jason's love for her, no matter what the future brought!

God knows, he'd helped her get well and he's supported her attempts to find Kristina. He had spared no expense in the attempt to locate Florine's daughter. Rumors about girls who resembled Kristina had come from New Orleans, St. Louis, Natchez, and other cities. All had been checked. Florine had been very hopeful when the private detective she'd hired had dug up information on a young lady, who fit Kristina's description, in San Antonio.

Jason had traveled there himself, at Florine's insistence, because she had told him Kristina might have suffered so at the mercy of the four scoundrels who'd taken her with them that she was ashamed to come home. Florine could understand that. Nightmares had haunted her since her daughter had disappeared.

She knew the kind of bastards who'd taken her daughter enjoyed debasing a beautiful, proud young lady like Kristina. How well Florine knew that, for she had experienced her share of that kind. Dear God, how she wished she'd told Kristina more about the ugly side of life instead of creating a fairy-tale world for her.

She'd been wrong—horribly wrong! Solitaire had been so much smarter. She'd known that Florine had been obsessed with giving Kristina the wonderful world of which she herself had been deprived.

But she would not believe that Kristina was forever gone from her. Not after tonight! Regardless of the fact that no clues or rumors had filtered back to El Paso, she knew Kristina had survived. Whatever had happened that night long, long ago, somewhere her daughter was alive.

No, she wasn't crazy! Let anyone think what they chose, but she was as sane as anyone, Florine told herself. She'd heard her daughter's voice calling to her, and Florine had felt that Kristina was a long way from El Paso. If only she knew where?

It pained Florine that she had made her beautiful Kristina so helpless. Of all people, she should have been smarter than that.

Chapter 14

Señora Lucía Navarro had expected Kit to be as exuberant about their trip to Austin as Delores had been, but it seemed that the two young girls had switched personalities. Kit had become quiet and moody, while Delores was the bundle of energy.

Now, that they had spent three days in Austin at Danton's house and the shopping spree was behind them, it was becoming clear to the *señora* what was troubling little Kit. Until now she'd been reviewing all possibilities.

At first, Lucía had wondered if this part of Texas was a familiar sight to Kit and she was absorbed in trying to recall her mysterious past. Perhaps, she was haunted by something she'd seen. Both girls had stared out the window of the train as it had rolled over the Texas countryside from Pecos to Austin.

But Lucía had dismissed that possibility for she remembered that the two girls had chattered away like two magpies during the journey. And Danton had been a most hospitable host to Kit, so she was not uncomfortable in his home.

The weather had been just marvelous for traveling especially so with spring bursting forth. Lucía always welcomed the springtime after the long winter months.

On their arrival in Austin, they'd gone directly to Danton's house, and Lucía had had to confess that she'd been wrong to question his decision to buy this property. At the time, she'd thought the purchase ridiculous, but she now saw that the cozy charm of the place would appeal to her son when he was away from Silvercreek.

Compared to the spacious, rambling ranch house, it was small. The tiny courtyard was enclosed by a ten-foot fence, within which there was a shady veranda and a sparkling, hand-carved stone fountain. Lucía noticed that Danton had acquired numerous tropical plants since her last trip to the house.

She could imagine the magnificent aroma that would waft up to the railed gallery when they began to bloom, which would be soon now.

She could not help feeling pride in the tasteful changes and additions Danton had made to the place. The tile floors had for the most part been left exposed. They'd been highly polished instead of covered with carpeting. Lucía liked that effect. She also liked the easy access to the courtyard from the rooms that encircled that small, serene area. She knew she would spend some pleasant moments out there.

There were only three bedrooms in Danton's house, so Lucía had one to herself and the two girls shared a room. The ladies were left to unpack their own clothing for Danton's house staff consisted of only two servants and both were men. One was a young Mexican youth Danton had nicknamed Abeja. Abeja worshiped Danton for he felt that he owed his life to his employer. Danton had fished the lad out of the river one night about two years ago.

Danton's housekeeper and cook was an old drifter who'd been down on his luck. Danton had offered him the position just to help the old man out for a while. As it had turned out, however, the arrangement was now going into its fourth year. Waco Martin, a former drover, could cook a beefsteak just the way Danton liked it, and he could bake an apple pie that rivaled Drusilla's.

Abeja lived up to his name, the bee. He was always busy putting Danton's home and clothes in order so it was a well-run household whether Danton was in residence or not.

The first evening Lucía heaped praise on both Waco and Abeja, and it pleased both men for the dignified *señora* to be so gracious with her compliments. The next morning, however, she wasted no time in taking the two girls on the first of their shopping sprees as soon as Danton departed for his office.

It was while they were at the dressmaker's shop that Lucía noticed Kit's moodiness, and her concern about it mounted as the afternoon and evening wore on. The girl must be coming down with some illness, for she just wasn't herself, Lucía decided. Danton must have noticed it too for he was showering her with attention. Abeja was going at a mad run to serve all of them, but he couldn't keep his admiring eyes off the pretty auburn-haired Kit, Lucía noticed with amusement.

The second evening they also were served a delicious dinner, but the ladies were left on their own for Danton had an evening business appointment.

Lucía could not contain her curiosity by their third day in the city. "Are you not feeling well, dear?" she asked Kit.

Kit hastily replied, "Oh no, señora. I guess it's just—just the excitement of being in a new place. At least, I don't think I've been here." How all-knowing the woman is, she thought to herself! Kit wished she could mask her feelings more, but strange images were plaguing her and no matter how hard she tried to sweep them aside they returned. Shadowy images of people she knew seemed to mesh with strange faces, and a

132

storm of perplexing emotions assaulted her.

If only she and Danton could slip away from the others, if he could hold her in his arms, she would be reassured but there was no possibility of that and the days had rushed by. The thought of leaving with Delores and Señora Navarro left her desolate.

She realized what a miserable, ungrateful minx she must seem to the generous lady who'd been like a mother to her. Dear Lord, there were four new gowns in the armoire—gorgeous gowns! There were under-garments made of frosty white batiste, and yards of delicate lace, three pairs of slippers, and a pair of highly polished leather boots. Why, the *señora* must think she would be with them forever.

Even though springtime was upon them, Lucía had insisted that she needed the soft French wool cape to warm her shoulders because there would be times when the wind would have a chill to it. What a fortune that had cost!

Delores had let out a howl of protest about the riding outfit Lucía had chosen for Kit, and the señora had laughed and told the dressmaker they would take a warm rich berry-colored one for the pouting Delores. Kit's was a sober black one, but the matching vest was delicately embroidered with multicolored designs. It made a most striking ensemble when enhanced by Kit's warm copper-colored hair.

Under her breath, Kit now vowed she'd be gay and light-hearted for the rest of their stay in Austin, even if it drained her to do so. The last thing in the world she wanted was to cause Lucía Navarro concern.

Kit's good intentions and plans were torn asunder, however, on their last evening in Danton's home. Lucía felt she had finally learned what was troubling Kit. Lucía had seen the monster of jealousy in Kit's lovely green eyes each time she gazed at one of Danton's dinner guests. Little Kit was infatuated with her son,

133

Señora Navarro concluded. She felt compassion for the lovely child whose formidable competition during the evening was Estellita Valero, a breathtakingly lovely woman who was poised and self-assured.

Lucía actually seemed to be feeling Kit's pain before the evening was over. She was rarely impatient with the usually considerate Danton, but tonight he irritated her. Could he not see what was going on? Was he blind? Lucía sometimes wondered if men pretended to be insensitive to protect themselves. Had her beloved Victor not done that on occasion?

Later, Lucía's feelings mellowed somewhat. When she and Danton were left alone after the girls had retired for the evening and his guests had said their farewells, she learned that it had not been Danton's idea to invite Estellita. Over a nightcap of cognac, her son told her that the charming widow had been going out with the nephew of Señor Valdez. When he had invited the Valdez family he hadn't known that their nephew, Ramon, had been visiting them.

Danton appeared to be vexed because his mother had not told him of Ramon's presence. He knew she'd visited her friend, Consuela Valdez since she'd come to Austin.

"I'm sorry, dear, that I didn't tell you Ramon was staying with his aunt and uncle. He seems like a nice gentleman to me. I know it made two extra guests, but I must compliment your man, Waco. He presented us with a delicious meal nonetheless. A handy man you have there, Danton. He and Abeja do a marvelous job."

"Hhmm. Yes, they do that," Danton responded. He could have wrung the sultry Estellita's neck, for he'd seen the green fire in Kit's eyes.

As he lit a cheroot he wanted more than anything to be completely alone, but he couldn't be rude. And if he were alone, there was no way he could be with Kit for she shared a room with Delores.

Lucía's keen instinct told her to drink her cognac and leave Danton to himself. He had an air about him that urged her to give him the solitude he obviously needed. She rose from the chair and gave Danton a pat on the shoulder.

"Good night, my dear. It was an enchanting evening and I enjoyed it. The magnificent food and the superb wine has made me pleasantly lazy. I must get to bed."

Danton kissed his mother's cheek as he bid her good night. He wished her a good rest before she made the trip homeward the next morning.

"You rest well too, son. We'll say our farewells in the morning before you leave for the office," Lucía told him as she turned to leave the room. Thoughtfully she mounted the winding stairway, wondering if she was losing that touch of hers. What was going on under her very nose that she'd been missing?

Now it was Danton who had her puzzled!

As soon as Delores' head hit the soft fluffy pillows sleep overtook her. Being around Fernando for the evening had stirred up such excitement in her that she was exhausted.

Kit was restless, however. Feeling that she'd scream if she didn't get out of the room, she leaped out of bed and searched in the armoire for her brand-new cream-colored cape. It seemed rather stupid to go through the rigors of getting back into the frock she'd worn for dinner so she just flung the cape around her.

As she closed the door of the bedroom, she noticed the light dimming under the doorway of the señora's room. The rest of the hallway was dark and lifeless so Kit assumed that Danton had also retired for the night.

She just hoped that the two servants, Waco and Abeja, were in the quarters they occupied. The carriage

135

house at the back of the property had been converted into their quarters.

She maneuvered her way through the hall and into the formal dining room, heading toward the French doors opening into the courtyard. She'd fallen in love with Danton's house almost as swiftly as she had with him. The fact that it was small appealed to her. Since being here, she'd realized how little she knew about Danton Navarro.

He was so much older, worldly wise. Why he must look upon her as a mere child like his sister. But, a voice reminded her, he'd never make love to Delores.

The image of the alluring Señora Valero came back to haunt her, and she had to agree with Delores that she was the type Danton would pick to stand by his side as a wife. The very thought annoyed her so that she slammed the French door harder than she'd intended as she stepped out into the darkness of the courtyard garden. She stopped and grimaced. Of late, Kit was learning things about herself. She had a horrible temper when she became riled!

The sound echoed loudly in the quiet of the night, and Danton reacted swiftly by stomping out his cheroot and dashing around the corner of the house to see what in the devil was going on. Waco and Abeja were in their quarters, so it wasn't them.

There by the fountain she stood, like a lovely goddess. She was draped in a long cape and her glorious, wavy hair cascaded down her back. He came to a sudden halt, and stood for a moment admiring her, savoring her presence.

It was as if his silent prayer had been answered. There she was, waiting for him to come to her. God knows, he wanted to see her, to be alone with her on this last night before she returned to Silvercreek.

Chapter 15

He moved quietly toward her, like a cat cautiously stalking its prey, until he stood directly behind her. Kit was not aware of him. Preoccupied in thought, she had no hint that his towering figure was coming out of the shadows toward her.

His deep voice broke the silence of the night and Kit's musings. "How did you know, little one, I wanted to see you?"

As she turned to look up at his solemn face, his eyes pierced hers. "I didn't know, Danton."

She was consumed by conflicting emotions as they stood so close to each other. A part of her wanted to close the slight distance separating them, to press herself to his strong, firm chest.

Yet another side of her demanded that she be aloof and cool for she was still feeling the hurt because of Señora Valero's presence at dinner. Pangs of jealousy lingered within her.

His arms snaked around her waistline, and he nudged her closer. She felt the heat of his male body penetrate her light woolen cape and the sheer gown she wore. It made her very conscious that she had practically nothing on beneath the wrap.

Danton could have sworn that no woman alive was so tantalizingly desirable as the divine little Kit he held in his arms. So wee, but so tempting. No despicable corsets marred the feel and touch of her flushed flesh. No layers of petticoats camouflaged the curves and valleys of her feminine figure.

Already his passionate nature was aroused, and he bent to kiss her. But this time Kit told herself she must prove to Danton that she was no easy conquest; she must not allow him to have his way anytime the urge came upon him. She could not be his just for the taking. Dear Lord, it was not going to be easy to deny him what he wanted! She hungered for his sensuous lips to kiss her, to go on kissing her. However, she pushed the palms of her hands against his chest.

In an impatient voice, husky with desire, he mumbled against her hair, "Wha . . . what is the matter, Kit?"

In her own way she was as flustered as he. She stammered, "I-I don't know. I just—"

He did not allow her to finish what she was about to say. Instead, like a man in a daze, he led her away from the garden courtyard. "Let's walk," he snapped, feeling the need to get her away from his house or whatever it was that was troubling her.

So they ambled through the garden gate and down the dark, deserted street, clinging together as they walked. Kit had no idea where they were going and even Danton would question himself later as to why he'd aimlessly led her toward the little park situated close to his house.

In the center of the area stood a massive live oak, and its limbs and branches seemed to enclose them when they finally stopped to lean against its trunk. Kit was thinking that they seemed to be in a room alone at last, secluded from the rest of the world.

When Danton bent his dark head down to kiss her, she did not fight him. She didn't know what had come over her all of a sudden—whether it was magic or madness. It seemed a spell had been cast on her. Nothing mattered except Danton Navarro and the ecstasy he gave her.

"Oh, Danton!" she cried breathlessly as he released her lips, but continued to devour her with his eyes.

As if he sensed what she was feeling, he murmured softly against her cheek, "It's this old, old tree, *querida*. I guess that's why I brought you here tonight. Strange legends have gone on for years about this particular old oak."

"Oh, Danton," she sighed, "I'm no child." She thought at first he was playfully teasing her, but she knew no child would feel about a man as she was feeling right now. When she leaned back to look at his face, however, she saw she was wrong for he was quite serious. "You aren't teasing, are you?"

"There are those who believe that the leaves of this live oak had magic in them. It is said that if they're brewed for tea and the tea is drunk it will keep you safe from any harm. There is the story that vows made here come true and endure forever."

"And is that the reason you brought me here, Danton?"

"We're here, so what can I say? It must have been that, little Kit. Damned if I know. But I do know I've never felt for any woman what I feel for you." He clasped her tighter in his strong arms urging, "Swear it is the same with you, *querida!*"

With a guileless look in her green eyes, she murmured softly, "I've never known any other man, Danton. None but you. Even though I can't recall my past I vow to you I've never felt this way before."

He held her close, wishing that he'd never have to let

139

her go and feeling an overwhelming tenderness swell in him. He admired her openness and honesty. Weeks ago, when Danton had asked himself how he felt about Kit's past he'd realized that he didn't give a damn about who she might have been. He loved her.

The unwitting pressure of her soft, satiny body made him forget everything he'd intended to say next. Making love to her consumed him.

He wanted to share the rest of his life with this woman. He had been on the point of asking her to be his wife before he had become enthralled by their lovemaking. Yes, there was magic about this old oak— the Treaty Oak. It was under this tree that Stephen Austin had made his treaty with the Indians years before, and it had been called the Treaty Oak ever since. Danton had been about to make his own pact with the auburn-haired girl who'd stolen his heart back in the mountains near old Emil's cabin.

Instead of speaking the words he'd meant to say, he gave way to his overwhelming need of her, and as they sank to the ground, his hands felt her naked body beneath the sheer gown, and a craving for her swept over him.

Kit's cape became their coverlet as they lay in rapturous seclusion under the live oak's protected branches. His hands and lips spoke the words of endearment he had not uttered, and understanding, Kit answered him eagerly and willingly.

Her soft moans of delight and her sensuously arching body told Danton that her need for him was as fierce as his need for her. They swayed together, their senses so alive they never wanted this interlude to end.

Danton tried to get his fill of the tantalizing little goddess lying beneath him. Everything about her stimulated his craving: the fragrance of her hair, the more subtle scent of her soft flesh, and the feel of her curvaceous, young body. The most exquisite silk from China could not have felt more smooth to his touch. When his hands trailed up and down her valleys and mounds, and when his lips touched her most sensitive places, he felt her quiver with unrestrained excitement. She was enjoying his lovemaking, and he sought to please her more. He caressed her with unhurried gentleness.

The thrill of his lovemaking made her forget that they lay upon the ground, concealed only by her cape. Danton's expert hands were already slipping her sheer nightgown down to her waistline. She marveled at how fast he removed her gown, but she put out of her mind the thought that he had obviously undressed many other women. It pained her and it would have destroyed their pleasure.

She trembled as she felt the tips of his fingers pushing the thin material of the gown past the curves of her hips and as the heat of his hand trailed back up her thighs once he'd freed her body of the garment. How adept he was at making her hunger for him. Now that she knew this man intimately, it gave her a feeling of power to know that she excited him so.

The throbbing force of his manhood had already made itself known to her, and now she was teased by the anticipation of what would come to pass.

With an effortless motion he carried her with him as he rolled onto his back and as she towered over him he grinned. "Now, my little kitten—you make love to me," he dared her.

"You want me to?" Her eyes were wickedly bright.

"I want it very much, *amada mía!*" He guided her round hips into a sensuous motion and she quickly obliged him.

The moonlight revealed the mischievous smile on her face. "I like it this way, Danton. It feels so good!"

she declared.

As he arched upward to please her even more, he laughed. "I hoped you would. I want to love you in many ways." He planned to do just that, but he intended to savor every precious moment with Kit for she was like no other. They would have a lifetime of nights such as this one.

Then ecstasy was his as her velvet heat consumed him! He reached up to capture the rosy tip of her breast with his lips, and she responded with a delighted cry of pleasure. Her body moved in a faster tempo causing Danton to moan.

Her sensuous movements were swiftly bringing him to that point where his strong will power could no longer exert control. She was that rare, wonderful female he'd dreamed about finding. Such a tiny little vixen!

She was every hot-blooded man's fantasy! She was his!

Finally his strong body shuddered its fulfillment, her legs clinging to him as though she could not possibly let herself be released.

"Querida mia! Querida mia!" he gasped huskily, his broad chest heaving.

"Yes, Danton. Ohhhhh, God!" she responded breathlessly. Her body glistened with dampness as she surrendered to the sweet exhaustion that follows lovemaking.

"Mine! That's what I vow, Kit. You will always be mine." He held her fast.

The glow of their love made them oblivious to the world outside the secluded low-hanging branches of that live oak tree.

Later, the two lovers strolled leisurely through the gate of the courtyard, having no inkling that their return was observed.

Lucía Navarro did not approve of what she saw. She knew instinctively what had happened between them. So sure was she, she would have laid a wager on it. Now, many things were made clear to the dark-haired matron. It was possible that this was not the first time. Strange as it might seem to those who knew her, she was not as concerned for Danton as she was for Kit.

Her son knew what he was doing, but Lucía would as quickly have sworn that Kit had been a virgin as she would have vowed that Delores was a sweet innocent. This bothered her. For it was Damien, not Danton, she'd watched with a protective eye.

Once again, Lucía questioned the protective feeling she had for her young guest. She could hardly fault a virile young man like her son for being tempted by the sight of such a ravishingly lovely young maiden! He had hot-blooded Latin ancestry and he was a part of her, she mused.

Lucía was not so old that she could not recall the days of her bold, daring past—the years before she'd met and married the handsome, arrogant Victor Navarro.

It was ironic that the aunt she had hated had been instrumental in bringing about her meeting with her beloved Victor.

She would probably have lived her entire life in the Louisiana parish where she'd been born if her dear mother had not died. When that had happened, her aunt, Celeste, had come to live with them. Lucía recalled how miserable she'd been. With the overbearing Celeste ruling the house, Lucía had felt doomed to be unhappy for the rest of her young life.

The venomous hatred she'd felt for Celeste and her father had been devastating to the fourteen-year-old Lucía. It was inconceivable that Celeste and her sweet mother, Celine, were twins. To Lucía, they did not look

143

anything alike, and certainly their ways were not the same. Nevertheless, in less than two years after her mother's death her father had married her aunt and Lucía was quickly becoming a stranger in her own home.

Influenced by her overbearing, greedy aunt, Lucía's father had demanded that she marry a French Creole gentleman of their parish. Lucía had flatly refused, was determined that her aunt would not have her way. Celeste had already done her enough harm, and she was too young to be bound to the obnoxious, middle-aged Paul Moreau. He was not only old; he was ugly; and her father's insistence on the match drove Lucía to make a bold move.

She stole away in the night, and with an abundance of luck and a multitude of lies, she managed to make her way to Texas, unharmed and unmolested. For months she stayed with the family she'd hitched a ride with, in the hill country of Texas.

Lucía, however, wanted more from life than the backbreaking work this humble family seemed content to endure. She loved Archie and Bess Larrimore very much, and she worked hard on their little farm to repay them for what they'd done for her.

But the raw-boned stout Bess Larrimore had pointed out to her that she was far too pretty and smart to settle for a life of grubbing for a living, and after six months, Lucía certainly agreed with her.

Once again, fate took a hand in Lucía's future. An old Mexican drifter stopped by the Larrimores' small ranch, and he taught Lucía the game of Spanish monte. Over the three weeks he remained there, he taught her other card games and he told her fascinating tales about the fortunes he'd seen won at the green-cloth gambling tables. The old bewhiskered Mexican painted such a fascinating picture of this strange world that night after night Lucía lay on her cot in the back room of the Larrimores' small house, imagining herself in a fancy gown like the ones the old Mexican had said the ladies in the gambling halls wore.

In her spare time, she'd try unusual hair styles, a cluster of wildflowers in her black curls for an adornment or even a feather that had dropped from the Larrimores' multicolored rooster.

Lucía learned many things from Bess Larrimore, for in the Larrimore home nothing went to waste. An old deep blue blanket, ragged and torn almost in half, became a very striking short cape for Lucía when Bess's skilled hand was finished with it and a trim of black braid had been added.

Lucía had spent over fifteen months with the Larrimores when she informed them that the next time Archie made his trek into San Antonio to sell his fresh-grown vegetables and eggs at the market place on the plaza, she would go along. It was time she was seeing to her future. A tearful Bess knew what she meant, so she didn't try to stop the young girl.

Her youth and her refreshing beauty were assets for Lucía in the busy, bustling city of San Antonio. She never could figure out why she'd given herself the name she had when she got to San Antonio, but she knew she hadn't dared to use her real name, Lucía. So she became Lolita—Lolita Gomez. Perhaps, she chose Gomez as a tribute to the old Mexican man she'd met at the Larrimores'.

She took a room at a boardinghouse and within the first week found herself a job as a dealer at one of the gambling halls. After a few months, looking far more sophisticated than her seventeen years, Lucía was the main attraction at the Palace. She was realizing that her dark, sultry beauty was the biggest asset she had, and she didn't waste it.

Her expertise at monte and faro was the talk of the city, as was her beauty. But she became a cool, aloof lady when she left the Palace each night. She went home alone and she slept alone. Such behavior only whetted desires of the gentlemen gamblers.

After almost two years at the Palace, Lucía had acquired nicer living quarters for herself and an exquisite, elaborate array of gowns and jewels. She did not regret leaving her home and Pointe Coupée. In fact, she never intended to return to Louisiana as long as she lived.

The wealthy gentlemen of San Antonio admired her elegance and her self-assured, regal air. They vied to be her suitor or her lover, but Lucía didn't accept their offers. Only when a devastating Latin with masterful ways appeared at the Palace did Lucía's heartbeat become erratic. Victor Navarro completely bewitched her with his Latin charm, and it was love at first sight for this bachelor whose wealthy family was known throughout the state of Texas.

Suddenly, without any notice the sultry Lolita was no longer at the green cloth. Her dainty fingers no longer flipped the cards with that special touch. Her admiring swains were devastated to find the black-haired beauty missing, and the Palace lost its allure.

But Victor Navarro figured he'd won the whole world when he carried Lucía home to his vast ranch miles away from San Antonio.

Now, this lovely lady stood by the window of Danton's home watching her son and a young lady, and she knew she saw two people in love just as she and Victor had been so many years ago.

She had nothing to fret about, she gently admonished herself. Would she have changed anything? The answer came loud and clear. Certainly not!

Chapter 16

Danton Navarro found it more difficult than he'd expected to maintain a casual air as he bid Kit, his mother, and Delores goodbye when they boarded the train to take them back to Silvercreek. He could hardly feel impersonal after the glorious night he'd shared with the auburn-haired Kit.

As he strolled away and the train began to pull away, he realized he was already anticipating traveling southward to Silvercreek for his mother's big annual shindig. But he reminded himself that in the meanwhile he had some scores to set straight right here in Austin. At the top of his list was the grasping widow, Estellita Valero.

He would not tolerate a repeat of her performance as his dinner guest. Her intimation of familiarity with him had hurt Kit, and he knew it was inevitable that these two women would meet again. Danton was certain that he wanted Kit for his bride, and a portion of their time would be spent right here in Austin, Texas's capital city.

These thoughts occupied Danton's mind as he ambled away from the station toward his carriage. He took no notice of the fast-paced gentleman trying to catch up with him, and only when he heard himself being summoned did he turn in the direction of the voice calling out, "Señor Navarro!"

He found himself facing the good-looking Ramon Valdez who was as trim as a bullfighter. Ramon wore a warm friendly grin on his dark face as he came up to shake Danton's hand, and Danton returned his greeting with equal warmth. He liked Valdez, who was a few years younger than he.

"This is a pleasant surprise, *señor,* and it gives me the opportunity to tell you what a wonderful evening I spent at your home. It was the highlight of my visit here in Austin. You see, I leave today for San Antonio," Ramon told him.

"Well, it was my pleasure, Ramon. As you know my mother and your aunt have been friends for many years now. She always looks forward to visiting your aunt when she is in Austin," Danton remarked.

Whatever dalliance had been going on between Ramon and Estellita, it was obviously over now if he was leaving for San Antonio, and with Estellita, absence did not make her heart grow fonder. Danton had found out long ago. When he'd become infatuated with the sultry temptress, he'd quickly found out that she was a born flirt, and from the first, he'd taken their relationship lightly. Yes, he'd used her just as willingly and lustily as she had him, so Danton figured neither was the loser. But he knew for all her trimmings of wealth and her high position in Austin society, Estellita was a tramp—a wanton, wily whore!

Now he planned to make perfectly clear to her that he would not tolerate any of her cunning tricks, not at the expense of the unsophisticated Kit. In very firm, straightforward tones, he intended to inform her that he planned to marry Kit in the very near future.

"You have time for a cup of coffee, Señor Navarro?" Ramon inquired as they began to walk along.

148

"I do, if I can request that you just call me Danton," Danton chuckled.

Navarro considered Ramon's offer a mere gesture of appreciation for being his guest the night before, and he had to admit that Valdez appeared to be a nice, well-mannered young man. He was also quite handsome. Although Delores' dark eyes had been glued on Fernando most of the evening, Danton had spotted her giving Ramon a couple of scrutinizing glances.

Indeed, Delores was the subject on Ramon's mind, and she had been ever since he'd walked into Danton's tiled hallway and seen her. Her beauty matched the most glorious yellow rose he'd ever seen.

According to the traditions demanded in his family and because Danton was Delores' older brother, Ramon wished to approach him about courting Delores. He wanted desperately to talk to Danton before leaving Austin for he had lost his heart last night. Ramon had never been so affected by a beautiful *señorita* before.

"Very well, Danton. Perhaps, we might go by the Plaza? Would that be convenient for you?" Ramon asked.

"Sounds perfect to me. It's on the way to my office too."

"I don't want to pose any problem or delay you."

"No, no. It's very convenient to be your own boss, Ramon." Danton grinned; then he headed toward his carriage.

They traveled down the street toward the Plaza, one of Austin's oldest hotels. The style and structure of the magnificent stone building reflected an Old World charm. Its generous grill work, high ceilings, rich dark woods, and overhanging galleries were impressive, and as Danton and Ramon entered the hotel's dining room, bright sunshine streamed through its many windows.

149

The tables were draped with frosty white tablecloths and on each sat a tiny vase holding one perfect little blossom.

The usual crowd of businessmen sat at their favorite tables, enjoying coffee and indulging in a morning chat before heading for their respective places of work.

Ramon and Danton picked a table sheltered by a giant betel palm, and as he sat Danton decided that the cool serenity of the room was enhanced by the hanging pots of ferns, begonias, and ivy that were judiciously placed throughout.

By the time their coffee was served and Danton and Ramon had settled into a relaxed, casual conversation almost an hour had passed. Ramon had commented on everything from the elegance of Danton's fine bachelor domain to the striking loveliness of Señorita Kit Winters. "Did I understand correctly . . . she is a guest with your mother at Silvercreek? A friend of Señorita Delores?" Ramon was trying in his way to broach the subject of Delores, but Danton's black brow arched sharply at these questions. He wondered why Ramon was so interested in Kit.

"That's right! The *señorita* is my mother's guest," Danton's voice was edged with irritation.

Ramon's next words made Danton tense even more, but he relaxed as his companion ended his statement. "I hope you won't think I'm presumptuous, Danton, but I wish to speak of your sister." Ramon sat back in the chair, tensely awaiting Danton's answer.

"Delores?"

The shrill tone of Danton's voice made Ramon hastily declare, "In the most honorable way, Danton. I . . . I find your sister a most beautiful, charming young lady and if I have your approval, I'd . . . I'd like to call on her." Dear God, he was stammering like an idiot and fidgeting in his chair. It had been far more difficult to plead his cause than he'd imagined.

Nodding his black head and trying his best to conceal his amusement, Danton drawled, "I see. You are interested in my sister, Delores?"

"Yes . . . yes, I am. Our families have a mutual respect for each other and . . . and I feel that is in my favor, but I wanted to know how you felt. I am aware that your mother values your opinion, Danton." Ramon's face was so serious. Danton saw the struggle he was going through as he awaited the verdict Danton would pass on to him. The young man's sincerity impressed Danton tremendously, and there were several aspects about Valdez that made him a suitable suitor for the little Delores. He had a fine family background, one very much like Delores'. He was certainly good-looking and he had a pleasing personality.

"What about your cousin Fernando?" Danton could not help testing him a little. How much was he willing to do to win Delores' affection?

Ramon favored him with a crooked grin. "Danton, who am I to tell you that all's fair in love or war?"

"*Sí, amigo,*" Danton let out a husky, throaty laugh. "It is true. I like you, Ramon, and I give you my heartiest approval to court my little sister. Be warned though, she may prove to be a handful!"

"*Gracias,* Danton! I had hoped you would feel this way."

"My pleasure. I have only one request and that is if your courtship leads to the altar, name your first son after me," Danton teased. He could have sworn that Ramon blushed, and feeling the need to make up for his jesting remark, he suggested that Ramon Valdez come to the annual Navarro fiesta. Ramon eagerly accepted the invitation.

"You will see me in July. Please give your mother

151

and sister my best regards when you see them."

"I will, Ramon, and I'm glad we had this opportunity to get acquainted. However, I had better get to my office or I might as well declare the whole day a holiday," Danton declared, pushing back in his chair.

When he left Ramon, Danton suddenly realized that the talk with Ramon had helped him as well. It had eased the pain of saying farewell to Kit, and it had lightened his own mood. Danton was certain that Ramon Valdez would be counting the days until the fiesta.

At the door of his office building, Danton was seized by a reckless impulse, and he gave way to it. His broad shoulders were halfway through the swinging door when he turned sharply on his heels to go back onto the street. He decided to pay a call on his old *compadre,* Constantine. He wished to have a piece of jewelry made for him, and the skills of this old goldsmith were incomparable.

The seventy-year-old Constantine had few years left in which to produce his exquisite pieces, each unique and special. Danton had been introduced to him by his own father when Victor had desired Constantine's services for a Christmas gift for his wife and daughter. The dainty, little gold crosses on delicate gold chains had been his last seasonal gifts to his wife and daughter because he had died before the next Christmas came.

On three occasions, Danton had come to the goldsmith for special gifts; he had purchased two pieces of jewelry for his mother, and he'd had a gold bracelet made for Delores' last birthday.

It was then that the wizen-faced old Mexican had told him sadly, "I'll not be making many more of these little lovelies, son. The eyes are fading fast now. A year perhaps, or two if I'm very, very lucky."

With this in mind, Danton felt compelled to have

him make something Kit could cherish forever.

When he came to Constantine's obscure shop, which was situated on a side street some distance away from the hub of the city, the goldsmith's young helper ushered Danton in.

When he entered the room where Constantine sat at his workbench, Danton didn't have to be told that the old jeweler's sight was worse for his head was bent so low over his work that his thick, rumpled white hair looked like the tangled mane of a lion.

"Good day to you, Señor Constantine." As Danton greeted the old man, he removed his hat.

Constantine looked up at the tall, handsome Danton Navarro. His eyes were failing him, but he recognized him immediately. Victor could be proud of the son he'd sired, Constantine concluded. The jeweler had always felt that Victor Navarro had truly appreciated his skill. So naturally he'd taken pride in perfecting anything he'd made for the Navarro family over the years.

"Hello, Danton. So good to see you. Come! Come in." Constantine motioned him over to the seat beside his workbench. "Your family—how are they, eh?"

"Oh, fine, Señor Constantine."

"Good! Good!" Constantine nodded his tousled head and smiled.

"You are busy as usual, I see," Danton remarked.

"Never too busy to do something for the son of Victor if he wishes it," Constantine responded.

Danton wasted no time in telling him what he wanted made. Constantine listened as Danton described the piece of jewelry he desired for Kit. As he'd done when Danton had ordered a gift for his sister, Delores, Constantine wanted to know, "Tell me about this little señorita, Danton. Peridots, eh?"

"She has a ring with that stone in it, and I've noticed it seems to match the green of her eyes. So I thought,

153

señor, a pair of earrings with peridots in them would be perfect."

"Ah, yes," Constantine slowly drawled. "Green eyes you say?"

"Yes, *señor*—the greenest."

Constantine privately thought that these must be a very special pair of earrings, and a few minutes later, after he'd listened to Danton describe the young lady, he knew they had to be a work of perfection for they were a gift of love.

The jeweler happened to remember the magnificent pale pink tourmaline, very rare. Quickly, his hand and finger sketched out a design of what he was already envisioning and he pushed the drawing over for Danton's approval.

"A pink tourmaline of magnificent quality with the teardrop, a peridot, dangling gracefully from your lady's dainty ear, eh? What do you think? Do you like Constantine's idea?" The old man's smile was wide, for he was already excited about the piece he was about to create.

As Danton surveyed Constantine's sketch, the jeweler observed him intently. "Perfect, Constantine! Just what I wanted . . . exactly what I had in mind!" Danton restrained the impulse to ask him just how soon he could have the work completed. That would not have set well with Constantine, and Danton knew it.

Instead, Danton slowly rose from the seat and he tactfully remarked, "I leave the creation of it in your capable hands, Señor Constantine."

"Would the end of June be agreeable?"

"That would be just fine, *señor.*"

Constantine scratched his thick mop of hair, and then he winked. "Ah, for you, Señor Danton, I'll get it done by the middle of June. It would be a shame to make a beautiful lady wait longer than necessary for a piece of jewelry such as this one will be." There was great pride in his voice, but Danton could not fault the man for that. Constantine was one of a rare breed, and his pride was exactly what made his work so superior.

Danton knew a young woman like Kit was also rare and special. No gem, no matter how exquisite, could compare to her. But it was fitting that she wear something uniquely beautiful.

Suddenly he didn't relish the thought of returning to his house that evening. Kit was no longer there, but on her way back to Silvercreek. The reality of her departure sank in. He would be more than a little lonely tonight.

Part II

The Fire

Chapter 17

The week had seemed endless to Kit. Since they'd returned from Austin, when each day ended she'd told herself that was one less before Danton came up the drive. Was he missing her as badly? Well, she hoped so! To be truthful, she was praying that he was just as miserable without her as she was without him!

Actually, her temper had been waspish. She'd chided herself because she'd snapped at Damien when he had not deserved it. But his mischievous taunting and teasing had irritated her. But the good-natured Damien had merely flashed her a grin, showing off his pearly white teeth, and he'd cajoled her.

When she'd offered him no hint of relenting or giving way to laughter, he'd coaxed. "Chiquita, I'll be handy at the party if old Danton gets mobbed or if that promiscuous Estellita preoccupies him."

"Is that woman coming?" Kit could barely restrain her anger.

"Oh, if I were betting on it I'd say it was a sure thing. Fact is, Danton could just bring her when he comes. Estellita has a multitude of acquaintances among our guests. You see, this little shindig has been held every year at the Navarro ranchero. But then I tend to forget that you couldn't know all this. It's a funny thing that we all just assume you've been here forever."

"That's sort of the way I feel too, Damien," Kit mumbled, hoping to make up to Damien for being so hateful. Besides, it wasn't Damien who should be punished because she was irked by the thought of Danton's lady love coming to the fiesta. She was really angry at Danton.

How could he possibly ask that woman to accompany him to the ranch after her behavior at dinner in Austin?

Damien noticed the look on Kit's face, and he took pleasure in knowing he'd instilled doubts about Danton in her. He'd make a point of adding fuel to that fire during the next few days, he decided.

His arm went around her shoulders as they took their stroll. For once he'd managed to do so without that pest, Delores, tagging along. "Why, Kit, you are family as far as the Navarros are concerned. You know that!"

He gave her a little squeeze, pressing her close to him, but Kit was not disturbed by Damien's affectionate gesture. At that particular moment, she found herself in need of his display of affection. Like many things that could not be explained, Kit felt a sudden surge of light-heartedness, and she mellowed toward Damien. In doing so, she found herself enjoying his companionship.

Tossing her lovely head to the side and gazing up at him, she inquired curiously, "Tell me, Damien, what is it like to be a twin?"

She took him by surprise. For a minute it was Damien who took on a rather subdued air. Then, with a serious voice, he replied, "Strange, in a way. There are two of you and you look at the other one and say, 'that's me.' Do you understand what I'm saying, Kit?"

160

"I guess."

"No, you really couldn't. I guess if you aren't a twin you can't. When you're a twin you can swear you know what your counterpart is thinking. It's eerie sometimes. That changed when Danton and I grew up, but it was that way when we were children."

Kit listened with intense interest for she'd never seen Damien so sincere. In this mood, he reminded her now of Danton, and that had never happened before.

Kit was amazed to find herself so abruptly drawn to Damien. Actually, he was very likable, and she realized she probably had not given him a chance to show her this side of his personality. For all of his trickery and teasing, there was a very serious side to Danton's twin brother.

"I've never had a sister," she candidly remarked with an air of certainty. She stared ahead as she spoke so she didn't see the disconcerting frown that appeared on Damien's face.

"But how can you be so sure?" He held his breath as he waited for her answer. Only a moment ago Damien had admitted to himself that if it wasn't for that damned incident back at the Crystal Castle he could find himself very much enamored with this copper-haired little darling. She certainly was a very tempting female. Damien liked the fire that smoldered in her eyes, hinting at the passionate nature he was sure she possessed.

"It's just something I know, Damien. Deep inside me I know that I have no sisters or brothers." She laughed softly. "Damien, I have been having some visions—crazy ones. They're all mixed up, but I just know it's going to clear up someday. Maybe very soon!" Kit had not mentioned this to Delores. She had not planned to breathe a word of it to anyone just yet, but on an impulse she had confided in Damien.

161

Any triumphant pleasure Damien had derived earlier from baiting Kit with insinuations about Danton and Estellita had now been replaced by tormenting concern for his own hide. He urgently wanted to get her back to the house and to be rid of her. It was inconceivable for a man like Damien Navarro to wish to rid himself of a gorgeous female, but this was no ordinary young lady. Kit could ruin him! *Madre de Dios,* she could be the death of him!

"Shall we return to the house, Kit?" He smiled down at her. If Kit thought those dark eyes gleamed with genuine affection, she was very wrong. Damien was feeling anything but affection. His heart was cold and his mind was calculating and indifferent. A cunning idea had already sparked in Damien, a plan to rid himself of the threat the beautiful redhead presented. It was a deadly plan—deadly for Kit!

Yet the guileless, unsuspecting Kit strolled by his side down the pathway having no inkling of the vile thoughts parading through her companion's head as they approached the house.

When they came to the steps of the long, roofed veranda, she turned to him and smiled sweetly, "Thank you, Damien, for our nice walk and for being so sweet to me. I . . . I'm just beginning to realize how very nice you are."

Damien moved backward on the flagstone walk. A flashing grin lit his handsome face as he bid her farewell; then he hastily turned and strolled away.

Rancor filled Damien as he marched toward the corrals where Santiago and some of the ranch hands had gathered. Their guffaws and their loud talk caught his attention. He kicked at the earth, cursing his twin brother. Had Danton never brought that girl to Silvercreek, he wouldn't be forced to do what he was planning. Damn him! Danton could thank himself for the girl's fate.

Santiago caught sight of Kit and Damien returning from their afternoon stroll. It seemed to the old foreman that Kit had spent a lot of time in Damien's company since her return from Austin. He didn't think Señor Danton was going to be too pleased to hear it. Santiago had mixed feelings about just how much information he should relay to Danton. There was much to consider. He did not want to be the spark that ignited a wildfire where those two boys were concerned.

As deep as his feelings for Danton ran, and as much as he admired the young man, he had been put in a position he didn't relish. Like Damien, Santiago almost wished the likable little Kit had not come to Silvercreek, yet Santiago was instantly guilty over having such a thought. He was as susceptible to Kit's winning ways as Danton or Damien.

When Damien joined the circle of hired hands and took a turn at tossing the dice, Santiago unobtrusively slipped away. The old man recognized something in Damien's manner that frightened him. Damien was tense and he'd seen him that way before. At those times Damien reminded him of a mountain cat ready to spring on its prey. Damien Navarro had the look of a killer in his black eyes on this afternoon. Santiago saw the danger, and he decided to avoid it.

It came as no surprise to Santiago the next morning when the newest of their hired men, a young man by the name of Blake Nash, was sporting a black eye. Upon inquiring where Blake had won that little trophy, Santiago was told: "That Damien and his goddamn hot temper—that's where!" The lean, lanky man shook his head, still befuddled by the incident. "Wish someone hadda' clued me in on that crazy son of a bitch! *Señora*'s son or not, I'll kill the bastard if he every lays a

163

hand on me again. Got no use for that one, Santiago."

Santiago stood in the morning sun and watched Nash saunter on toward the barn. Now he knew he'd been right about young Navarro. It was times like this he yearned most for old Victor.

These incidents involving Damien made Santiago ponder how the young man could have been sired by such an honorable man as Victor Navarro. As the foreman went about his usual morning chores, his thoughts kept drifting back to Damien's disgraceful act. Such behavior was not good for the morale around the ranch hands.

An hour later, Santiago spotted the *señora*'s buggy dashing down the drive. Lucía was in the driver's seat, and he paused to admire that attractive lady. To Santiago, she was like a queen, so proud and regal. In her simple black outfit, a black wide-brimmed hat atop her black hair which was now sprinkled with gray, she made a striking image. One could not help being impressed by the sight of her.

She was going to the neighboring Morilla Ranch, Santiago was certain of it because of the turn she took at the fork in the road. He knew she had made it a habit to visit with the depressed Antonia Morilla at least twice each month since the death of Antonia's son. Her considerateness was one of the qualities which endeared the *señora* to those who knew her. She was compassionate and caring.

Lucía Navarro was in especially high spirits as she traveled through the countryside this particular morning. The pasture was spotted with the brilliantly colored wildflowers, the Indian Paintbrush which always came into bloom in the springtime. She was sparkling with almost girlish excitement over the fiesta traditionally held at Silvercreek. It would always be special to her for she and Victor had initiated it early in their marriage.

The pleasant drive to the neighboring Morilla ranch found Lucía enjoying the day and reflecting on the delightful evening she and her family had shared. What a blessed woman she was! She was engulfed with a feeling of well-being for life had been kind to her. It was wonderful to have her family gathered around her table as they had been last night. She thought about Delores and Kit, two beautiful young ladies, and then Damien who had been his most flamboyant self. How utterly charming and entertaining he could be when he chose to do so. Perhaps, some of her happiness could rub off on her dear friend, Antonia, she thought as she saw the Morilla's two-story home come into sight.

Had Lucía Navarro known what had caused Damien's strange exultation she would have been shocked. Damien's high spirits had come from the sadistic pleasure he'd derived from slamming cruel blows into poor Blake's face. The blows and punishment Damien yearned to inflict on Danton, he'd executed against the ranch hand, who didn't deserve them.

For Damien, beating the man was stimulating. It gave him a wild, wonderful sensation he would have been hard put to describe. Actually all the frustrations he harbored were suddenly released, and like a gusting rampaging wind, they rushed out of him, leaving quiet and peace in their stead.

After such an act Damien felt sated. For him it was almost like the sweet release he felt after he'd bedded a beautiful woman. Conquest was always Damien's goal. Women had always been pawns in the games he played. Love had no meaning for him.

Perhaps, that was why the beautiful Kit's presence

was so disquieting to Damien. She excited him as no other woman had, and she challenged him. But he dared not use her as his toy, and he sensed that she was the one lady his Latin charms could not entice into playing his little game.

This made her all the more desirable to Damien Navarro!

Chapter 18

Days before the fiesta the preparations began, and the activity mounted daily. Drusilla was assisted in the house and kitchen by three extra Mexican women. Since the Valdez family would be overnight guests the guest rooms had to be cleaned and aired, and fresh linens put on the beds.

Delores bubbled with excitement as she told Kit the surprising news that Ramon Valdez would be accompanying the Valdez family for the two-day visit at Silvercreek. "Seems he and Danton ran into each other after we left Austin, and Danton extended an invitation. Can you imagine? He's coming all the way from San Antonio to attend our fiesta!"

To herself, Kit muttered that she just hoped Estellita Valero didn't come all the way from Austin. But to Delores she said nothing.

Kit must have taken her gorgeous gown out of the armoire a dozen times to admire it. It was far more beautiful than she'd realized when they'd purchased it in Austin.

She could have sworn those dainty little rosettes were actually miniature real roses; they were so perfectly made. They certainly enhanced the beauty of the green organza gown which was underlined with green taffeta of the same shade. The long, flowing skirt was molded around her hipline and then gathered into a bustle at the back, while the flattering bodice came to a point at the waistline in the front. The neckline, cut deep to show just a hint of cleavage, was edged with a sheer, frothy ruffle. As a final touch, in the flounces of organza at the hem of the skirt the little rosettes nestled. Another cluster was attached at the side of the waistline.

Kit had no memory of the beautiful gown she and Florine had picked out for her birthday in this same season only a year ago. Nor did she recall that the lovely peridot ring on her finger had been a birthday gift from her mother, but instinct told her the ring was a significant link to her past life.

Kit had told no one about the mysterious phenomenon that had happened the last time she'd taken the gorgeous gown out of the armoire to gaze upon it and feel its diaphanous softness. She was convinced they'd think her crazy if she spoke of it, so she'd kept it her little secret.

Nevertheless, she could not forget what had happened, nor could she put it out of her mind.

Suddenly, the gown hadn't been a gown at all. She had become detached from it, and the green gown had become a lush green field filled with lovely pink wildflowers, like the rosettes on the gown. She, Kit, was romping amid those knee-high blooms, and from time to time she would reach down to pluck one and put it in the wicker basket she carried over one arm.

She had laughed gaily as she'd turned to a lady who stood at a distance, watching her frolic. The lady had a look of delight on her dark, tawny face, and she'd waved to the girl. The lady was lovely, a beauty rather like Señora Lucía Navarro. But she was darker of skin, and she was not as tall and stately. She wore a bright-colored kerchief tied around her hair, and the hair showing was as black as midnight.

When her caprice in the meadow came to an end, the girl rushed to the woman who waited for her with open arms, and she went into them. The woman encircled her protectively and murmured her name. But Kit, standing away from the scene, could not hear the name she spoke. Oh, how she wanted to hear that name! But she could not!

When the scene had been played to a finish and the green meadow was no longer a meadow but a gown, Kit felt very drained and weak. Her dainty hands trembled, and her legs felt as if they were melting. She was forced to sink down on the canopied bed until she regained her strength.

These strange visions had to be jagged parts of her forgotten past. More than ever Kit wanted to fill in that great gap in her memory. How long would she be forced to wait? Señora Lucía's doctor had told her there was no timetable for such a thing. It could come about suddenly, or there could be gradual recall of events in her past life. But when would the shadows and the mist clear away?

In her impatience, Kit could not appreciate the fact that some power within her was striving desperately to restore her memory at that very moment. The strange phenomenon she'd experienced was a memory of the meadow just outside El Paso where she and Solitaire went when they took their weekly rides into the countryside. Kristina had loved to go through the fields picking the beautiful wildflowers.

Her mind was working when she watched Lucía playing cards at the little teakwood table, for she had often observed Florine sitting and playing the game of solitaire. The feisty little roan, Scarlett, was a reminder of the fine prancing bays that pulled her mother's fancy gig around the city of El Paso.

A part of her mind worked tediously to reveal that she was Kristina Whelan not Kit Winters.

In the meanwhile, she could only struggle. Being in a perplexing state of limbo went against her nature.

The day before the Valdez family arrived at Silvercreek everything was in readiness for their visit and for the fiesta the next evening. The brass beds gleamed like brilliant gold, the linens were spotlessly clean, and vases of fresh flowers brightened the rooms.

The grand staircase in the entranceway had been polished, and the wood shone from the rubbing Drusilla had given it. Lucía's front parlor was elegant and it was the perfect formal setting in which to entertain the Valdez family on the evening of their arrival. The mahogany sofa upholstered with a deep rose brocade sofa and the matching chairs were comfortably arranged. Matching vases sat at either end of the marble mantel of the fireplace, each holding a lovely combination of white and pink flowers.

The cozy comfort of the back parlor was enhanced by Lucía's greenery and by the large gilded cage that housed her singing canaries. Because they appealed to her, Lucía had vivid colors in this room. The chairs were upholstered in bright red velvet and the matching settees were covered with a print of red and gold. There was a native stone fireplace in this room, and over the mantel hung a portrait of the younger Lucía. Victor had painted it after the birth of the twins.

While the spacious house was in order, the kitchen was still a busy beehive what with the baking and the preparation of the sumptuous fare for the fiesta. Drusilla and the additional help still had many tasks to accomplish.

Lucía was more than pleased at how perfectly the household was running by the time her dear friends arrived from Austin. For Señora Navarro, it was an ideal situation to have one evening alone with Alberto and Eugenia Valdez before her other friends and neighbors gathered at the ranch the next evening. Her only disappointment was that Danton did not arrive with them.

Her friendship with the Valdezes was one of long standing, over twenty-five years now. She and Eugenia had warmed to one another the minute their Latin husbands had introduced them. Like Lucía, Eugenia was not of Latin descent, and like Victor, Alberto was several years older than his pretty wife. Lucía and Eugenia formed an instant bond of friendship.

So it was very pleasant for Lucía to share a delightful dinner with her friends. After dinner, she, Alberto, and Eugenia slipped away to her back parlor to chat and enjoy her beloved Victor's favorite brandy. They reminisced about times gone by, times that the two couples had shared.

Fernando, Ramon, Damien, Delores, and Kit occupied the main parlor, and Damien entertained the group by playing the guitar and singing. Then Delores played the piano. There was a very relaxed feeling to the evening, and Kit was enjoying herself far more than she'd expected.

In the festive atmosphere, Fernando went to sit on the piano bench beside Delores, and he played the bass as she played the treble of a song. Then they began to harmonize by singing it together. Without consciously doing so, Kit joined in. She knew the words.

Damien's attention was immediately captured for he hadn't heard her sing since she'd been at Silvercreek. When the song ended, he complimented her lavishly.

"You never cease to amaze me, *chiquita!* You sing like a little bird. I think, perhaps, you've been holding out on us."

His praise naturally pleased Kit, but he was no more stunned than she was. "I . . . I thank you, Damien. You're very kind."

"Kind—no! Honest, yes!" Damien had seen a new quality in this auburn-haired beauty when she was singing—a sensualness . . . the eyes and the mouth.

"Sing a ballad for us, Kit," he insisted. He mentioned a little love ballad very familiar and well known. Kit had started to plead off, but she suddenly felt like doing it. While Damien picked up his guitar and began to strum it, Kit moved with a slow, catlike grace to sit on the arm of his chair. When she began to sing, Damien was entranced by her. She taunted and tantalized him until he felt like a man being seduced by a lovely enchantress. Kit was now standing up so she might give vent to the deep emotion she was feeling as she sang her song.

She was a bewitching siren now. He saw in her no resemblance to the sweet innocent who'd been living under the same roof for months. By the time her song was over, Damien ached to have her. By God, he would—one way or the other!

When the song ended Kit was in a trancelike state. She was experiencing another one of those strange feelings. How frequently they were coming now, she thought. She knew those songs, both of them. She had certainly sung them before, but the face of the man sitting at the piano was not Fernando's and no one had been strumming a guitar. But the haze refused to lift for Kit. She could not recall the nights she'd sung downstairs at the Crystal Castle while Sid Layman had played the piano.

Suddenly Kit looked up to see a towering figure in

172

the archway. His coat was swung carelessly over one arm and the neck of his shirt was unbuttoned. An unruly lock of black hair fell over one side of his forehead, and his dark eyes pierced Kit's green ones. She wanted to rush into Danton's arms, but his demeanor discouraged it. The black fury in his eyes made her wary.

Her long lashes dropped to avoid the punishing stare he was inflicting on her. Damien was very aware of Danton's displeasure. He wondered just how much of the scene his brother had witnessed, obviously enough to put him into a black mood.

"Danton! Oh, good—you got home! Come and join us." Delores greeted her brother warmly. Her own mood was too gay to be dampened by her solemn-faced brother.

Slowly, Kit raised her head to see if Danton would stride to her as she hoped he would, but he'd already turned away from her. He was walking toward Ramon and Fernando Valdez. In his gallant way, he forced a pleasant smile as he extended his hand to Fernando.

"Nice to see you, Fernando. Ramon, you made it, I see. I'm glad," Danton noticed that the two good-looking young men were sitting close to his sister. He didn't have to be told that Delores was enjoying herself this evening for her pretty dark face was radiant. But then, she had not been the only one who was thoroughly enjoying herself. Kit was most assuredly having a good time from what he'd observed.

Dear God, the seductive siren she'd revealed was someone he'd thought only he was privy to see. The fire and passion she'd exuded while singing were the same he'd felt when they made love. No other man had a right to see that. Fury blazed up in him and he had a wild desire to slap Kit's beautiful face and to bury his fists into Damien's ogling eyes.

He did not know what was being said as he stood there with Ramon. Like a man walking in a thick fog, he heard the conversation, but he didn't absorb the words. It was impossible for him to concentrate on what was being said.

When Damien's arm snaked around Kit's back as if to console her, she didn't try to move away for she felt that she would faint were it not for Damien's support.

She couldn't understand how Danton could possibly treat her so cruelly and coldly after what they'd shared. How could he if he cared for her as he'd said he did?

Had she been only a moment of pleasure for Danton? Perhaps he no longer desired her, now that he had had his way with her!

She must not be naïve and trusting. Whether she wanted to or not she would have to give some thought to Damien's pointed innuendoes about his twin brother. Oh, yes, she had most assuredly just seen with her own eyes the obstinate and unyielding side of Danton Navarro.

He could be cold and despicable!

Chapter 19

The brandy did nothing to numb his mind or to stop his tormenting thoughts. Even smoking cheroots and pacing the floor did not ease Danton's frustration. In fact, now he was even more miserable!

He'd tarried below no longer than hospitality and cordiality demanded, and out of respect for his dear mother he'd see the fiesta through somehow. Although he knew it would be torture, he was determined to exert more willpower than he normally demanded of himself.

But for Lucía Navarro, he told himself, he'd leave the first thing in the morning for Austin. He knew the next twenty-four hours would try his patience to the limit and it would be best if he stayed away from Damien and Kit as much as possible.

It was a black night outside for the moon was shrouded by the clouds that were moving over the Texas countryside. Danton was not the only one wakeful.

Lucía lay on her bed, praying that the weather would cooperate with her plans for the next day. Thunderstorms and rain would ruin everything. But then, she knew the Texas weather. Like a chameleon it could change so swiftly.

She was delighted that Danton had arrived, and she was equally pleased that he'd not been accompanied by Señora Valero. Perhaps, she'd not credited her son with the ability to look beyond that woman's lacquered loveliness to the vicious vixen underneath. Lucía knew Estellita's kind. She knew such women well!

Señora Valero's wiles were deadly. Indeed, Lucía had confessed to her dear friend just this evening, "I don't want Danton to be beholden to that woman, Eugenia, if he does seek to throw his hat into the political ring."

"I know what you mean, Lucía. She used poor Ramon to get to go to Danton's dinner party, and I knew it. She has always been that way, ever since I've known her—even when she and Manuel were married."

Lucía also confessed to Eugenia her great relief that Estellita had not accompanied Danton from Austin. But Eugenia had responded with a warning.

"Oh, don't count Estellita out yet. She's like a bad penny, as they say. She could turn up before tomorrow night is over, Lucía."

"Somehow, I don't feel that she will, Eugenia," Lucía had replied.

"Lucía, a woman like Estellita has no pride. She will do anything to get what she wants, and she does want Danton. She has since she first laid eyes on him. It is common knowledge that she was having an affair with one of Governor Roberts' advisors—one of the most respected too. The man was a devoted family man before Estellita got under his skin. Oh, you cannot take the witch lightly, Lucía."

"Then I must pray that Danton will see through her cunning ways," Lucía told her friend, but she did not add that she hoped it was the spirited little Kit who had

176

stolen Danton's heart.

However, at this late hour Kit was not very spirited. She yearned for sleep, but it would not come. How she was going to make it through the gala fiesta the next evening, she could not possibly imagine. It had taken all her self-control to hold back her tears until she made a quick exit from the parlor. At least the others had not seen them.

She knew nothing about this man she encountered tonight. This was not the man she'd given herself to with such eagerness. This man was cold and cruel; he was a stranger she didn't recognize at all. Why, he'd given her a perfunctory nod of his head and a restrained hello as though he didn't even want to greet her.

How could she have been so completely taken in by him? But was she? Had he not rescued her, been the good samaritan who'd picked her up by the wayside and then given her shelter and food? Had he not been the caring protector and finally her tender, gentle lover? Her honesty demanded that she answer truthfully, and he had done all this.

But what had caused this stranger to appear before her tonight? Her conscience was clear, she told herself. She had done him no wrong!

Accepting that fact, the spitfire temper she'd inherited from her Irish mother emerged. She was suddenly consumed by a fury that matched Danton's fierce anger. Damn him! she thought to herself. She didn't have to take such an insult from him or any other man. Maybe she didn't know who she was, but she knew what she was and she was not some man's doormat!

Well, she'd show him, she vowed! Tomorrow he would learn that two could play his game. Never again would she bow her head in pain and hurt, nor would

177

she shed tears or sob.

Her eyes suddenly became heavy with sleep, for she was now looking forward to the dawning of the next day. No longer did she wish to run away and hide so she would not have to look upon Danton's smirking face. She'd challenge him with her own brand of cool indifference.

Lucía was devastated to find the skies were still overcast and gray the following morning but she tried to maintain a feeling of optimism. While Alberto Valdez and Fernando accompanied Danton to the stables to look over some of the prized Navarro horses, Ramon seized the opportunity to be alone with Delores. The pair took a long morning stroll in the courtyard gardens, and he was thrilled to have this time with her.

Eugenia kept Lucía company as her friend made her final inspections and gave last-minute instructions to Drusilla.

Damien lingered near the house hoping to catch a glimpse of Kit. He knew the deep hurt Danton had given to her the night before. It suited his plans perfectly. Unknowingly, his brother had eased the way for him to ingratiate himself with the naïve Kit. Ah, this could be a most memorable night! Perhaps before the night was over and the gay festivities had ended, he might have the delectable darling in his arms and his bed. Now that would be the ultimate revenge. Damien was quite proud of his prowess with the ladies, but last night, Kit revealed a provocative side of her nature that he'd not suspected. Who would have thought that the curly haired girl he and his pals had taken from El Paso as their hostage had concealed the sensuousness she'd exhibited in the front parlor last night. He had to give old Dake Davenport credit. He hadn't been so stupid after all.

Now, Damien knew why the dude was so hot for the girl after the night ride to their campsite. Hell, he would probably have been the same.

For the thousands he'd lost at the monte table in Florine Whelan's gambling hall, he'd bet she'd paid with heartbreak tenfold. He had had his revenge. Mlle. Whelan had spent many sleepless nights.

Christ, if only he could have been certain that this girl hadn't seen enough of his face he could have saved himself many nights of torment. He'd tried to recall just how the events of that night had occurred. At the Crystal Castle, he could recall that Dake had dragged her into the hallway, but he could not remember whether he'd pulled the mask back over his face when he and Jesse had scurried out of the bedroom after Florine had been shot. Florine had been in shock and so she might not have seen him clearly.

He clung to the hope that the dim campfire had distorted his features once he'd encountered her. Damn, if only he could be sure! Only Kit could tell him, and if she did it would be too late.

He couldn't chance it. He had to insure his safety, and to do that he must rid himself of Kit!

The night of fiesta was always a time of reflection for Señora Lucía Navarro. It was the special time too, a time when she gave way to the rare urge to put on one of her more fancy gowns and to wear a more lavish display of her fine jewels. Her beautiful sapphire and diamond necklace and earrings were what she'd chosen for tonight, as accompaniments for her pearl gray gown with its overlays of wide black lace flounces. The neckline of the gray bodice was square, and the unlined

179

sleeves of black lace were fitted at Lucía's wrist. She wore gold bracelets on her right wrist, and they gleamed brilliantly against the black lace material.

She was pleased with her appearance as she took a final look at herself before joining her friends, Alberto and Eugenia. Victor would have approved of the way she looked tonight, she mused, smiling into the full-length mirror. It was a wicked smile. Someday, she should tell Eugenia about the other Lucía—the Lucía Navarro only Victor knew existed. Oh, Eugenia would be shocked and tongue-tied for a minute but then she'd be amused, Lucía concluded. One day, she might just tell her friend of her past.

With a serene expression on her fine chiseled face, she threw back her head. "Beautiful *condesa!*" That was how the handsome Victor had addressed her on the night he'd approached her table in the famous gambling establishment in San Antonio.

The Palace had been famous, but the lady called Lolita had been its main attraction. Her striking, sultry beauty and her expertise at Spanish monte and faro were almost legendary. The elegance of her dress and her fabulous collection of jewels set her apart from the few well-known lady gamblers of the area. In the years since she suddenly disappeared from that world into the seclusion of her life with Victor, no woman had taken her place.

One had come close, and it was ironical that that woman had been taught her skill at monte by the famous Lolita—Señora Lucía Navarro!

Lucía had often thought about the vivacious Florine Whelan. She had taken the younger girl under her wing at the Palace in San Antonio and she'd taught her to handle the cards. The pretty auburn-haired young girl had been an eager pupil, and she'd had a natural talent. Lucía could recall Florine's long nimble fingers.

180

Where had life led the provocative, vivacious redhead, Señora Navarro wondered? Most of the better known lady gamblers seemed to end up broke and down on their luck. They were a sad, sorry lot. Lucía prayed that Florine Whelan had not been one of the unfortunate ones.

Then she turned away from her mirror and her past life. It was time to go downstairs to greet her guests.

As she walked down the thick carpeted hallway and started to descend the winding stairway, she smiled. She felt Victor's presence. She was his beautiful *condesa,* and she assuredly looked the part. No queen could have looked more regal in the fine gown set off by old Constantine's jewelry. The sapphires and diamonds were exquisite. The old artisan would have beamed with pride if he could have gazed upon the *señora* this evening.

The stairway would be graced by many lovely ladies that evening, but none would outshine the breathtaking vision Kit made as she followed Lucía a short time later. She needed no jewels to enhance her beauty. At the side of her head, a cluster of pale pink rosettes that matched the ones on her gown was pinned, and her curls, pulled back from her face, cascaded down her back. But for the ring on her finger, she wore no jewelry. In her hand she carried a dainty fan edged with a delicate French lace.

If one looked at Señora Navarro and imagined a queen, to look at Kit one would have certainly envisioned a royal princess. Like Lucía, she found herself in a festive mood. As distressed as she'd been at the end of the preceding night, she now felt quite gay. Her vivacious air made her face glow.

She had no apprehensions about facing Danton. In fact, she anticipated doing just that. She'd show him he could not ignore her and get away with it as he'd done the night before. According to Señora Lucía's guest list many gentlemen were coming to the fiesta this evening. Of course, there was always the happy-go-lucky Damien. He had stood by her last night when she'd needed someone.

She saw Ramon's smiling face looking up at her as she slowly descended the stairs, and she suspected that he was waiting for Delores to come down. Nevertheless, his dark eyes flashed with admiration at the sight of Kit.

"*Señorita,* may I say how beautiful you look tonight!" Ramon exclaimed.

Kit took the hand he gallantly offered to assist in the final step from the stairway. "And you certainly look very handsome, Ramon." With the air of a coquette, she declared, "All the young ladies will surely be vying for your attention." She gave him one of her sweetest smiles.

He chuckled, "Well, I'd settle for one particular one, Señorita Kit. I suspect you know who I mean?"

Tilting her head to the side, she admitted, "Delores, I think."

She could have sworn that he blushed. With a very serious look on his face, he then implored her as they ambled toward the main parlor, "Do you think, *señorita*—do you think I possibly have a chance?"

"I'll tell you what I think if you promise me something, Ramon."

Ramon responded with boyish eagerness. "What? Anything?"

"Please just call me Kit, and I think, Ramon, that you have a very good chance with Delores. I can't think of anyone who could stand in your way."

"You don't think Fernando . . . that she . . ."

"Not if you give her a hint about how you feel." Kit smiled. It amused her to talk with such authority to

Ramon who was probably a few years older than she. Yet, to Kit, he seemed much younger.

From the smile on his dark, swarthy face she knew he was pleased with what she'd said, and the two of them entered the archway with radiant smiles on their faces, smiles that could easily have been misinterpreted. Kit was still on his arm, her hand placed at his wrist, and they were smiling at one another from the result of their confidential conversation.

In the candlelit elegance of the formal parlor the señora and Alberto and Eugenia Valdez were enjoying a glass of champagne. Over in a remote corner sat Fernando and Danton; they were engaged in private discussion. An abrupt silence came over the spacious room.

Openly displaying their admiration for the beautiful sight Kit made as she entered on Ramon's arm, Alberto and Fernando rose in unison. Danton sat like a starstruck youth, frozen to his seat. Finally, he rose from the chair and a tide of emotions rushed over him. She took his breath away; he damned well couldn't deny that! But as he stood there watching her walk in to join his mother and her friends, he seethed with jealousy. Would she ply her bewitching charms on Ramon tonight, he was asking himself. Dear God, she was a wicked, little vixen!

Danton was not the only one who had to brace himself against powerful emotions. Lucía smiled that usual serene, lovely smile of hers as she complimented Kit on how lovely she looked, but she was glad to be seated on the rose brocade sofa. Otherwise her legs would have been like jelly. This auburn-haired beauty was the image of Florine Whelan. Now Lucía knew why she'd warmed so to the girl when she'd first arrived at Silvercreek. No two could look so alike unless— Dear God, was it possible? Could Kit be related?

183

Florine's younger sister perhaps? Her daughter?

But Kit's eyes were no longer looking at Lucía Navarro. She gazed in Danton's direction for he'd remained at the side when Fernando joined the group. Her voice was soft but confident as she greeted him, "Good evening, Danton."

As her green eyes teased and taunted him with daring boldness, every fiber in his body pulsed with desire. There was not enough willpower in him to fight it!

With her head held defiantly high and a look in her eyes that said she dared him to try, she continued to let her eyes pierce him. To herself, she vowed silently that before the evening was over she'd make him regret that he'd ignored her so completely! She would make him aware of her presence.

Chapter 20

The long drive to the Navarro home was aglow as the guests arrived. The golden orange flames of the burning flambeaus lent a festive atmosphere to the grounds. As carriages rolled up the drive and stopped at the gate of the walled garden courtyard, Santiago and four of his handpicked men took charge of the equipages as the guests paraded through the gate into Lucía's beautiful garden which was decorated with colorful hanging lanterns strung among the branches of the trees.

Strolling musicians in their colorful attire, sombreros on their heads, were already playing their guitars to entertain the Valdez family.

Lucía had arranged for the tables and chairs to be placed so that they would accommodate her guests when they dined under the long, roofed veranda. The tables were distributed under the curved overhead arches so that each was lit by a lantern, and they were covered with bright red cloths. The veranda was an inviting sight.

Since they were seated at adjoining tables, Roberto Morilla chatted with Mister Langford and his daughter, Molly. Roberto's daughter, Carmella, was too busy searching the garden for the handsome Damien whom she'd not yet spied. Molly Langford didn't interest the lovely Carmella at all.

After Lucía introduced them to the neighboring rancher, Pete Stockton and Alberto and Eugenia Valdez joined Morilla since the rancher was alone.

Danton stood with his mother, greeting their guests, and Antonia Morilla had lingered beside them. It pleased Lucía to see Antonia chat with Danton, for she was certain the woman had not spoken with anyone other than the members of her own family since her son's death. Lucía knew what drew Antonia to Danton. Miguel and Danton had been the same age and they had been lifelong friends.

Lucía wondered what was holding Damien up. She'd seen the rest of her little brood milling around the gardens, but not Damien.

The sight of Arthur Cameron and his daughter, Della, coming through the garden gate was a relief to Lucía. As Eugenia had mentioned earlier, Estellita could have popped in with the Camerons for she and Arthur had been very close friends. It might have easily turned out that way that Estellita "just happened" to be a guest at Arthur's ranch.

With a feeling akin to gratitude, Lucía shook Arthur's hand and declared, "So glad you could come, Arthur. You too, Della my dear."

"Wouldn't have missed it for the world, Lucía!" Cameron turned to Danton and remarked, "Glad you got home, son. Got something to talk to you about tonight, Danton."

"All right, Mister Cameron. Della, nice to see you."

"You too, Danton. Delores in the garden?"

"I think you'll find her over there by the fountain, Della. She and Ramon Valdez are together, I think." Danton had directed the girl to the area where he'd last

186

seen Delores.

Della smiled, and after asking her father and Lucía to excuse her, she started to rush away. Suddenly, she turned back to Danton and remarked, "Oh, Danton, I can't wait to meet your friend, Miss Winters. Delores has me so curious."

Danton did not answer her. He merely nodded his head. At this point, he was a little curious about Miss Kit Winters himself! But the nice little Della didn't deserve a sour reply because of the way he was feeling about Kit, so he bridled his tongue and gave her a smile. He'd known Della all her life, and he almost looked upon her as a younger sister.

For the next several minutes guests continued to mill through the courtyard gates, but when there was finally a lull in the greeting and handshaking, Danton suggested to Lucía, "Why don't we begin to enjoy ourselves, Mother? May I get you something refreshing to drink?"

"Yes, Danton. That sounds like a good idea. Champagne. A glass of champagne, dear."

Danton gave his mother a crooked, mischievous grin. "Are you sure? Keeping a tally?"

"Be off with you, Danton! You aren't that old yet, my handsome son, to try to boss me," she admonished him light-heartedly. Then she reached out her be-jeweled hand to him and declared, "You do look quite handsome tonight, and doesn't our little Kit look like a walking dream?"

"Yes, Mother. She . . . she looks stunning." He turned sharply away.

Slowly, Lucía walked over to sit down at one of the lantern-lit tables to await her son's return with her champagne. She wondered what was plaguing Danton, for now that she thought about it she realized that he had not sought out the pretty Kit this evening. Not that

187

she didn't appreciate his playing the role of host, which Victor would have been doing if he were here with her this night, but Danton had not sought out Kit at all. Another question gnawed at Lucía as she enjoyed the luxury of resting her feet after standing so long. Where was her other son?

The sounds of light laughter and deep voices engulfed the huge courtyard garden now. Melodious music mingled with them, and tempting aromas wafted through the night air, along with the scents of honeysuckle and jasmine.

As it usually happened at Lucía's fiestas, everyone seemed to be enjoying the get-together. Most of the people present had known each other for years. There were two exceptions this time—Ramon Valdez and Kit—but they seemed to have found one another fast enough, Danton thought to himself, as he moved closer to the refreshment table to get his mother some champagne.

Standing beside it and pouring herself a glass of white wine was the gorgeous Kit. Danton was momentarily stunned by her radiant loveliness. She looked so damned innocent, as if she were flaunting the fact that he'd misjudged her.

"Well, hello again, Danton."

There was a flippancy in her tone that Danton quickly detected. He hoped she hadn't imbibed too much wine this early in the evening for there was a long night ahead.

"You seem to be enjoying yourself, Kit," he said, trying to mellow his deep voice.

"I am!" Her chin seemed to rise a little higher. "It promises to be a most exciting night. Señora Lucía looks so beautiful, and I'm certain her fiesta will be remembered for a long time."

Their nearness to one another had already begun to

work its particular magic. Danton could not tear his eyes away from her lovely face, and the glass of champagne he was taking to his mother was forgotten. The fact that he took a sip of it a moment later was due to the distraction she'd instigated in him. He and Kit stood watching the crowd approach the food-laden banquet table. Alberto and Eugenia had initiated the move at Lucía's suggestion so the guests could start enjoying Drusilla's delectable dishes of food. The serving girls and young ranch hands scurried back and forth with trays of drinks and carafes of steaming hot coffee and tea.

"Kit, why don't you join me for some of Dru's tasty goodies?" Danton felt he was doing her a favor if what he suspected was true and she had drunk too many glasses of wine on an empty stomach.

With his warm black eyes dancing over her face that way, she would have followed him to the ends of the earth. So she nodded her head and mumbled a soft acceptance, taking his arm as he led her through the line.

Greedy to have her all to himself, Danton guided Kit to the last table along the long veranda and it was only then that he noticed the almost-empty champagne glass and he realized he'd drunk the champagne intended for his mother.

They both gave way to a gusto of laughter before he excused himself for a moment to get both he and Kit another serving.

When he returned to the table, Kit was still smiling and her spirits now soared. He placed the glasses by the sides of their plates and then his eyes devoured her. "You are enchanting tonight, *amada mía,*" his deep voice murmured softly.

"And you've never looked so handsome, Danton," she told him in a slow, hesitating voice, for as he stood there looking down at her she felt almost breathless. His fine male body was molded into the tailored cream-colored pants and the shirt of the same shade. At his throat he wore a scarlet silk scarf. The neck of his shirt was open, and he wore no coat or jacket since the night was mild. She recalled the compelling power of this magnificent, virile man who'd made love to her with such fierce passion. Dear God, how she remembered it! Sitting there, she felt a flaming liquid heat creep over her.

Slowly, he bent lower and lower across the narrow table until his lips touched hers, and then he hungrily took the sweetness they had to offer. He cared not if they were observed by his mother's guests, for he was helpless to curb the wild impulse throbbing within him.

When he finally broke away, his dark eyes glanced at the inviting, sensuous mounds of her breasts, now slightly exposed, and his groin ached to have her right then and there. But he sank down into his chair and took a generous sip of champagne. With a soft moan of his anguish, he said, "Oh, God, *querida,* what you to do me!"

Her hand reached across the table to caress his cheek. "Danton, don't you know it is the same with me?"

He released a labored chuckle, "I hope to hell I do."

She gave him an impish smile, "Well, you do and you know it, I'd suspect."

His black eyes took notice of the little sparkling peridot ring, as it glowed in the lantern light. He thought of the earrings in their little velvet case back in his room. What a perfect time to have presented them to her and he didn't have them with him!

He captured her hands in his. "You must know how much I care for you, don't you, Kit?" Just because he was without the exquisite earrings did not mean he could not accomplish what he'd intended to do that night under the old Treaty Oak back in Austin. This was the perfect setting with the silvery moonlight and the festive atmosphere of the fiesta. Somehow, Danton knew that if Victor were here he would have approved.

The last hour had convinced Danton Kit was the only woman in the world for him. Why waste any more time thinking about it, he knew what he wanted. He wanted Kit to be his wife.

In this very romantic setting, he would propose to her. Perhaps, it was his Latin heritage that stirred such sentimental ideas or maybe the girl Kit brought them to the surface. Danton wasn't sure, but he knew how he felt as he gazed upon her loveliness in the silvery moonlight.

No matter how stylish she might look he would cherish the vision of a wandering waif on a mountain trail—Kit on the day he'd first come upon her. His eyes had been captivated by the sight of her, and his heart had been captured as well. Her green eyes had gleamed so vividly that Danton had known she had been trying desperately to hide her feelings of helplessness and fear. The once-lovely gown she'd had on had been a pathetic pile of rags. Its condition had aroused a feeling of compassion in Danton, who had sensed that something most unpleasant had happened to her. Never would he forget that little girl!

Someday the lawyer in him would demand that many questions be answered, and the mystery would be untangled, Danton realized. But that didn't have to delay their marriage.

Again he wondered how she happened to be on that trail and who had brought her to that spot and deserted her. She had been helpless, easy prey for the wild animals that roamed the woodlands in that remote area. But who would wish to do harm to such an enchanting creature?

In due time he would have his answers, but tonight, he only hoped that she would say yes when he asked her to be his wife.

He took Kit's tiny hand in his and brought it to his lips, letting them play over it leisurely before murmuring softly, *"Querida,* I adore you! I find myself crazy with wanting you every time I'm around you. Do you know that?"

She was completely entranced by his words, and she was at the point of saying that she felt the same way when the intrusion of exotic perfume and the rustling of crinoline diverted her eyes from Danton's handsome face. Looking over his shoulder, she saw the provocative Estellita with Damien beside her.

They had mocking smiles on their faces.

Danton's words of undying love remained locked within him, impatient to be spoken, and Kit was denied the opportunity to voice the endearments she'd intended to express.

The smug smiles brightening the faces of the intruders seemed to say that they both sensed Kit's and Danton's intimate feelings and they were finding devious joy in destroying this precious moment!

Chapter 21

Amidst all the gaiety and celebrating going on in the gardens as her guests praised the fiesta and the sumptuous refreshments, Lucía was swept by a wave of apprehension. She felt chilled, as though a sudden oppressive breeze had invaded her courtyard. The effect was so intense that she moved slowly away from where she'd been sitting with some of her guests to move around the long line of tables.

Then her nose sniffed the air. She had detected a particular perfume, an unusual scent: sandalwood, tearoses, and spice. She knew who wore that unique fragrance. She knew Estellita had come even before she spotted her scarlet gown moving through the crowd as Damien escorted her quickly to the secluded corner of the courtyard where Kit and Danton were cozily seated. The wealthy widow had managed to get her way.

Lucía happened to be near the table where Arthur Cameron was seated with Mister Langford. She remarked very casually, "You didn't mention that Estellita was down here, Arthur."

"Damned if I thought she was going to come over here tonight. You mean she's here now? That's one fickle lady. Told me and Della that she'd have to miss your party 'cause she was feeling poorly when she arrived late this afternoon. Son of a gun! I still don't see her."

"Oh, she and Damien just arrived, and they are going to the back of the veranda to join Danton and Kit I think." Lucía smiled a forced smile. She had no doubt about where that pair were headed. Lucía seethed. She wished she could tear into that woman's upswept hairdo as she'd seen some of the bar girls do years ago at the old Palace Gambling Hall.

Politely, she excused herself from Arthur and Langford's presence to amble just a little closer to Kit and Danton. What she saw made her clench her teeth and hiss under her breath, "You bitch!"

Lucía could easily read the displeased expression on Kit's pretty face as she looked up to see Estellita standing beside Danton, and at the same moment the meddlesome woman bent down to plant an intimate kiss on his mouth. Although Danton's back was turned to his mother, Lucía got the impression her son felt caught in the middle of a precarious situation. She rather hoped so! He had best rid himself of that grasping, cunning female if he didn't want worse problems later. She certainly did not want Estellita Valero for her daughter-in-law, and she suspected that her devilish son, Damien, had had a hand in this little escapade.

Danton had not one shred of doubt about Damien's part in the affair when Estellita stood behind him and boldly grabbed his face to kiss him. But his lips remained tight and unresponsive for he did not intend to join in her cunning little horseplay. He wasn't in such a stunned stupor that he hadn't noticed the gratification on Damien's face. This was why his brother hadn't appeared earlier at the fiesta. He'd been traveling to the

194

Cameron ranch to pick up Estellita. Damn her and damn Damien too!

Kit didn't try to hide her feelings. It was plain to see that she was thinking exactly what the promiscuous widow wanted her to think.

"Watch him, Kit darling. These devilish Latins have a way with words, you know. Born lovers . . . from the time they're in the cradle, I do believe." She laughed lightly and pinched Damien's cheek.

Until this had happened, Kit had almost convinced herself that Estellita meant nothing to Danton and that the things she'd observed back in Austin were all one-sided. But she was determined not to let Estellita get her goat. She, too, smiled smugly. "Well, I'm sure if anyone would know that, *you* would, Señora Valero. Perhaps, by the time I'm your age and have as much experience, I, too, will be more knowledgeable about Latin lovers."

An awesome silence settled around the table where Kit and Danton sat and Damien stood holding Estellita by the arm for Damien had noted the fiery response Kit's words had sparked. His eyes were wary. He felt Estellita's arm tense as if she would like to strike the lovely girl seated below her.

Danton, who had not yet made the gentlemanly gesture of rising, stared across the table in disbelief at the wide-eyed Kit whose eyes were locked into Estellita's. Now she was playing the innocent and he damned well knew it.

Estellita tried to gain the control that usually came so easily to her. "My, the little kitten has sharp claws, *querido*," she purred, her flashing black eyes going to Danton.

Kit was now the one aflame with anger for she immediately recognized Danton's term of endearment.

Danton could not see where this was leading for he

was still dazed by Kit's surprisingly acid remark. He was privately applauding her, but he did not want the friction between the two spirited women to get out of control. As he rose slowly from his chair, the uncompromising look on his face was observed by Damien. What was Danton preparing to do? Damien wondered. He was very displeased with Estellita's brash display. But more evident was his resentment at Damien for helping to pull this little shenanigan.

"Let me offer the two of you this table since I'm assuming you haven't eaten yet, Damien," Danton said, then his eyes fell on Kit. Her look was fathomless, and he wasn't quite sure what she was feeling at that moment. Danton felt that he must get her away from Estellita Valero before there was hell to pay.

"You had finished eating, had you not, Kit?"

Danton moved around the narrow width of the table to assist her from the chair. Kit nodded her assent, eager to make an end to the unpleasant scene.

Danton's aloofness only whetted the malicious streak in Estellita, however. Damien was now wishing he'd not put himself in league with this cunning, complex woman for he might have been enjoying a frollicking evening with Carmella or Molly who had both been darting glances in his direction. Estellita was too complicated a woman, and Damien didn't have the patience to deal with her on this particular evening. He actually wanted to swat Estellita's temptingly rounded hips when she pouted in order to get her way.

"You mean to tell me, Danton Navarro, that you intend to desert us. Why, I've come all the way from Austin! Anticipating the pleasure of your company was part of the incentive." Hoping to goad Kit and feeling the need to even the score with the auburn-haired minx who'd pricked her vanity sorely, she shrugged a bared shoulder and the movement provided

196

an ample display of her flesh and of her voluptuous breasts. In a very confidential tone, she then said to Kit, "You know, this is the busiest young lawyer in Austin these days. His . . . services are always in demand."

Kit felt the firm pressure of Danton's hand on her arm, and there was a possessive air about his manner. Under other circumstances she would not have resented Danton's masterful attitude, but now it did not sit well with her. If she could have known the words Danton had been about to say before they were aborted by Estellita's and Damien's appearance, she would not have felt as she did. Danton already possessed her heart, but her pride was involved when the conceited Señora Valero was scrutinizing her so intensely.

She rose, however, and immediately Danton's arm went around her waist. The force and power of his touch made her anger mellow. Danton's eyes turned on her but there was no smile on his face.

While his old girl friend and his brother had come at an inopportune time, Danton found it opportune that the music was starting up and the dancing was beginning as he and Kit left Damien and Estellita. His disgruntled mood was already gone, and his festive exhilaration was returning.

"I claim the first dance with you," he declared, flashing a boyish smile down at Kit.

He gave her no time to answer, but immediately guided her gracefully to the platform that had been set up for the dancing.

As they moved to the beat of the music provided by the violins and guitars, Kit was very much aware of his impressive height for she had to strain to look up into his face. Her arms were almost extended full so her hand might rest on his broad shoulder, and she could not have pinpointed the moment he'd pressed her close to him. When they'd begun to dance they were slightly apart, but she was suddenly aware of his heated closeness and of the aroma of the cheroots he smoked. Her hand could feel the firm, flexing muscles in his shoulder through the thin, fine tailored shirt he wore, and since he had no jacket on, she was aware of them when he made the slightest motion in guiding her around the floor, which he did with expertise. She hoped that she danced as well as the other ladies he'd held in his arms on a dance floor.

Oh, Kit wished for a multitude of things. She yearned to have the polished sophistication of Estellita Valero, to possess her voluptuous figure. She stared at the *señora* who sat in the fireglow of the hanging lantern at the table she and Danton had so recently occupied, and she even longed for the daring scarlet gown that sheathed Estellita's curvaceous body.

Then the strange feeling washed over her, as though she'd already lived this scene. As pretty as she had thought she looked in her new pale green gown, she now felt dowdy, little girlish. At some other time Kit had experienced this feeling. She had felt inadequate when she'd compared her feminine body to that of a full-figured lovely woman who was in the arms of a handsome man. But the haze still clouded her memory of the past. She didn't recall pressing herself against the balustrade on the second landing of the Crystal Castle while she stared at a blonde beauty in a fancy low-cut gown. That woman was being embraced by the man whose arms were now around her.

That night she'd so wanted to be held like that, and now that wish had been granted she could not know it. In fact, she'd been loved so completely and intimately that anything she'd have imagined that night was now pallid by comparison. That night she'd yearned for only a kiss!

Danton saw the starry-eyed look on her oval face. "Having a good time, *querida?*" he asked.

"I think so."

"You think so?" A crooked grin split his face, and he gave her a full, wide swing on the dance floor.

"I was having a marvelous time until Señora Valero came," she drawled, almost sneering as she spoke Estellita's name.

She looked so young and so tempting to Danton when her pert little chin jutted out with distaste and he was pleased to detect signs of jealousy over Estellita's bold familiarity with him. God, if she only knew how little she had to concern herself about the widow. In Danton's scheme of things, Estellita had meant a moment's pleasure. Never had his intentions been serious. That was the reason their affair had lasted as long as it had.

Estellita pursued sex as a man would, Danton had recognized that the first time they'd gone to bed together. More than once at his men's club in Austin he'd listened to her escapades being bandied around by various men.

When he guided Kit back to him after twirling her around, he once again drew her close. Then he bent his head so that his cheek pressed against the side of her face and his nose nuzzled the softness of her hair. The perfumed fragrance of her was intoxicating. Desire flamed in him as his body responded to the closeness of hers.

He whispered softly for her ears only, "I adore you, my little one. So much that I'm crazy with wanting!" His voice was husky with the sudden ache that consumed him.

He held her so close that she could feel the forceful need of his male body, and there was no denying that it fascinated and also pleased her to arouse such overwhelming yearning in the handsome Danton Navarro. He made her feel all woman—all powerful too. His obvious desire swept away any apprehensions that had been stirred by the sight of Estellita Valero. Kit was appeased by knowing that she, too, possessed her share of feminine charm and allure. Otherwise Danton would not be so affected by dancing close to her.

Feeling the need to even the score just a little because she'd been forced to watch Estellita kiss Danton and because he had made no effort to fend the woman off, she decided to be coy. "Please, Danton! We're not alone. What will your mother's friends think?"

"Who the devil cares?" he mumbled, leaving his head close to hers.

The last chords of the melody were being played, but Danton had not noticed. Nor had he been aware that his mother and Arthur Cameron were on the dance floor beside him and Kit.

When the movement of the dancers slowed, Arthur's voice stopped Danton just as he was preparing to take Kit to some remote spot in the courtyard and express what he'd intended to say when Damien and Estellita had interrupted him. He was determined to make his proposal before this night was over.

"Young man, I can't allow you to hog this pretty lady all night," Arthur said teasingly. Lucía stood beside him, smiling at the young couple. She was happy to see that Danton had whisked Kit away and had left Estellita's side.

Before Danton could protest, Arthur had Kit's hand in his and he was leading her back onto the dance floor, a big grin on his ruddy face.

Danton took his mother's arm and led her onto the floor. Lucía saw the deep frown on her son's face. "Dear, is dancing with your mother so distressing?"

Distracted, Danton mumbled an apology and he forced a pleasant look on his face for his mother's sake. Lucía was a very good dancer, and he would have normally enjoyed dancing with her as he always did at these affairs.

But his separation from Kit was only beginning. From Cameron's arms, Kit was claimed by Fernando Valdez and after Fernando she danced with Ramon, who was pleased to tell her, "Señorita, I am eternally grateful to you."

"Me, Ramon? What did I do?" Kit let a soft, puzzled laugh escape her.

"I did what you suggested and I think—I think—Delores likes me. At least enough to give me the courage to keep trying to convince her just how much I adore her," he smiled.

"Ah, I'm so glad, Ramon." Kit sighed. He was such a nice young man and so lovestruck over her little friend, Delores. They made a very striking couple, she thought, for she had observed them strolling around the fountain in the garden earlier in the evening. To her, some couples were well matched and others were not. Delores and Ramon seemed perfect for one another.

Kit did not realize that the sight of the stunning Estellita had brought a foul taste to Ramon Valdez's mouth as well. He was trying to shy away from the woman, wanting nothing to put him in a bad light in the lovely Delores' eyes. He knew Delores must remember that he'd escorted Señora Valero to Danton's dinner party in Austin.

Ramon was not a worldly-wise, sophisticated man, nor had he had the experience of Danton Navarro, but he'd felt very uncomfortable around the widow, whom he'd considered too brazen.

As the tempo slowed and Ramon glanced over to the

side of the dance floor, he saw a flash of bright scarlet sashaying seductively toward them. He hurriedly jerked Kit off the floor. His unintentionally rough tug on her arm put Kit into a quandary, and as he pushed her through the huge green-leaved shrubs she wondered whether Ramon Valdez was the gentleman of quality she'd thought him.

But then he drew in a deep breath and apologized. "Forgive me, Kit. I didn't mean to be so ill mannered just now. Please, say you forgive me."

Wide-eyed and wondering, Kit looked up at him. "I . . . suppose I forgive you, Ramon, but would you please tell me why we made that wild exit?"

He sighed, and a weak smile came to his dark face. *"Madre de Dios,* you are the only one I could possibly say this to, but confidentially, Kit, I didn't want to be waylaid by Estellita Valero. I know I am being very ungentlemanly, but the woman . . . she makes me . . . well, I don't care for her."

Kit could not restrain her delighted laughter, and she raised up on tiptoe to plant a sisterly kiss on Ramon's face.

"Ramon, you are a very smart man, and I share your feelings about Estellita Valero. I don't like her either! You are most assuredly a gentleman! She is just no lady!"

On the other side of the white flowering oleander shrub, a pair of jet-black eyes pierced the couple on the other side. The thick branches and the green leathery leaves prevented his eyes from seeing clearly, but there was no denying that he saw Kit eagerly kiss Ramon Valdez. She was certainly not being urged to do so by Ramon, nor was she fighting him off. No, this girl was bold and aggressive. Her heart could not belong to him alone obviously!

Angrily, he dug his booted heels into the ground.

Why should he deny himself a pair of waiting arms then? Kit obviously wasn't denying herself!

He turned his eyes back toward the courtyard and the sight of that bright red gown. He knew the pleasures that awaited him with the lascivious lady wearing that gown. To hell with a lifetime of love, all he sought right now was a moment of lust!

Chapter 22

Estellita Valero didn't try to analyze Danton's mercurial behavior. She only wanted to enjoy him while he was with her, dancing to the stimulating beat of the music. The piece being played happened to be one of her favorite songs. Its rhythm aroused the senses when a man and woman merged.

Estellita did not waste the advantage given to her as Danton guided her around the floor. She'd always considered him a magnificent dancer, but tonight he seemed to be trying to exploit the two of them. She knew they were being observed from the sidelines and that the other couples on the floor ogled them as they moved aside.

Whatever it was eating away at the moody Danton, she loved it. He'd approached her with a forceful, menacing look on his face, but as he'd come up to her to ask her to dance with him his striking Castilian features had softened some. However, a wicked gleam had remained in those dark eyes of his.

She figured that he and his little kitten might have had a falling out, but whatever she did not really care. Perhaps, he was infatuated with the little auburn-haired miss staying with the *señora*. It could be that her

204

naïveté and youth whetted his male appetite. But right now, Estellita's body was sending him a message and he didn't have to say a word in reply for Estellita knew that his magnificent manhood was answering her.

A lusty, knowing smile slowly etched his face as she looked up at him, giving him the full benefit of her long-lashed dark eyes.

When Ramon and Kit came out of their little secluded spot, he eagerly reunited himself with Delores, and Kit quickly realized her presence was no longer needed. Besides, it seemed like hours since she'd been whisked away from Danton to dance with Arthur Cameron. She scanned the sea of people noting that the night's gaiety was in full thrust. Everyone appeared to be more jovial and light-hearted after Lucía's delectable feast and fine wines and champagne had been enjoyed.

Now, the evening's reveling would go on as long as the musicians kept playing. The merrymaking was more lively and spirited.

Kit noticed instantly that more people were dancing now. Suddenly, she watched as couples moved to the sides of the square platform, leaving in the center of the floor the sensuously swaying Estellita. As people continued to move back, her partner was revealed—a handsome, tall man in a cream-colored shirt and tight-fitting trousers. The red silk scarf around his neck seemed to match the scarlet of Estellita's gown. They looked like professional dancers, so well did they move. Kit stood there like one in a trance. Every fiber in her body rejected the scene, but she could not turn away.

Admiration and envy consumed her. The look on Danton's face, as his black eyes gazed so lustily on Estellita, sickened Kit, but she could not make herself leave.

A deep chuckle echoed behind her, "Damn, they are superb! But then practice does make perfection."

She whirled around to see Damien standing close behind her. In the shadows, he could have been Danton except for the different color of his attire. He wore a vest over his fine linen shirt. But his tailored black pants clung to his muscled body enhancing his fine physique.

He moved to stand by her side. Like Danton, he had to bend low to whisper in her ear, "You are a breathtaking creature, tonight. Do you know what? You've not danced with me so I claim the next one."

"No, Damien. I . . . I don't think so right now."

"Hey, you mean you don't want to follow their little exhibition? Listen, *chiquita,* you just let me lead you and we'll put them to shame. The way you looked the other night when you sang those airs in the parlor was more exciting than all the wiggling old Estellita's doing out there. Trust me, Kit. I'm a damned good dancer." He laughed and gave her a wink.

He was so arrogant and assured as he took Kit's hand and led her to the floor that she found herself believing him. Her reluctance faded as Damien approached the musicians and made his request known to them. He gave Kit another broad grin, and by that time she was feeling amazingly cocky and self-assured too. They stepped onto the dance floor.

Molly Langford or Carmella Morilla would have confirmed Damien's boast that he was an excellent dancer; now they both sat at their tables, envying Kit. Both knew what Kit couldn't, that whether she was a good dancer or not Damien would make her look as graceful and agile as a gazelle. He had that knack.

Lucía suspected that her handsome son was going to perform flamboyantly. She had witnessed these little contests before between her twins. It puzzled her completely, however, that Danton was leading Estellita toward one of the little flagstone paths and that he appeared to have no interest in observing his brother and Kit. Lucía could have sworn that Danton had been enamored of the ravishing little redhead earlier. Oh, how she wished that despicable Estellita had not come to the fiesta!

Danton had seen his twin brother and Kit approach the musicians, and he knew Damien was requesting the special song he wished them to play. Danton knew exactly what the melody would be. He knew also that by the time the dance was finished every man in the courtyard garden would desire the lovely Kit. He had no intention of putting himself through the torment of watching her. Nor did he trust the volcano smoldering within him, for he had a most urgent desire to yank Kit out of his brother's arms and to turn her over his lap and paddle her, and then to sock Damien's smiling face.

Lucía gave way to the churning impulse gnawing at her. She had never been a conniving mother and it was a little late to change her ways, but her instincts told her that where Estellita Valero was concerned she must fight fire with fire. She felt that she could read the widow's thoughts as she watched Estellita maneuver Danton in the direction of the courtyard's back gate. She knew they would then go in the direction of the Navarro stables.

She left the Morillas and walked hastily toward Danton, calling to him, "Dear, could I get you to run and get my lace shawl for me. Antonia and Roberto are preparing to leave." Lucía had such a lovely smile on her face no one could have imagined the anger brewing in her. "Estellita, dear, Antonia wants so to meet you. Come, let me take you over there while Danton goes for my shawl. She said you two had a brief meeting at

207

Arthur's ranch some time ago." Lucía's hand went to Estellita's arm, and she could almost feel the firm tenseness there. It had taken great self-control for Estellita to contain her temper. She silently cursed Señora Navarro.

As Lucía marched Estellita away and Danton went to do his mother's bidding, the *señora* had no qualms about aborting that little peccadillo. In fact, she was amused and pleased with herself.

By the time Lucía and Estellita joined Antonia and Robert on the veranda, the dance was over but exuberant applause was resounding throughout the garden.

"You missed it, Lucía. They were absolutely magnificent! I tell you they were fantastic!" Antonia raved on and on.

"Oh, I would have loved seeing them," Lucía lamented.

A laughing Kit clung to Damien's arm as the pair left the floor amidst a shower of compliments. Kit was elated for she, too, knew they'd looked fantastic.

She stretched up to whisper in Damien's ear, "You're wonderful, Damien! I can't believe it—really! You made me look good. I'm not a great dancer and I know it."

"See, *chiquita*. I told you so. Maybe you'll believe me next time, eh?" He could not help thinking it was a damned shame that fate had dealt him such a harsh blow. To have to waste so much woman as there was in this little lady was truly distasteful to him. She had looked so ravishing when they'd danced!

He suggested they enjoy a glass of champagne after their strenuous dance and Kit instantly accepted. Both of them noticed that the Morilla family was leaving and that their departure seemed to prompt the other guests to make an end of the evening. Slowly, the garden was emptied of guests.

Quiet descended over the garden then, except for the muted sounds of the servants cleaning up after the festivities. One by one the bedrooms went dark and the occupants retired, exhausted, to their beds. Finally Damien bid Kit good night at the bottom of the stairs.

Kit lay in her dark room, wide-eyed and very much awake. Could she have been so wrong? Had she misjudged Damien? He had made her feel so good tonight and she certainly had needed her spirits bolstered!

Maybe, it was childish of her, but she hoped Danton had seen her dance. However, he'd been so entranced by the widow he might not have noticed. She tried to convince herself that she didn't care.

What had happened during the evening didn't matter for she had ended it in a blaze of glory, Kit thought as she lay there looking out the windows of her room. Once she and Damien had begun to dance, she'd felt utterly at ease. The nerves and apprehension that had plagued her beforehand were quickly swept away.

She wondered if maybe she had performed for an audience in her early life. After all, Damien had raved about what a beautiful voice she had, and he hadn't been the only one. The next day Delores and Ramon had mentioned it.

It was ironic how things had turned out, that it was Damien who'd given her a good-night kiss when he'd left her at the base of the stairway a short time ago. She would have sworn it would have been Danton.

Earlier, when the happy-go-lucky Damien had jestingly stated that they were so good they could go on the theater circuit, she'd surprised him by confessing a momentary flash of her past.

"I see a huge room, Damien. I swear it is so clear. A massive crystal chandelier is suspended from the very center of a very high ceiling, and there are plush bright carpets you sink into when you walk."

"And where was this place, *chiquita?*" he prodded.

"Dear God, I wish I knew," she dejectedly moaned. "If I knew then I'd know who I am!"

"Is . . . is there any more to the vision you can see?"

"Yes, there is laughter and gaiety as there was here tonight. Beautiful ladies in fancy gowns and fine gentlemen. There is music and dancing in one part of the room. Another room, as large, has many people in it, and there are tables covered in green."

"Tables with green tablecloths?" Damien cunningly baited her.

"No . . . not that. I . . . I'm not sure. No, Damien. I'm certain it's not a tablecloth of green." She was disturbed by her own confusion at that point, and Damien soothed her tenderly, urging her not to plague herself about it.

Damien feared if she kept talking and talking the fogs and mists in her head might suddenly lift and he could not encourage that. So he had taken his leave, gently admonishing her, "Sleep, *chiquita*—that is what you now need. So do I."

But sleep was not in the cards for Damien after he left Kit. He had some thinking to do and he went back down the steps to the library just as his father, Victor, used to do when he had some serious thinking to do. Like Victor, Damien desired some of that fine old Napoleon Brandy.

Soon . . . soon he must carry out the deed facing him. Once he'd removed the threat of Kristina Whelan from his life he would finally be free. Weeks ago, he'd come to the indisputable conclusion that Florine Whelan had not gazed upon his unmasked face that night or the law would have come after him. In any case, Damien had decided that it would be Danton who was left vulnerable, for he had established a firm alibi with old Mack. The man would swear that Damien was at the cabin with him doing some hunting.

Like everything else involved in his scheme to revenge himself against Florine Whelan, nothing had fallen into the proper place. The only satisfaction Damien had gotten out of the robbery was the return of the money he'd lost at Florine's gaming tables. The rest of the cash had gone to his cohorts. Now it seemed that his plan for his twin brother to be accused of the crime was not to be realized.

Once again Danton's halo fit snugly atop his head. Damien's envy and resentment of his brother had been fanned higher this evening when the chattering Estellita had revealed the plans already in the making of influencal local ranchers like Arthur Cameron and prosperous businessmen in Austin. They were going to propose that Danton throw his hat into the race for senator.

A new rage was igniting in Damien!

Chapter 23

The two brothers missed encountering each other in the library by a couple of seconds. Danton had taken a generous serving of the fine brandy and had selected one of his favorite cheroots from the walnut chest. Then, intending to take a stroll before retiring, he'd ambled on out through the side doors into the garden moments before Damien opened the oak-carved door to enter the room from the deserted hallway.

As it had always been with Danton and Damien, their tastes were similar up to a point, but from that point on they strayed far afield. After that point, an ocean might have divided them.

Danton didn't really know what he was doing down in the garden roaming aimlessly about when he should have been getting some sleep. He chided himself. Then he firmly decided he was leaving the first thing in the morning. There was no question about it. He had to get away from Silvercreek and that slip of a girl, Kit Winters. Kit Winters—hell! That wasn't even her name. That was just his little creation. He was beginning to wonder if she was entirely a figment of his imagination. He'd seen a different girl at Silvercreek this time, not the one he'd discovered on the mountain trail or at the magical spot down by the creek or under that special old oak back in Austin. This new lovely lady had tormented him. She had teased and taunted him unmercifully. Damned if he liked it!

He must clear his head so he could think intelligently about Arthur's flattering offer and map his future plans. He could only do that back in Austin, away from the beguiling distraction of Kit.

There was more to Arthur's proposal, he'd concluded, than the race and his established popularity around Austin and the state. He would not sell his soul or submit to the grasping claws of Estellita Valero. No one had to tell him that Estellita need say only a few little words to certain parties in Austin and she would make or ruin a politician.

She was a wicked, vindictive bitch when she wished to be, and her influence could not be denied. Danton found it hard to understand her worshiping horde of friends, which stretched from Austin to San Antonio. Perhaps they were still paying undying homage to her late husband, Manuel Orlando Valero.

Danton prided himself on having too much intelligence to permit himself to be her slave. He didn't want any yoke hanging around his neck, not where the promiscuous widow was concerned. Danton had decided that before he took this campaign too seriously he'd better put his cards on the table before Cameron. While Danton had always respected the older rancher, he was certain the man had knowledge of Estellita's lascivious nature. Hell, how could he not?

Estellita Valero was so bold she made the dance hall girls look like shy violets. The only thing he could surmise was that her vast, inherited wealth had bought her a ticket to respectability. How hypocritical!

Finally, deciding that he had no answer to his various dilemmas, and the dawning of a new day was already coming, Danton went inside.

The next morning, after only five hours of sleep, he managed a swift departure from Silvercreek. His hastily concocted story seemed to satisfy his mother even though she was a little stunned by his announcement. She realized that Danton was a sought-after young lawyer, so she didn't question him. But she was disappointed by his leaving so early.

Danton felt great relief at being able to ride down the long driveway and out to the main road without having to say his goodbyes to the various house guests at Silvercreek. He was especially glad he didn't have to face the girl whose ravishing loveliness would haunt him all the way back to Austin. Once the buggy was a mile away from the ranch, rolling down the dirt road that would take him to the Cameron ranch, Danton relaxed and leaned back in the seat.

Once again, he was gambling on luck being on his side. When he arrived at Cameron's ranch he hoped he would not encounter another female, who he had no wish to face. Arthur was an early riser, Danton knew, so he'd make his stand on the issues known and take his leave.

When his buggy turned in through the gate to the Cameron property and he saw that Arthur was having his early morning stroll and puffing on his pipe, he was pleased.

"Danton, my boy, this is a surprise! Thought I was the only one who got up with the chickens. That was a shindig to remember over at your place last night. Hey, son, you're too early to see Estellita, I'm afraid."

Danton leaped down out of the buggy. "It's you I wish to see, Arthur, before I get on to Austin. Truth is, I'd just as soon we go to the barn or over by the corrals so she won't see me. I'm in a bit of a hurry . . . if you don't mind."

His direct, straightforward manner was not questioned by Arthur Cameron. "Sure, son. We can go inside the barn if you want." Danton secured the buggy and followed Arthur.

"Tell you something, young man. You're going to rile that lady sleeping upstairs when she finds out you're on your way back to Austin without her. If you didn't know it, she was planning on traveling back with you."

In a curt tone that made old Arthur raise his skeptical brow, Danton bluntly remarked, "Then the lady upstairs presumed too much. I didn't invite her to accompany me back, nor did I inform her of my plans."

Arthur chuckled uneasily. "Well, you know how women are at times."

"Arthur, I thought I'd tell you that I'll stop by and try to talk some sense into old Jim Longley. I'll try to pound some sense into his head in the hope of stopping this senseless bloodshed. At the same time he could save himself the trouble of restringing that barbed wire along that one-mile strip of his land."

"Hell, he's got over a thousand acres and enough of that damned Pedernales River to share just a hair of it with his neighbors. Besides, the railroad track is going through there whether he likes it or not."

"I think I can make him see that."

"If you can't, no one can for he thinks highly of you, just like he did your dad."

"Well, we'll see, Arthur. There is another matter I need to talk to you about since I'm not too sure when I'll be returning to Silvercreek. I consider it an honor that you and the others want me to run, and I would promise to do my very best to win. However . . . This doesn't apply to you, Arthur, for I've known you all my life, but I can't say the same for some of the others. To make it sweet and simple, I guess what I'm telling you is that I'd be no one's pawn—no man's and no woman's!"

"That's a hell of a mouthful, son!" Cameron scratched his head with a lazy gesture as though he were thoughtfully absorbing Danton's declaration. He knew exactly where Victor Navarro's son was coming from and what he was saying. Damned if he didn't admire the young man. But politics was a whale of a game, and Cameron had played it long enough to know the rules.

"It had to be said before I go any farther. Weigh it for the next few weeks, Arthur, and so will I. My professional life is very important to me, but my personal life is far more important."

Arthur Cameron gave Danton's words his full attention. He'd watched this young man grow from a small boy to a stripling youth who reached the same height of his father. He recalled the day when Danton and Damien had reached their eighteenth birthday, how he'd envied old Victor who had not one but two fine sons.

But the last six or seven years, Cameron's opinion of Damien had changed. Danton, on the other hand, had earned more and more of his respect. Feeling so strongly about him and knowing what his youthful energy and level-headed wisdom could do for the state, Cameron was certain Danton could go far. Yet now he was reluctant to say what he felt he must, to warn the young Navarro.

As Danton rose to depart, Cameron felt the overwhelming impulse to give a warning when he told Navarro goodbye. "Danton, I'll respect your decision, whatever it is. You know that already. But I've got to remind you there's a hell of a lot of power upstairs there." He nodded toward his house.

Danton broke into that familiar crooked grin of his, knowing Cameron referred to Estellita. Then he let out a husky chuckle as he started to walk back toward his buggy, "Yeah, and there's a hell of a lot of problems, too, Arthur. Problems I don't intend to take on!"

He gave his old friend a final wave of his hand and leaped onto the seat of the buggy, prepared to urge the bay into action.

Cameron watched the buggy roll down the road and through his gate. When it was out of sight he turned away from the road to enjoy the quiet of the countryside on this summer morn. He expected a turbulent storm when Estellita awoke and found out Danton Navarro would not be her companion on the trip back to Austin. She would certainly not be pleased.

Suddenly, a random thought hit Cameron like a bolt of lightning. Thinking about Danton and the night before, Cameron remembered Lucía's little auburn-haired guest. He recalled how he'd taken her away from Danton for a dance and what a cute little filly she was. Damned, he'd bet his best mare that young Navarro had his eyes on that one! Yes, sir! That was it!

The morning quiet echoed with Arthur's laughter, deep and loud as a lion's roar. What a beating that would be for the conceited Estellita's pride, Cameron thought to himself.

Delores' soft lilting laughter rang out as she strolled with Ramon in the garden courtyard that same morning. They'd spent the breakfast hour together, and it had been Ramon's suggestion that they take a stroll. He'd jovially confessed he'd eaten too many of Drusilla's flaky biscuits. The truth was he'd eaten very little for his heart was heavy at the thought of leaving Silvercreek, and Delores, in a few short hours. Since last night, however, he felt that he had a chance with the beautiful *señorita*.

Delores had already held hands with one or two young suitors, but she found Ramon different. Perhaps, that was due to his serious personality and the

217

fact that he was a few years older. She knew that he made her feel grown-up, however, and so she sought to act like a young lady as Damien was always attempting to chide her into doing. She liked the feeling she got when he held her hand as though he never wanted to turn loose of it. And she liked the way his dark eyes seemed to worship her when he gazed so longingly at her.

Last night, she'd seen an almost boyish shyness about him. At one moment when they'd stood in the secluded corner of the garden shrouded in darkness, she knew he was about to kiss her. But some approaching footsteps made him abruptly draw away. She sensed his nervousness, but she'd appreciated the shyness in him. She felt at ease with him and that pleased Delores.

His cousin, Fernando had certainly attracted her, but now that she'd been with Ramon and gotten to know more about him, she knew a courtship with Fernando would not have endured long.

Delores' heart fairly leaped with joy when Ramon voiced her sentiments exactly, "I shall be very sad to leave you tonight, Delores. This . . . this has been the most wonderful time of my life."

She never questioned his sincerity for the look on his finely chiseled face could not have been that of a liar. She, too, was sad when she thought about him leaving when they'd had such a brief period together. "I . . . I will miss you, Ramon. I think I shall miss you terribly," she candidly confessed.

Ramon knew she meant it, and that knowledge gave him the mettle to be bolder than usual. He pulled her close to him and his free hand held her waist. Then he let out a bittersweet sigh. "Oh, Delores . . . can I . . . dare I hope—"

"Oh, yes, Ramon!" She gave him the loveliest,

pleased smile.

"Oh, Delores, I don't take love lightly. I . . . well, I've never been in love before, but I feel so much love in my heart for you I don't know how to express it."

Delores stood close to him, her heart pounding wildly. His declaration of love filled her with such deep emotion it urged her to boldly suggest, "Express it, Ramon, by kissing me. If you don't, I think I'll just die!"

He needed no more urging and eagerly did her bidding. His lips took hers, letting the sweet rapture of their kiss linger and linger. He wanted to savor this tender moment until he could hold her in his arms again.

When Ramon finally released her, Delores was almost overcome with the wonder of it all. She made a soft sound, "Ramon! Oh, Ramon, I've never been kissed like that before."

He smiled, exalted and pleased. He could have owned the whole world in that magical moment. "I'm glad, Delores! I plan to claim all your kisses from this day forward. May I?"

"My kisses shall belong to only you, Ramon. I vow it!"

When Delores finally came out of her romantic daze, long after Ramon had left Silvercreek, she sought out Kit. She had to talk to someone about the exciting thing that had happened to her on this wonderful summer day, and it was Kit with whom she wanted to share her secret.

Was it possible for someone to explode from sheer happiness? Delores felt she could have! She wanted to proclaim to everyone that she was in love. For the very first time in her life, she was in love. But right now, she decided to say nothing to anyone, but Kit!

Chapter 24

Santiago was not a man who tried to fool himself about his age, and this summer he'd noticed that the hot Texas sun demanded he start his siesta earlier than in previous years. But he would not admit that the heat had affected his brain so he was not thinking clearly. For the last couple of weeks he had been aware that young Damien was keeping an eagle eye on the little Señorita Kit.

He'd admit to being a suspicious man, but he always tempered that suspicion with a share of common sense. Yet he felt so strongly about this gut feeling gnawing at him since yesterday that he was tempted to give Señorita Kit a warning the next time he had the chance.

Since the day Kit had arrived at Silvercreek, she'd been warm and friendly to the Mexican foreman. He'd been the first person she had met when she'd arrived with Danton and they had exchanged a friendly smile when Danton had introduced them. Afterward, when they had chanced to meet on the ranch conversation came easily. Santiago's feelings for the girl had grown stronger and deeper during her months at Silvercreek. There was something about the girl's down-to-earth way that made him even more loyal and devoted to her than to little Delores. While that didn't seem logical, Santiago knew it was a fact.

He knew, too, that if Señor Danton did not pick her to be his bride one day the young man was a fool. Why, all Santiago had to do was look into her green eyes when the two of them were together to know how she felt about Danton.

The thoughtful gesture she had made yesterday would be forever remembered by Santiago. Kit had obviously noticed that while the heat of the midafternoon had been searing the countryside Santiago sat under the old oak, fanning himself with his sombrero. Since she sat on the long veranda enjoying some lemonade Drusilla had served her, she poured a glass of the delicious beverage to take to Santiago.

She smiled and handed him the cool drink. "You look like you could use this, Santiago."

Grateful for the liquid refreshment and appreciative of her concern, Santiago sighed. *"Ah, gracias, señorita. Gracias!"* He took his wrinkled kerchief from his neck and wiped his damp brow. He had been surprised by her next move. Unceremoniously, she had sat down on the grassy knoll beside him. Such spontaneous gestures endeared Kit to Santiago. He could not have imagined Señorita Delores sitting down with him like that.

"You should be more careful, Santiago. The day is so warm," she admonished him gently.

"It is and I tend to forget that I'm not a young man anymore," he smiled over at her. She sat quietly, her arms encircling her propped up knees. She wore a long flowing floral skirt and a soft cotton blouse with a drawstring neckline. As her long, thick hair fell around her shoulders, she swept it back from her face with her finger.

She had a faraway look on her lovely face as she

221

scanned the countryside. When she spoke there seemed to be a melancholy tone to her soft voice. "This is a lovely place. When I think of Silvercreek I'll always think of you, Santiago."

A frown creased Santiago's swarthy face. "Why, *señorita* . . . you . . . you sound like you are leaving Silvercreek?"

"It is inevitable, Santiago. There will come a day when I will." She laughed softly. "Oh, you will have to put up with me for a while yet."

As they sat there, lingering over their easygoing chatter, she asked him a multitude of questions about the Navarros and about his own life here at Silvercreek. Santiago loved to talk about those subjects. He spoke in such glowing terms of Victor Navarro that Kit could picture the man quite vividly. As they shared the lazy summer afternoon, Santiago's eyes chanced to gaze in the direction of the barn door. A tall figure stood beside it—Damien. For some reason he couldn't put his finger on right then, he pretended to not notice. He got the impression that Damien had been watching them for some time, and he wondered why a Navarro would find it so interesting to linger there and spy on an old Mexican like himself and on Kit.

Out of the corner of his eye Santiago kept checking to see if Damien was still observing them, but he gave Kit no inkling of what he was about. It seemed very strange to him that Damien should be so curious.

But when Kit finally rose from the ground and told him goodbye, Santiago was in more of a quandary than before. When he looked over toward the barn, the towering figure had disappeared. It made no sense. This is why it worried him and he couldn't dismiss it. He was reminded of that old tomcat in the barn that sat for hours awaiting the right moment to pounce on an unsuspecting little mouse.

Santiago didn't want that little mouse to be Kit. But what could he say to warn her? Could he possibly tell her to watch Damien for he was the devil's own? The old Mexican was bothered every time his thoughts drifted back to the incident.

For the next few days Santiago kept a sharp eye on Kit, and on Damien Navarro's comings and goings.

When the countryside was drenched by rain which lasted throughout the day and night, Santiago welcomed its arrival. It meant more to him than relief from the heat. All that day Kit remained inside, and Santiago realized just how much extra trotting around he'd been doing to protect her. He was worn out!

Kit had no inkling of the commotion she was causing for old Santiago, but she would have been terribly grateful had she known that he actually cared so much about her.

After the busy days of preparation and the excitement of the fiesta, the calm that followed it had lulled Silvercreek into a lazy pace. Señora Lucía Navarro now had much time for idle thought.

Since she had no knowledge of the numerous strange flashes of memory Kit had experienced, she felt there must be something someone could do for the girl.

A pretty young lady did not just disappear from the face of the earth without someone missing her. It just didn't make sense to the *señora*. Since Danton had obviously been unsuccessful in obtaining any information about Kit, Lucía decided she was going to play the physician.

Her opportunity came when they were left alone for dinner one rainy evening. Delores had taken to her bed with the sniffles and Damien was absent from the dinner table. Lucía thought nothing about Damien missing dinner. She'd learned a long time ago that there was no point in dwelling on his absences.

223

Since the night of the fiesta Lucía had been unable to shake her thoughts about her own past and her remembrances of a young woman by the name of Florine Whelan. Oh, she knew her suspicion was remote, but stranger things had happened. So maybe she was a more imaginative person than she'd considered herself to be, but when an idea stuck with her as this one had she couldn't just shrug it aside.

After they had dined, Lucía urged, "Come, Kit, keep me company. It's a good night for a card game with all this rain coming down. What do you say, dear?"

"I'd love to, Señora Lucía," Kit said. The day had been a long one. They were confined inside, and Delores had been feeling so miserable because of her cold that she'd been in no mood to talk.

Kit could not seek out Santiago with the rain so heavy, and Damien had been out of sight all day. So she had read an entire book, which was unusual for her. Perhaps, such quietness after all the festivities had put a tinge of gloom on the house, Kit had decided.

Furthermore, she was feeling hurt because Danton had not told her goodbye when he'd left. The way he'd behaved at the end of the fiesta had made it perfectly clear that he cared nothing about her.

But then, she had reasoned, how could he have acted so amorous when they'd dined earlier, and when he'd taken her into his arms to dance there why had he had the look of love on his handsome face. But all that had changed once she'd left his arms to dance with Arthur Cameron. Kit was perplexed. What had changed the loving, adoring man she'd left to the sour-faced, smirking one she'd next seen. But for Damien's rescue, the evening would have left a bitter taste in her mouth.

When Delores had informed her the morning after the fiesta that Danton had departed from Silvercreek bright and early, Kit's lingering hopes had been quashed.

Without the distracting torment Danton stirred in her, Kit was able to think about herself and about the state she'd lingered in for months. She'd come to the conclusion that she obviously was a nobody, for no one had sought to find her. Surely, by this time, there would have been some inquiries.

She now settled herself at the square teakwood table across from Lucía. The older woman noted her intense concentration immediately. "You seem far away this evening, Kit dear?"

"Oh, I guess I am, *señora*. Kit was depressed by the state of limbo she'd endured so long now. "I'd hoped my memory would have returned."

"I'm glad we are alone tonight, Kit, for I'm beginning to feel just like you. I was certain that we could have done more for you by now."

"Oh, I didn't mean to infer that you'd not been doing enough for me. I could not ask for more consideration and kindness than you and your family have shown me, Señora Navarro."

Señora Navarro rose up from her chair and moved toward the liquor chest to pour herself a glass of sherry. She invited Kit to join her. "You know, Kit, I've thought about you a great deal lately, and I don't feel you are from this part of Texas. In fact, I feel you lived far away. A pretty girl like you would have been sought. If your family lived in this area, there would have been inquiries. Doesn't that make sense?"

"Yes, it would seem so," Kit slowly drawled. She wondered what was on the *señora*'s mind for she sensed that Lucía Navarro was weighing something.

"Does the city of San Antonio ring any kind of bell with you?"

"The city where Ramon lives?"

"Yes, dear."

"No, ma'am."

"I see." Lucía set her glass down and offered the

225

other glass to Kit. Slowly lowering herself into the chair, she picked up the deck of cards and gave them a quick shuffle. "Kit, I have a confession to make to you. You remind me of a lady I used to know. The likeness is almost eerie. Perhaps it is a crazy idea, but what do we have to lose, eh?"

"Not a thing that I can see. Who was the lady?"

"Does Florine Whelan mean anything to you?"

Kit pronounced the name slowly not once but twice before Lucía noted the fascination gleaming in Kit's eyes as Señora Navarro's hands performed her witchery with the cards.

"No, Señora Lucía. I know no such person that I can recall."

Lucía shrugged her response aside and remarked, "Well, it was just a remote possibility, dear. You do remind me of her, but that was a long, long time ago. However, Florine could have a daughter your age. Shall we play some cards?"

Kit smiled and nodded her head. But the name Lucía Navarro had shot at her remained, echoing over and over again.

Later, after she'd retired for the night her dreams were haunted by a lady named Florine Whelan with hair like flames and eyes like emeralds.

Once, she woke suddenly and sat up in bed, trying to sort out the reality from the dream. The lady's lovely smiling face was as clear and real to her, as Danton's was. How could it possibly be so real? she asked herself as she sat there in the dark, if she didn't know her quite well.

Dear God, how long must she travel down this long, endless road of not knowing who she was?

226

Chapter 25

When Damien had returned home after the dinner hour was observed at Silvercreek, he'd made his way from the barn to the quiet house, entering through the kitchen door. By that time there was no one in the kitchen. Drusilla had finished her evening chores long ago and had departed for her quarters.

At first, Damien had thought his mother, sister, and Kit were already upstairs, but he soon heard female voices coming from the back parlor and he moved on down the darkened hallway toward the open doorway.

He chanced to hear his mother speaking of a lady whose very name pricked him sorely—Florine Whelan. He lurked by the door to listen.

As his mother spoke of Florine Whelan, he recalled the episode at the Crystal Castle in El Paso and it was a thorn in his side. What torment and havoc it had caused him!

What he'd thought a perfect way to get revenge on the high and mighty Florine Whelan had ended up by haunting and disrupting his whole life. All three of the women—Florine Whelan, Kit, and his own mother, Lucía—God, he detested them all!

Although he credited Señora Lucía Navarro with being the most clever woman he'd ever known, that didn't diminish the hatred he'd harbored for her during the last few years. When he heard her express the feeling that Kit came from another part of Texas, he smiled to himself. Pretty smart of you, Mother dear, he thought to himself. But when she mentioned the city of San Antonio, Damien bristled sharply. San Antonio, he recalled bitterly, was where his father had met and married her. It was also the city where Damien had, quite by accident, learned about the life his mother had led before she'd married Victor Navarro. That had happened over six years ago. When he'd returned to Silvercreek, the stately dignified lady had never looked so grand after that. For Damien, she had fallen off the pedestal he'd placed her on. Why, she was no better than the dance-hall girls in Pecos, his mother.

From that day, Damien defied her, refusing to allow her to instill in him any of her righteousness or her upstanding ideals. Hell, that was a laugh! But it perplexed him that his esteemed father had taken her as his bride. Damien swore no woman would ever bewitch him. He'd use them all for what he wanted, he decided, for he had come to think all women were whores.

From then on, he had taken sadistic delight in meting out his own brand of punishment to the lot of them. Of course, one of his victims had been Florine Whelan so when he heard his mother mention her name he froze in a state of shock. While he'd known something of Lucía's past in San Antonio, he had not known about her connection with Florine Whelan.

Damien slipped back down the hallway after hearing that part of the conversation. He needed to know no more of what his mother or Kit said. By now, his numb body had awakened to pound with mounting rage. He made straight for his room and the bottle of whiskey he kept there.

When Kit's long lashes fluttered open under the invading rays of the bright morning sun, she lay quite still for a moment, making no effort to move. The dawn and the promise of a sunshiny day had lifted her spirits now that the dismal darkness of night had faded. Along with the night, she dismissed her tormenting dreams as she moved to the edge of the bed.

Anticipating that she might go for a ride after breakfast, she dressed in the pretty black riding ensemble Lucía had purchased for her. There would be no need to wear the vest, she decided. The soft batiste blouse was all she needed on this warm day. She quickly brushed out her hair, deciding to wind her thick tresses into a double coil like the *señora* wore. That would also be more comfortable than letting them hug her neck or fall over her shoulders and face.

Before she left the room, she grabbed the black flat-crowned hat. As she rushed into the hall, she was tempted to peek in on Delores to say good morning, but she thought better of it. Delores might be sleeping.

In the dining room, she found the *señora* breakfasting alone. Lucía looked up and greeted Kit. "Well, my dear, it seems we are the only ones in the house this morning too. Delores still has a fever and Damien gulped down a fast cup of coffee to rush away, God knows where."

"Well, I'm glad I didn't disturb her when I came down just now."

Kit had barely taken her seat before Drusilla came through the door with a cup of black, steaming coffee which she placed before her. "Your usual, *señorita?*"

"Yes, Drusilla. That will be just fine."

Kit was eager for the taste of the coffee. Its steaming aroma teased her nostrils. Something she couldn't put her finger on was prodding her this morning. She was anxious to get out of the house, to enjoy the glorious day after the constant rain of yesterday and last evening. She only wished she and Delores could have shared the ride she was planning to take. But since neither Delores nor Damien were here, she had no intention of lingering in the confines of the house. The beautiful courtyard, breaktakingly serene as it was, could not satisfy her need to wander over the open countryside.

Lucía sensed the high spirits of the girl sharing the morning repast with her. At least, little Kit seemed light of heart today. She wished she, too, felt that way. It was not Lucía's nature to be depressed, and she could not pinpoint the cause. Her mood on awakening was in drastic contrast to Kit's.

She felt tired and weary. This was the morning she'd promised Antonia Morilla that she'd pay her a visit, but she did not feel like doing so. She wished Danton were home. She felt a need to speak with him.

Something most puzzling had happened last night. She'd pondered it long after Kit had retired and she'd retired to her own rooms. She knew Damien had lingered in the dark hallway to eavesdrop on her conversation with Kit, but what he'd done made no sense to her. He had obviously forgotten about the mirror in which from where she'd been sitting she had noticed his towering figure.

But why would Damien not announce himself? Why would he unobtrusively listen to them? Why would her conversation with Kit hold such interest for him? She did not understand any of it, nor did she understand his nervous manner this morning. But she was thankful that the bright, smiling Kit was sitting with her now. Maybe some of Kit's cheerfulness would rub off on her.

When Kit declared her intention to go for a ride, Lucía confessed her own lack of energy, "Maybe my night of fiesta is just catching up with me. I was supposed to go over to Antonia's and take one of Delores's dresses. The Morillas' seamstress is going to copy it for Carmella, but I just don't feel up to it. Isn't that terrible?"

Kit giggled softly. "Not at all. That was my mood yesterday."

"But yesterday was the type of day to make one feel lazy. Today should inspire one to go out and enjoy it."

"You are not feeling ill, are you? I hope you aren't going to catch Delores' cold." Kit hoped not. She knew the vivacious *señora* had not taken to her bed one day since she'd been at Silvercreek.

"No, my dear. Just a little lazy." Lucía quickly sought to ease Kit's mind, although it was nice to see her genuine concern.

"Well, I could run your errand for you, take the dress to the Morillas if you like. It's a nice ride from here to their ranch," Kit volunteered eagerly.

"Well, of course. Yes, Kit. That would be just fine. It is the yellow one with the white lace trim. You'll find it in Delores' armoire."

"All right, and I'll give you a report on Delores when I come back down too," Kit told Lucía as she rose from the table.

With spritely movements, she mounted the stairs, slowing her pace only when she reached the door of Delores' bedroom. She turned the knob cautiously so she would not disturb Delores in case she was sleeping.

"Well, I was wondering if you'd forsaken me," Delores' soft voice chided her, and the teasing glint in her dark eyes told Kit she was feeling better.

Kit laughed. "I see you're getting back to your old self. I'm glad! The truth is I wish you were up to going riding with me this morning. Have you looked out your window?"

Dejectedly, Delores grumbled, "Yes! Wait until tomorrow though."

Kit sat down on the side of Delores' bed and after scrutinizing her friend, she remarked, "Well, you still look a little pale, but a day in the sun will take care of that." She remarked that she was going to the Morillas' ranch to take the gown Lucía had promised to bring over for Antonia.

"So Carmella is going to copycat my yellow gown, eh?"

"I guess so."

"She is lucky I'll let her have it after the outrageous way she was flirting with Ramon the other night."

Kit could not help laughing at her little friend. "So you are the jealous type? I must remember that!"

"Oh, Kit—never of you. I'd never worry about you being around Ramon." Delores patted Kit's knee. Then with a confidential air, she asked, "Don't you think he's good-looking, Kit? Honestly?"

"Oh, incredibly!" Kit declared, knowing that was what Delores wanted to hear, but she added quite sincerely, "Ramon is such a nice young gentleman too, and I know how much he adores you."

Delores' delicate-featured face glowed. "Oh, Kit, I'm so in love with him. It's . . . it's so nice to have you here to talk to. That's why I couldn't wait to rush upstairs the other day and tell you about Ramon and me."

Kit rewarded her with a pleased smile, but Delores' talk about Ramon brought her bittersweet thoughts of Danton. Since she could not discuss her innermost feelings with his sister, she went to the armoire to get the gown she was to take to the Morilla's.

232

"I've a question to ask you, Kit," Delores called to her as she stood at the armoire.

"What is it, Delores?"

"Why do you think Damien would not like Ramon?"

Kit whirled around. "Damien? Damien doesn't like him? Is that what you're saying?"

"Well, he certainly gave me that impression. I . . . I was shattered the other day when I mentioned to him how much I liked Ramon and Damien made one of his smirking remarks. I couldn't believe it. I was so mad at him I wanted to slap him. I think I've changed my mind about my brothers. I always worshiped Damien and his fun-loving ways, but Danton's arrogance and his seriousness intimidated me. Still, he would have never been as nasty as Damien was."

Kit suddenly realized just how hurt Delores was by her older brother's crassness. "Perhaps, Delores, he didn't mean it and his mood was just sour?"

"So his mood was sour. He didn't have to deliberately try to hurt me. No, I rather got the feeling that Damien enjoys hurting people. I've seen this trait in him many times, Kit. I guess it just made a deep dent in me this time because I care so much for Ramon. It hurt so because I've always loved Damien so much."

"It always hurts more if you care for a person who seeks to hurt you."

"Why do people want to be cruel, Kit?"

"I imagine it's because they aren't too happy themselves so they want to make others unhappy too, Delores."

"Are you saying Damien isn't really so happy-go-lucky?"

"I'd say that's a very good possibility. If he were a cocky and self-assured person he wouldn't have been cruel to you. I'd say Damien is discontent."

"Oh, Kit, I didn't realize how wise you were. I wish I were smart. I guess I've got a lot to learn."

233

Kit prepared to go, the yellow gown flung over one arm. "Oh, Delores, I'm not so clever, but I thank you for the compliment." She bid her little friend farewell and left the room.

As she started to descend down the stairway, she mumbled to herself, declaring that if she were smart she would have figured out the complicated, frustrating Danton Navarro, who seemed to adore her one minute and abhor her the next. No, little Delores, I'm not so smart, she thought as she reached the base of the stairway.

Chapter 26

Señora Lucía Navarro watched the two ride out of the barn. Dear old Santiago—what would she do without him! More to the point, she asked herself why had she made a point of suggesting that Kit have Santiago accompany her on the ride to the Morillas' ranch. Whatever had provoked the suggestion, Lucía was glad that Kit had done as she'd suggested.

As Lucía stood at the window and watched the pair ride off, she would have wagered that the girl's suggestion that he ride with her had pleased the dear old Mexican. Santiago was not one to disguise his feelings, and he liked Señorita Kit very much. But then, Santiago's appraisal of people and animals had always been superb. He wasn't easily fooled by man or beast.

Observing them as they rode out of sight, Lucía had to confess that one would hardly guess the age of the aging Mexican foreman. He still sat straight and proud in the saddle, and the beautiful Kit was a striking companion for him. Her wide-brimmed black hat was set cockily on the side of her head. She was a proud little minx, and Lucía admired her for that. Maybe she had assumed too much about Danton's feelings about the girl, but she still thought Kit was the type of girl he needed.

Finally, Lucía turned from the window to go upstairs and look in on Delores. Perhaps, her daughter might enjoy a little company before her lunch tray was brought, she thought. In fact, she might just tackle the tedious chore of brushing out Delores' thick mop of black hair since the young girl who'd been helping Drusilla had not come to the house this morning. Santiago had sent her to administer to one of the cowhands who'd mangled a finger late yesterday afternoon. Young as she was, the Mexican girl, Yolanda, and her healing herbs were much praised at the ranch.

Santiago had been pleased by Kit's invitation, although if she hadn't requested his company, the Mexican would have ridden protectively behind her. After they had trotted a short distance down the road, however, Kit remarked quite innocently that Lucía had suggested he accompany her. Santiago shrugged his shoulders and casually replied, "Well, I put everyone to their chores and I was going to give myself the day off. I am a pretty smart fellow, *sí?*"

Kit giggled. *"Sí, Santiago!* A very sly one, too."

"Ah, *niña,* I think I don't fool you, eh?" He chuckled. "Not a bit!"

In unison, they spurred their horses to a faster pace, giving way to the light-hearted mood they shared. Age and years slipped away from the old Mexican, for the spirited young miss made him feel young and carefree. Her vitality was intoxicating and contagious.

Kit was enjoying herself with him too. His dark eyes looked at her with such devoted affection, and his husky, accented words were always laced with sincerity. She never doubted anything Santiago told her.

When they arrived at the Morilla ranch and tied their mounts at the hitching post, Santiago excused himself to go to the barn and seek out one of the many hired hands he knew; then Kit went up the walk to the front door.

Once she had assured Antonia Morilla, who met her at the door, that nothing was wrong with Lucía, Señora Morilla ushered her into her parlor. "This is a very nice surprise for me, Kit, and of course, I'm relieved that Lucía is not ill. I can well understand why she would be exhausted after that mammoth undertaking. I'm sure she's already told you she does this every year. I told her just the other night, that one day she will have to discontinue it."

Antonia proved to be a chatterbox during the next half-hour, and Kit knew that Lucía would be delighted to learn that Señora Morilla had been lifted out of the morose mood she'd lingered in so long after her son's death. Maybe Lucía's fiesta had been responsible for that.

When the time came for Kit to leave, Antonia invited her to call on them again. "You are a most divine addition to our countryside, Kit dear. I must tell you that all of us have talked about you constantly since seeing and meeting you the other night. You are the most beautiful young lady we've seen around these parts. Mercy, I'll be embarrassing you if I keep on."

Kit gave the friendly woman's shoulder a gentle pat. "Hardly that, Señora Morilla. I consider you most kind and charming. It is never embarrassing to be told you're beautiful."

"Well, do come again . . . please. I'm just sorry Carmella was not here. She would be delighted to see you."

"I will come again and thank you for your hospitality." Kit gave Antonia a warm smile; then she turned to go down the steps. She waved her hand since Antonia still stood at the door, and then she broke into a jaunty walk that befitted the good mood she was in.

Whether she knew who she was or not, today she really didn't mind so much. It was glorious to be alive, and everyone she'd encountered had been so sweet. Maybe that was all that counted after all!

When Santiago saw her coming, he told his friend, Juan, farewell. As Kit approached, he realized that she was something to behold. He'd seen many a frisky, fiery filly in his lifetime, but seeing Kit with her head held high, her hat resting on her shoulder blades, and her curvy body swaying sensuously as she walked, he knew that any red-blooded man would yearn for her. *Madre de Dios,* he wasn't even so old that he couldn't appreciate the little temptress.

As she drew closer, he could see her beautiful eyes gleaming like precious emeralds. Ah, yes, it was easy to see that the little *señorita* was in a capricious mood.

"Ready, *niña?*" he asked her when they met.

"Ready, Santiago," she replied. "Did you finish your visit with your friends?"

"Oh, *sí.* It was nice to talk to Juan, for I haven't seen him in three or four weeks."

As soon as they'd mounted up they rode off toward Silvercreek, and because the afternoon sun was becoming exceedingly warm Santiago suggested a different trail rather than the main road.

"It will provide us with more shade, I think," he said.

"Sounds good to me, Santiago." She allowed the old Mexican to guide her, reining Scarlett to a slower pace.

It was cooler under the trees, and a few squirrels were at play, scampering up and down the trunks.

"Santiago, are we riding on Navarro land now?" she called to him.

"*Sí, señorita*—I think now we are. It's a little hard to

tell right here. Señor Morilla and Señor Navarro never needed to put fences or borders between their spreads. But yes, I think this is Navarro land."

"Navarro land," she echoed slowly. "It must be nice to own so much land."

"I guess, *señorita.* I will never know about that, but I've been happy to live here all these years with the Navarro family. They've been good to me."

Kit was following along at a slow pace, enjoying the quiet of the trail, almost soundless except for the thudding of their horses' hooves. It couldn't have been a more pleasant day. Riding through the wooded area was a good idea.

The sharp explosion suddenly destroyed the serene peacefulness Kit and Santiago had been enjoying. Santiago's head jerked back and his sombrero fell off as his eyes darted around to check on Kit. Her panic-stricken mare whinnied, swung her head to the side, and then lunged forward, ramming into Santiago's horse.

Though the Mexican was an excellent horseman, his instant reaction could not keep his horse under control. The stallion reared.

Kit didn't know how she'd landed on the ground. Her mare hadn't reared as Santiago's mount had. She could only remember that her feet suddenly left the stirrups and she had fallen to one side, out of the saddle, onto the ground below. A split second after she landed, she had looked up dazedly to see Santiago fighting to gain control of his frenzied stallion.

Although Santiago's skill and strength were taxed to his limit by the effort it took to show the horse who was the boss, his thoughts chilled him to the core of his being. He knew a rifle shot when he heard one, and he knew this was no accident. Someone had taken a shot at them—someone who had stalked them on their way from the Morilla ranch. That scared the devil out of the old Mexican—not for himself but for Señorita Kit.

It troubled him to think he'd failed her, but he wasted no time in calming the horse. Then he leaped off and went to where Kit lay. Her eyes were wide with fear. "Dear God, Santiago!" she gasped, her disbelief reflected in her flashing green eyes.

"Stay low, *señorita*. Let's just stay right here for a minute." Santiago considered it wiser to let the bastard think his bullet had hit its target. His ears strained to pick up some sound that might tell him whether a horse was moving away from them or approaching them. The ambusher might want to check out his handiwork. Santiago sent up a fair share of prayers in the space of a few seconds. He knew his limitations as a protector— he was an old man—and he was worried about Kit.

"Santiago?" she whispered, leaning closer to him.

"Sssssh, *señorita*," he whispered.

Finally, when he'd heard that telltale sound he'd prayed to hear, he inquired of the girl, "Are you just shaken, *señorita?*"

"I . . . I think so. How about you, Santiago?"

"Oh, I'm all right. My old heart is just pounding too fast for a man my age." He suggested that they mount up. He was certain he'd heard a rider depart from the woods. "I feel the need to get back to Silvercreek as soon as possible."

Kit pressed the palm of her hand down on the ground as she started to rise. She winced. The pain traveled right up to her elbow. "Oh . . . I must have landed on that wrist. It hurts like the devil."

"It's most likely sprained, *niña*," Santiago told her. "Here, let us make a cradle for it, eh." He took off his bandanna and tied it around her neck like a sling. "There, slip your hand right through there."

"Thank you, Santiago. I . . . I'm sure glad you were

with me."

"So am I, *señorita*," he mumbled, extending his hand to her as she started to rise from the ground.

She smiled gratefully; then she gasped and suddenly became dead weight.

"Damn! My ankle, Santiago!"

Kit flinched, and Santiago saw the pained look on her face. *"Madre de Dios,* don't even try to stand on it. Sit down." She obeyed him eagerly for taking her weight off it did soothe the aching at her ankle.

"All right, *niña*. We've got to get you on your horse by putting as little pressure on that ankle as possible. At Silvercreek I can get some help and we'll carry you into the house."

Santiago knew that he was not going to leave her to get a wagon. He pondered for a minute or two before he spoke again.

"Grasp me under the shoulders and I'll rise on the good leg, Santiago," she said. "Then if you let me lean on you I can hop to my horse."

Santiago complied. When they got to her horse, he knelt and told her to sit on his shoulder. As he rose Kit was able to fling a leg over the horse and land in the saddle. She sighed with relief. Then she turned to the old Mexican.

"What are you waiting for, Santiago? Let's ride!" she said teasingly, then she laughed. Her coiled hair had come loose, and it hung down over her back and shoulders. Santiago laughed too, from relief that the girl was alive! The very idea that this vital young woman could have been lying on the ground with a bullet in her petrified Santiago. But by the time they reached Silvercreek, the chill in his bones had turned to hot rage.

He knew what he was going to do as soon as he'd gotten Señorita Kit into the capable hands of Señora

Lucía. A fleeting qualm made him ask himself if he might be wrong. What if he found nothing out of order in the Navarro barn when he checked out the horses?

If the black stallion had just been ridden then Santiago knew he had the answer to his question. That thought did not sit well, but neither did being shot.

He noted Kit's quiet mood as they rode back to the ranch. Was the incident having an impact on her too? Was she horrified by her suspicions?

Chapter 27

Pain didn't plague her as much as confinement. Once Kit and Santiago had arrived at the courtyard gate, the attention showered on her had overwhelmed her. Lucía had insisted that the same young doctor who'd attended to Kit when she'd first arrived at Silvercreek come to the ranch to check out her injuries.

Dr. Rojas' diagnosis was exactly what Santiago had claimed back in the woods. She had to stay off her foot for a week or so and her wrist had a sprain. But long after those injuries were attended, Dr. Rojas sat, asking Kit a multitude of questions.

Later, when he went downstairs to the privacy of Lucía's back sitting room, as the two of them shared a cup of coffee he confessed, "I was hoping that this shock or the fall might have jarred her memory. Sometimes, it happens. I'm sorry to tell you it didn't. However, *señora,* I am happy to report that she will be just fine. Bed rest will heal her ankle. Luckily neither she nor Santiago was shot. I'm glad it was not a wound I was dressing. I'll report this to the sheriff when I get back into town if you would like me to."

"I most assuredly would," Lucía said. Such a despicable deed would not go unpunished if she had her way. Her anger had mounted as the afternoon had worn on. The old Mexican's welfare was important to her and Kit was becoming more dear to her with each day.

Dr. Roja drank the last sip of his coffee; then he picked up his hat and rose from the cozy chair he seemed almost reluctant to leave. "I will see to it. Señora Lucía, it is always a pleasure to see you and to serve you. If you should need me, you have only to let me know and I will be here. My best regards to your family."

"Thank you, Doctor. I wish you could have come to our fiesta," Lucía told him.

"I had hoped that Señora Linsley's baby would wait, but the little fellow just wouldn't cooperate." He grinned.

"Then may I invite you to dine with us some evening when you come out this way to see one of your patients? Please . . . it would be my pleasure."

"I accept. Now, I must be going."

Lucía escorted him to the front door and bid him farewell. Her first opinion of Dr. Rojas had remained. He was an outstanding young man and a devoted doctor.

Each of the Navarros paid a visit to her room during the evening. Delores trotted across the hall. She was feeling much better herself even though she was still lounging about in her nightgown and robe.

"Tomorrow, I'm dressing and going downstairs," she delightedly informed Kit. "I promise, though, Kit, to help you pass the time you must spend in your room."

"That's sweet of you, Delores. Maybe Dr. Rojas will be wrong in saying I must rest my ankle a whole week. I might just fool him," Kit confidently replied.

They talked casually for a few minutes before the servant rapped on the door bearing a tray with Kit's dinner.

Delores asked to have her tray brought to Kit's room so they might dine together. "Poor Mother must be having a lonely dinner if Damien is out again this evening."

At that moment, her brother's husky voice drew the attention of both of the girls to the doorway. Laughing good-naturedly, he informed his sister, "But Damien isn't out again tonight." Then he chided his younger sister. "You're going to convince Kit that I'm a thoughtless ogre. By the way, how are you, Kit? I was so sorry to hear about your accident this afternoon."

Kit was looking down at her tray, trying to arrange it in a more balanced way on her lap. "Oh, Santiago wouldn't call it an accident, nor would I, Damien. It was hardly an accident."

Damien shrugged his shoulders and remarked, "Surely it must have been. What would make you think otherwise? That old Mexican is prone to wild imaginings at times."

Kit bristled instantly, "Santiago and I agree about what happened, Damien."

Damien took a step closer to the bed. "But who in hades would want to harm you or old Santiago?"

"Someone obviously." Kit told him, taking a bite of her food. She was so hungry that she couldn't resist the tasty-looking food on her plate.

Noting that her interest was on eating instead of talking, Damien excused himself politely and left the bedroom. Taking a cue from Kit, Delores had already begun to eat.

As Damien descended the steps, he played nervously with the gold cuff links of his shirt. He wasn't relishing the hours ahead, not with the sagacious Lucía Navarro eying him across the dining table.

245

But this wasn't the time to be out of favor with the obstinate, strong-willed lady he knew his mother to be. So he must do certain things even if he found them distasteful. He had to let his happy-go-lucky charm shine tonight. He must be gay but not too gay, for she must feel that he was concerned about this afternoon's incident. Damien was very aware of Lucía's devotion to Santiago and of her loyalty to and her sincere affection for Kit.

He would cajole and flatter her as they dined. His conceit blinded him to the fact that his Latin charm was not infallible. He did not even consider that it might not be effective on Lucía Navarro. The *señora* was one lady Damien should have made an exception, especially on this particular evening. The devil himself could not have charmed her, for there was too much weighing down her thoughts.

The existence she'd lived in her youth, the very one Damien abhorred, had fortified Lucía Navarro with lessons about living that her son could not begin to appreciate at this time in his own life. She was far too shrewd and clever to be fooled by Damien's charming ways. It was he who was naïve, though he'd thought himself clever on numerous occasions.

Tonight Lucía was ready for him. By the time Damien joined her for dinner she'd had a brief discussion with Kit, and a longer one with Santiago.

She understood, after what had happened only hours earlier, that her old friend was definitely disturbed. It must have been very harrowing for him. But she didn't quite understand why the wily old Mexican was holding something back from her. She and he had always been able to talk without restraint, so the old man's manner puzzled the *señora*.

The possible cause of such a situation disturbed her greatly. Once again, she wished very much that Danton were here at Silvercreek.

When Damien joined her he found her unusually quiet and thoughtful. His mother had a reputation as a conversationalist, but tonight she was reserved.

"Are you feeling well, Mother?" he asked, for her manner intensified his own anxiety.

"Yes, Damien. Please forgive me, dear. I didn't mean to be so aloof or preoccupied. But I am and I guess you can imagine why."

"Of course, Mother. All of Silvercreek is upset about what happened, or could have happened, to Santiago and to Kit."

"Thank God, nothing did. But this incident isn't going to be dismissed. Never! Dr. Rojas promised to report it to the sheriff."

Damien sat, saying nothing. He could have been a statue, so expressionless and lifeless was he. His mother's remark had taken him by surprise. He hadn't thought she'd take this incident so seriously.

When his temporarily numb brain slowly began to function again, he thought about the craziness of what he'd done. If the bullet had hit its target the sheriff would have been summoned, but not for this. Fear stabbed Damien.

Once again, he was struck by a damning consequence of his act. Suppose his jet-black stallion had been seen coming out of the grove near the spot where the ambush had happened. He sat in a foggy daze, so absorbed in the troubling thoughts parading through his mind that he was not paying attention to what Lucía was talking about.

"I won't tolerate such a thing on this land. Why Victor would have been appalled, and so am I." She turned her attention back to the food on her plate, not noticing the deep frown etching Damien's handsome face. When she spoke next, she once again perplexed him. "Damien, you have not rubbed someone the wrong way lately, have you? I've wondered if this would be an act of revenge directed at the Navarro family. I'd swear Santiago has no enemies in the countryside and certainly that sweet girl doesn't."

Damien retorted sharply, "No, Mother. Not enough to make someone do something this drastic."

"Well, Damien, I know you're devious, but I'd hate to think you'd stir up this much wrath in someone. More to the point, I'd hate to think someone else might have paid for some misdeed of yours." She could not have known what she was doing to Damien in that moment. Had she stuck a knife in his gut, twisting it without mercy, he would not have hurt less. Her eyes seemed to be searching the depths of his soul, but he reminded himself that he must not flinch.

His black eyes met her black ones, and behind his warm and gentle smile, a black hate smoldered. How he hated her in that moment as she sat there prepared to be his judge and jury. Silently, he acknowledged his consuming dislike of her.

That endless dinner hour finally came to a point where Damien could gracefully excuse himself to go outside and smoke a cheroot, or so he told her.

As he ambled away from the table, Lucía's voice called after him, "I enjoyed your company at dinner, son. Too bad we had to speak of such unpleasant things. Tomorrow will be better, I hope."

"Yes, Mother. Tomorrow will be better."

After he'd left her, Lucía sat awhile before she called to tell Drusilla that they were finished. It was a little thing, Lucía tried to tell herself. But it was something Damien never failed to do when he left the table, and that was to bend down and plant a kiss on her forehead or cheek. To her, it was very significant.

Something she'd said had disturbed Damien terribly.

Chapter 28

It had been a long ten days since Danton Navarro had ridden away from Arthur Cameron's ranch to head north for Austin. Many a mile separated him from Silvercreek this night as he sat poring over a mountain of paperwork, but he was determined to finish what he'd set out to do before calling it a night. He intended to return to Silvercreek just as soon as he could.

There was a letter to get off to Arthur Cameron in which Danton would be happy to report his success. He had stopped by the L and J Ranch, and his talk with Jim Longley had gone amazingly smoothly. The truth was, he'd ended up being delayed an extra day and night in getting back to Austin. He'd thought he known the old hard-nosed Texan, but Danton hadn't been prepared to deal with the proposition Longley had handed him.

When he and Jim had sat down to discuss the situation Danton hoped to talk the stubborn rancher out of blocking roads and fencing in his land. Danton hoped to stop the bloodshed that would result because the smaller ranchers needed water from the nearby river and they had the right to use the road old Jim had closed off.

Danton never figured the old fox would dump it all in his lap. At first, he thought Longley was just being a little eccentric as a lot of people accused him of being, but he soon realized the rancher was dead serious. For a man who owned thousands of acres a mere two hundred and sixty-nine acres were nothing.

"You take that strip, Danton. You handle it any damned way you want. I wash my hands of it," Longley barked gruffly.

"I can't do that, Jim," Danton protested.

"Why the devil can't you? It's mine and I can do what I want with it. Don't like the idea for it to be given to you? Then I'll sell it to you. What you got to say to that, Navarro?"

Two hundred sixty-nine acres was not a big ranch, but the strip was bordered on the Pedernales River by a multitude of pecan, sumac, and oak trees. The rich black soil would grow anything. Danton couldn't believe what he was hearing, but he took Jim's bait. "All right. What do you want for the land and the headaches it's caused?"

"I want a dollar, and I call it damned good riddance."

"You've got it! Of course, I may be feeling like you do a year from now." Danton grinned at the rancher.

"Sorry, Danton, I won't take it back. You'll be stuck with it." Longley laughed good-naturedly. In the following hours Danton came to realize that the gruff old man had a light jovial side to his nature.

Danton enjoyed the day spent with Jim Longley. The two men walked over some of the land Danton had unexpectedly acquired, and by the time they'd ambled down the grassy pasture toward the bank of the Pedernales River, which was lined with weeping willows, Danton wondered how Longley could possibly want to sell this spread.

Old Jim had a very logical reason for doing so, however. "What the hell do I do with all I've got, son? Got more than I need for this lifetime and the next. Me and my dear Laurette wasn't given the chance to have any kids. That damn Indian half-breed took care of that. Course, I know you know that. I never wanted to marry again so that's the way it is."

They'd come to a bend in the river, and Danton paused, figuring Jim was ready to walk back to their horses. But Longley urged him to continue on around the bend. "Got one other little thing to show you about this particular section."

A gentle breeze rustled through the low-hanging branches of the willows, and Danton's ears picked up a humming sound. Jim noticed the expression on Danton's face.

"Pretty, isn't it?" he asked. "That's why my dear Laurette gave it the name of Whispering Willows. See over there—the little stone cottage. That was our first home when we got this land." Longley went on to explain that his wife was a sweet, simple woman. "She gave names to every and any thing she liked. She liked the sound of the rustling willows. Told me as we stood here that day it seemed like they were whispering to us."

Danton felt very privileged that Jim Longley would confide in him. "Your wife had the soul of a poet. She must have been a very special person, Jim. I'm sorry I never got to know her."

"Yeah, that would have been nice, Danton," Jim told him, as he kicked at the earth with his boot. Danton figured Longley's eyes had darted downward because of the tears gathering in them. He had noticed the quick gesture Longley had made, swiping his hand across his face.

"Come on, son. Let's be heading back to the house.

Feel the need for a drink," Longley's voice was crisp and snapping. He sounded more like the gruff, hard-nosed Texan he was reputed to be, but Danton would forever think of him as the man he'd come to know that day.

Danton spent the night at the L and J Ranch, leaving at the crack of dawn the next morning. Not only had he successfully accomplished his mission for Cameron and his group of rancher friends, he was already making his own plans for the Whispering Willows.

Once he'd arrived back in Austin, he'd worked like a demon to clear away the pile of paperwork, but his mind was elsewhere. He caught himself staring out the window of his office, giving way to whimsy and daydreaming.

He turned down two or three social invitations during the next week, and twice he shrewdly out-maneuvered the wily Estellita Valero, escaping her by a few seconds. Finally, she'd stormed through his front door to be told by his faithful Abeja that Señor Navarro had left a couple of hours earlier to return to Silvercreek.

The giggling Abeja had then rushed up the stairs to Danton's bedroom to find Danton sitting casually on his dark balcony and watching the señora angrily exit from his dark courtyard. Abeja whispered, "Ah, *señor,* that is one mad woman, I think."

Danton grinned, "I've no doubt, Abeja."

When they both heard the harsh slamming of the iron gate, Abeja confessed, "I . . . I don't know whether I'd like to have to lie too often to that one. She has the fierce look of a *bruja,* Señor Danton."

Danton laughed gustily for he realized that Estellita's fury had, indeed, instilled fear in the young Abeja. Danton apologized to him, "I promise not to put you in that position again, Abeja."

Mindful of Estellita's intimidating ways, he felt sorry for the youth although he'd warned his young servant earlier that she might do just what she'd done. Actually, he hadn't exactly lied for he did intend to go to Silvercreek in another day or two.

Lucía Navarro's garden was a profusion of glorious colors: white and pink, lavender and deep rich purple mingled with the greenery. The petals of some plants gleamed with such luster they could have been silk. Lucía watched the graceful mist of the spray from the fountain provide a happy bluejay with a cool bath. The bird perched, unmoving, beneath the water, allowing itself to become drenched.

Delores, eyes closed, lay on the wicker chaise lounge. Lucía enjoyed having her daughter's company, and she was glad that Delores was feeling better. It made her a bit guilty to think that poor Kit had to remain upstairs, however, while they enjoyed these delightful pleasures of the summer day.

It was the quiet period of the day when the servants took their siestas, but Drusilla never rested. Long ago, Lucía had quit nagging her to go lie down like the others. This afternoon Drusilla had insisted that she had to make a cake, Delores' favorite, chocolate.

Dear, devoted Drusilla! Lucía could not have managed without her. Like Santiago, she was a part of the Navarro family, of Silvercreek.

Señora Navarro's private musings were interrupted by Delores' lazy soft drawl, "Momma, I've something to ask you."

"What is it, Delores? I was being very quiet because I thought you were napping."

"No . . . not really. It was just so nice out here and so good to be out of bed again."

253

Delores raised herself up slowly. She didn't quite know how to go about asking her mother what she thought of Ramon Valdez. What if Lucía said she didn't like him? But how could she possibly not like such a gallant young man like Ramon? Delores' courage rose. But as she was about to pose her question a tall, towering shadow fell across the flagstone patio and she turned to see her brother standing nearby.

"Danton . . . what— What are you doing back here?" she exclaimed.

"Well, I can't say that is a very cordial welcome!" A devious grin appeared on his tanned face as he swept a straying wisp of black hair off his forehead. "God, how wonderfully cool it feels out here!" He bent down to give his mother a gentle kiss on the forehead.

But the face he wanted to see and kiss was missing from this little gathering. As he rose, he inquired about Kit's whereabouts. The possibility that Kit and Damien were together had made jealousy flare in him.

Lucía tried to choose her words carefully. "There was a slight accident, Danton dear, but let me hastily add that she is just fine. She will just have to stay in bed a little longer." Lucía had only to look at her son's flashing, black eyes to know that this news had shocked and disturbed him.

"What the hell kind of accident was it?" he snapped.

"My goodness, Danton! Kit has a sprained ankle and her wrist was slightly strained, but it is fine now. Dr. Rojas is allowing her limited movement now. He just doesn't want her attempting the steps yet." Lucía was secretly pleased at his display of concern. Actually, she felt smug because she'd been right in her assumption that he cared very much for Kit. Regardless of what she'd witnessed the night of the fiesta, what had gone on between Danton and Estellita, now she knew that had been nothing serious.

When Danton abruptly whirled about, hastily excusing himself, Delores giggled and then Lucía exploded with laughter.

"I think Danton is stuck on Kit, Momma. Can you believe how excited and anxious he got when you told him about her getting hurt?"

Lucía smiled slyly. "Yes, I'd say he was just a little upset. So you think your brother likes our little Kit, Delores. Well so do I."

"I saw him kiss her once up in the hall, and I didn't think too much about it. I figured any man would love to kiss her. She is so beautiful! I know Damien probably feels just like Danton." Delores sighed dramatically. "Oh, that would be a mess, wouldn't it, Momma, if they both insisted on being Kit's suitor?"

Lucía laughed softly. "Ah, yes, *niña*—a horrible mess!"

Kit had strolled to the window looking out over the inviting scene below. The sight of Delores lying so contentedly on the wicker lounge while Señora Lucía sat serenely nearby made her swell with envy.

She turned from the window, feeling there was no point in tormenting herself by looking down at them and wishing she were sitting with them.

She sauntered over to the dressing table and grabbed the silver-handled hairbrush. Then she flung herself down on the bed, taking her frustrations out by furiously stroking her tangled hair.

When she struck a snarl, she gasped. Then she looked across the room at the mirror on her dressing table. What a mess she was! Her hair looked like a mop, and it needed to be washed. All the luster and gloss was gone. It looked dull and lifeless.

Her disheveled appearance was so depressing that

she decided to do something with her hair. She flung off the cumbersome wrapper to sit cross-legged on the bed in her sheer, pale green gown. She did feel much more comfortable as she began to brush her hair again, using the brush more gently.

In his anxiety to satisfy himself that she was all right, Danton forgot his good manners. He did not knock before opening the door.

His unexpected entrance provoked a shriek of protest from Kit. "Who—what—Danton Navarro!" She sat with half-opened lips, taunting him with her eyes, those lovely green pools he wanted to drown himself in, while he stood before her with a wicked smile on his face. His eyes danced lustily over the sensuous curve she displayed so bewitchingly until she snapped angrily, "Well, Danton, are you through leering at me?"

"Ah, *querida,* I'll never be through with looking at you, but looking is not enough," he told her in a deep, husky voice as he strode toward the bed.

As he moved closer, she sat like someone spellbound. Their gazes fused, and as he lowered himself to sit down beside her on the bed his overpowering essence permeated her so completely that she felt light-headed and dizzy.

She opened her mouth to speak, but no words came for Danton's warm lips captured hers. As a smoldering liquid fire spread through her, she wanted him to make love to her. It was futile to tell herself that she shouldn't feel that way.

He felt her body arching toward him, and he pressed his huge hands against her back to draw her closer.

Holding her so, Danton knew she was why he'd needed to get back to Silvercreek. He felt wonderfully content just holding her in his strong arms and whispering words of love in her ear.

With Danton holding her and loving her, Kit no longer felt alone. She never would, not when Danton Navarro was telling her that he loved her. But then Danton's mood changed quickly.

To hold her was not enough for the hot-blooded Danton, whose desire had mounted at the sight her green gown revealed—the rosy tips of her jutting breasts which pressed against the diaphanous gown. His hands moved to lower the straps so his lips might caress the luscious satiny tips of her breasts, and Kit moaned with pleasure. Instantly aroused, she pressed herself against him as he leaned over her.

Her body seemed to have a will of its own, though she had sworn he'd not conquer her so easily. It pained her, but she forced herself to withdraw from the sensuous touch of his lips. "No, Danton! Damn it! No!" Her eyes were wide and her lashes fluttered as she moved back out of his reach.

"What's the matter with you? You know you wanted me to do just what I was doing," he declared, his black eyes sparking. It was a stunning blow to Danton's ego that she should act like this.

He looked so arrogant, so full of conceit, that she realized how easily he'd had his way with her. Now, he figured she was there for the taking whenever he chose. Her temper exploded, and she bolted up, tilting her head defiantly. "I'm not your plaything, Danton Navarro!"

"Holy Christ, whoever said you were?" It was Danton's turn to become riled. What had happened to the girl he'd left here at Silvercreek? He sure didn't recognize this one!

He rose and sauntered away from her, heading for the door. "I don't need a toy, sweetheart. I'm a man, and it's a real woman a man wants!" He couldn't see the startled, hurt look on her face because his back

257

was turned.

She leaped out of the bed and placed her hands on the tiny waistline that enhanced the alluring curves of her hips. It took all her strength and determination to put a smile on her face for there was excruciating pain in her ankle due to the pressure her careless movement had put on it. But her temper got the best of her.

She sensuously flaunted her lovely body, defying him to say she wasn't a woman. "You dare say I'm not a woman, Danton Navarro?" When Danton turned around, she looked like the most ravishing temptress he had ever seen.

Slowly, he took a step toward her. His dark, menacing eyes pierced her, and she could not prevent a tremble from running through her as he moved toward her like a dangerous cat ready to strike. "I intend to find out, *querida.* I have an insatiable curiosity and you've just whetted it."

"You . . . you wouldn't . . . you . . ." She didn't finish what she was about to say because Danton interrupted her by declaring, "The devil himself wouldn't stop me now!"

The expression on her face as she moved backward sparked Danton's desire and his determination to convince Kit that she'd never wish to deny him or his lovemaking again. As she fell back upon the bed, he pounced on her, straddling her, his boots tangling in the coverlet.

"Damn you, Danton," she muttered as he grabbed her flying fists.

He easily subdued her, and then he laughed. *"Chiquita,* I thought you were so sweet and innocent."

"The conceit of you, Danton Navarro. I was a virgin until I met you. That we both know, don't we?" There was a sneer on her angry face, but it only tended to heighten Danton's passion.

His lips captured hers, teasing them, penetrating them, demanding the return of his ardor. "Don't tell me you didn't like that? The Kit I know isn't a liar. Tell me, Kit—tell me?"

"Why should I?" She pretended a distaste that she was not feeling. His forceful body, fully clothed, was holding her down, and the feel of it was having an effect similar to what his lips had just aroused.

"Because I want to know."

"And you always expect to have your way, don't you? Maybe I like to, as well," she curtly declared.

"Kiss me then as you know you want to," he dared her.

To show him she could kiss him and turn aside afterward, she met his challenge boldly. As she did so, Danton moved his hand to cup her exposed breast, and his finger rubbed its hardened nipple with lazy strokes. In spite of herself, Kit's body responded instinctively. Immediately, Danton's other hand started to yank away his shirt, and he moved slightly away from her to rid himself of his pants. Then he realized he still had his boots on.

She could not restrain her laughter for he looked like a frustrated, little boy, perplexed by the dilemma he found himself in.

"Laugh, you little witch. You do put a spell on me, I confess. I won't lie to you, *querida*." He quickly flung each boot aside and then recaptured her in his arms. "Now, show me what a woman you are, eh?"

She did just that!

She knew the ways of lovemaking now, for her teacher was an expert and she was an eager student. Her lips tantalized him, and she moved her body over his in a manner that was a sweet, sensuous torment to him. Danton was ablaze, flaming out of control. As her hands played a magic melody on his body, he sighed.

259

He could dwell for a lifetime in this paradise.

"*Querido* . . . I'm a woman . . . yes?"

"*Mucho* woman!" he swore, laughing huskily. "The woman I want for the rest of my days. You, *amada mía*—you are the woman I wish to marry."

As he rolled her over onto her back to show her that she was with a man, the only man for her, she whispered, "*Sí,* I will marry you and love you as no other woman could."

He waited no longer to bury himself deep within her. Then searing flames devoured them until the inferno of passion had died down to smoldering embers. Still they lingered, contented and sated, in one other's arms.

They knew, without words being uttered, that she was his woman and he was her man!

Chapter 29

If Delores could have read her mother's mind she would have been shocked, as any young lady would have been, for the young tend to forget that their mothers and fathers were once young and often reckless in affairs of the heart. Lucía was recalling the sweet abandoned feeling of being held in a man's arms, of making love. Victor had been a man of passion and a fascinating lover.

Her son's hasty departure to rush up to Kit had not surprised her, nor had the fact that he'd not returned to the courtyard though an hour had passed. Perhaps, she should have played the indignant mother and marched upstairs. But she would not do that to Danton and Kit for she was certain they were lying in one another's arms.

Was she wrong? No. How could she cast an accusing stone at them when she and Victor had indulged in lovemaking before they'd married? She'd be lying to herself, even now, years later, if she said those were not the most exciting memories of their glorious courtship. So she sat in the garden with her daughter, chatting about other things while her secret thoughts wandered into yesteryears.

Only when they finally left the courtyard did Lucía promise herself that she would talk to Danton that very evening. Son or not, he'd not use Kit sorely under her roof, although she couldn't really believe Danton would do that.

Two hours later, the parlor was quiet, awaiting the members of the Navarro family who would congregate at the appointed dinner hour. Damien had been the first one to descend the steps, but he had gone into the adjoining room, Victor's study, to help himself to some brandy. He wanted none of the wine his mother usually had Drusilla bring out before the meal was served. His mood had been foul since he'd returned from his afternoon romp with the pretty Molly Langford, and old Santiago had seemingly taken great joy in announcing to him that Señor Danton was home again. Damn Señor Danton. He'd cursed under his breath as he'd left the barn to come into the house as twilight was descending over the countryside.

Wasting no time, he'd quickly changed his clothes so he could get downstairs and have a couple of drinks before the rest of the family assembled.

Before Danton had finally forced himself to leave Kit's side, he'd presented her with the gift he'd intended to give her the night of the fiesta. With boyish enthusiasm, he'd insisted that she put the earrings on immediately, even though she had on only the sheer, green nightgown. That mattered not to Danton as he stood back and raved about the perfection of Constantine's handiwork.

"Stark naked you'd make them look great for they were not picked to complement any fancy gown, but to suit you, *mi vida.*"

Kit gave out a lilting little laugh as she looked into

the mirror. The gift was exquisite, a perfect match for her little peridot ring. The fact that Danton had given such thought to the jewelry he'd chosen for her made her treasure it even more.

"Oh, Danton, I love them!" She turned her head to one side and then the other, her finger flicking back the long strand of hair that obscured her view of one of the earrings.

"More to the point, *chiquita*—just love me."

"But I do. I loved you anyway, Danton Navarro. You know that!"

"Had things not gone so wrong the night of the party it was my intention to give them to you then. You must have more faith in me, Kit, for I will tell you this only once. Estellita Valero means nothing to me and never has. I was about to ask you to marry me that night just before she and Damien intruded. The earrings were in my pocket awaiting your pretty ears."

Kit sighed deeply and confessed, "I got so . . . so jealous of that woman!"

He could not resist playfully rumpling her hair and laughing, "Good! I like you being jealous! Just don't make us pay such a price the next time, *querida.*"

But she dared to banter with him, the look of a coquette on her face and a challenging glint in her eyes. "Then don't you ever give me reason to think I should get jealous!"

"Hush, before we are at odds again. Now, you start getting yourself pretty because I want you to dine downstairs with me tonight."

"But, Danton, I'm not supposed to go down the steps yet," she feebly protested.

"Who said you were going to walk down? I will carry you up and down the steps. I want you there with me, Kit, when I announce my intention to marry you."

His eyes were so warm and loving they took her

breath away.

"Oh, Danton, I love you so very much," she declared. But the smile on her face slowly disappeared and a slight frown replaced it. "Danton, what about . . . well, you know? What about the problem of not knowing who I am? How will your mother feel about your marrying a girl whose background you know nothing about?"

He took her hands in his. "You don't have to be concerned on that score, Kit. Unless I'm completely wrong, Mother adores you. In case you haven't noticed my mother is a very unusual lady—far ahead of her time. Now, I'm going to leave you. I'll summon Yolanda to assist you in getting dressed. You have her come and get me when you're ready."

"Yes, sir." She smiled light-heartedly. Secretly, she was adoring his masterful way of taking charge. Of course, she was elated that he was so eager to tell the *señora* and the rest of his family that the two of them would be married.

Nothing mattered to Kit now that Danton had vowed his love for her and had proved it by asking her to be his wife. Her doubts about his sincerity were all swept away. She knew it had not been foolish fancy when she'd felt he cared for her, not her romantic heart just wishing it was so. He did love her as she loved him!

Danton, for all his sophistication and polish, was just as exhilarated. The girl of his dreams had promised to marry him. Her lips and her body had told him of her love, responding to him in such sweet surrender, giving him such overwhelming ecstasy.

He bent to kiss her one more time before leaving the room. "I'll be expecting you to agree with me from now on," he teased.

"Don't expect that, Danton my darling." There was a wicked gleam in her eyes as she looked boldly up at him. Now she had that seductive air he'd witnessed the night he'd strolled into the parlor and seen her singing while Damien played the guitar. She was a fascinating little creature who amazed and intrigued him.

"We'll see, *querida,*" he replied cockily. "Send Yolanda for me when you're ready to go downstairs. Oh, yes, wear the earrings tonight . . . for me."

"I wouldn't appear without them. They're so beautiful I'll wear them whether I'm dressed or not." She laughed softly.

"I can attest to that, little one." He paused. "You're so beautiful, Kit. If I didn't say so before, I'm telling you now." He grinned.

She grinned too, and then flushed as she recalled their torrid lovemaking right after he'd put the earrings on her.

As Danton's tall figure was about to go through the bedroom door, she called out to him, her voice almost a purr, "I love you, Danton Navarro."

"And I love you too, my little Kit," he replied, his tanned face warmed with adoration.

Kit went through the motions of dressing in an euphoric state. Her thoughts revolved only around the man she loved. Yolanda could see the glowing radiance on her lovely face as she helped her into a beautiful pale pink gown appliquéd with green and rose embroidery.

"Oh, *señorita*—you look so beautiful tonight. It is no wonder Señor Danton has lost his heart to you." Yolanda sighed as she put the last touch to Kit's hair. "There, *señorita.*"

"Oh, thank you, Yolanda. I wish I had your talent for fixing hair."

"Oh, it is not that difficult, *señorita.* I'll show you the little tricks I use if you wish me to, and you will see just how easy it is." Yolanda offered eagerly.

"I'd like that. Oh, yes!"

Yolanda stood back to survey her work. Since she'd been spending more time at the Navarro home and observing the members of the Navarro family, she had her favorites. Although Señorita Kit wasn't a Navarro, she was the nicest, with the exception of Señora Lucía.

Perhaps, that was because Señorita Kit was almost the same age as Yolanda so she felt more at ease around her, but she did not have the same feeling for Señorita Delores. Delores Navarro was not haughty or demanding, Yolanda admitted to herself. It was just a matter of choice. She liked Señorita Kit better.

"You have a fine man in Señor Danton, Señorita Kit," the young Mexican servant girl declared. Her opinion of the other Navarro brother would not have been the same. Damien Navarro instilled great fear in Yolanda, and she tried to shy away from him.

She'd found that out as soon as she'd come to work in the main house. Before that, she'd only observed him on the grounds, or out by the corral or the barn, as she'd done her daily chores for old Santiago at his little cottage. Old Santiago's cottage did not take much effort to keep clean and he was a dear soul, demanding little of her time. The truth was, she'd rather return to doing that, for she had felt safer. But for the threat of Damien's lecherous ways and his wicked eyes and overeager hands, Yolanda would have been delighted with her new position.

"We certainly agree about that, Yolanda," Kit replied to the servant girl. "He's wonderful!"

Yolanda busily shook out the flowing skirt of Kit's gown now that she was standing up, making certain it fell properly. "But, *señorita,* I must add that I think he's a very lucky man to have won the heart of one so beautiful as you."

Kit smiled and gave the girl a warm hug, urging her to announce to Danton that she was ready to go downstairs to dinner.

Yolanda nodded her dark head excitedly, and scurried out the door. Kit was left alone to ponder on how Danton's news would be received. If Señora Lucía did not approve, Kit knew she'd be crestfallen. Señora Navarro's opinion was very important to her, and she wondered if the woman had someone else in mind for her son to marry.

Life here at Silvercreek would be unbearable if that was the case!

Chapter 30

How stately she looked sitting there in the rose brocade chair, Danton thought, observing his mother as he entered the parlor. Except for Lucía, he was the only one present. He was almost tempted to announce to her his intention to marry Kit. Only the desire to have Kit with him when he told his mother stopped him.

As Lucía turned toward her son, motherly pride swelled in her bosom. What a strikingly fine figure of a man he was, and how proud Victor would have been at that very minute. She regretted that her husband had been denied that pleasure.

She noticed immediately that Danton had dressed in his finely tailored black pants and a linen shirt, not his usual attire at Silvercreek where he relaxed after the faster paced life in Austin. Again, she was reminded of Victor as Danton strolled into the room. He looked so masculine and virile, as though his body had been molded into the pants and shirt.

She had not noticed in the garden this afternoon, but now her astute eyes perceived that her son's hair had grown longer. She decided to caution him about working too hard. Obviously he had not had time to see his barber. But his face had no hint of weariness. In truth, he had never looked happier or healthier.

"Good evening, Mother. May I say you look most charming in your black gown." He bent down to give her his usual kiss on the forehead.

"You may, my son, and you are especially handsome tonight. I must ask you if you intend to leave in a few minutes to go over to Arthur's for dinner."

"No, I wouldn't think of going over to Cameron's tonight. You're stuck with me," he teased her.

"Well, wonderful! A sherry with me? As you can see we are the only ones down. I can't make any promises for your unpredictable twin, but Delores will be down shortly."

Danton went through the motions of pouring himself a glass of sherry, which he didn't relish at all because he was pondering her remark about Damien. Taking a seat in the chair across from his mother's, he inquired about his twin's erratic habits.

"Doesn't he share the evening meal much?"

Lucía replied, "Sometimes. Then again we may not see him for two or three evenings in a row. Of late, he's been dining here more often."

"Perhaps, you should have a talk with old Santiago. He knows everything that goes on around Silvercreek. If I'm ever in need of news I always go to Santiago."

"I've talked with him, but Damien is a secretive imp where Santiago is concerned. They've never been comrades as you and Santiago have, Danton. We'll speak of this later, son." She heard someone approaching the parlor.

It was Yolanda coming to announce to Danton that Kit was dressed and ready for him to bring her down. Behind Yolanda, Delores and Damien trailed into the parlor, having met at the same time on the second landing.

"She is waiting for you, Señor Danton," Yolanda announced. She had aimed her dark eyes directly in Danton's direction as Delores and Damien had moved on by her as she'd stood in the doorway arch. Oh, it was not that she was unaware of Damien's presence as near as he was to her! She was very aware of him, and his proximity upset her.

She only began to calm down as she trailed the towering figure of Danton Navarro back up the steps to fetch his pretty, waiting lady. Her bad feeling, like a chill, subsided; and her superstitious nature marveled at how swiftly it faded when she was out of the sight of Damien Navarro.

The seventeen-year-old girl had not thought anything about her so-called special powers until she'd been brought here to Silvercreek where the ranch hands swore she had healing powers because of her uncanny knowledge of the right kind of herbs to use in broths and salves. Before she'd just nursed people that way because it was natural. She'd had no awareness that it was some kind of gift.

When her ministrations had aroused so much comment, she'd begun to think about what she did and she'd decided it was a heritage from her half-breed mother. From her Yolanda had learned how to make her tonics and ointments.

But now her dark, olive face and her heart were light and gay. In her soft, accented voice, she exclaimed to Danton Navarro, who was always kind and considerate to her, "She will take your breath away, Señor Danton; she is so beautiful tonight."

He grinned, "I don't doubt that at all, Yolanda. I get the feeling you rather like Señorita Kit, eh?"

"Ah, yes! I enjoy very much doing that lovely hair of hers."

A pleased look lit Danton's face as he remarked to

270

the servant girl following him, "You might give some thought to being her maid in the future. I think Señorita Kit likes you too." He was thinking about his and Kit's future. They'd be leaving Silvercreek soon, and he knew that old Santiago had taken in the girl, Yolanda, some months ago. One of Santiago's relatives had sired the girl with a half-breed woman from a neighboring county. Yolanda had lived all her life in a little settlement just outside Fort Stockton until she'd been brought to Silvercreek after her parents had died within a month of each other.

Although she was an orphan, Yolanda had fared better than she had before at Silvercreek, and the young señor's suggestion that she become the personal maid of Señorita Kit was very attractive to her. Gratefully, she told him so. "Oh, I would be honored, Señor Danton if . . . if she wishes it. If Señora Lucía approves, too."

"We'll see, Yolanda." He politely dismissed her as he turned to enter Kit's bedroom for her services were no longer required. He was taking charge now.

But when he opened the door and saw Kit sitting on the bed, the lovely gown spread out and her beautiful face smiling so sweetly, his knees became weak. From her ears Constantine's magnificent peridot earrings dangled, sparkling brilliantly as the light hit them.

The pink gown seemed to give Kit a rosy glow, or perhaps she was flushed with excitement as he was. He was glad Yolanda had styled her hair so that the earrings could be seen and admired. His eyes danced like firelight over Kit, and before he said a word she knew how pretty she looked tonight.

"You take my breath away, Kit," he murmured, his deep voice laden with emotion.

"Oh, Danton," she let out a pleased sigh.

He came to her, saying no more, and he proceeded to

271

lift her into his arms. His black eyes warm with passion, he whispered, "Mine. You'll always be mine. Now that I've found you I'll never let you go." Then his lips sealed his vow with a kiss.

A wonderful feeling flooded Kit as his arms enclosed her for it was in them that she wished to remain forever. But she didn't have to tell Danton that. The look in her eyes and the love she felt was on her face for him to see.

Their entrance through the parlor arch brought forth varied reactions from the other members of the Navarro family.

Lucía smiled approvingly when she saw Danton with the beautifully gowned Kit in his arms. She was overjoyed to know the young woman would be joining them for dinner.

Delores was less restrained. She let out a shriek of approval, then said, "Kit, I didn't expect to see you down here tonight. How clever of you, Danton, to think of carrying her downstairs."

Damien managed a bland smile, and he remarked, "I am only sorry I didn't think about carrying you down, Kit. I beg your forgiveness."

"You're forgiven, Damien." Kit laughed.

Danton placed her on the settee so he could sit beside her. But Drusilla came in a moment later to announce that dinner was served. With a broad, warm smile on her face, she added, "Nice to have you with us again, señorita." Danton had informed her earlier that Kit would be down for the meal so Drusilla had already set a place for her.

Kit wondered just when Danton would choose to tell his family that he'd asked her to marry him. Possibly, he'd do it at the end of the meal, she figured.

It was nice to eat at the table instead of from a dinner tray in her room. Somehow the food tasted better than it had on a tray. She'd missed the company, and she

272

was enjoying dining by candlelight. Even Lucía's colorful centerpiece of sweet-smelling blossoms delighted her.

But Kit wasn't able to concentrate on the chatter going on around the table. The only thing real or meaningful to Kit was Danton. She and he constantly exchanged glances, and she was so completely magnetized by the overpowering nearness of Danton that no one else existed for her.

Delores was amused by how lovestruck her brother was, and she smiled slyly in her mother's direction.

Damien, too, was cognizant of something in the air. He'd obviously been unaware of just how far the relationship between his twin brother and Kit had gone. He knew the looks they shared were those of lovers. In a way, he found that amusing, and he decided that all was not lost even though the woods incident had not worked out as he'd anticipated.

To make Danton pay in the most painful way and to satisfy his own taste for revenge—surely he could do this through Kit. Why not? he pondered. It had worked with sweet Molly Langford; it could work with Kit.

Damien's face brightened as a wave of excitement flooded his veins. Devious as always, he turned his attention to Kit, remarking, "You are as radiant as a bride tonight. Your bed rest has obviously enhanced your loveliness. Don't you think so, Mother dear?"

Lucía laid her napkin in her lap and agreed with Damien's appraisal. "Yes, Damien, we certainly agree about that, but what made the bed rest necessary still galls me." Lucía let her eyes shift hastily from Damien to Kit. "I've not had a chance to tell you, Kit but they've not turned up one lead from what Santiago was able to tell the sheriff although he took him to the spot where you two were ambushed."

Kit wanted no morbid thoughts or conversation this

evening so she shrugged aside the subject by saying, "I still find it amazing that someone like me or Santiago was a target. Perhaps whoever did it will never be found. Maybe someone daft in the head was just riding through the countryside." She chuckled, hoping to bring a light-hearted touch to the dining table.

"Well, it goes without saying the man who did it was crazy—or stupid—maybe both," Danton's deep voice was harsh and resolute.

Kit had only to look at Danton to know the subject had sent him into a foul mood, and she could detect his hot temper beginning to smolder. She didn't want the evening spoiled. "But Santiago and I are just fine, Danton." Her hand reached out to his on the table. "Let's just be grateful for that."

Her touch softened him. Her slightest wish was his desire tonight, so he smiled and winked at her. Instinctively, she knew what he was about to say.

With her hand clutched in his, he rose slowly. "I think this is the proper time to tell you, my dear family, that I've asked Kit to marry me and she graciously accepted." His black eyes darted down to her smiling, happy face, and like Kit, he waited anxiously for a response.

The exuberant Delores was the first to react. She jumped from her seat and rushed over to hug and kiss Kit. Then she embraced her older brother. "Well, I couldn't have done better if I'd hand-picked your bride, Danton! I just want you to know that." She stood beside her brother, smiling with excitement at his marvelous news.

Lucía, despite her calm serene manner, was just as jubilant as her daughter. Dear God, my prayers have been answered and life is truly good, she silently mused. Delores had most certainly voiced her exact sentiments.

"My son, I think you could not have pleased me more. I don't think I have to tell you, Kit my dear, that I've considered you a part of my family for a long time. But let me say tonight that I already love you and it will be nice to have another daughter."

"Oh, thank you, Señora Lucía," Kit murmured, tears coming to the corners of her eyes. "I—I could not have been treated any better all these many months by my own mother, so you see we have a mutual admiration for one another."

Damien rose from his chair, his wineglass in his hand and a dashingly, handsome smile on his face. "To Kit, a beautiful addition to the Navarro family!"

The others drank to his toast, but Damien remained standing.

"To Danton, who has always had luck on his side!"

Again, everyone sipped the wine, and then there was a light chorus of amused laughter.

In that jester's way of his, Damien sank down onto his chair, and grumbled, "I shall try to not be a sore loser, Danton old boy."

Danton wasn't so sure Damien's clowning was not sincere, but he laughed. "Well, I'll not say I'm sorry, *amigo*. Kit stole my heart long before she ever set eyes on you."

Behind Damien's smiling face, he calculated that his brother was dead wrong about that, but he would let him remain ignorant of that little tidbit.

As the two Navarro twins bandied back and forth, teasing each other, one of those eerie strangenesses flooded over Kit. The black silk scarf on Damien's neck had brought it on. Why? For a fleeting second when she'd casually glanced across the table, she could have sworn she saw it over his face and above it his piercing black eyes. But in the next moment she saw nothing but his tanned, smiling, jesting face.

275

She was like a puppet when she raised her glass to respond to the toast, but when Danton's sensuous lips caressed her cheek she forgot everything but him!

Neither of them noticed Damien's cruel smile, nor could they have known the evil scheme hatching behind the handsome mask of his face, a matching reflection of Danton's.

Chapter 31

News of the betrothal of Kit and Danton Navarro swept over the countryside like a raging fire, and neighboring ranchers and friends came to Silvercreek to congratulate the young couple. It was a golden time for Kit who was showered with attention by friends of the Navarro family. She might have been a nobody, not wanted or cared about, but that didn't matter anymore. The Navarro family would be her family.

She and Danton took long, leisurely strolls, holding hands and discussing their plans for their future. He told her about the acquisition of Whispering Willows, and she was so impressed by Jim Longley's story about his sentimental Laurette that tears came to her eyes.

They also went on a picnic, which Kit suddenly realized they had never done before. She told Danton they'd have to do that more often when they spent time at the little stone cottage on the banks of the Pedernales River.

Kit knew she'd forever consider this a special time in her life, but Lucía had not realized the excitement the announcement of Danton's wedding would stir. She suddenly felt a new zest for life, and thoughts which had been troubling her were swept away. She told Kit that she only hoped old Constantine, the goldsmith the Navarro family prized so highly, would still be able to make the wedding ring Lucía was certain Danton would request of him.

"Someday, my granddaughter will wear those gorgeous earrings you now display, Kit," she remarked, appraising them.

"She may have to wait a long time, Señora Lucía, for I fear I will be selfish about relinquishing them to her," Kit had confessed.

In her light-hearted mood, Lucía then teased Kit, saying she would be a very cautious grandmother and not play favorites where her own cherished pieces of jewelry were concerned.

Kit was in such a blissful state she could hardly believe that Danton had been at Silvercreek a week. When he told her he had to get back to his neglected office in Austin, a crestfallen look appeared on her pretty face.

"After all, *querida,* I'm getting ready to become an old married man," he teased.

"Don't you forget that for a minute, Danton Navarro, while you're so far away from me."

Even though she didn't say it, the glint in her eyes told him she referred to Estellita. For the first time since arriving at Silvercreek, Danton thought about Estellita; about her reaction to his marriage to Kit. There could be one hell of an explosion! Estellita could be vicious!

To Kit, however, he replied, "Your beautiful face is constantly with me, *chiquita.* Constantly! Your love is all I need to make me happy ever. Always remember that. Whether I'm at your side or miles away, you have my heart."

"Oh, Danton! Danton! I love you so very much. I think I would die without your love."

"Then you shall live forever!" he told her, taking her eagerly in his arms and kissing her.

During the week that Danton and Kit had enjoyed their lovers' paradise, Damien had sunk deeper and deeper into the blackest of moods. His brooding and drinking had ended later each night. On the evening before Danton was to return to Austin, Damien had watched the lovers who were in the courtyard garden. Already, he'd drunk generously from the bottle of whiskey he kept in his room.

His mood was a reckless one, enhanced by the bravado initiated by liquor. In one moment of crazy whimsy, he decided, irrationally, to do something he'd wanted to do since the night Kit had broke into song while he played the guitar.

Taking another generous drink from the bottle, he mumbled, "By God, I can do it! I'll bet that red-haired little bitch won't know the difference." He broke into an evil, boisterous laugh in anticipation of his little escapade.

Kit's state of bliss would have been shattered if she'd known the vile plot Damien was hatching as she was saying good night to Danton. She did not, however, and almost as soon as her curly head hit the soft pillows, her eyes became heavy. Her long lashes fluttered once or twice and then they closed in sleep.

A cooling breeze floated through the open windows, and the sheers fluttered gently. The soothing songs of the nightbirds were serene and peaceful, giving no hint of the evil brewing in the Navarro household. Already it was lurking a short distance away from Kit's bedroom door.

Coolly patient and calculating, Damien wanted to make his move at just that right moment. A salacious look on his face, he slowly moved out of his doorway and slipped cautiously down the darkened hallway.

His drunken stupor was not so numbing that he didn't look under each door he passed for a glimmer of light. Satisfied that there was none, he moved on toward his destination.

Noiselessly, he turned the knob of Kit's door, opening it just enough to slide through before quickly closing it. He could have been a prowling cat, his barefeet padded so quietly over to the bed. Underneath his black robe, Damien's finely muscled, naked body was stirred by what he was about to attempt. Arrogance and insatiable resentment ruled him.

The lusty thoughts engulfing him made him smile as he sank down on the bed beside Kit. Her gorgeous hair fanned out over the pillows, and she made a soft kittenish sound as his nude body eased in next to hers and his thighs touched her silken flesh. Damien felt himself swell with instant desire.

She lay slightly on her side, and he shifted her to bring her firm, rounded hips to the front of him. At that moment, Kit's eyelashes fluttered and she became aware of the heated male body against her. Dear God, Danton had come to her as she'd yearned for him to do.

Eager for his love on this last night before he went back to Austin, she moaned out his name and turned over to face him. A husky flow of love words came to her ears as strong arms enclosed her and heated lips captured hers. She could feel the wild pounding of his breast, and the hair on his chest teased her breasts, bared now since he'd pushed the straps of her gown aside.

Kit arched against him sensing the hunger in his kisses and his body for they'd had no chance to steal a private moment alone. Danton was definitely being the impatient lover tonight.

His lips traveled down her throat and sought the hardened tip of one of her breasts and she moaned, letting her arm snake upward to go around his neck.

She heard him give a light chuckle of his pleasure as her fingers trailed through his thick mane of hair, then moved with a lazy motion over the contours of his features, stopping at the corners of his sensuous mouth.

Damien suddenly felt her body go taut. She drew in her breath sharply as though she were gasping for breath. At the same moment, the palms of her hands violently rammed against his chest. Utter revulsion surged through Kit. Her fingertips had not found that telltale scar on Danton's face. All too well, she knew why! It was not Danton but Damien who was making love to her. Outraged, she lashed out at the grinning face staring down at her, her long fingernails deadly as the claws of a wildcat. Then she cursed the man hunched over her.

Her frenzied attack took Damien by surprise. The scratches on his face stung and when he touched his cheek his own blood moistened his fingers. As a shrill voice called him a bastard, he hurriedly leaped from the bed.

"Get out of here, you despicable son of a bitch!" Kit screamed.

Kit didn't have to tell him that for Damien was in a state of panic. He knew those nails of hers had burrowed deep into his handsome cheek. All numbness of the liquor had left him, and his head was miraculously clear of any deceptive bravery. He could have been a frightened young tot as he scrambled to the safety of his room to survey the damage done to his face.

Once his door was closed, gasping and trembling, he lit the lamp, turning it only high enough to see himself

281

in the mirror. Four furrows scarred his face and he frantically dampened a wash cloth to wipe the oozing blood away. He speculated on the possibility of being permanently scarred for life and he cursed the whore who'd done this to him. Only after he'd sunk dejectedly into a chair did he realize that he had to get away from Silvercreek before dawn broke. He couldn't encounter anyone around the ranch for awhile. If he did his life wouldn't be worth a cent.

He'd take refuge up at the cabin he knew about for a few days. He'd leave a note on the credenza in the hall, telling his mother some concocted tale. In a few days, his face would surely not look the way it did now.

He could always explain it away when he returned from the shack by saying he'd tangled with a mountain cat. By all that's holy, he'd felt like a damned wildcat had jumped on him when Kit had lashed out at him like some she-devil. Even in the dark room, he could have sworn he'd seen green fire shoot out of her eyes.

He still could not understand how she knew he wasn't Danton. Dear Lord, she'd been so eager and willing for him to kiss and caress her. Her body had undulated so sensuously, his for the taking. It never entered his mind that the scar on Danton's lower cheek was the clue that had given him away.

Such a little thing, but for Kit it was a world of difference between the man she loved with all her heart and the man who was to be her brother-in-law. For one brief second, she had felt she was going mad!

The sprawling, spacious house was dark. It appeared to be peaceful and quiet, its occupants asleep. At least, that was what the wandering Santiago thought as he ambled around his cottage at the midnight hour as he often did when sleep evaded him.

Such was not the case for two people in the house, however. Damien hurriedly flung on his shirt; then he drew on his pants. Gathering a few other odd pieces of clothing and a jacket, he made ready for a swift departure from Silvercreek.

Kit, meanwhile, pulsed with a need as urgent. She'd attempted to wash away Damien's kisses and caresses, but doing that was not enough to quiet her tormented soul. Only one thing could soothe her—the healing balm of Danton's strong arms. She desperately wanted them around her.

With her wrapper clutched tightly about her, she tiptoed barefooted down the long hallway. When she opened the door to Danton's bedroom, the moonlight illuminated his face, and the mere sight of him had a calming effect on her.

She sank down on the bed beside him, snuggling next to his still body like a forlorn kitten. The assuring warmth of his closeness calmed her immediately.

Only then, because she felt safe, did Kit allow the tears to flow. As she lay looking at the face of the man she loved, instead of the face of the man who'd been in her room only minutes ago, her trembling subsided.

Tomorrow, she'd think about the nightmarish incident that had just occurred. For now, she wanted only to lie beside Danton.

Chapter 32

His long, muscled body stretched languidly between the bed sheets. He was in limbo, slightly awake and yet still dazed with sleep, but certainly aroused. What a fantastic erotic dream he'd been having about his little goddess of love! It came as no shock to Danton for she was the last thing on his mind before his eyes had grown heavy with sleep. On this, his last night at Silvercreek, he'd yearned more than anything to make love to her but somehow the announcement of their marriage had made a secret interlude harder to manage.

He flung his strong arm out across the bed, and felt flesh, no sheet or pillow. It was softer and more silken than any bed he'd ever lain on. Danton's rippling muscles flexed. His long-lashed eyes opened wide, and he drawled disbelievingly, "*Querida* . . . do I dare to hope this is not a dream?"

In a faltering murmur, she asked, "Are you angry?"

He chuckled. "Angry? Ah, Kit! I dreamed of holding you like this tonight. Now you're in my arms where I want you." It made Danton swell with passion to know she yearned for him so intensely she could not resist coming to his room. What a little jewel he had in this

284

woman—a rare, exquisite jewel!

He pulled her close to him, her body fitting to his as his hungry lips sought hers. The soft, sweetness of her mouth was like nectar.

As forcefully as she'd rejected Damien's intimate caresses, she now pressed against Danton wanting to absorb the whole of him and to be filled with the essence of this man. Suddenly engulfed by raw passion, she clung to him, feeling his strong hands move up and down her back, tingling with excitement as his strong thighs encased her.

How strong his thighs felt as they pressed around her legs, their touch searing her flesh. His lips touched her face ever so lightly as he whispered, "Can't get that sweet body of yours close enough. You feel so good, Kit—so very good."

The clusters of the hair on his chest tickled and titillated her breasts as they lay pressed together, his male body powerful and demanding. She knew well the intense desire pulsing through him, and it made her own need mount.

Her body cried out to be filled by him, and fired by her own passion, she flung her leg around his firm, muscled ones. At that moment Danton knew she was surely the most wildly, exciting woman his arms had ever held.

"Ah, chiquita—chiquita! Yes! Yes!" he moaned as her soft body enclosed him. Tonight, that golden body was going to know the depth of his love. No part of it would go untouched. His tongue sought to tease and taunt her until Kit felt giddy, frenzied by the magnificent magic he created.

"Dear God, Danton!" she moaned, amazed by this unknown rapture devouring her whole being. She was now the greedy one for her whole body was burning. Never had she known such sweet, sweet agony!

His mouth was magic, creating new and wonderful sensations which made her gasp with pleasure. She cried out from sheer ecstasy as their mounting passion carried her to boundless rapture.

"Ah, *querida* . . . you are such a woman of delight!" Danton rasped, his own desire blazing and building.

No longer could he resist burrowing himself in her velvet softness. He had to feel her flames consume him. Kit arched with greedy eagerness, undulating her flushed body to match the sensuous tempo of Danton's. The rushing, rampaging river of their passion carried them more and more swiftly, around one bend and on to another. Finally, they reached the edge of love's precipice and tumbled into space, plunging down as though in a cascading waterfall.

Their descent had left them breathless, but a sweet languor flooded through them and they were now content to idle in still water. What a rapturous river they'd traveled down!

Danton enjoyed the sweet feel of her as she slept in his arms for the next few hours. It did not matter that her curly head rested on a muscle, making his arm ache now that he'd roused. But he knew he had to get her back to her room before dawn broke, much as he detested the idea of parting from her.

Danton Navarro knew theirs would be no long engagement!

He slipped into his pants, knowing what he must do. Then he opened the door of his room to make certain that no one was in the hallway. All was still as he quickly lifted the sleeping Kit in his arms and hastily scurried down the hall with her.

He placed her on her bed, and when he bent down to plant a kiss on her lips, she purred kittenishly. Her long lashes fluttered but her eyes did not open. Danton smiled down on her. He knew he'd cherish the memory of how she looked at this moment, fondly carrying it with him while he was away from her.

By the time Kit woke three hours later, Danton was well on his way to Austin. She had awakened with a bit of a shock when Yolanda entered the room, for it was a moment before Kit realized that Danton had brought her back to her own bedroom sometime during the early morning hours.

Another detail put her into a quandary: he had forgotten to put her nightgown back on her. She lay with her shoulders bare and exposed. When she'd heard Yolanda opening the door, she'd frantically jerked the sheet up to cover herself, but Yolanda's perceptive eyes had not missed her attempt to hide the fact that she was obviously nude under the sheet. In fact, the Mexican girl did her best to hide her amusement. After all, last night had been Señor Danton's last at Silvercreek before his return to Austin so it didn't shock or surprise Yolanda that these lovers would seek to have a romantic rendezvous. A hot-blooded young couple like Señor Danton and Señorita Kit must surely enjoy many torrid moments, she thought.

"Would you like me to bring you a breakfast tray this morning, Señorita Kit, or would you rather go downstairs?" Yolanda cleverly asked.

"I'd like a tray, Yolanda. Yes, I'd like that very much, I think," Kit replied quickly. Yolanda turned to leave the room, a broad grin on her face. She did not doubt that by the time she returned Señorita Kit's gown would be covering her bare body.

She could not suppress a giggle as she agilely skipped down the steps and headed down the tiled hall toward the kitchen. As she burst through the kitchen door, the busy Drusilla demanded, "Well, what happened to you, Yolanda, to give you such a glowing, smiling face?"

Swishing her long floral skirt playfully and looking

287

like the cat who'd swallowed the canary, the servant girl replied, "Oh, Drusilla, how I wish it was me something exciting was happening to. But it isn't me!"

Slapping her dish towel down on the counter and feeling impatient with the frivolous girl who was so saucy and full of life this morning, Drusilla grumbled, "Well, I've got a couple of chores which might just excite you, missy."

A giggling Yolanda gave Drusilla's chubby waistline a hug. "I'll do them for you, Dru, just as soon as I return from taking Señorita Kit's breakfast tray to her. All right?"

The girl buzzed around the kitchen like a bee before flying back out the door. As it closed, Drusilla shook her head and broke into a smile. The Navarro household is on one of its hectic schedules this morning, she thought.

The young *señor* had swept through her kitchen to gulp down a hastily sipped cup of coffee. Neither Señorita Delores nor Kit had come to the breakfast table. Señora Lucía had preferred a tray in her room. God only knew about Señor Damien because as yet she had not seen hide nor hair of him!

She puttered and fumed, examining the possibility that age was catching up with her after all her years of service here at Silvercreek. Lord, the years did come and go so quickly!

Then an arrogant look came onto her round face, and to the empty kitchen she mumbled, "They'd be lost without me—couldn't do it without me!" The truth was Drusilla would be lost if she wasn't playing mother hen to the Navarro family as she'd done for over twenty years.

Drusilla was not the only one who'd not seen hide nor hair of Damien Navarro this morning. Damien had ridden away from Silvercreek as fast as his black stallion would carry him, heading southward toward Cienega Mountains. How long he'd be gone he didn't know as he galloped down the drive leading him away from the dark house and his family. The desperate need to be far away from Silvercreek was Damien's overpowering obsession as he hastily gathered a few articles of clothing and then slipped out of the house to the barn.

He'd left a hastily scribbled note to his mother on the hall credenza, a habit he'd gotten into when he'd started taking off some years ago.

Having found it there when she'd emerged from her quarters to go about her morning chores, Drusilla had placed it on the señora's breakfast tray. The house-keeper didn't know which of the twins had left the message.

As Danton journeyed toward the east, Damien rode to the south. His real destination was not old Mack's cabin as he'd stated in his message to his mother. He wanted the solitude of the shack up in the Cienega Mountains, the shack he and Dake Davenport had stumbled on a couple of years ago. Its remoteness appealed to Damien, for he had some thinking to do. He never doubted that if Kit told Danton what he'd done his life wasn't worth two cents. But would she? Would she be too embarrassed to confess just how far she'd allowed him to go? He had lain next to her luscious naked body and kissed those sweet, sensuous lips. His hands had fondled her supple breasts and by God, she'd been aroused by his touch. She'd be lying if she denied that his touch had not made her liquid fire flow. Damned if he knew what had dampened her passion and made her become an ice maiden!

His curiosity about that would plague him for a long time to come.

Nothing plagued Danton Navarro as he got closer

and closer to his destination. One of the first items on his agenda once he'd arrived in Austin was a visit to the goldsmith's shop. He wanted Kit's wedding ring to be a Constantine creation.

The other item on his mind was the restoration of the stone cottage, Whispering Willows. With some additions and renovations, it would be a livable home. He was a young man, dreaming of his future and of the beautiful lady he planned to share it with. Not once had he thought about his political aspirations or his law practice, he realized with amazement.

By the time the sun was sinking in the Texas sky Danton had reached his destination, but his twin brother had not. Damien had decided to make camp for the night before continuing the steep, rugged climb to the secluded shack above in the mountains. A shimmering purple haze was already shrouding the countryside below him.

He and his black stallion were weary for Damien had driven the horse and himself long and hard. The idea of making his campsite by the small creek whose cool waters flowed down from the mountain appealed to him. He recalled that a short stroll up the creek led to deeper water and a swim would be nice before eating and crawling into his bedroll.

By the late afternoon hour, Damien had relaxed because of the miles he'd put between him and Silvercreek. Now, he felt a certain kind of exhilaration in the deepening solitude of the mountainous terrain.

When he'd seen to the tether of the stallion and taken his gear to the spot where he planned to bed down for the night, he took the silver flask from his saddlebag and drank generously of the whiskey. Its pleasant, soothing effect made him take another swig, and then he flung his black flat-crowned hat carelessly over atop his bedroll. He let out a light-hearted gust of laughter as he unbuttoned his shirt to strip down to his pants.

Then, flask in his hand, he sauntered down the pebbled path bordering the creek whose clear waters rippled along slowly and unhurriedly. He didn't have to walk too far before the creek branched into a stream of much deeper water. Beside it, Damien took off his pants, and he laid the flask on top of them.

As his muscled, naked body let the cool waters wash over him, his torment and anger seemed to wash away too. He dipped his face and head into the water, raising up to shake his head vigorously. His fingers ran through his thick black hair sweeping it back from his face. God, he felt great!

In this little paradise, in his little mountain retreat, he planned to forget about the formidable Danton and what he might do when he found out what Damien had tried to do to Kit. Out here he was free from the devastating torment of Kit's presence. No one at Silvercreek knew about this little hideaway.

Madre de Dios, he didn't even have to listen to the whining and nagging of Molly Langford every time they lay in that hayloft together! If that cute little blonde thought he was going to marry her she was mad!

Caramba, he'd never go back to Silvercreek, not if it meant marrying Molly Langford!

Part III

The Fury

Chapter 33

Here in Texas, the autumn day was as warm as a summer day elsewhere, and the flowers seemed to be in their fullest, most colorful bloom as Lucía took her leisurely stroll in the garden courtyard. She didn't know where the young ladies were or what they were doing. Most likely they were sequestered, chattering about their two young men.

Lucía was pleased that Kit and Delores were so close. She smiled, thinking about the two of them and all their romantic talk—Kit praising Danton and Delores oohing and aahing over Ramon Valdez. Oh, it was wonderful to be young and in love! Yes, she could envy them and yearn to live it all over again!

She halted along the flagstone path to lift her deep blue, sprigged muslin skirt so she might lean over to pluck a huge golden aster which caught her eye.

Clutching the stem in her hand she ambled on her way. Across the garden, the barnyard cat was being attacked by two angry bluejays. As Lucía watched they swept down on the fleeing tomcat and she exploded with laughter.

Just then, the sound of pounding hooves alerted Lucía Navarro to the approach of riders. She wondered who her visitors might be as she began to walk back toward the courtyard gate. Whoever they were, they'd been coming in at a furious gallop and that whetted Lucía's curiosity.

By the time she reached the gate, Joe Langford had dismounted and was coming through it. The three men accompanying him were still mounted, and Lucía recognized them as his hired men. In fact, they were three of his roughest, toughest-looking ranch hands. One of the burly, solemn-faced men was the half-breed, Lucía noticed. She knew Langford always praised that man highly. He was the one Langford called Hawk.

Instinct told Lucía that this was no social visit her old friend was paying. All she had to do was observe the men's expressions to know that, especially the ire on Joe Langford's ruddy face. These were angry, riled men.

A wiry, small-boned man, but tough as nails, Joe Langford had an iron determination that Lucía admired. For as long as she'd been in this part of Texas, she'd either known or heard her beloved Victor praise his old friend, Joe Langford.

"Mornin' to you, Lucía," he greeted her, taking off his old weather-beaten hat.

"Good morning, Joe. Good to see you on this beautiful day. Isn't it glorious?"

Joe's fury could not be concealed, but he tried to gentle it for Lucía's sake for it was not directed at her. "Lucía, my dear . . . I fear you won't think the day so beautiful when we get through talking, but talk we must." He took her arm to guide her back into the garden area and out of the earshot of his men.

Lucía's brow lifted skeptically and she searched the weathered face of Langford as they walked to the bench under the large oak tree.

"But for your sake, Lucía, I wouldn't have wasted a

296

minute to explain anything. You know my great respect for you . . . and God rest Victor's soul."

A puzzled look was on her face. "Of course, Joe. We are friends—friends for years."

"Damn I know it!" He shook his head and clenched his fists, such desperate frustration was filling him. "I can't make this come out easy for you, Lucía. Hell fire, I can't do it so I'll just tell you what I'm going to do. I met Santiago a minute or two ago as we were riding over, so I know Damien isn't here. I'm tracking him down, Lucía. I'm tracking him—and there's going to be a shotgun wedding, come hell or high water!"

"Wedding, Damien? You . . . you've got to mean Molly then?" She hesitated for her mind was befuddled and confused at that moment.

"That's right, Lucía. There's no way I'll stand still and let Molly bring shame to the name of Langford. Pardon me, Lucía, but not even a Navarro bastard is worth that. So Damien will marry her—or I'll kill him, so help me!"

She bowed her head and reached for his wrinkled, tanned hand, patting it. She said nothing for a moment or two. She didn't have to ask whether Langford was certain Damien was the father of Molly's expected baby. She knew it was probably just as Joe said.

When she finally raised her sad dark eyes to gaze at him all she could say was, "I'm sorry, Joe. So very sorry. I can't fault you or your feelings."

"Oh, hell, Lucía," Langford moaned, obviously in anguish. "Damn it, I don't like this at all."

"I understand, Joe. I understand. Victor would have been the same if he were alive and it happened to Delores."

Joe Langford always had respect for Señora Navarro, but he had even more on this day. She was one fine, genteel lady!

"Lucía . . . don't you fret for a minute that I'd kill your son." He gave her a hug around her shoulders. "Now, I ain't promising I won't scare the cocky rascal a bit. You wouldn't hold that against me, would you?"

Lucía managed a weak smile for her old friend. "I won't hold that against you at all, Joe. We . . . we grandparents must stick together, mustn't we?"

"We will, Lucía. We will surely do that." Langford rose from the bench, his hat in his hand. Then, in a gallant gesture, which surprised and amazed Lucía, Joe Langford bowed like a cavalier and remarked, "Lucía Navarro, I think it's time I told you what a fine, remarkable lady I think you are. Victor Navarro had to be the luckiest son of a gun in the state of Texas."

She said nothing. She didn't have to speak, for her lovely smile expressed her thanks to Joe Langford. Long after his departure, Lucía remained in the quiet solitude of her garden. Later, during the evening meal, as she dined with the two younger ladies, she did not mention the purpose of Joe Langford's visit to Silvercreek.

Almost two weeks would pass before Lucía Navarro would set eyes on Damien again. When the buggy came up the drive bearing him and his new bride, Molly, his black stallion hitched to the back of the rig, Lucía asked no questions of her son.

True to his words, Joe Langford had tracked him down, and some sort of legal marriage had been performed to satisfy Molly's father. Now, Damien was forced to bring his bride to Silvercreek, and Lucía had only to look at the shy Molly to feel very sorry for her. There would be no happiness from this union. It had been made only to legalize the poor baby soon to be born. Lucía was filled with compassion for the girl.

When Damien excused himself to take his gear

298

upstairs, Lucía invited Molly to join her in the back sitting room and she graciously welcomed the girl into the Navarro family. In a gentle voice she tried to assure the young bride of her welcome at Silvercreek. "I'm so very proud to have you for my daughter-in-law, Molly dear."

Molly's blue eyes gleamed with mist as she told Lucía, "I'm so glad you approve, Señora Navarro. I . . . I was afraid maybe you wouldn't."

Lucía affectionately hugged Molly, aware of her need for assurance. "Mercy, such a pretty little thing as you! Why Molly, I've known you all your life and I couldn't be happier. If that son of mine doesn't treat you right I'll kick him out of the house."

Señora Navarro's jesting actually brought some subdued laughter from Molly, but Lucía was far more serious than Molly could know. She did not consider Damien's behavior humorous.

In a state of amazement, Molly Langford Navarro sat there with that charming lady who was her new mother-in-law. Her tenseness was easing, and it was Lucía Navarro who'd made that happen, certainly not her new husband. Damien's surly manner had depressed her. But she was feeling more positive now.

As they talked and drank the coffee Drusilla served them, Lucía had no idea just how much she'd done for this desolate young girl.

"Why, Molly, you'll be astounded at the miracles we'll perform on Damien by putting our two heads together." Lucía was consoling her still.

"Señora Lucía, you've already performed a miracle and I do thank you from the bottom of my heart," Molly declared, a warm smile on her face. "You've made me feel so welcome here at Silvercreek."

"You are a Navarro now, Molly. Remember that, my dear." Lucía patted the girl's dainty hands.

Damien, Lucía mused, will do well to bear that in mind.

Damien had stormed upstairs to drop off his gear. That gave him an excuse to avoid spending time seated by his new bride while they chatted with his mother. He didn't need her eyes undressing him, laying him bare. He still had the telltale signs of Kit's long, raking fingernails on his handsome face. Oh, the ugly redness was gone, but the little furrows were still noticeable.

He thanked God when they'd arrived that Delores and Kit hadn't been present along with his mother. At least, he had not been subjected to their two smirking faces. When he entered his room, the thought of putting up with Molly night after night was abhorrent to him.

The mere thought of her made him stand in the center of his room and snarl. Already, he was thinking about how he'd ease the pain of having her around. He'd be spending many late nights in town at the saloon and in the rooms above it with little María or Margie.

He sauntered over to the chest and opened the drawer to get the bottle of whiskey he kept there. Opening it, he took a generous sip. Then he sat down on the bed, and took another sip of whiskey because he needed it. His fist slammed the bag he'd just tossed on the bed.

"That damned Langford! That old son of a bitch is going to rue the day he forced me to marry his daughter!" he muttered angrily.

He also cursed Langford's half-breed whose damned sniffing nose had tracked him with such expertise. But Damien could not overlook the fact that he'd made one stop along the way which had most likely sent them in his direction. If he hadn't done that, the bastards would never have found him sleeping soundly in his bedroll by the creek at that early morning hour. If he'd gone up into the mountains and not lingered by the creek, he would have heard four riders coming up the steep mountainside.

When he finally moved off the bed and prepared to leave his room, a smoldering volcano of emotion churned within him. He was ready to lash out at anything in his path.

A deafening reverberation made Kit whirl around as she left her room. Immediately, she realized that Damien had emerged from his room and given the door a mighty slam. She thought of hastening back to her own room and securing the door. The feeling that she should gnawed at her, but her daring spirit said otherwise.

She crossed the few feet to the stairway, but in that brief space of time, Damien's long striding steps had brought him to her. He stood, towering menacingly in front of her. His black eyes glared down at her, a lascivious gleam in them, and a lustful smirk twisted his mouth.

The full impact of his raging fury was on his face, and Kit was truly frightened!

Chapter 34

The four small lines etching Damien's tanned face were a grim reminder of the night he'd intruded on her bed, and for a fleeting second, Kit could not move. Fright did not remain with her long, however, for her own fury mounted as she looked into his face. She turned her back on him to close her still-open door, ignoring him. It was Damien who should be apologizing to her after such a disgusting display of behavior, Kit reasoned.

But she had hardly reached for the knob when her small body felt the strong force of his hand push her, without a hint of gentleness, back into the room. Her hip scraped the wood frame of the door and she reacted immediately by demanding, "What the devil do you think you're doing, Damien?"

A lusty smile lit his face, "I'll show you, *chiquita!*" He surged toward her, an evil chuckle escaping from his lips.

Kit knew he wanted to inflict pain on her. His objective was plainly written on his face, yet she felt helpless against his brute strength and the wildness of his manner. She had never seen this side of Damien before.

"Dear God, Damien . . . have you gone mad?" Kit shrieked frantically.

The answer she received was a savage blow of his open hand as he struck her across the side of her head. Kit swayed.

"You . . . you are crazy!" she choked out, her head wobbling as she spoke. But her words riled him even more, and he raised his hand to inflict more pain on the auburn-haired woman whose defiant eyes glared at him with such bold insolence. He was determined to humble her.

"You've done nothing but cause me trouble since the day I laid eyes on you, you whore!" Damien hissed.

A split second before he struck her, Kit thought of a rattlesnake. Then under the force of the second blow she sank to the floor, overcome by a stunning spell of weakness she'd not experienced with the first harsh slap to the other side of her face. Her thick hair had somehow cushioned the first one. Instinct told her not to rile him further or he would surely kill her.

But an urge more powerful, one she could not control, struck her. A new, bold person suddenly replaced the crumpled, petite girl sitting on the floor. Her soft voice spoke in a positive, direct manner leaving no shred of apprehension on her part. "You . . . you are the one I saw at the Crystal Castle. You are the black-haired man who abducted me from my home in El Paso."

A stunned look came to Damien's face, but he drew forth every ounce of will power he possessed. "And just who are you?" he asked, his heart pounding erratically.

"You know who I am! I'm Kristina Whelan from El Paso."

For a few minutes, Damien was like a man floundering in deep water. The sight of her perplexed him. There was a certain air of tranquility on her face as

303

though she were alone in a private little world.

"No, *chiquita*. I hate to disappoint you, but you are wrong about one thing. It was Danton, not me, in El Paso. I've never been there."

"You lie, Damien." Her voice was harsh and stern.

"I know you want to believe that because you love him and you think he loves you. Danton never loved you or anyone else. He's cool and calculating. That's why he and Estellita make the perfect pair. If he does eventually marry you, that won't stop his relationship with her."

"You're the devil's spawn, Damien Navarro!" Kristina spat at him.

"Ah, I may well be, but what I say is true. You're naïve, Kristina my sweet. Why do you think Danton wants to marry you? It is because a wife can't testify against her husband. Do you think for a minute that Danton isn't smart enough to have figured out that you could ruin his political ambitions if your memory returned and you recognized him? God, Kit—or pardon me, I should say Kristina now—Danton is a shrewd bastard. That's why he's a lawyer and I'm just the fun-loving caballero."

Damien's spirits surged when he saw that his cunning scheme was working. Kristina was thinking about what he'd said.

"That is something for you to think about, Kristina. I had to even the score with you for those vicious scratches you gave, no? You see, *chiquita,* my only guilt is wanting to love you." Damien was rather enjoying himself as he used his old familiar charm on this very vulnerable young lady. "You see, Kristina, I fell in love with you when Danton introduced us here at Silver-creek."

He turned on his booted heels and exited the room, leaving her on the floor to stare at empty space. An evil grin remained on his face as he slowly ambled down the hall toward the stairs. He was so elated he could now challenge the indomitable Señora Lucía Navarro.

A deep throaty chuckle broke from his throat as he took the first step.

Yolanda stood in the hallway, prostrate because she was helpless to do anything for Señorita Kit. She had chanced to come out of one of the rooms in time to witness Damien pushing Kit back into her room, and she knew that trouble brewed.

She'd listened outside the closed door because of her deep concern for the pretty *señorita*. She genuinely liked Kit. As she listened, the depth of her hate for Damien intensified.

When she had heard Damien go down the steps, she slipped out of the alcove in the hall and took the liberty to enter Kit's room without knocking. Her heart broke to find the pretty lady lying on the floor and dissolved into tears. She rushed to comfort her and take Kit in her arms. "Oh, *señorita* . . . if only I could have helped you. Ohhhh!"

Kit cried and cried until she felt drained inside, and she made no move to leave Yolanda's consoling embrace. But even as she wept, thinking all the time how easily her happiness had been marred by Damien's revelation, she decided what she must do. It tore her apart to leave, but she must not remain at Silvercreek. Without Danton's love, there was nothing here for her.

When her tears ceased, she finally looked into Yolanda's concerned face. Then she wiped her eyes and heaved a deep sigh.

"Yolanda, I need your help. Will you help me?"

"Oh, *señorita,* you know that without asking. What can I do that would help you? You just tell Yolanda and it will be done."

"All right. Listen carefully. Promise me, Yolanda, that you will do exactly as I say." When the young servant girl nodded her assent, Kristina continued. "I want you to fetch me a tray for dinner. Just tell the *señora* that my ankle is troubling me slightly. Make it sound convincing, but not drastic. I cannot possibly see the *señora* this evening. In case she does come up, I shall leave my hair loose so I can sweep it over this left cheek, if I must. My right side is passable. It is the left side of my poor head that got the brunt of Damien's hand."

"Oh, that will be no problem, and perhaps, having a new daughter-in-law here tonight will occupy the *señora.*"

"But, Yolanda, that is only one minor detail. I've more to ask of you."

"Sí, señorita?"

"I must leave here tonight. If you heard everything then you know that I've regained my memory. I must get back to my home in El Paso just as soon as possible. For reasons I cannot go into, I intend to leave just as soon as I can slip out of the house."

As Kristina's mind was churning, so was the little Yolanda's head whirling with ideas. "I will help you, Señorita Kit. Oh . . . you must be patient with me, *señorita*. It will take me awhile to get used to calling you Señorita Kristina."

"I fear we won't have that much time, my dear little friend." Kristina Whelan smiled sweetly at the servant who'd been so kind to her. She had no inkling of what little Yolanda had already been conjuring up in that busy head of hers.

"I'm honored, *señorita,* that you consider me a friend. I . . . I feel that you are my friend too. We are very good friends, *sí?"* Her dark, warm eyes sparkled

306

brilliantly and she smiled sweetly at Kit.

Kit patted her hand and laughed softly. *"Sí, Yolanda.* We are very good friends. Now, let me tell you what I need you to do once it is dark outside."

Then Kristina told Yolanda of her hastily concocted plan to be gone from Silvercreek before this night ended. As she did so she suddenly became aware of the excitement sparking in Yolanda, and when the girl began to speak Kristina knew why.

"Oh, we will make it, *señorita.* I know we will!"

"Yolanda! Yolanda! What do you mean by 'we'?"

"Oh, *señorita,* please let me come with you. We are friends, *sí?* I have no one here—not a dear friend like you. I will work so hard for you and my presence, even though I'm not very big, will add to your safety. It can be very dangerous for a pretty lady to travel alone."

"But, Yolanda, I don't—"

"Oh, please . . . please! I have nothing to keep me here after you leave. You would be doing me the greatest favor."

For a moment, Kristina said nothing. But at a busy place like the Crystal Castle she knew there had to be some job for a girl like Yolanda, and she sincerely wanted to come with her. Furthermore, what Yolanda had said was true, even a maid traveling with her mistress provided some protection.

"All right, Yolanda. You get your things together, and while the Navarros dine we shall make our getaway from the house. They'll think that I'm dining up here in my room, and knowing their evening routine as I do, my absence might not be discovered until morning."

"I have little to take, *señorita.* But I'll go now and prepare my bundle before Drusilla sets me to doing some chores. Then we can be ready to go swiftly, yes?"

"Yes . . . and Yolanda, I will have a letter for you to place later in Señor Danton's room, along with

307

two others."

Yolanda gave an excited nod of her dark head before she bounced excitedly out through the door. Kristina gave her a warm smile; then, without further ado, she turned to her little writing desk to compose the letters she intended to leave behind when she left Silvercreek.

The first was easy to write. It was addressed to Señora Lucía Navarro. It read:

> Dear Señora Lucía:
> Forever, my heart will be filled with the deepest affection and love for you. I will never be able to repay your kindness to me.
> Forgive me for leaving this way, but it was necessary.
>
> Sincerely,
> Kit

Kristina deliberately did not sign her message to Lucía as Kristina Whelan, nor did she sign Danton's letter with her real name. She signed only Damien's letter as Kristina. Damien Navarro already knew who she was, but he had good reason to conceal that fact.

But she sensed that something was jumbled in this crazy puzzle, and her head whirled with conflicting feelings. Perhaps, it was she who was not thinking straight now that her memory was restored. She strained, trying to recall the conversation she'd had with Damien Navarro, but his words were lost in all the confusion of this harrowing day.

"It matters not," she mumbled to herself as she moved around the room. "I must get home and see Momma." Suddenly it dawned on her that all these long months her dear mother must have thought she was dead! That realization made her desire for a hasty departure from Silvercreek even more urgent, but she knew she must wait until darkness came to the Texas countryside.

Thinking of Yolanda's remark about having little to take, Kristina packed very few things for she'd come to Silvercreek with only what she'd had on her back. Tears came to her eyes as she reluctantly removed the peridot earrings Danton had given to her, but she intended to leave them behind.

Now, she knew why the little peridot ring was so cherished by her. She could recall the occasion when it was given to her—her birthday.

One memory recalled another, each a link in Kristina's past. Throughout the remainder of the afternoon into the twilight hour, these recollections engulfed the girl named Kit, who often scrutinized herself in the mirror to look at Kristina.

Oh, dear Lord, it was so glorious to be able to say her name and to remember all the people so dear to her— the devoted Solitaire and Cara, Sid and Jason.

Having the past to dwell on made the present easier to bear. As for the future, Kristina gave a happy-go-lucky shrug of her shoulders and then murmured, "Time will have to decide that!"

Chapter 35

Silvery moonlight gleamed down on the winding dirt road the little gig traveled, lighting the trail for them. "Borrowing" the gig from the Navarros didn't set well with Kristina. She felt a pang of guilt about that. She promised herself that she'd find a way to right that wrong, but she could not allow herself to fret about that now. She had to get home to El Paso.

She took the route Yolanda had suggested, not the one she'd planned to take. It seemed a wiser choice. Since the Navarro lands lay halfway between the towns of Pecos and Fort Stockton, Yolanda had felt they should catch the early morning stagecoach westward bound. It would carry them directly to El Paso, from Fort Stockton.

"If they discover us gone, Señorita Kit, it will be to Pecos they'll ride. I feel most strongly we should go south instead of north when we get to the bend just ahead. I truly do!"

Kristina could not take the serious look on Yolanda's face lightly. "I'll do as you say, Yolanda, if you feel that's the best way."

"Oh, yes. I do!"

"South we shall go." Kristina managed to laugh

lightly, even though the two of them were starting out on what might be considered a reckless venture for two young women. "Besides, I've heard of your powers with herbs and your uncanny instincts. I must take the suggestion seriously."

"Oh, I lay no claims to any powers. I just do what comes easily for me, and if it works or helps someone, I'm very grateful and happy," Yolanda replied.

Both young women were dressed in dark clothing. Kristina had worn her black riding ensemble and a soft cotton blouse. Atop her head she'd placed the wide-brimmed, flat-crowned hat, and she wore her hair in double coils at the nape of her neck. Yolanda had on a comfortable batiste blouse and a calico skirt with a black design printed on it. A black shawl covered her tiny shoulders, and her long black hair was braided into two plaits.

Nevertheless, the pair could not help being conspicuous if anyone observed them. Two women did not travel about at night.

Yolanda's instincts proved to be on target. When they arrived at Fort Stockton and left the Navarros' gig at the livery, from which Kit arranged to have it returned to Silvercreek in a few days' time, they had little time to wait before boarding the early morning stage.

When they rolled away from the depot in the coach, Kristina leaned back against the back of the seat, suddenly realizing just how weary she was. It had been an exhausting twenty-four hours. It seemed that one life had faded and a new one had been born, she mused thoughtfully as her eyelids became heavy with sleep.

Yolanda sat looking out over the countryside. She, too, thought about the new life and world into which she was venturing. She was far too excited to sleep— just yet! But she folded the old worn shawl and tucked it behind her head. She silently thought that she'd have died if the *señorita* had refused to allow her to come along.

Yolanda only regretted to leave dear old Santiago. But the tremendous threat that Damien Navarro would have his way with her—it no longer existed. That was enough to delight her!

But there came a time when the quiet of the stagecoach and the soothing movement lulled Yolanda. She relaxed and laid her head back against the seat, letting the rhythmic swaying of the stage induce sleep. The little Mexican servant was very happy.

For the next several hours the stage made poor time for it traveled that winding road through the Barillo Mountains. No passengers boarded the stage when it made two brief stops, but it was not until they'd stopped at the town of Van Horn to switch to a fresh team of horses that the stage was occupied by anyone other than Kristina and Yolanda.

The two young women had a ravenous appetite as they ate the simple fare that the station house offered. Then they walked around a bit before journeying the next long stretch to their destination.

Kristina was now feeling as elated as her little companion, for it seemed that the long journey home was going smoothly. She was well aware that many things could have gone wrong.

She hugged Yolanda impulsively and then laughed, "We've done it, Yolanda. Thanks to you! I couldn't have managed without you. I'm glad you had the money for our passage on the stagecoach. I'm beholden to you, Yolanda, and I'll pay you back when we get to El Paso."

This declaration was music to Yolanda's ears and she excitedly exclaimed, "I'm glad too, Señorita Kristina! So very glad!" It dawned on her a second later that

312

she'd called her mistress Kristina twice now, and she suddenly said, "See, it was easy after all, *señorita*."

"Oh, Yolanda, I'm realizing many things about you. I've no doubt I'll find you a jewel to have around."

Kristina was really glad she'd brought little Yolanda with her for the girl's presence had kept her from thinking about her unconventional departure from Silvercreek. Maybe the presence of poor, pathetic Molly would so occupy Lucía that that kind woman wouldn't have time to feel too harshly toward Kit. Oh, Kristina prayed that would be so. Señora Lucía Navarro would always be dear to her.

When it was time for the two young ladies to board the stagecoach for that last, long jaunt, they found that they were not to have the coach all to themselves.

Inside the stage sat a strikingly handsome gentleman who had a very inviting smile on his face. His deep voice added to his particular charm which most ladies found fascinating. Neither Kristina nor Yolanda could help returning his warm greeting. He extended a hand to them in turn, assisting them into the coach.

In his black broadcloth suit, he was a suave, dapper figure of a man. He wore expensive gold studs on his linen shirt, and a sparkling diamond stickpin adorned his gray and black silk ascot tie. His piercing gray eyes appraised Kristina as though he were savoring the sight of her. Then he gave her a lazy smile as he continued to stare at her.

Yolanda's sharp dark eyes kept darting from Kristina to the handsome stranger accompanying them, and she wondered just how long he was going to stare so lustily at her little mistress. The little Mexican servant assumed a protective air, and her pleasant expression changed to a frown of disapproval.

The man noticed the lovely lady's companion staring at him as intensely as he'd been staring at her

313

beautiful mistress. Gallantly, he apologized, "Forgive me, please, for staring. I just haven't gazed on such beauty as yours before, ma'am. I apologize."

Kristina gave him an understanding nod, but she made no comment. She felt the little Yolanda relax slightly and lean back against the seat. The girl's closeness was a comfort. Kristina realized that this situation would be quite uncomfortable if she had been alone.

The man smiled. "And once again, I apologize for not introducing myself. Ladies, you have the services of Dan Recamier at your disposal. All jesting aside, I'm Dan Recamier."

"Mister Recamier." Kristina gave him another nod and acknowledgment. For reasons she didn't comprehend at the moment, she replied, "I'm Kit Winters and this is my maid Yolanda." She heard Yolanda's sudden intake of breath, but the girl uttered no other sound.

"A name as interesting and as rare as you, ma'am," Recamier remarked in his silken smooth voice.

"You think so, Mister Recamier?" Kristina retorted. She was finding the man's piercing eyes most disconcerting by now. The lazy movement they made as they trailed her face to the opening of her soft, sheer blouse made her want to reach for the sleeveless black vest lying on the seat beside her.

"I find your name most interesting, *mademoiselle,* and it does fit you." He turned his head at an angle, and a quizzical demeanor etched his handsome face. Kristina noted the thin line of a brown mustache over his upper lip as he proceeded to inquire, "Would you, by chance, perform on the stage, Miss Winters? There is something very familiar about you, now that I've absorbed the loveliness of your face."

Yolanda grimaced, thinking to herself it was a lot more than Señorita Kristina's face he'd been absorb-

314

ing. She'd already formed an instant dislike of this handsome *hombre* who overworked his silver tongue. She just hoped the *señorita* wasn't falling for all his grand talk.

"No, Mister Recamier, I've never been in the theater."

"I wasn't necessarily talking about the theater."

"Then, once again, I must tell you I've not performed in any place where you could have seen me."

"I see." Dan Recamier shook his curly brown head in amazement, accepting her declaration. "Well, I could have sworn I'd seen you." Undaunted, he posed another question. "May I be presumptuous enough to ask if you've ever been to Kansas City or Wichita?"

By this time, Kristina was finding Dan Recamier's insistence that he'd seen her amusing. Even if it was just his way of trying to charm a lady, he was devilishly good at it. So she broke into easy laughter.

"No, again, Mister Recamier."

"Well, that is amazing, ma'am, because somewhere, or somehow, I've seen your face and your glorious auburn hair. I know it."

Ironically, Dan Recamier was telling a part truth. For all his roguish ways with the ladies, which he plied quite successfully in many cities over the country, he was being honest about trying to place Kristina as a gorgeous redhead he'd known. But it was hard for Dan Recamier to pinpoint a town or city, for his trail had taken him through so many: Wichita, Kansas City, and Dodge City; Natchez, Memphis, and New Orleans. Wherever there was a high stakes poker game, Dan appeared, and he'd learned over the last ten years that the pickings were best when a political convention was held in a city.

Dan Recamier had long forgotten how many fortunes he'd won and lost. But that never cooled the fever in his blood, and Dan knew it never would. It was born in him for his father, Dion Recamier, had been a gambling man all his life. Up and down the Mississippi River he'd ridden, plying his skills. The sad misfortune of one pretty Mississippi miss was that Dion Recamier had stopped long enough in her city to sire Dan. Dan had never known his father, and his mother had died when he'd been a lad of sixteen. The only heritage Dan had was an inborn skill at gambling, and he'd used it for fifteen years. There was one other thing he'd inherited from his gambler father, the striking good looks which had proven to be a worthy asset.

When he'd boarded the stagecoach in the little hamlet of Van Horn, he'd never expected to meet such an exciting little creature as Kit Winter. In fact, he'd been prepared for the jaunt to El Paso to be a weary, boring one with only the anticipation of the game he planned to sit in on whetting his appetite. Now, he found himself excited about more than just the poker game.

The fever in his blood right now had nothing to do with the poker game. It was caused by the girl with flaming red hair!

Even his partnership in the saloon, the Bird Cage, which he and three cohorts from Kansas City had just purchased, even that had not thrilled him like this lovely damsel in the stagecoach did. El Paso seemed more inviting to Dan Recamier now. She was going there!

Chapter 36

It was not in Danton's nature to be deterred when he'd set a goal for himself. Some called this hardheaded stubbornness, but Danton liked to think he was just damned determined. Whether as a lean, lanky youth he'd been attempting to break a cantankerous bronco that the other *hombres* around Silvercreek swore he couldn't manage or whether as a young lawyer he'd decided to show up three seasoned, Austin attorneys by winning his client's case, Danton refused to lose.

When he'd returned to Austin and arrived at his home in the city, Abeja's sad news that the old goldsmith's shop was closed had been a bitter blow for Danton. His hopes to have Kit's wedding ring designed by Constantine were dashed, but he was glad he'd purchased the magnificent earrings for her while there was still time.

"The boy, Poncho, brought you this yesterday, Señor Danton. He says it is a message from Constantine himself. He told me if you have trouble making out his poor attempt at writing that Señor Constantine wishes to see you as soon as you can come to him."

"Yesterday . . . you say this was delivered, Abeja?"

Danton took the message and the crude scribblings told him of the old man's struggle to write the brief note to him. But for the fact that the hour was so late, Danton would have gone to Constantine immediately.

But the next morning before he went into his office, he guided his gig down the quiet little back street toward Constantine's old shop. He knew the goldsmith's quarters were the back of his workshop. He recognized the little street waif everyone knew as Poncho standing at the corner, the same young boy who'd delivered Constantine's message to Abeja. For a long time, Danton knew, little Poncho had been a priceless treasure to the old man, running constant errands that old Constantine was too feeble to see to anymore. For that reason it was Danton's habit to hand the youth a generous fistful of coins whenever he was in that neighborhood. This day was no exception, and Poncho skipped away, exclaiming exuberantly, *"Gracias! Ah, gracias, Señor Danton!"*

When Danton entered the shop he was pleased to see that Constantine's longtime aide, Ruffino, was still there with the blind goldsmith.

"May I go on up, Ruffino?"

"Of course, he will be so very happy to see you. I think that he will be greatly relieved that you've come so soon." He guided Danton up the step to the raised level which Constantine had curtained off as his living quarters many years ago. Here he had lived his bachelor's existence.

"Señor—it is Señor Danton come to see you," Ruffino called to the white-haired old man who sat in an overstuffed chair which was badly in need of recovering. Danton could see that Constantine's hands were busy doing something. As he drew closer he saw that the goldsmith was whittling on a piece of wood. Indeed, the shapeless piece of wood was already

318

assuming the image Constantine sought to bring out of it. It resembled a cat, and Danton would have sworn it was patterned after the old tomcat that had been curled around Constantine's feet when he was so diligently working on his jewelry.

Danton recalled how sad it had made the goldsmith when a wagon had rolled over the cat as it had slept in the alleyway. That had happened about a year ago.

"*Mi amigo!* Constantine . . . how good to see you!" Danton strode over and gave the old man a pat on his humped shoulders. Constantine's wrinkled hand immediately clasped Danton's. His gesture revealed the affection he felt for the young man.

"Ah, Danton. Good to see you. I can tell you are feeling fine, eh?"

"Yes, *señor.* I've never felt better. I'm to marry the most beautiful girl in the world, the one I love with all my heart. What more can a man ask?"

Constantine chuckled. "Nothing! Absolutely nothing! But then I knew this weeks ago, and that is why I wished to see you. You see, Danton, anticipating such an occasion as this, I made a wedding ring for your bride. In fact, I began to work on it the minute I'd finished the earrings. Should you not believe in destiny, let me convince you it exists, for when I put the last finishing touch to that magnificent ring, I knew I would never see again. But I was well pleased! A sublime peace came over me, Danton. My last and my best work I did for you and your bride."

Danton was completely overcome with emotion, and he unashamedly allowed a tear to come to his dark eyes. For a couple of seconds, it was impossible for him to express his feelings to Constantine.

"I . . . I have no words to tell you what this means to me, and I know my bride will feel the same way, Constantine. Someday, I want the two of you to meet."

"Ah, we will meet, Danton. Rest assured, we will."

The goldsmith moved slowly to rise from his chair, and although Danton wished to assist him, he made no move to, appreciating the proud nature of Constantine.

Instead, Danton watched him move over to a nearby chest and pull out the small center drawer. The old man fumbled for a moment before his hand found the object he was seeking—the tiny velvet pouch in which the ring nestled. Then Constantine held it out for Danton to take.

"Your wedding ring, Danton for your beautiful bride."

Taking the pouch, Danton loosened the silken tassel and a most lustrous golden splendor greeted his eyes. A delicate filigree of flower petals centered the band, and flawless diamonds encrusted each petal. The diamond at the center was a most brilliant emerald.

"Dear God, Constantine, this is magnificent!" Danton released a deep, breathless sigh of amazement. He had never mentioned to the old goldsmith that Kit's eyes were green, yet it was this stone the old jeweler's hand had picked. Why he had done so?

"You picked the emerald for the center stone, Constantine. May I inquire as to why?"

A smugness radiated from the old man's face, and there was arrogance in his voice when he replied to Danton, "Ah, because I knew it should be the emerald. Is it not so?"

"It most assuredly should be, for my lady's eyes are as beautiful as any emerald and as green."

"You see!" Constantine chuckled, but Danton was still left to wonder at the old goldsmith's ability to have made such a perfect selection.

An hour later when he left the shop after he and Constantine had both indulged in a glass of wine, he was still pondering this strange mystery.

His day, spent in his law office, went by pleasantly, but it could have gone no other way after its delightful beginning at Constantine's shop. Danton's thoughts dwelled on what he could do to see to the old man's comfort. Now that Constantine was blind he did not want him to need for anything, yet he had to bear in mind that Constantine was a prideful soul. He must handle this situation with considerable care. He'd find a way.

There were numerous messages piled on his mahogany desk, but his young assistant, Alan Markham, had ran the office efficiently in his absence. Many of the messages were from Estellita or her little clique of cohorts. Danton experienced the bitter taste of politics when he considered that he must constantly mingle with Señora Valero, but he smiled slyly as he sat at his desk and tossed aside all the social invitations, knowing damned well he wasn't taking time out for any of them.

Now, that his visit to Constantine was over, Danton was ready to throw his energies into the restoration of Whispering Willows. It would be a wedding gift for his bride. With an almost boyish anticipation, he envisioned taking her out there. The furnishings and décor he'd leave to her taste, but the repairs, inside and outside, he wanted to accomplish by the time they'd returned from their honeymoon.

He knew the man he needed to get in touch with to achieve the results he desired at the cottage by the Pedernales River, the man who had worked on his house in Austin. He jotted down the name of the architect, Percival Vale, to remind himself to see to the mission the first thing on the following day.

But Percival's services might not be available, Danton realized. He knew Oran Roberts had sought

321

the fine architect's skill for the rebuilding of the capitol building, which had been destroyed by fire a short time ago. Danton knew his little cottage out on the Pedernales wasn't a monumental project like Governor Roberts' capitol building.

But he would certainly put his bid in for Percival's highly valued skill!

Danton Navarro's spirits were soaring so high he could have been on the peak of the highest mountain. For him, nothing was beyond the realm of possibility on that wonderful September day when he finished working at his office and got into his gig to go to his house.

He was content to be going home to spend a quiet evening and to enjoy one of Waco's hearty meals, hopefully a good beefsteak with a bottle of red wine. If he could not share his bed with his little green-eyed minx then he would endure his solitude by anticipating the glorious nights to come.

The same September twilight that was shrouding the capital city of Texas was also descending on the countryside around Silvercreek. Walking side by side in that purple-hued twilight hour were the mistress of Silvercreek, Lucía Navarro, and her devoted Santiago. In the many years he'd spent on the Navarro lands, Santiago could recall having seen the señora shed tears only once, when her Victor had died. This evening when they'd chanced to meet and she had invited him to stroll with her she had cried once more.

"I need your company, Santiago," she had unashamedly confessed to him.

No one had to tell him that the *señora* carried a heavy burden of concern and worry. All he had to do was look at those soulful dark eyes, and his own heart ached for her. She did not deserve such a useless, heartless son as Damien. Oh, he'd witnessed the tall young man staggering into the hacienda in the early morning hours. Sometimes, he'd sung aloud at the top of his voice when his tearful, young bride had met him at the door. At others, Damien's devilish laughter had echoed back into the darkness, or his snapping irate temper had exploded like thunder.

Oh, yes, Santiago knew what was tearing the *señora* to shreds, but he was unable to help her. Once again, he wished that that robust mountain of a man, Victor Navarro, was among them. He recalled vividly witnessing Victor take Damien out to the barn and whip him soundly for some act of disobedience.

Madre de Dios, that would be a fitting punishment for Damien now, for he was acting as irresponsibly and foolishly as a child!

As they walked along, Santiago and Lucía did not have to voice their thoughts, but Lucía finally broke the silence by saying, "What is that old saying, Santiago . . . about when it rains it pours? Dear God, we've had a damned cloudburst lately!"

A weak smile came to Santiago's weathered face for he knew the true depth of her despair when she uttered that curse word. It hadn't shocked Santiago because for all the *señora*'s grand dignity it was her earthy quality which made her unique.

"That is the saying, *señora.*"

"I miss her, Santiago. I miss our little Kit very much, but as sad as that made me I respect what she felt she had to do. It was just very hard to write that letter to Danton telling him what had happened."

"I don't think he'll take it too lightly. Those two were meant for one another. As sure as the sun rises in the east, I know it, *señora.*"

"I know it, too. I think I knew it from the minute she

323

arrived at Silvercreek with Danton." She paused for a minute, and Santiago halted too. "You know, my old friend, I feel much better all of a sudden." A sublime smile brightened her lovely face which, to Santiago, no longer seemed drawn with tenseness. Santiago didn't know what had brought the change in her, but it gladdened his heart.

"Ah, I am so glad you feel better!" he exclaimed, realizing his own spirits were now lighter too.

"The sun always shines brightly after a storm. Is it not so?" she released a lilting, soft gust of laughter.

"Sí, Señora Lucía." Santiago's laughter mingled with hers.

"And the sun will shine again here at Silvercreek, Santiago. I must believe that! Victor would be disappointed in me if I didn't. We won't disappoint him, will we, Santiago?"

"Never, Señora Navarro. Everything will be fine. You and I will make it so." The old Mexican smiled at the lady strolling by his side. In her own way she was as strong willed and determined as her husband.

Santiago thought that Danton Navarro was deserving of two such parents. Yes, thank God for Danton! he said to himself.

Chapter 37

Lucía kept asking herself why Danton didn't arrive at Silvercreek as she would have expected. It wasn't like Danton at all. Several days had gone by since she and Santiago had taken that evening stroll around the grounds and she confided in him that she'd procrastinated for a couple of days before writing Danton that Yolanda and Kit had left the ranch in the middle of the night.

She had been reluctant about informing Danton by letter instead of face to face. Now, she was very apprehensive about how he'd reacted to the startling news. Was he so crushed that he didn't wish to face the family? More repulsive to Lucía was the distasteful possibility that he was drowning his sorrows in the arms of Estellita Valero.

Danton was a prideful man, just like his father, and she had no doubt his ego would be painfully wounded.

She could do nothing about that, but she was determined that the constant shenanigans of Damien wouldn't drain her. She'd made herself develop a cold indifference to Damien's comings and goings, for she knew that was the only way she could deal with the situation without permitting a shroud of gloom to engulf her.

Her energies were directed toward the red-eyed, weeping Molly and to her daughter, Delores. Of course, there was always that sweet solace of Santiago.

For Damien the final straw was the reproach reflected in his little sister's eyes after his nights of drunken revels. After years of thinking of her as his doting little lap dog, Damien was stunned when she had recently shrugged him aside and made a snapping retort. That just wasn't like Delores—not the sweet, docile Delores. Hell, he'd caroused for years!

But he didn't take into consideration that Delores had developed a genuine liking for the gentle Molly. By chance, she'd witnessed Damien's disgusting behavior toward his young bride, and brother or not, she wouldn't excuse it!

The displeased look in Lucía's eyes did not plague him in the least, nor did old Santiago's snarls, and as far as Molly was concerned, she could go to hell. For some ridiculous reason, however, Delores' chilling manner gnawed at him intensely. Little Delores, of all the people in the world!

Damien, like so many people who deceive themselves, had gotten caught in the web of his deception. He could not yet detect the toll his nightly drinking bouts were starting to take on his handsome face. His dissipation would leave far longer-lasting scars than the ones Kit had given him. Had his mind been clear of the fog remaining from his nightly drunken stupors, he would have realized that Delores' hero worship had turned to disapproval. She now saw him as weak. Instead of a hero, she saw him as a scoundrel.

When Damien was around the house or grounds of the ranch, he gave no hints of the light-hearted, happy-go-lucky personality he'd formerly projected. He was a sullen, moody individual just itching for a fight.

Perhaps, Lucía Navarro had unconsciously prepared herself for that night when there was a knock on her door. When she responded to it, she found a tawdry-looking lady of middle age before her. The woman introduced herself as Maggie, and then she asked Lucía if she might speak to her about her son, Damien. Lucía invited her inside.

"I apologize, Señora Navarro, for having to bother you. I know you don't have the likes of me in your home." Maggie Montgomery was intimidated by this startling, stately lady, and she nervously played with the fringe of her shawl. It was due to her frenzied nerves that Maggie chattered on as Lucía ushered her into the entrance.

"I didn't know what to do for him but take him upstairs to one of the girls' rooms and get him to bed. Then I sent for the doctor."

Lucía saw the woman's tenseness and she quickly assured her, "It is the Navarro family who owe you a token of gratitude, miss. What is your name by the way?"

"Maggie, ma'am. Maggie Montgomery. I work at the Lady Luck Saloon in town."

Lucía did not have to be informed of that. One glance at the woman's tired-looking, overadorned gown and at the frazzled feathers attached by a rhinestone pin to the woman's brassy blond hair had told her that. Furthermore, Maggie's full-breasted figure was hardly concealed by the gown, but Lucía couldn't overlook the good streak in the woman. She had traveled all the way to Silvercreek to bring her word about Damien. Lucía felt grateful to Maggie.

"Please, Maggie . . . may I get you some coffee or tea? We will go to my sitting room and you can tell me what's happened to Damien."

The two women walked down the hall and as they

entered the back sitting room, Lucía noticed the woman's eyes dart over to the small liquor chest. "Or maybe something stronger would fit the bill after your long trip, eh?" Lucía inquired.

"Oh, yes ma'am . . . that sounds good to me," Maggie replied eagerly. "A little whiskey would be fine, I think."

Lucía walked over to the chest and to fortify herself for what she knew was to be unpleasant news, she picked up two glasses. "I'm having a brandy. Would you, perhaps, like that instead of whiskey, Maggie?"

A slow, stunned smile came to Maggie's heavily rouged face, and she hastily answered, "Oh, sure! Sure I'd like a brandy!" She stared at the fine lady, amazed. How could such a no-good bastard like Damien come from such a gracious, kind lady like the *señora?* Why, she wasn't a bit snooty or overbearing! Maggie leaned back on the comfortable soft-cushioned seat, and her busy fingers were no longer fidgeting by the time Lucía handed her a glass of brandy and then took a seat near her.

"Tell me, Maggie . . . what happened tonight?" Lucía implored.

"Well, I should have sent for Hubie before it got so far out of hand."

"You mean Sheriff Howard?"

"Yes, ma'am. I'm sorry I didn't do that, but it ain't any big thing for a fight to break out in the Lucky Lady. I thought a bloody nose or face would be about it. As it ended up, though, Damien got shot in the leg by that crazy Davenport. He ended up killing Davenport, which ain't no loss anyway."

"And Damien, Maggie? Was it a serious wound? What did the doctor say?"

"Well, ma'am, that's the reason I've driven out here in the buggy. Doc figured he'd best be kept still so I thought I should let his family know since he wouldn't be showing up home," Maggie explained between gulps of the brandy.

"That was very thoughtful of you, Maggie. I appreciate the extreme burden all of this has put on you, and I intend to see that you are compensated for everything."

"Ah, wasn't nothin', ma'am," Maggie declared, shrugging her shoulders. Lucía moved to fill the woman's glass with more brandy. She felt with the lateness of the hour she should offer the woman a night's lodging instead of letting her drive back into town alone at such an ungodly hour, but Maggie refused the offer politely. As she did so, she told herself that the girls back at the Lucky Lady would swear she was lying if she told them she could have been a guest in the fine Navarro hacienda.

She found Lucía stubbornly determined, however, that she take a generous pouch to pay for Damien's care. "I'll send two of my men to the Lucky Lady with a buckboard padded with quilts for Damien's trip home, if that is agreeable with Dr. Rojas. My foreman, Santiago, will accompany them. Is that agreeable to you, Maggie?"

"Ah, fine, *señora!*"

"Good. I'll also prepare Damien's bride for the situation."

Maggie let out a deep sigh. "Sure was glad it was you who answered my knock instead of her, I can tell you. Lord, I was hating the thought of telling the poor girl."

"Truthfully, I'm glad too, Maggie." Lucía gave her a smile and patted her arm. Then she opened the front door and ushered Maggie out onto the front veranda. After she exited, Maggie paused. "Señora Navarro, we will probably never meet again, but it's been a real privilege for the likes of me to meet such a fine lady like

329

you. A really grand privilege!"

Again Lucía smiled warmly as she lightly touched the woman's shoulder. "I like you too, Maggie Montgomery, and who's to say we won't meet again. I wouldn't take bets on that." She laughed infectiously then, and Maggie with her.

"Mercy, I'd like to think so!"

Maggie hesitated a moment, and then Lucía felt herself being given a genuine hug. Maggie hastily broke the embrace, but she called back to Lucía, "You did something for me tonight, Señora Navarro. You made me feel like a lady and I ain't never felt that way before. God bless you, Señora Navarro!"

Into the night she fled, but Lucía stood on the veranda for a few moments deep in thought. Out of bad had come good, Lucía mused. She valued the sentiments of the dance-hall lady. The practical, honest side of her confessed that she could have been a Maggie Montgomery!

On the following afternoon the buckboard bearing Damien arrived at Silvercreek. Dr. Rojas had allowed him to be brought from town to the ranch. Rojas didn't concern himself with Damien's pain and discomfort. In his opinion the young *toro* deserved some punishment—and pain!

Rojas was certain, although he did not enlighten Damien about it, that the young man might not regain the use of one of his legs. The path Davenport's bullet took, having been shot from a pistol as Davenport lay on the floor, made this likely. It had traveled upward to penetrate Damien's side. If the doctor's suspicions proved to be true, he would soon have to inform his patient that one of his legs was going to remain stiff for the rest of his life. Damien Navarro would be using a cane to walk if he was lucky enough to get out of a wheelchair.

But Rojas said nothing about that to Damien on the day he was taken from the saloon, nor did he say anything to Señora Lucía on the following day when he paid a visit to Silvercreek. Luck was with the young doctor. He had no more calls to make, so he was finally able to enjoy a fine home-cooked meal at Lucía's table.

More delightful for Arturo Rojas was the pleasure of Delores Navarro's presence. Her lovely Latin charm appealed to him. Arturo's dedicated life had not allowed him much time for entanglements or affairs of the heart, but he was a romantic young Latin and the beautiful Delores aroused his desire.

By the time the meal was finished, he'd seen her evolve from a shy, bashful young lady, who stared up with doelike brown eyes, to an adorable, vivacious miss who was conversing easily with him. She intrigued him, so it was a pleasant surprise when she invited him to walk in the garden after the meal.

Lucía was amazed by her daughter's sophisticated air in the young doctor's company, but it rather pleased her for she knew how much Delores had missed Kit. Lucía had also been pleased by the support Delores had given her in recent days when her daughter had sensed her depressed state. Lucía felt a strong sense of motherly pride in Delores, who was showing she could be a very responsible person. She needed the comfort of knowing that two of her children were turning out as she and Victor would have desired.

She and Molly went to the parlor after dinner, Lucía insisting that the young woman needed a break from Damien's sick room. Lucía suspected that the time Molly spent there was not too serene, for Damien was a grumbling, complaining patient.

"Let him fret alone for a while, my dear, and then maybe he'll appreciate all of us more," Lucía declared teasingly to her daughter-in-law.

331

"He has been a handful. I can't seem to please him whatever I do, Señora Lucía," Molly dejectedly told her.

"Then quit trying, Molly. If he's going to act like a spoiled child, then treat him accordingly," Lucía told her quite seriously. "Ignore him."

Molly knew she would have been miserable at Silvercreek if it had not been for the dear *señora*. She had been so homesick she'd wanted to die, and she'd prayed that after the baby was born her father would let her return to his ranch. In the meantime her only consolations were Lucía and Delores.

Damien hated her. She knew that by now, and she was very close to hating him after this brief time as his bride. Yet Lucía Navarro had been an inspiration to the pretty blonde-haired Molly in ways the older woman could not imagine. When Molly thought about it she even found their present conversation ironic because she'd decided just this afternoon to do exactly what Lucía had suggested. She was going to ignore Damien. Now she even had Señora Lucía's support.

After all, she was Joe Langford's daughter, and as such more honor and respect than Damien Navarro had given her was her due.

"I plan to do just that, Señora Lucía. As you've suggested, I'm going to ignore Damien until he becomes a man instead of a child." She smiled and laughed softly.

Lucía liked the spunky look on Molly's pretty face. It made her look different, almost radiant.

"Miracles do happen, Molly dear. Shall we have ourselves a glass of sherry? It's far too early to retire, don't you think? We still have a guest strolling the gardens with Delores."

"They do make a handsome pair, don't they, Señora Lucía?" Molly remarked, referring to Delores and

332

Dr. Rojas.

"Molly, you must have been reading my mind." Lucía had poured the sherry, and she now raised her glass in a toast, saying, "Here's to happier times, Molly."

While Molly drank the sherry, she was making her own resolutions about her future. All her romantic, girlish illusions had been swept away and only ugly ashes were left. She could thank Damien Navarro for that!

Chapter 38

Delores Navarro could have sworn that her heart belonged to Ramon Valdez so utterly and completely that no other man would ever interest her. But now, she could not be so sure of that! Arturo Rojas had changed all that. By the time the evening meal was over, she'd found his presence so compelling that she could hardly take her eyes off him. She wondered if his being such a dedicated doctor was what impressed her, but she'd soon realized it was far more than that.

It amazed her that she had been so bold as to ask him to walk in the garden with her. With Arturo, there was not that shyness she'd felt with Ramon in the beginning. Her pulse had raced when Ramon had kissed her, but wildfire raced through her when Arturo's strong, sure hand held her arm. Dear Lord, how would she react if his sensuous lips touched hers here in the dark garden? Like a wanton? She wanted him to kiss her as they stood so close in the moonlight, the only night sound the hoot of an owl perched in the huge oak tree.

She felt that she was soaring up to the silvery moon when he asked if he could come by to see her again when he had a free moment, and she eagerly consented.

When he departed from Silvercreek and Delores ambled up the long stairway, dreamy and starry-eyed, she yearned desperately for Kit Winters. At that time she'd have given anything to have Kit to talk to, but Kit was gone. Delores missed her so.

There was pain in Kit's heart when her thoughts went back to Silvercreek. As hard as she willed herself not to feel that way and despite the pampering adoration she'd had since she'd walked through the door of the Crystal Castle with the wide-eyed Yolanda that afternoon over two weeks ago, she could not forget Silvercreek and the Navarro family.

When the stage had arrived in El Paso in the midafternoon, it had been an emotional time for Kit, for she was returning to her home and her life as Kristina Whelan.

In order to arrive at the Crystal Castle posthaste, she'd gladly accepted Dan Recamier's invitation to escort her and Yolanda to her mother's establishment. She did not think of questioning the fact that a carriage and driver were waiting for him. When he, however, sought to question her about her destination, she had politely answered him, but she'd revealed very little about herself.

"Oh, I have a friend to meet there," she'd told the dapper Recamier.

"H'm, a fortunate friend he or she is," he'd quipped, a charming smile on his mustached mouth. Recamier had become more and more intrigued by the gorgeous auburn-haired miss with each mile they'd covered along the way, and by now, his curiosity was really aroused.

Kristina chose not to expound on the subject of whether it was a man or a lady she was to meet. She saw the curiosity in Dan Recamier's steel-gray eyes, and she found it amusing.

But when he lifted her down from the carriage and, in turn had gallantly helped Yolanda descend, Kristina was so overcome with emotion her knees felt so weak. She looked up at the familiar two-story structure which had been her home and she fought back tears, not wanting to cry in front of Dan Recamier.

As soon as Yolanda stood beside her, Kristina bid him a curt, quick farewell. Then she turned swiftly so he couldn't see the mist gathering in her eyes.

As his carriage rolled away, he called out to her, "Not goodbye! I'll be seeing you again. You can bet on it!"

Once Kristina saw that his carriage had rolled out of sight, she took Yolanda's hand and urged her to come with her. They went around to the private entrance, instead of using the main entrance where Recamier had left them.

"Where we going, *señorita?*" Yolanda inquired as Kristina yanked her along.

"Home, Yolanda! Home!" Kristina exclaimed, more excited with each step she took.

Perched on a cane-backed chair in his appointed spot, his hat masking his face, was the napping Rollo. When Kristina rapped on the door and then peered through the long panel of glass, the old black man came alert. As his eyes took in the smiling, auburn-haired apparition staring at him with tears rolling down her cheeks, Rollo came out of his frozen trance and lunged for the door. No ghost cried! None he'd ever seen!

Yolanda watched from the side as they embraced, crying and laughing. No one had to tell her what these two thought of each other. It made her happy just to watch the happy reunion. How wonderful it was to be cared about and loved!

"Lord God Almighty, Miss Kristina! Never thought

to see your pretty face again in this life!" Rollo declared in a cracking voice as he finally broke their embrace and held her out from him, looking at her in stunned amazement.

Despite the tears dampening her cheek, Kristina laughed gaily. "Well, you're seeing it now, and it's good to be seeing yours, Rollo."

"Everyone thought you dead, Miss Kristina—everyone but madame. Madame Florine kept telling everyone you was alive. By the Jesus, she was right! Lordy, is she goin' to be one happy lady."

"Oh, I can't wait to see her, Rollo!" Kristina almost vibrated with excitement. She suddenly noticed the grinning Yolanda and called to her to join her. "Come here, Yolanda. I want to introduce you to my friend. Rollo, this is another friend, Yolanda. She's going to stay with me."

The old black man gave the little Mexican a gallant bow and declared, "Nice to meet you, Miss Yolanda. Nice to have you with us."

"It's nice to be here with my dear friend, Señorita Kristina, and to meet you, Rollo," Yolanda said. The little black-eyed girl smiled up at Rollo, and he returned her smile with a broad grin.

After Rollo there was a long procession of reunions: Sid Layman, Sally O'Neal, and the others. It was from Sally O'Neal that Kristina learned of Florine's marriage to Jason Hamilton. Her mother was now living outside El Paso at Jason's ranch, Sally told her. Then Sally escorted Kristina and Yolanda to the living quarters on the second floor.

"Never could bring myself to take over Florine's quarters after she went to live at the ranch. She told me I might as well but I couldn't," Sally told her. "Christ, you've changed so. You look just like your mother did when I first came here, Kristina."

"Really? Well, for that I thank you, Sally. Momma

337

was always so beautiful."

Sally suddenly realized Florine's daughter did not know—she couldn't know—all the changes in her mother's life other than her marriage. Sally reasoned that Kristina should at least have a refreshing bath and a good meal before traveling out to the ranch, even though it was a short distance.

"Why don't I send up some refreshments to tide you and Yolanda over until you can refresh yourselves and rest awhile, Kristina? Would you like that?"

"Oh, yes I would, Sally. I'd like to look a little better than this when I go to see Momma."

Sally took a string of keys out of the pocket of her royal blue, brocade robe. "I keep it locked all the time except when the cleaning woman goes in to clean and dust."

When those heavy oak doors were flung open, Kristina's past rushed out of the lavishly furnished quarters which provoked so many memories of her childhood and youth. Her earlier life swept over her like a gusting breeze, and she stood like one in a trance while Sally went into the room to open the velvet drapes at the windows. Yolanda walked around Kristina to enter for that perceptive instinct of hers told her that the little señorita was savoring and absorbing the sweet sights of her home.

Noting that Kristina had let the small bundle she'd been carrying slip to the floor, Yolanda obligingly picked it up and placed it alongside her own bundle on the magnificent settee. Already her eyes were taking in the opulence surrounding her. Señorita Kit had obviously lived in as fine a style as the Navarro family did.

By the time Sally had left them, Yolanda was roaming through the quarters. She had sighed at least a dozen times at the luxurious furnishings. While she wandered about one room, Kristina moved into

338

another. But when they met again in the pink and white boudoir, Yolanda didn't have to be informed that this was the *señorita*'s room. Kristina sat on the bed listening to the little music box Jason had given her for her birthday, and as she did so she realized that she'd had another birthday in this long, lost interlude of time.

Her head whirled with a million memories as the music box played. Seeing the little teakwood table in the other room, Kristina could visualize her mother sitting there and playing her game of solitaire. But as she sat on her own bed, she remembered another lady sitting and playing her game of solitaire—Lucía Navarro.

The many times at Silvercreek when her past had striven to break through that maze of lost memory were crystal clear to her now. No wonder, she took so easily to singing along with Damien as he'd strummed his guitar, for here at the Crystal Castle she'd sung along as Sid had played the piano. Lucía's cardgame was also a familiar sight, and that time she'd seen the image of a tawny-skinned woman in the fields as she'd been picking wildflowers certainly made sense to her now. It was one of the many trips she and Solitaire had taken into the countryside. Solitaire had always let her pick a basketful of wild verbena and Indian Paintbrush.

But the biggest torment Kristina felt as she sat, assembling the tidbits of her life, was the bittersweet memory of a handsome black-haired man. The first time she'd seen him down in the El Paso street, the second, downstairs in the Crystal Castle. As he'd embraced the lovely blonde, her heart had been lost. But was that man Danton or Damien? She loved Danton, but she could not be certain that he was not the one who'd robbed her mother and kidnapped her on that night so long ago. Damien swore it was

Danton, and Kristina could not help questioning whether that was why Danton was so good to her. Damien was right about Danton's being cool and calculating. Twice, she'd been deeply hurt by his chilling aloofness. He most assuredly had a cruel side to his personality when he chose to reveal it. She'd felt the sting a couple of times!

Suddenly Sally interrupted Kristina's thoughts by announcing, "Missy has your bath all ready for you, Kristina. I hope you won't take this wrong, dear, but I couldn't help noticing how precious little you and your little friend brought along with you. I fetched one of Missy's little calico dresses for Yolanda, and, Kristina, there are enough gowns in your mom's armoires to dress a dozen women."

"Oh, thank you, Sally." Kristina giggled. "And Sally, when I've settled down a little I'll tell you about my adventures."

"God, I hope so. I can't deny I'm curious to know what happened." Sally wore only her robe for her working hours didn't begin until later in the day. She sat down on the bed beside Kristina and patted her hand. "So good just to have you home, honey. You know, Kristina I looked on you as a kid before you were taken away. These experienced eyes tell me that you are a woman now. A darned ravishing one too!"

Kristina smiled at Sally. "I don't know how ravishing I am, but you are right. I'm certainly no child anymore. I am a woman."

There was a sophisticated air about her as she spoke, and Sally knew instinctively from looking into her bright flashing eyes that Kristina Whelan was no virgin either. "Yeah, you are very much a woman, I'd say." If Sally knew anything about men and women, and she thought she did, Kristina was a woman of fire and passion. She was most assuredly Flo's daughter!

340

Chapter 39

It was late afternoon when Kristina boarded the buggy with Rollo, who was driving her out to the Hamilton ranch. She had needed only the light refreshments and the relaxing, sweet-scented bath to refresh her. As she'd told Yolanda, there was no way she could have taken a short nap while the anticipation of seeing her mother again churned in her.

She appreciated the wisdom Yolanda displayed by suggesting that she go alone to her mother while Yolanda remained at the Crystal Castle. In fact, little Yolanda seemed to be quite at home there after only a few hours.

Sally had suggested that Yolanda take Solitaire's old quarters for the time being. Now, in Missy's calico gown with the lace-edged puffed sleeves and the flouncy bustle, the saucy little Mexican girl looked most appealing, Sally thought to herself as she accompanied Kristina downstairs to depart.

"Can't believe how you've suddenly filled out that blue frock of Florine's. Looks great on you, Kristina!" Sally remarked, letting her eyes travel from the young lady's wasplike waist and curvy hips to her provocative bustline. She might have been more petite than

Florine, but Sally had to admit that Kristina was even more alluring and appealing. She had never thought she'd see a woman more seductive than Florine Whelan with her flaming red hair and her striking green eyes. Now, she had—and it was Florine's daughter.

Sally watched the buggy roll around the corner onto the road to the outskirts of El Paso. What a glorious night this was going to be for her dear friend, Florine!

Sally's blonde head whirled with all kinds of whimsical thoughts as she turned to go back upstairs to put on her finery before going to work. Sally was worried about the business, but she had just had an inspiration. It was sheer folly to ever think that Florine would allow it or that Kristina would do it, but, dear God, what an attraction it could be!

If that gorgeous redhead sat on a stool and sang while Sid played, every man in the gambling establishment would be panting for her. Sally would wager such a move would pull a lot of the old bunch back to the Crystal Castle. Most of the old crowd was now patronizing the Bird Cage, which was owned by a guy named Thornton. He'd imported himself some fancy gals whose pleasures could be bought, and this sideline filled his gambling tables. He also ran high-stakes poker games in private rooms. Having ladies of pleasure in her establishment had never been Florine's policy, so the added attraction the Bird Cage offered had hurt the business of the Crystal Castle.

Sally had approached Florine about the idea even though it left a foul taste in her mouth, but Florine had responded with a firm no. In a way, Sally was glad, but she knew if business didn't pick up soon the Crystal Castle was going to have to close its doors. She, Sid, Brenda, and all the other employees would be hunting jobs. Old Rollo would be the only one Florine would be able to place out at the ranch if the place shut its doors.

On their pleasant journey out to the Hamilton ranch Rollo let this little calamity be known to Kristina. "Ain't saying that Miss Sally don't try hard enough and work like the very devil, Miss Kristina. But it just hasn't been Madame Florine in there bustling around those tables. Know what I'm saying?"

"I . . . I think so, Rollo," she replied. "You're saying the special atmosphere Momma created is missing?"

"Yes, ma'am. Guess that's it!"

As if Kristina were voicing Sally's private thoughts, she said to old Rollo, "But if there was a new attraction, a drawing card, to get the crowd into the Crystal Castle again, business would prosper. Wouldn't it, Rollo? She didn't sell the place to Sally, did she?"

"Oh, no, ma'am. Why that would be like selling herself, Miss Kristina," Rollo said. "That's one of the problems with that new bunch that's come into El Paso. All them painted women they've brought in. Madame Florine never did allow that in her place."

Kristina was thoughtful for a moment, weighing carefully what the old man had said, but already an idea was forming in her pretty head. If it was good enough for her mother to do all those years, it was certainly not below her dignity to attempt it. It would be up to the patrons to judge whether she was as good as Florine.

She knew she could capture an audience and hold them with her singing. Why, even as a sixteen-year-old girl she'd had the full attention of the late-night gentlemen. She was no naïve young miss now. Danton Navarro had taught her many ways to excite a man. At first, it had been startling to learn that she håd the power to attract a man like Danton. That knowledge had excited and thrilled her tremendously.

When she voiced her idea to Rollo, his eyes flashed with sudden awakening. This girl he'd known all her life, she was no little girl child anymore. She was a grown-up lady!

Kristina then said in a firm, determined tone, much like Florine's, "Well, Rollo, I think we've got to fight fire with fire but we'll do it with class and good taste—in the Whelan fashion! We'll need no ladies of pleasure either."

Rollo's dark eyes darted swiftly in Kristina's direction. Her head was held high, and her delicate features glowed with such a cool loveliness she reminded him of some untouchable goddess. She could tempt any man to desire her, yet he felt she could remain elusive, unattainable. Rollo suddenly realized that Miss Kristina was as rare a woman as Madame Florine. They were alike in many ways, but each was unique.

"I like the way you talking, Miss Kristina. Yes, sir! I surely do like the way you talking." Rollo laughed and nodded his fuzzy, graying head. Lord, he wondered how that sweet, little thing had ever learned about such things as ladies of pleasure. She'd never encountered one around the Crystal Castle so he, like Sally, wondered just what had happened to Kristina Whelan while she'd been away from her home all these long months.

As he drove along, deep in thought, the magnificent display of gold and rose on the horizon deepened into purple as the sun sank in the western sky. Rollo marveled at this colorful panorama as he reined the buggy into the drive of the Hamilton ranch. His spirits had lifted. Now that Miss Kristina was back with them where she belonged, all was right with the world. The old black man said a little private prayer of thanks for her return.

Lamplight already glowed from the windows of the sprawling stone and adobe home of Jason Hamilton.

Rollo still found it hard to call this Madame Florine's home. To him, the Crystal Castle was her home. It was not that he didn't like Mister Hamilton. Rollo could not have asked for a gentleman who was more considerate and kind to his mistress. It just seemed strange that she lived out here now.

When Florine had been able to leave her wheelchair and walk slowly with the aid of a cane, she'd made regular visits to the Crystal Castle, but she'd stayed only for an hour or two. It wasn't the same, nor would it ever be, Rollo realized.

Florine Whelan rested on a very high pedestal as far as Rollo was concerned. No one would ever replace her!

As the old black man and Kristina walked up the steps to the front entrance, Kristina apprehensively murmured to Rollo, "Mercy, I . . . I hope I don't shock her too much, Rollo."

"Well, honey, it's going to be the best shock she ever had—one she's waited for." He gave her an assuring pat on the arm.

Wild anticipation mounted in Kristina as she heard the door being opened. Then, standing there in the reflecting light was the willowy mulatto, her head covered with a bright-colored kerchief.

"Solitaire!" Kristina shrieked with joy.

"Miss Tina? *Mon Dieu,* Miss Tina? It is *you!*" Solitaire shrieked, now convinced. Grabbing the petite miss to her bosom and holding her so tightly Kristina could hardly breathe, Solitaire wept so hard that Kristina could feel her body throb. Kristina wept too. Even Rollo joined in their emotional reunion by letting a tear or two fall.

The muffled sounds of the commotion at the front of the spacious house reached Florine's ears. She ambled to the hall at the slow pace she'd accustomed herself to

345

endure. It was a darned sight better than being confined to that miserable wheelchair. Jason, with his doting ways, had bought her an array of fancy canes, and they had laughingly made a game out of picking the right cane to match her frock.

Tonight, she was dressed in a pearl gray peau de soie gown so she'd picked the silver-handled cane Jason had obtained on his trip into Mexico. She was the picture of elegance as she walked down the black- and white-tiled hall to see if it was Jason arriving with their dinner guests.

Black onyx earrings dangled from Florine's ears, and the exquisite onyx choker that encircled her throat enhanced the pearl gray gown. The regal arrogance Florine had displayed for the patrons of the Crystal Castle was still evident. She held her head with the same proud dignity now that she was Florine Whelan Hamilton.

By now, she caught a glimpse of Solitaire's trim figure embracing someone, and of course, there was no mitaking the humped shoulders of old Rollo. Although Kristina's petite figure was concealed, Florine knew instinctively who Solitaire was holding in her arms, and she strained to make that leg of hers move more quickly.

"Kristina! Oh, my darling Kristina, I knew you could not be dead!" Florine called out though she was still some twenty feet down the tiled hall. Kristina broke free of Solitaire's enclosing arms and rushed to her mother.

"Momma! Oh, Momma!" Her arms clutched Florine tightly, and tears mingled with laughter as Solitaire and Rollo watched the rejoicing pair. Florine's months of speculation and sorrow were finally at an end for little Kristina was home, very much alive.

Solitaire finally stepped forward to guide the two

ladies into the parlor, feeling the emotional strain, joyous though it was, could take its toll on Florine.

Several minutes of silent wonderment had to pass before Florine and Kristina finally spoke; then they became like two magpies. As the grinning Solitaire slipped unobtrusively away, she invited Rollo to join her in the kitchen. "We got something to celebrate, eh, Rollo? Good times coming back. All the bad times are gone now."

Rollo shook his head in agreement. "You right, Solitaire! Lordy, ain't she pretty? Guess I'd done forgot just how pretty she was, Solitaire, and that must mean old Rollo is getting old and forgetful."

"No such thing! You couldn't forget what wasn't there, Rollo. That enchantress isn't the little Kristina we knew before. That's a woman, Rollo—a woman full of ginger and spice!" She laughed wickedly yet melodiously.

Chapter 40

The portly, dignified Jason Hamilton was utterly amazed at the miracle taking place under his roof. He knew it was not just wishful thinking or whimsy that Florine's step was more lively, and having her long-lost daughter back with her had to be the reason Florine's face glowed so radiantly. Jason sincerely concluded he'd never seen his wife look more beautiful. Dear God, that made him a happy man!

Amused, he promised himself never to doubt that red-headed woman of his again. Her uncanny instincts had proven him wrong, along with all the so-called detectives he'd hired to search for Kristina. By all that was holy, he'd cast his lot with his beloved Florine from now on. He couldn't deny that he'd felt compassion for her grit and determination when she'd refused to believe Kristina was dead, but he'd believed the girl was. Well, it showed how wrong he could be.

Jason, like her other friends, saw that Kristina was like a completely, different young lady now that she'd returned to El Paso. Before she had been the young daughter of Florine, a sweet-faced, little angel her mother worshiped and adored. Now, his eyes saw an utterly gorgeous young woman, in full bloom, and so alluring it overwhelmed him.

He had followed Florine's guidelines and not pressed his stepdaughter for anymore details than she'd sought to reveal to them, but Jason knew there was much Kristina was not telling. Whatever her reasons were, he abided by Florine's wishes. He did not prod Kristina even though he had to admit he was very curious.

Despite Jason Hamilton's worldly, sophisticated lifestyle, he was impressed by Kristina's poise and by her self-assured manner. He saw more in her than the spirit he'd seen in the willful miss who'd been around when he was courting her mother. She was her own woman now, taking orders from no one!

When she'd abruptly announced to them that she had to get back into town to check on her little friend, Yolanda, Jason had noticed a disapproving frown crease Florine's face. Kristina had caught it too, and quickly seeking to appease Florine she'd said, "Now, Momma, I'll come back tomorrow. I just don't want poor little Yolanda to think I've deserted her. Besides, I want you and Jason to meet her because, as I've told you, Yolanda helped me get back to El Paso. Without her, I don't know whether I could have made it."

Florine knew Kristina's mind was made up so she didn't insist that her daughter stay a few more days before going back to town. But she couldn't help being greedy for the sight and closeness of Kristina after so many months' absence.

Smiling graciously, Florine confessed, "Ah, my darling daughter, I suddenly realize I can't be too selfish about you, but be patient with me for a while."

Kristina gave Florine an understanding look, and then Jason offered to drive her to the Crystal Castle when she wished to leave the ranch.

When Jason and Kristina, in turn, gave Florine a

349

kiss before departing for El Paso and the Crystal Castle, Florine sought the quiet veranda from which she watched the buggy roll out of sight. Jason's big, shaggy collie, King, ambled up to keep Florine company. His damp nose nudged at Florine's hands, urging her to pet his head, and she obliged the lovable collie, whose loyalty for her had grown since she'd come here to live at the Hamilton ranch.

Patting King's head and looking out at the countryside now washed by the gathering darkness, she felt very fortunate to have her daughter back, safe and sound. She'd never ask for more from life, she privately vowed.

Yet a restlessness gnawed at Florine tonight. She'd known this feeling before, since she'd married Jason. Despite the devotion he showered upon her and the luxurious life he provided, there was a void he could not fill.

The magic and gaiety of the Crystal Castle's evenings were far more exciting and stimulating to the former gambling lady than the more elegant affairs she attended with Jason or parties they'd hosted at the ranch after she'd gotten out of her wheelchair.

Dear God, there were those who would call her insane, and she could understand that. Only one person would not—Solitaire. Florine had often told her faithful friend that she yearned for one more glorious night like the ones of the past.

"I know, *mam'selle*. I, too, miss our Crystal Castle," Solitaire always confessed to her mistress.

The two women reminisced. Florine Whelan Hamilton now wondered what she'd have done or how she'd have endured without her devoted Solitaire.

Sometimes, the collie, King, was privy to Florine's private thoughts, and tonight she patted his head and confided in him. As she was at the point of clasping her silver-handled cane and rising out of the wicker chair to go inside the house and bid good night to King, she felt the dog tense. He instantly rose and pointed his head toward the front gate of the drive, but Florine saw no one, nor did she hear a horse approaching.

"Your girlfriend calling you tonight, King?"

The collie wagged his tail slightly and gave Florine his attention for only a moment before turning his head back in the direction of the woods a short distance away.

Florine slowly moved out of the chair and ambled toward the door. "Behave yourself, boy." She went inside leaving King to go his way.

The collie was a sensitive, smart dog, and it was no roaming bitch he'd scented over in the woods. King's gentle nature turned vicious if anything threatened the property of Jason Hamilton. He instinctively knew the hired hands from an unwanted intruder.

The man astride the huge black horse was a threat as far as King was concerned. Florine had not been observant. If her mind had not been so preoccupied, she might have noticed the flickering glow of the cheroot the man was puffing on.

He'd observed Jason and Kristina leave the ranch, and he'd lingered to watch the other red-haired lady come out onto the veranda. When Florine went inside, he flicked the cheroot to the ground and prepared to ride back into El Paso.

The rumors floating around El Paso that Florine Whelan's daughter had returned were true. It was just as Jack Crawford had told him when he'd arrived in town.

A devilish smile creased his face as he spurred the horse to a faster pace. He knew what his next move would be. He'd seen all he needed to see to decide on that.

*   *   *

As soon as Jason had seen Kristina to Florine's former quarters, he took his leave and started back home. Yolanda gave her Señorita Kristina an exuberant welcome back to the Crystal Castle, but Kristina didn't have to be told that the saucy, little Mexican girl had nested in quite easily. She didn't have to concern herself in the least about whether Yolanda had gotten accustomed to her new surroundings.

The servant girl flitted around like a busy little bee, showing Kristina the various little chores she'd accomplished while Kristina had been visiting her mother.

"I'll take you out there the next time, Yolanda. You and Solitaire will like one another, I think."

"Solitaire?" Yolanda looked puzzled for a moment until she remembered it was Solitaire's quarters she was now occupying. "Oh, yes . . . Solitaire!"

"Yes, she is my mother's friend and companion as you are mine, Yolanda."

"Sí, Señorita Kristina. I understand. Solitaire is your mother's devoted servant and friend."

"For years and years!"

A smug look came onto Yolanda's pretty dark face as she assuredly announced, "As we shall we, *sí?*"

"Of course, Yolanda." Kristina giggled, then she hugged the young girl to show her affection. Yolanda had no one who truly cared about her as Kristina did, and Kristina was filled with compassion for the eager, humble girl who was so willing to do anything asked of her.

She promised herself that someday she must learn how her own mother and Solitaire had joined forces as she thought of the circumstances that bound her to Yolanda.

The music echoed from below and caught Kristina's attention. No longer did she have to sneak out the door to go below, she thought with amusement. She could go anywhere she wished. Taking notice of the clock sitting on the Italian marble mantel, Kristina was seized by an intriguing idea, and she urged Yolanda to help her.

"You what? You are going to what? Oh, *señorita,* I just bet your mother will not approve," Yolanda muttered.

"My mother is not here to approve or disapprove, is she? Besides, Yolanda, I am a woman now and I can do as I wish." Kristina was already kicking off her shoes and unfastening the waistband of her skirt.

When she glanced up, Yolanda was watching her, her hands at her waist. "You going to dress up and go downstairs?"

"I am! Look in the armoire and find me the prettiest gown in there," Kristina ordered.

Yolanda whirled around without saying a word. She opened the doors of the armoire and started checking out the array of magnificent gowns hanging inside. Any one of them would have been a perfect choice, and all were in colors flattering to Kristina. Yolanda surveyed the lot of them before going back to lift out the bright emerald green one. It was made of a soft sheer material, and it had a taffeta lining. A double tier of ruffles went across the bustline, and the sleeves could be worn off the shoulder. The soft flowing skirt was gathered into a flouncy bustle at the back.

"Señorita Kristina? You like this one?"

"Yes, that's just fine, Yolanda. Check the slippers because if I remember correctly Momma always had slippers to match most of her gowns."

Yolanda once again started to survey Florine Whelan's extensive collection of shoes, and she found a pair of green ones with sparkling buckles made of brilliants. *"Sí,* I found some."

Busily, the two of them attended to Kristina's toilette, and an hour later, her auburn hair was piled high atop her head and set in glossy curls, and she was ready to step into the gown Yolanda held for her. Wriggling into it as Yolanda pulled it upward, Kristina heaved a deep sigh when Yolanda was finally ready to adjust the ruffles over her shoulders.

"I couldn't be bigger than Momma," she muttered.

Yolanda giggled. "Well, you sure better not eat any more tonight or you'll burst this out." The girl appraised Kristina for the gown fit as though it was molded to her petite body. Florine desired a snug fit in her gowns, knowing how flattering and alluring an image it created, but Kristina's gowns, those sewn by Lucía's seamstress, were far less restricting. Naturally, Kristina felt slightly uncomfortable.

"Eat? I don't know if I can even breathe," she remarked, starting to walk around the room.

Yolanda sighed delightedly. "Ah, then don't breathe, Señorita Kristina, cause your figure is *maravilloso!* The gown looks good on you!"

Kristina could not help laughing at the excited, little creature whose flashing black eyes admired her. "All right, Yolanda . . . I'll . . . I'll just not breathe."

Placing a final dab of perfume at each ear and on each wrist, Kristina bid her little friend goodbye and moved out the door. She drew in a deep breath before going down.

As Kristina Whelan descended the steps, Sally O'Neal was awestruck by the ravishing vision she presented. The tight gown demanded that Kristina walk slowly, but the effect was sensual. Her movements were more tantalizing to the patrons than Kristina could possibly know.

Sally O'Neal instantly recognized in Kristina the solution to the Crystal Castle's dilemma. Here was the attraction they needed.

Sally was unaware that Kristina had already made a decision to be just that, and the reaction of the gentlemen staring at her confirmed her resolve.

Displaying the same flair, elegance, and sophistication of Florine Whelan, she lifted her skirt slightly to negotiate the last step and she smiled her prettiest smile. Tilting her head slightly, a flirtatious sparkle in her green eyes, she greeted her worshiping admirers, "Good evening, gentlemen! Welcome to the Crystal Castle."

From that night on Kristina's presence lured the gentlemen gamblers to the Crystal Castle. It became a tradition to watch the beautiful auburn-haired maiden make her descent down the stairs and welcome them.

Business suddenly started to flourish at the old gambling establishment.

Chapter 41

When Jason Hamilton returned to his ranch and found Florine still up to greet him, she suggested that they sip some wine before retiring. He could not have been more pleased.

Florine was more like the vivacious woman he'd fallen in love with. He'd considered it a blessing when she'd been able to discard that wheelchair for a walking cane. The truth was, in the beginning Jason could only pray the beautiful woman he'd adored for so long would live. But during the last couple of days another miracle had happened.

"I'd like to talk to you, Jason, about Kristina," Florine told him.

"Of course, darling." His arm went around her waist, and he planted a gentle kiss on her cheek. "Solitaire and I agree that you have never looked more beautiful."

Florine responded with a soft laugh. "You and Solitaire are both prejudiced."

Jason confessed that that was true.

When they were finally settled in the small sitting room just off the parlor of the spacious house and Jason had served their wine, Florine wasted no time getting to the subject she was puzzled about. "Jason, we've always been honest and straightforward with one another or else we'd never have made it this far. I'm perplexed about Kristina, Jason. Perhaps, it's because of what's happened to me that she wouldn't want to worry me, but I have the feeling she's told you more than she's told me. Is it true?"

A stunned expression came to Jason's face. "Christ, Florine! I probably don't know even as much as you do. The answer is a definite no, Florine darling. What brought that on?"

"Do you realize just how little she did reveal, Jason?"

"I do, but I didn't seek to pry. I figured the first two or three days she was just so damned happy to see you and Solitaire—just to be home."

"In a way you are absolutely right, Jason, but she was gone months—many months. She told me how she slipped away from the men who'd robbed me and taken her with them. She says she remembers falling down a high cliff in a mountainous area and when she finally came to she had no memory. Some nice people rescued her, she told me; then, she quickly shrugged any other questions aside."

Being a shrewd gentleman, Jason Hamilton knew the young lady was concealing something, but he hesitated to say anything to Florine. Instead, he sought to ease any concern his wife was harboring. Whatever experiences Kristina had lived through during her year away from them, he could not know, but he suspected some had been painful.

"Your daughter is a lot like you, Florine. When she's ready to discuss those months, she'll tell us what happened. Until then, I would suggest that we do not nag her. She's as stubborn and headstrong as another pretty lady I know," Jason teased playfully.

Florine smiled, knowing that Jason spoke with

wisdom. "She has changed so much. She's beautiful, isn't she?"

"Ah, most assuredly!" Jason agreed.

"I wasn't a bad-looking woman when I was that young, but Kristina's face is so much more delicate. Her hair and eyes are like mine, but her features and her darker complexion are, much as I hate to mention him, like those of the man who fathered her."

Jason's eyes were warm with emotion as he pointedly addressed his wife. "Suppose you'll ever tell me who he was? I've never made an issue of it, as you know."

"I may . . . someday, Jason. I've appreciated your understanding about that."

"I've never felt any reason to be jealous of the man, Florine. That was long before we met."

"That's true, Jason. Long before we became so close when you were advising me about some of my business matters. If you remember, a couple of gentlemen became too presumptuous about Kristina while they were trying to woo and win me. You'll recall they didn't remain long."

Jason roared with laughter, recalling the two suitors who'd happened to be friends of his. "Oh, do I remember. Old Broderick was crushed to the core."

Florine smiled, "It was nice, the way our friendship grew into love, Jason. It was slow, but enduring. No flash in the pan that fizzled once the fire and passion were spent. That kind of attraction never lasts long."

Jason patted her hand affectionately and vowed, "Ours will last, Florine. Ours will last forever. I've never been so happy as I have since you became my wife despite all our problems and ordeals. I think they've even made you dearer to me, my darling."

As Florine leaned over to kiss her handsome husband, her fingertips caressed the silver at his temples. "Jason, I couldn't have endured these last months without you. You've been my strength—my everything! I shall love you all the days of my life."

He enclosed her in his arms, deciding not to tell her yet that he must leave for a few days to travel to Fort Worth on business. Somehow, he felt it would be best to wait until tomorrow morning.

When Kristina returned to the living quarters of the Crystal Castle in the early hours of the morning, she found Yolanda sprawled on the settee. Her heart was filled with affection for the little Mexican girl. Like a trusty puppy dog, she'd waited for her return.

Had it not been for the distorted position of Yolanda's body, Kristina would not have disturbed her. Reluctantly, she shook the listless Yolanda's shoulder until her eyes opened wide.

"Go to bed, Yolanda."

When the girl was about to ask her mistress how her evening had gone, Kristina quieted her with the promise that they'd talk in the morning.

Watching as Yolanda wobbled down the hallway, Kristina realized that morning was already here and that she would sleep until early afternoon. But that night had had a thrilling effect on her, one that remained long after the crowd had responded with their rowdy applause when she'd sung her songs.

She now knew, if her mother would teach her the skills of monte and faro, she could lure the sporting gentry back to the Crystal Castle.

While Kristina was patting herself on the back for the inspired idea of singing to the patrons, she'd decided to be a faro dealer like her sophisticated mother. Actually, Kristina's ideas were not unique. Another lady had used a similar approach years earlier at the old gambling establishment in San Antonio called The Palace.

Instead of wearing the outrageous gowns and heavy makeup that were the trademark of cheap, wanton women, Lucía Navarro had draped her curvaceous body in exquisite gowns. She'd worn fine jewels and she'd let her dark sultry beauty whet the desires of the big spenders and the high stakes gamblers; but she had remained a mysterious, elusive lady whom no one could claim. She had challenged them, but she had remained untouchable.

Years before Kristina was born, Lucía was doing exactly what Kristina was secretly plotting to do. It had been exciting to Florine's daughter to provoke the response she'd aroused tonight. The small crowd had become a larger one before the night was over. The word had drifted across the street to the establishment called the Bird Cage, and men had left the tables over there to come to the Crystal Castle.

She could not deny the exhilarating power she'd felt as she'd sat on the stool and watched the gentlemen amble in to assess the rumor about her. It was stimulating!

Now, as she lay in bed thinking about her future and the future of the Crystal Castle, her course seemed obvious. She would save the place for her mother if she could.

If the patrons of the gambling establishment desired to possess her body or if they found her lips so luscious they wished to kiss them, that was their problem not hers. Only one man had been permitted to take those liberties—Danton Navarro. Dear God, how she'd ached for him since leaving Silvercreek! But until her uncertain heart could know without a shadow of a doubt that it was not Danton she'd seen here at the Crystal Castle that night long ago, she had to forget about him. She wanted Damien to be the guilty one, not Danton!

No man would possess her, she vowed. She might have a wicked glint in her green eyes at times, but the pain would be the man's and not hers from this day forward.

Never had she loved or appreciated her mother more than now, for she could understand a woman giving herself to a man and being sorely rewarded for it. She could have been left with Danton's child after any of their torrid love interludes. Obviously, that was what had happened to her mother. Someday soon, she planned to tell Florine about Danton, but not just yet. She knew there would be no shocked look on Florine's face. Her mother would understand all too well.

What Kristina was more concerned about was Florine's reaction when she approached her about learning the elements of monte, which she knew was very similar to the game of faro. She had some grave misgivings about that. She wondered if Florine would accept her becoming a dealer.

Dan Recamier was even more interested in the beautiful redhead now. The little minx had lied to him on the day they'd arrived on the stage. Not only was she a beauty, she was a foxy one! He liked that in a woman.

The day after they had arrived in El Paso, he'd gone back to inquire about a Miss Kit Winters only to be told that no such young lady was there, but Dan Recamier was not a man to give up easily. He'd asked his various contacts in El Paso about a certain beautiful lady who'd arrived on the stage with him. As it happened in the midst of a poker game a couple of nights ago, his old acquaintance from Kansas City, Jack Crawford had supplied him with a lead on such a girl.

"Hell, you're talking about Florine Whelan's daughter, it sounds like. Rumor's going around the town that she's suddenly reappeared after about a year's absence. I wasn't here when she disappeared, but I heard it was a hell of a thing—rocked the town for days. Me and Talbert didn't drift down this way from Kansas City until a few months later after all that took place."

"Fill me in, Jack. Sounds interesting," Recamier urged his old crony. He knew why Crawford and Talbert had left Kansas City because he'd left for the same reasons. The Anti-gambling legislation in 1881 had ruined the city for the sporting gentry.

Jack Crawford puffed on his cheroot for a second before going into his tale. "Well, the truth of the matter is that damned bad luck hit old Florine and put her out of commission. That was what prompted your partners to open the Bird Cage. Without Flo there to ride herd, the Castle began to slip. Sally O'Neal is a fine, hard-working gal but she ain't got class like Florine."

Dan Recamier nodded his head and muttered, "I wonder what had caused the sudden decline of the Crystal Castle. For years, as you know, Jack, even back in Natchez and New Orleans, the reputed Crystal Castle was the talk around the green cloth, right?"

"Damned right! But the Crystal Castle was Florine Whelan, know what I mean?"

At Recamier's urging, Crawford told him the tale he'd heard about Florine's daughter being abducted the night she was shot and robbed. Recamier listened with intense interest, and when Crawford was through talking he inquired about Florine's whereabouts, asking where the Hamilton ranch was located. Then, without delay, because Recamier was becoming more and more intrigued by the auburn-haired beauty, he went in search of this mystery lady.

In the seclusion of the woods, he sat astraddle his horse observing the grounds and the house at the Hamilton ranch. The first afternoon, he was not rewarded by the sight of her so he rode back into El Paso. On the next afternoon, at a later hour, he rode out again to take up his watch behind the concealing underbrush bordering the Hamilton property. This time his vigil paid off when he saw the lady he sought get into a buggy with an older dignified gentleman he presumed to be Jason Hamilton.

He watched the occupants until the buggy traveled out of his sight, then just as he was about to head for El Paso another woman caught his attention. She had the same burnished, coppery colored hair, and there was something about this woman on the veranda which entranced him too. Oh, this was not that consuming sensual desire he felt for the girl named Kit, but the feeling was just as demanding and powerful. The cocky, arrogant Recamier was a little puzzled, but he didn't fret about it. He just gave way to the impulse gnawing at him, and he sat there a moment longer and observed the woman.

When she finally moved off the veranda and entered the house, Recamier rode back into El Paso.

But Dan Recamier could not dismiss the silhouette Florine had presented when she'd lingered in the doorway, the light in the hallway reflecting on her coppery hair and outlining her trim figure. In the twilight her face was indistinguishable but not her hair and figure.

It wasn't until he was cantering his horse down the street in El Paso, intending to sit in on a game of poker, that Dan knew what had fascinated him about the woman he'd watched only moments ago. Two dapper men in the traditional gamblers' attire had just crossed his path.

One of the flashy gents he'd just seen had reminded him of his own gambler father, Dion Recamier. From him, Dan had received little: gambling skill, good looks, and a winning way with the ladies. Like his French father, he was possessed of an overwhelming conceit about his prowess with women. The other thing Dan had that belonged to his father was a gold locket with a small miniature of an auburn-haired lady.

Chapter 42

Hundreds of miles separated the two men, but one woman dominated the thoughts of both. Each man was determined that the beautiful Kristina was going to yield to his indomitable will. Interestingly enough, the two shared many similar characteristics. Dan Recamier was as reckless and as undaunted by the possibility of failure as was Danton Navarro.

Both men were tall and handsome. Their dark, good looks urged ladies to succumb to their charms. But there was a sharp contrast between the two men's natures. Dan was easygoing compared to the hot-tempered Danton Navarro.

Danton's mood was now dark. Too many devastating things had occurred, and all of those at the Silvercreek ranch had been aware of his wrath from the moment he'd arrived.

Lucía's letter had been delayed by two weeks because Danton had not been in Austin to receive it. He'd been camping out at Whispering Willows so he could oversee the work done on the little cottage he intended to present to his bride, Kit. His obsession with that project had consumed all of Danton's time.

The impact of his mother's letter, telling him of Kit's

sudden departure from Silvercreek, left him totally perplexed. Then he exploded with anger. Had he not known her at all? It was not gratifying to his male ego to realize that she'd played him for an idiot. But what else could he believe? She knew he loved her! How could she doubt that after he'd asked her to marry him?

His first thought had been that Damien had pulled some conniving trick. The night after he'd returned to Austin and read Lucía's letter, he'd sought the solace of liquor to drown his pain. He'd hoped to numb his hurt, but he had been unable to do so. For a fleeting second he'd been tempted to take out his frustrations by going to visit Estellita Valero, but he'd never made it out of his house.

He never realized it when Abeja helped him up to his room and into bed. But the next morning as he paid the price of his folly with a throbbing head, he decided to go to Silvercreek to find out more than Lucía's letter was telling him. More important, he wanted to talk personally with Santiago.

The following day, with a much clearer head, Danton left Austin to journey south. Waco Martin and Abeja were not told when he would be back, nor was the young man at his law office. Danton didn't know when he'd return. He made one promise to himself, but that was not for the others to know. When he did return, he vowed it would be with the woman he loved accompanying him.

No other woman would share his life or the little dream cottage at Whispering Willows. Whatever her reasons were for fleeing, he'd find out. Wherever she'd gone, he'd track her down whether it took weeks or months. If some other man stood between him and the woman he loved, he'd eliminate that barrier too!

Anyone looking at his tense features that morning, lips set tight and black eyes afire, could not have doubted that. His long-legged stride was like that of a man marching into battle. Nothing was going to stop him!

At least, Danton Navarro was happy about one thing when he rode up the long, familiar drive of Silvercreek and that was the sight of his good friend, Santiago. He's already prepared himself to meet the challenge facing him when he arrived at the ranch—Kit wouldn't be there to greet him—but the sight of the old Mexican met with his approval.

He threw his hand up and called out to Santiago, *"Amigo!"* The Mexican waved at him enthusiastically. For more than one reason, Santiago was glad Danton had finally appeared. Frankly, it had puzzled him that he'd not arrived at least two weeks ago. Santiago would have wagered that Danton would have headed for the ranch the minute Lucía's letter had arrived in Austin.

Danton had only to stand by Santiago's side and look upon the old man's wizened, weary-looking face to know that times had not been good at Silvercreek. "I'm glad you happen to be out here, Santiago. I need to talk to you for a while before going in to see Mother. Still got that bottle of tequila stashed in the bin there in the barn, *amigo?*" Danton had a crooked grin on his face as Santiago nodded his head and motioned for him to follow.

The two ambled in through the door to go to a place of seclusion where they could talk without being disturbed, and enjoy a few nips of tequila as they'd done often enough before.

"Señor Danton, your mother has needed you very much. I kept looking for you day after day, but you didn't come," Santiago told him.

"I didn't get the letter until I came back to Austin

367

from Whispering Willows a couple of days ago, Santiago. Hell! Two damned weeks wasted when I could have been hunting down that little runaway."

Each took a sip of tequila. "What do you make of this, Santiago? Why would she have left like that?"

"I can't answer that, Señor Danton. But I think I know Señorita Kit well enough to know that it was something so urgent and powerful that nothing could have stopped her. It might make you feel better to know that Yolanda left with her, and the buggy she and Yolanda helped themselves to the night they stole away has been returned. It was at the livery at Fort Stockton. That is the last trace we've had of the little señorita and Yolanda."

"Fort Stockton, eh?" So Kit was heading toward west Texas, was she?

"*Sí, Señor.* Señor Danton"—Santiago's voice cracked and he hesitated—"I have the feeling you were not told about Damien."

Danton's black brows arched sharply and he almost spit the inquiry out. "You're not about to tell me he went with her?"

Such blinding rage lit up Danton's face that Santiago quickly soothed him by informing him that Damien was here. "I mean about his marriage to Molly Langford."

Santiago heard Danton heave a deep sigh before a quizzical look etched his face. "Santiago . . . are you saying that Damien and Molly are married? *Madre de Dios,* has the world suddenly gone insane?"

"*Sí,* I am telling you that. I've much more to tell you before you go to the house now that we've been given this chance to talk."

"I don't like the tone of your voice, Santiago. Are my mother and sister all right?"

"Señorita Delores is just fine and you would have

368

been very proud of her, Señor Danton. She has been a great comfort to your mother during the last few weeks—very trying weeks they've been, too."

"I get the impression that there's been nothing but trouble one way or the other since I left here," Danton muttered disgustedly. Selfishly he wondered if there would ever be a day when he could wash his hands of Damien. Would he get a reprieve when Delores married some gentleman who'd help take over the reins at Silvercreek?

Danton had reached that time when he was ready to go beyond Silvercreek. Silvercreek was Victor Navarro's proud obsession but Danton wanted his own place. He'd found it in Whispering Willows. As Victor had found his Lucía, Danton had found the woman he wanted to share his dreams with, or so he'd thought until he'd found out Kit had left. However, not for a minute did he consider the possibility that he'd not find her and get her back. Danton Navarro would not allow himself to be a loser! He never had!

He listened as old Santiago related to him everything that had come to pass at Silvercreek after Damien had brought his bride, Molly, home with him. He told Danton how the iron-willed Langford and his men had tracked Damien down and how they hadn't let him out of their sight until the wedding was performed.

"So it was a shotgun wedding?"

"*Sí* . . . it was."

"So old Damien's luck ran out on him." Danton gave a slightly amused laugh. Sooner or later, it had to happen that some irate father or husband would see that justice was done. Neither Damien's charm nor his glib tongue would get him out of this mess, Danton figured.

"Oh, *señor*, when his luck ran out it really ran out! He was drinking nightly in town, leaving his new bride alone. Your mother felt so sorry for her and as is Señora Lucía's way she took Molly under her wing. Then there was an incident at the saloon, and Damien got shot in the upper thigh. The bullet did damage to his spine. Your brother, Señor Danton, is now in a wheelchair. Your mother, she talks to me a lot, and there isn't much hope that he will walk again as he once did. He will possibly have to use a cane for the one stiff leg."

"Christ, this ranch has gone to hell in a hurry, hasn't it?" Danton raked his long slender fingers through his thick mop of black hair.

Then, figuring it was time he went on to the house, he rose from the pile of hay on which he and Santiago had flopped down to have their talk. Brushing off his fawn-colored pants to rid himself of the hay, he moved to leave the barn stall.

"Thank you, *amigo,* for preparing me for what I'm facing. Damn, a new sister-in-law, a brother confined to a wheelchair, and my beautiful lady missing!" As he and Santiago walked through the barn door, he saw a figure dash toward them and for one short moment he thought it was Kit with her petite figure clad in flowered muslin and her rustling petticoats lifted so she could move faster. But in the next instant, he knew it was Delores.

He caught his sister in the circle of his arms as she reached him. She was panting from rushing to meet him. "Oh, Danton! Danton! God, how glad I am to see you here." With her older brother hugging her, she felt secure and safe as she had when her father had swept away all her apprehensions and fears when she'd been a little girl. Now, Delores knew things around the ranch would be straightened out. On that score, she and Santiago were in accord.

When their embrace was finally broken, Danton saw a mist in his sister's big doelike eyes as she looked searchingly up into his face. "Santiago has told you everything, hasn't he?" she asked.

"Yes, sweetheart. He's told me everything but it will be all right, I promise."

"I know it will now, Danton. Now that you're home."

"You're a sweet girl, Delores." Danton grinned down at his sister, then gave her a brotherly kiss on the cheek.

She bristled slightly, and with a cute pout on her red lips, she corrected him, "I'm no child anymore, Danton. I know brothers don't notice that."

He gave her an affectionate pat and confessed, "I guess you are right about that, little Dee."

As Santiago turned to go toward the corrals, Danton and Delores crossed the courtyard garden, heading toward the house.

It was his new sister-in-law they first encountered when they strolled down the tiled hallway. The very sight of Danton, so tall and handsome as he strolled with his sister, made Molly's heart beat faster. It sparked her old feelings of infatuation for him. Dear God, she wondered why couldn't it have been Danton she'd ended up with? Now, there was a man—a real man!

Now, she knew only too well that Damien's charms were always so shallow—like a lacquered coating that hid a coarse surface. The twins' faces might be the same, Molly mused, but that was where the similarity ended.

Danton was making his own survey as he observed the pretty blond-haired Molly waiting to greet him. Before she spoke, he noticed the difference in the girl he'd known all his life, a girl he'd even escorted to a couple of social affairs. Her blue eyes sparkled brightly as they said their hellos and Danton graciously told her how happy he was to have her for his new sister-in-law, but Danton saw something else. There was a hardness in those eyes now. Danton sensed the change even more as the trio chattered light-heartedly while they proceeded to Lucía's back sitting room.

Lucía wasn't there so Molly offered to see if she was in the kitchen with Drusilla. "She'll be so happy to see you, Danton. Lordy, so happy!" Molly scurried away before he could reply.

"She's changed!" Danton voiced his thoughts before he realized what he was doing.

"She certainly has! I say good for her, Danton. Damien was horrible to her that first week, and now she takes no quarter from him. She and mother had become very close though, and I . . . I like Molly, too."

"That's good, honey. Got an idea she might have needed you two."

As Lucía Navarro observed her offspring, she heard Delores' comments to her older brother, and she felt an overwhelming surge of pride. Her daughter was a fine, young lady. Lucía was almost certain after the last few weeks that the young Dr. Rojas was going to be a part of Delores' future.

The two young people she was now watching and admiring did not leave her heart heavy with concern or worry. They would be just fine!

Finally she made her presence known. "My son . . . it is good to have you home."

Danton turned to see her standing there, and had he not known the troubled times she'd faced since he'd said goodbye, he would have not had any inkling of her difficulties. Always, she was a lady of dignity!

She favored him with her soft, pleasant smile and then stretched out her hands. As Danton took them his dark eyes locked with hers. What an indomitable spirit she was, her dark head held high and her chin angled with an arrogance of pride.

When Danton kissed her, Lucía knew there was no

need to speak of the unpleasantness evolving around them. Her son's manner told Lucía that Santiago or Delores had already filled him in on all the details.

Delores, however, wishing to allow the two of them to have some privacy, politely excused herself. She, too, wanted to speak to Danton alone, just as soon as possible. At first, Santiago's presence had delayed such a talk, and then they had encountered Molly just as she was about to tell Danton of the letter she'd come across by accident. For some reason, she had decided not to show the letter to Lucía. She had kept it her secret, but now she would show it to Danton.

At first, Delores had been shocked to see that it was addressed to Damien, and her hurt had been deeper for Kit had not written her a farewell message. She'd questioned just how sincere Kit's friendship for her had been.

But the more she'd pondered the mystery of Kit's sudden flight into the night with Yolanda, the more Delores had known that some driving force had impelled Kit to make a hasty departure from Silvercreek. The most startling piece of the puzzle was the way Kit had signed her letter to Damien. Her mother's message was signed by the girl they'd all come to know and love for many months. It was signed "Kit," but Damien's letter was signed "Kristina Whelan."

Why? Delores had exhausted herself trying to figure it out.

Somehow, Delores could not believe she'd been so utterly fooled about the auburn-haired Kit. That was why she was so eager to talk to Danton and see what he would make out of this strange business. Danton was smart and clever and Delores was confident he'd have an answer. Besides, Delores really believed that Kit and Danton had been very much in love.

Now, she must wait to speak to Danton alone.

Chapter 43

Convention would not allow her to return home to her father's ranch and desert a crippled husband, Molly Langford Navarro realized. Nonetheless, she had stubbornly refused to take his despicable treatment. He could no longer abuse her physically so his foul mouth was now his only weapon.

Once she found the new source of power within herself, she was undaunted by his childlike tantrums. She just walked out and left him ranting and raving. Molly had learned that she was a force to be reckoned with. This infuriated Damien, as Molly intended.

Molly was unaware of the growing respect and admiration the people at Silvercreek felt for her, but her allies, Lucía and Delores, made up for the humiliation and shame Damien had made her feel in the beginning.

On the first afternoon Danton was back home at Silvercreek, he spoke with a few of the hired hands and the gossip he picked up here and there told him that all sympathy lay with Damien's pregnant bride, not with Damien.

Danton figured it was time he went to see his twin brother. He knew he'd delayed the encounter because he was unsure of his own reaction to Damien. He was not cad enough to strike a man in a wheelchair, but Danton could not convince himself that Damien was not linked with Kit's departure from Silvercreek. It was unacceptable to him that she would want to leave him. Damn it, he knew she loved him!

His mother had let him read her letter from Kit and he'd read the letter she'd written to him. The mysterious little minx's letter had only left him in a quandary. He could not figure out the "barrier" she'd written about. Why would something keep them forever apart? Nor did he understand that she had to be convinced beyond a shadow of doubt before she'd dare let herself love him again.

Oh, *querida,* he moaned silently to himself, how can I convince you if I do not even know where you are? How can I prove to you that my love is eternally yours if you want it!

Perhaps when he talked to Damien these questions would be answered. Without further delay he left the barnyard and walked swiftly back to the house. As he was heading up the flagstone walk that led to the veranda, he heard a muffled voice beckon to him. His sister stood behind the oleander bush, anxiously gesturing at him.

"Little one, what are you about, eh?" Danton grinned because she looked so cute and impish as she had when she was a small child. He'd wondered where she'd run off to.

"I'm trying . . . I've been trying to get you alone since you got here three hours ago. I've got something to show you, Danton—something about Kit." Delores' manner and voice were too serious for Danton to take her words lightly.

His broad shoulders plowed through the oleander branches, and he took her hand, leading her over to the little wooden bench by the live oak at the back of the courtyard. "You know something I don't about Kit, Dee?"

"I didn't until I came upon this the other day," she replied, pulling the folded piece of paper from the pocket of her flowered muslin frock. "I think you should read it, Danton. Kit obviously regained her memory before she left Silvercreek."

Danton's hands were so eager they trembled as he took the paper and began to read. "This was written to Damien!" He grimaced, glancing at Delores.

"Yes, I was helping Drusilla up in his room the other day and it must have fallen off the chest onto the floor. I admit I was curious, Danton, because I saw it was signed 'Kristina.' At first, I wondered who the new woman was in Damien's life. Everyone here knows he doesn't love Molly. Mercy, I can tell you I was shocked when I realized it was Kit who'd written the letter."

All the time she chattered, Danton read. As he read the letter a second time, his shrewd lawyer's mind was whirling, trying to cipher out the meaning. At least, he now had something to go on for she had most assuredly regained her memory. He now knew her name and where she was going. That was all he needed to know!

He was puzzled by Damien's letter as he had been by the one addressed to him. However, he concluded that Damien was privy to the fact that she'd regained her memory before she left. Why else would she have signed her real name, Kristina?

More than ever now, he was anxious to talk to Damien, and if he had to wring it out of his twin brother, he was going to find out what Damien knew about all this.

He bent to give his sister a kiss on the cheek. "Thank you, honey. Thank you very much. Now I think I'd better pay a call on our brother." Danton turned

376

sharply and headed for Damien's room.

Delores was worried about the scene that would take place between her older brothers. There had been too many despairing days lately at Silvercreek; another tragedy was not needed. She knew that Danton could not possibly be prepared for the twin brother he was about to encounter. But then, Damien was not going to be elated to see his enraged twin either.

Danton was stunned by the sight of the man he saw in the wheelchair. It was eerie to gaze upon Damien's face, a copy of his own, and to see the bitterness etched deeply into his handsome features. There was a snarl on his mouth as he turned in his chair when Danton opened the door without knocking. Danton had been unwilling to risk Damien's refusing to allow him to enter his quarters. If Danton had ever had any doubts about his twin's intense resentment of him, they were now swept away.

Damien smirked. "Well, well, well—the great white knight comes forth to see the black knight, eh?"

"Damien," Danton's fathomless black eyes pierced his twin as he sauntered slowly up to stand in front of him. For one fleeting moment, a sense of compassion flooded over him. For the happy-go-lucky Damien to be confined to a wheelchair, to be unable to ride his fine black stallion or to go courting the ladies, that was a punishment worse than death.

"Pour us some whiskey, Danton, and have a drink with your old twin," Damien suggested. "A lot has happened since you were last here, wouldn't you say?"

"I'd say too damned much!" Danton went over to the low chest where he found the half-filled whiskey bottle. "You've obviously nipped quite a bit already, *amigo.*"

"I have," Damien snapped. "Come on, Danton, it's a little late in the day for either of us to call the other *amigo.* Hell, we haven't been friends from the time we

377

turned sixteen or seventeen. Victor Navarro saw to that."

That statement provoked a defensive response in Danton. "We were just different individuals by that age, Damien. Don't blame a dead man for that."

"I do and I'll continue to do so with just cause. Ridicule was all that old hardnose gave me while you got the praise."

"I got the praise for my skill at riding horses, but I damned well recall the very expensive guitar Father ordered for you and his raving over your magnificent voice. Hell, I couldn't sing. I never danced as well as you do either. Never could charm people like you could. I remember how I envied you when father and mother gave those annual fiestas and everyone gathered around you. You use Father as your excuse for everything, but he's not at fault. Your short-comings and mine are our own."

Damien laughed and took a generous gulp of the liquor. "Ah, so typical of you, Danton. The gallant paragon!"

"Paragon, hell! Never!" Danton, too, took a big swig of the whiskey.

A wicked twinkle came to Damien's eyes. "Don't you know, Danton, what an admired *hombre* you are? Why, my bride thinks you're a paragon! You're Delores' hero and Mother dearest thinks you can do no wrong. Mother dearest . . . that's a laugh!"

As if instinct told Danton that his twin was about to utter something derogatory, he pointedly warned, "Watch it, Damien! Watch that mouth of yours!"

Damien saw the black fire smoldering in Danton's eyes. "Figures . . . yes sir, it figures. She and your Kit have a lot in common. Ask her if you don't believe me, brother."

What kind of irrational gibberish is Damien spout-

378

ing? Danton wondered. "Damien, I'd call that a compliment to Kit." He rose from the chair and walked over to set his glass on the table. He wanted no more of the whiskey. Damien had been right when he'd said they were never friends. They didn't speak the same language or share the same feelings about anything. He had no reason to linger in this room that reeked with Damien's bitterness.

Sensing that his brother was preparing to leave, Damien yearned to taunt him about the beautiful Kristina. "Well, your little auburn-haired kitten skipped out on you, didn't she? Whores—all of them are just whores. Some just wear fancier gowns than others."

Like a raging mountain cat, Danton whirled around and lunged at Damien. One strong hand grasped the open collar of Damien's white linen shirt, and the other slapped Damien's face once and then twice before his control returned. The twins stared at one another. Damien was choking and gasping for breath as Danton, disgusted that he couldn't stand up and fight him like a man, hissed down at him, "You foul-mouthed son of a bitch! Cripple or not, I'll kill you if you say that again."

It was then, in a gasping, faltering voice, that Damien enlightened Danton about Lucía's past life. "Regardless of what you think of me what I'm telling you about Lucía Navarro is true."

Danton stood frozen in his tracks, recalling Damien's trip to San Antonio when they were eighteen. When he'd returned there had been a change in him. A sullen belligerence had settled over him for weeks after that.

Seeing the impact he was having on Danton, Damien took a devious pleasure in taunting him about Kit and about his little escapade in El Paso. He was so overcome with a crazed sense of power, so eager to torment and punish Danton, that he left out not one single detail of the whole episode. When it had been told, Damien laughed like a raving madman. It was a crazy man Danton stared down on!

Dazed with disbelief, Danton gazed at the pathetic soul sitting there. He was dumfounded. How could this devil have come from the womb of their mother along with him? Time stopped for Danton and he could only stare at his twin. Only Damien's shrill, crazed voice finally brought him out of his trancelike state.

"Kill me! Go ahead! I know you are itching to after all I've told you. Get me out of this living hell. You're the great savior! Come on! Do it!"

For one second, Danton's black eyes warmed as he stared down at his twin brother, but at the same instant, a slow, lazy grin appeared on his mouth. Revolted, Danton turned his back on Damien. He walked slowly to the door, and his deep voice, stern and unruffled and unrelenting floated back as he marched through it.

"You're not worth killing. You're having your judgment day and I'll not interfere with it."

Danton closed the door and Damien was left alone to seethe about his failure to outfox his twin brother. It was his last chance and he'd bungled it!

He could have sworn that Danton would draw his pistol and shoot him in a fit of rage, but he didn't know his twin brother at all.

Damien's despair was overwhelming.

Chapter 44

Danton felt the need to sequester himself alone in the quiet of the courtyard garden before talking with his mother as he knew he must. He could turn his back on Damien—his brother had made his own hell—but he wanted to know from his mother's lips what Damien's vile innuendos were really about.

Nothing Damien could ever say would destroy his great love and respect for Lucía Navarro. No woman who truly loved and gave of herself so unselfishly as he'd always known her to do could be the kind of person Damien was trying to make her seem. But no mortal was a saint. Lucía had instilled that awareness in him when he was growing up.

It was funny how her words came rushing back to Danton as he ambled slowly to the spot where he intended to sit for a while and gather his thoughts before going into the house. When he and Damien were stripling youths, she'd often told them, "Remember, my sons, always beware of people who try to paint themselves as Gods or saints. They aren't—no one is! There are serious flaws in such people, and they are invariably selfish."

Danton had recalled her words on many occasions

when he'd encountered such individuals. He had always appreciated his mother's wisdom and her sage advice. She couldn't have been the woman Damien described!

Lucía, meanwhile, had seen him go into that secluded corner of the courtyard garden. It had been anything but a pleasant homecoming for her son, she realized. The way he walked and the expression on his face told her he was troubled. Knowing that he'd just come from a visit with Damien, she wondered what had been the gist of their conversation.

The time had come, Lucía realized, to tell Danton about her past, the past that Damien had flung in her face so cruelly only a week ago. Dear God, how Damien had hurt her! She would carry that anguish to her grave. Victor had promised her years ago that he and she would stand together when they told the children about her gambling days at the Palace. Dear, darling Victor had made it seem so simple and uncomplicated as he'd gently shrugged all her apprehensions aside when she'd voiced her concerns about what their children would think when they learned that their mother had been a faro dealer. He'd coolly and calmly repeated that he'd be standing beside her, but it had not happened that way.

No, it had not worked out that way at all. Damien's vile slurs had cut at her like a knife slashing her body. He had enjoyed himself that miserable afternoon, and that was the most painful hurt of all. Now, she must find out whether her other son would hold her in contempt as his twin brother did, and if so, would she have the courage to deal with it? She must! she told herself.

She was a survivor. If she hadn't been, the early days of her womanhood would have been tragic. Regardless of Damien's devious efforts to make those years sound sordid, Lucía knew they were not. Oh, she was human and she had her faults, but she was an honest person!

For that honesty she had paid a tremendous price the other day when she'd taken her son's abuse. She could not help thinking that if Victor had heard Damien's vile language, he would have surely killed his son.

That afternoon she'd stood looking down at Damien in his wheelchair, and she'd thought to herself with agonizing honesty that her son was destructive and selfish. This left her heartbroken. But her stubborn will prevailed as she left his room, and she vowed he would not destroy her as he yearned to do.

Molly now carried her first grandchild, and her darling Delores was devoted and comforting. Soon, she was certain, she'd live to see her daughter married to the nice Dr. Rojas, and they, too, would have children. The Navarro family most assuredly would go on and on. There was Danton—his future lay ahead of him. Lucía felt very strongly that the auburn-haired Kit was not out of his life forever. She would not believe that for a minute.

Thus fortified, Lucía walked slowly across the grounds to the secluded corner in the garden where her son was. When she returned this way, she would be desolate or she'd rejoice. She hoped Danton possessed the wisdom she'd always tried to instill in him.

Her steps were slow, but determined, as she took the straight, direct path, her dark head held high. From the set of her lips and her dignified air no one would have guessed how nervous she was.

Because of the thick carpet of grass, Danton did not hear her soft footsteps as she approached the bower entwined with vines. Actually, as Lucía was about to make her presence known, he was preparing to rise from the little wooden bench to go seek his mother out. So when her familiar voice called out to him, he was pleased.

"Mother, join me. You must have been reading my mind. I was just coming in the house to find you. We've some things to discuss, I think, in private." He extended his hand to guide Lucía onto the wooden bench beside him.

Those piercing eyes of hers were busy surveying Danton's face as she spoke, "You are troubled, Danton. I can tell."

"Yes, Mother, I am troubled as I know you've been for weeks. I can only say that I'm sorry I was not here."

"You have seen your brother?"

"I have seen him. Talking about Damien will do little good at this point, I fear. My mistakes with Damien were made long ago when I began to shield him from the consequences of his many escapades." Danton's black eyes darted down to the hand which clasped his mother's. "I've . . . I've never felt right about the man I shot and killed in Fort Worth that night at the White Elephant Saloon. I just made it easier for Damien to do his next irresponsible deed."

"Danton, my darling, I will not allow you to blame yourself for your brother's wickedness." Lucía's hand went to his cheek.

"But it is true nevertheless, Mother, and you, of all people, taught me to be honest. Remember when I went to El Paso to drag him out of there before he and his no-good buddies got into big trouble and Damien lost all his money at the faro tables?"

"I recall the time, Danton."

"In that case, I have something for you to read because that incident had a far more drastic effect than you or I realized, I can tell you." He handed his mother the letter Delores had slipped to him—Kit's letter to Damien.

"You have your letter from Kit and I have mine; this

384

is the one she left for Damien. When you read it, you'll see exactly what I mean." He gave the paper to a perplexed Lucía Navarro.

She read the missive and then read it again. A giddiness washed over her as she finished the letter, for she now knew the instant affection she'd felt for the girl named Kit was rooted in the past. She was Kristina Whelan, the daughter of her old friend, Florine. Merciful God, what a small world!

Her dark eyes darted over to Danton. "Am I going crazy or does this mean what I think it means? Damien knew—all the time he knew that she was Kristina Whelan. Why, Danton, why did he not inform us?"

"Because, Mother, Damien didn't want her identity known. Kit's loss of memory was a blessing for Damien because she could have identified him as the leader of the gang who robbed Florine Whelan and abducted her daughter that night in El Paso."

"But Danton, her letter does not say all that. How did you find that out, my son?"

"From the horse's mouth, shall we say. Damien delighted in telling me the whole sordid mess. Damn! How he enjoyed himself! I could have killed him, Mother!"

Lucía heaved a desolate sigh. "Dear God, how could he have done such a despicable thing?"

"I can't answer that. Obviously, Kit was a young innocent girl who was frightened out of her wits on that night they rode out of El Paso, but she escaped from that bunch. Then, she must have fallen, hit her head so hard it caused her loss of memory. Damien couldn't enlighten me about how that happened himself, but he knew that the night she left with Yolanda, she had regained her memory."

"Oh, Danton! That poor, poor girl! What a horrible nightmare this is." Lucía bit her lower lip.

385

"Yes, it is a nightmare. If Damien wasn't in that wheelchair, I'd beat him within an inch of his life. But my brother has received his punishment from a higher power and he will pay for the rest of his life."

Lucía could not argue with that so she only nodded her head. Just as she was about to ask Danton what he intended to do about Kit, he volunteered the information.

"I'll be going to El Paso, Mother. I love her. I've loved her since I spotted her up on that mountain trail near Emil's cabin."

"I thought you did, Danton, and I'm glad to hear you say so. Whatever her name is—Kit or Kristina—I think she loves you too. Go to El Paso and tell her how you feel. There is nothing you can do here—nothing at all."

"Thank you, Mother," he said, bending over to kiss her. "You are quite a woman!"

His words reminded Lucía that she hadn't yet told Danton her story, and she knew she must even though it seemed to be the wrong time. Would his sentiments be the same after she told him?

"Danton, you've always been such a fine, devoted son and I've always taken great pride in you."

"Credit yourself, Mother, if that is so." Danton grinned for the first time since they'd been sitting on the wooden bench.

"It seems this is one of those strange days in a person's life, and so I must now tell you a story, a story that would have been told long ago if Victor had not died when he did. We had intended to tell it together, but fate doesn't always oblige."

Now it was Danton who had a perplexed look on his face so Lucía delayed the ordeal no longer.

"As you three were growing up you were always told my parents were dead and that is partially true. My mother is dead, and my father was dead to me long

386

before I met Victor. My father remarried shortly after my mother's death, and his new wife tried to push me into a marriage I didn't desire, to a man I detested. My father was so bewitched by his new bride that he also insisted I marry that man. So I ran away, Danton."

She told him about hitching a ride in a wagon with a family traveling from Louisiana to Texas, about working on their ranch when the family settled in the hill country, and about the old Mexican named Gomez who'd taught her to play Spanish Monte and faro. She described how, at the tender age of seventeen, she'd bid the family farewell and sought employment in San Antonio.

She watched her son's face as he listened attentively when she related how she'd become known as Lolita, the Queen of the Palace, a gambling hall in San Antonio. It was there the young bachelor, Victor Navarro, had met her and they'd fallen in love at first sight.

A slow easy smile came to Danton's face and he remarked, "I'll bet you were some beautiful sight for any man's eyes to behold! So father was smitten at once, eh?"

Lucía took her first easy breath since she'd started her tale, and she smiled. "Ah, my darling, he was not the only one smitten. The butterflies went wild in my stomach. I'd never seen such a magnificent, handsome man as my Victor was that night. I fell so hopelessly in love I felt I couldn't breathe."

The rest of her story was no ordeal, for Danton's response had obviated any concerns she might have harbored. "I was right, you know. You are quite a woman! I never realized how much of a woman until now! No wonder my father adored you all the days of his life, Mother."

"Oh, God bless you, darling!" Lucía smiled though

her dark eyes were misted, and before they parted, she told him about Florine Whelan, that she had been an acquaintance of hers in San Antonio. "It is startling, Danton, Kit's resemblance to her. I admit I had a funny feeling about that dear, sweet girl, one I could never quite explain to myself."

Mother and son now felt light-hearted, and Danton gave her a reassuring hug.

"Well, I think it's perfect that you and Florine are old friends," he said playfully, "since she's going to be my mother-in-law very soon if I have any say about it. Would you not agree?"

"I would and I'd say that you shouldn't let any grass grow under your feet. Get to El Paso, young man."

"Ah, rest assured, *mamacita*. I go the first thing in the morning, to El Paso and the woman I love."

Lucía Navarro smiled and nodded her head approvingly. Life at Silvercreek was good again! She knew Victor was smiling down on them.

Part IV

Forever, my love

Chapter 45

Miles separated Silvercreek Ranch from the town of El Paso, which lay westward, but in her dreams Kristina Whelan was at the ranch with the man she loved. In fact, the dream had been so real she sat up in the bed and pushed her long thick hair away from her neck in an effort to cool the smoldering flames which seemed to be consuming her flushed body.

Dear God, she moaned quietly. It was as if he was in the room with her! The heat of his lips had been so real as they'd caressed her breasts, and his magical touch had been just as real as he'd urged her to accompany him to the heights of rapture. She'd felt helpless, unable to resist yielding to his indomitable will.

Lips meeting, arms and legs entwining, and bodies fusing in frenzied, flaming passion—their lovemaking had been so vivid she was breathless and her heart was pounding wildly. It took a few moments of sitting on the side of the bed in her dark room to come to terms with the fact that it had only been a dream. Danton Navarro was not here in El Paso, not in her boudoir. He was miles away in Austin or out at Silvercreek.

"Oh, you black-eyed devil, why do you haunt me so!" she dejectedly mumbled. Then she rose, and still swishing the long straying strands of hair off the back of her neck, she lazily strolled to the open window to look out at the starlit night. Perhaps, it is morning by now, she thought as she stared out the window. The breeze felt good and the quiet darkness shrouded the grounds below. The household still slept peacefully.

For the first time since she'd returned home Kristina felt a pang of remorse because she'd left Danton. Had she been wrong? Had Damien deceived her? Had she thrown away something so precious she'd live to regret it the rest of her life?

For the last few weeks her time had been totally occupied by her effort to make the Crystal Castle the flourishing business it had been before the tragedy had struck—at the hands of a Navarro. For the first time, her heart cried out, declaring it could have been Damien and not Danton.

Yet she could not deny that Damien was always the carefree, frivolous twin who had nothing more on his mind than wooing and winning the favors of one lady or the other. He liked to revel and carouse, to ride his fine black stallion over the countryside. She knew he merely played at helping his mother run the ranch.

No, it was Danton who was shrewd and cool. He had the cunning, calculating mind. She could not dismiss the times when he'd perplexed her, when he'd shut her out of his life as though he'd found her offensive. The jealous streak in her could not forget the intimate closeness she'd witnessed between him and Estellita. So how could she credit Damien with telling the truth?

Whatever the truth was, she decided she wasn't going to discover it tonight or this morning. She had her own gambler's game to play, and play it she would. At least, she'd finally gotten her way with her stubborn mother. She was about ready to launch her newly acquired skill as a faro dealer.

Singing nightly at the Crystal Castle had won some of the old patrons back, but she hoped when she could assume her mother's former role at the monte and faro tables, she'd show that bunch over at the Bird Cage who was queen of gambling in El Paso.

Kristina had heard the rumors floating around town. She was already being called the Queen of the Crystal Castle. Well, that was all right! That was exactly what she intended. Dapper gentlemen could admire the sensuous curves her alluring gowns revealed and they could enjoy their wild fantasies about kissing her luscious lips or yearning to possess her nightly—but none would! Only she would know that the wicked glint in her green eyes was to bait them to spend their money!

Solitaire had admonished her severely just the other day, telling her, *"Mademoiselle . . . Miss Tina, you got a wicked streak in you, you know that?"*

In response, Kristina had giggled so spontaneously that Solitaire had been reminded of the little girl she'd once cared for. That Kristina was now so grown up momentarily amazed the mulatto.

"Now, Solitaire, don't you try to tell me that Momma didn't do the very same thing!"

Solitaire had hastily turned away from Kristina's prodding green eyes to hide her amused smile.

"Come on, Solitaire, be honest!" Kristina playfully insisted.

"Ahhhh, how come you got so smart so fast, missy? You just don't outsmart yourself. There's always some man out there that can make you forget everything good sense tells you to remember."

"I'll try to remember that in the future, Solitaire."

"See that you do, Miss Tina. Heart don't listen to what the head tells you," Solitaire pointed out.

"Oh, I've already found that out, Solitaire," Kristina

told the mulatto servant.

The look on Kristina's face and the faraway stare in her lovely eyes told Solitaire a lot.

"I had that already figured out, Miss Tina. That look of love's been all over your face since you got back home."

Kristina tried to put on a frivolous air. "Now, you are being too darned smart, Solitaire."

"Oh, yes, ma'am—always have been that! *Mam'selle* told me that many years ago just like you just did. But I was right just the same," Solitaire remarked in that smug, but adorable way of hers. Then she sashayed out of the room, flashing a mischievous grin at Kristina, a glint of mischief in her black eyes.

Kristina laughed at the mulatto, who would always hold a special place in her heart. Solitaire had been a second mother to her throughout her growing years. It was little wonder that the servant couldn't be fooled, Kristina realized.

Alone in her room, she tried to concentrate on her life here in El Paso, on the song she'd sing this evening, on anything but Danton Navarro; but all her strong will wasn't working.

She marched to the armoire. Which gown should she wear? The white brocade or maybe the royal blue one? There was that magnificent black one that always seemed to be admired. She knew its sophisticated elegance was enhanced by the exquisite choker of pearls Dan Recamier had presented to her the night before. She had promised to join him for a late dinner in one of the little private alcove rooms at the Crystal Castle after she'd finished her first set of songs.

Now why, she asked herself, couldn't I get excited about having dinner with this dashing gentleman? He'd come to the establishment the second night she'd started to sing at her mother's gambling hall. He'd been

394

nice and mannerly.

He was new to the El Paso scene, so she'd been told by Sally O'Neal. He'd come from New Orleans or St. Louis. He was a gambler and a high-stakes one, and from the way he threw his money around, he was a lucky one.

Recamier's manner sometimes reminded Kristina of Damien Navarro with his teasing black eyes. Only Dan's eyes were silver-gray, and as piercing as a sharp-edged sword. Yes, he was everything that should have made a lady's heart flutter excitedly, but hers didn't. Under her breath, she cursed Danton Navarro! Had he spoiled her for any other man? His haunting and taunting face invaded her dreams at night, making a man like Dan Recamier, for all his charm, look pale in comparison.

Two men traveled that early evening and both were obsessed by thoughts of Kristina Whelan. Danton Navarro journeyed toward El Paso, and he was impatient to reach his destination, like a youth going to court his first love.

Dan Recamier drove his fine gig down the streets of El Paso, just as eager to be finally sharing a private dinner with the luscious Kristina. She was a delectable female, and he was determined to have his way with her. She'd excited him beyond anything he'd ever experienced before.

His conceited ego reasoned that once he'd possessed her, she would be far more easy to fit into his plans here in El Paso. He and his partners could not allow her to continue taking business away from the Bird Cage. One little auburn-haired female wasn't going to mess up their carefully laid plans, not after they'd invested so much money in the Bird Cage. He'd convinced his three partners not to rough her up until he'd tried his own idea. They'd gone along, but the deadline was the end of this week. The cocky Recamier was sure he could pull off his plan, and have his pleasure too.

The arrogant young gambler would not have felt so self-assured had he known that the gorgeous young lady he was about to call on was wishing she had not made the date with him. Danton Navarro was all too real to Kristina Whelan this evening.

Just before Rollo was to drive her into town from the ranch, something happened that only intensified her tormenting thoughts of Navarro. Kristina hadn't intended to get into a discussion with her mother, but she had. As they'd talked Kristina had suddenly found herself spilling out the whole story—well, almost the whole story.

Now, as she sat back on the velour-covered seat of the carriage, she wondered if Florine had deliberately led her into talking about Danton. No one had to tell her how clever her mother was! She never expected to fill Florine's shoes on that score.

She'd merely walked into Florine's sitting room, as a lot of daughters do when they're all dressed up, to seek her mother's appraisal. She'd chosen the black gown and the lovely pearl choker, along with some pearl earrings.

Florine had nodded appreciatively. "Just a minute, darling—one finishing touch, eh?" She opened the drawer of her dressing table and pulled out the black aigrette decorated with seed pearls.

"This, darling, in your hair and you will look absolutely stunning! Oh, Kristina, I pray I won't regret the day I've gone along with this plan of yours. If it proves to be foolhardy and you suffer, I will feel very guilty."

Kristina stood, allowing her mother to place the aigrette at the side of her hair. "It will be fine. I've had a good teacher. You had no one and you did all right."

"Oh, I did not always do things right, but I learned from my mistakes and I certainly got smarter."

Thoughtlessly, Kristina said, "The price is painful sometimes." The instant she said it she felt Florine's fingers pause, and she knew her mother's green eyes were staring at the reflection on her face.

"I've never asked you, Kristina, because I felt—well, I hoped—you'd tell me, but I think there is a man who has caused you pain. Am I right, dear?"

Kristina was too much like Florine to try to deny it, and she replied with candor, "He has caused me pain but only because I love him. I doubt that I'll ever love anyone as I've loved Danton Navarro."

"Danton Navarro." The name echoed in Florine's mind and she uttered it over and over. She thought Jason had told her the obnoxious young scion of the wealthy Navarro family over in Pecos was named Damien. Because her thoughts were on the name of Damien, Florine remarked to her daughter, "So Damien Navarro is the man you love, my dear."

Kristina looked startled at her mother and sought to quickly correct her. "No, Momma—it is Danton I love. Damien is his twin." Her long-lashed eyes fluttered nervously, and she stared at her mother before she continued to speak. When she did speak Florine saw the depth of her daughter's emotion for Kristina could not hide the ache in her heart. The torment in her soul was revealed as she told her mother the complete story of her months of absence.

"But I must know without a shadow of a doubt which one was here that awful night. I must, Momma. You can see that, can't you?"

"Of course, darling. You pray it is not the one

you love."

"Oh God, how I pray!"

"You will find out, Kristina. You will. Perhaps, sooner than you think." She gave her daughter a reassuring hug and murmured warmly, "I'm so glad we finally had this long-overdue talk. So very glad, Kristina."

"So am I, Momma. Now I must go. I will be spending the night at the Crystal Castle for I have a late dinner date with a gentleman."

But before Florine could inquire about the man her daughter was seeing, Kristina was dashing madly from the sitting room and Florine's slow, tedious movements did not allow her time to move out of her chair. While Kristina rushed on down the long hallway and out of sight, therefore, Florine remained in her cozy, soft chair, and she smiled. She was content to have her daughter back. It was wonderful! It was the only nice thing that bastard had done for her years ago. Kristina was worth it all!

Chapter 46

There are men and women who receive instant attention when they enter a room. Dan Recamier was that kind of a personality, and tonight he'd paid special attention to his impeccable attire. He'd selected a deep gun-metal gray coat and a lighter shade of gray pin-stripe trousers. A black silk ascot provided the perfect background for his diamond stickpin, and on the cuff of his frosty white shirt were his cherished five thousand dollar cuff studs.

His expressionless face gave no hint that he was aware of the eyes aimed in his direction as he stood so nonchalantly in the foyer of the Crystal Castle. But he knew his image projected good taste and a touch of class. That was his aim.

Standing there, he had to admit to himself that Florine Whelan had at the Crystal Castle something he and his cohorts would never have at the Bird Cage, but then this was not what they were in the gambling game for.

There was grandeur here and sparkling opulence, elegance with a flair. By God, he gave the lady credit for that! He and his partners had drifted down from Kansas City after it had been drained dry and had ceased to be a gambler's haven, and they were out to make a fortune while they could because one day the gambling halls in Texas—those in Dallas, San Antonio, and El Paso—would go by the wayside just as they had back in the east. The move was toward the west.

He and his partners would move with the sporting gentry, anticipating the change, going from one prime spot to another. Whether they worked from a building or a set-up tent, it didn't matter so long as the gambling action was taking place.

But that was why this gorgeous, auburn-haired slip of a girl couldn't be allowed to dampen their thriving business here. Sally O'Neal had proven to be no obstacle, nor had the semiretired Florine Whelan, but they hadn't counted on the return of Florine's sensuous, voluptuous daughter. No doxie at the Bird Cage could make gentlemen enamored of her as Kristina had, yet all the little minx did was sit on a stool and sing her songs. That alone was enough to drive the gamblers wild with desire, and they fantasized their private yearnings as they watched Kristina Whelan.

The Bird Cage's overpainted ladies of pleasure were not providing enough competition for her beguiling beauty. Perhaps, her untouchable aloofness was a challenge to the gentlemen as it was to Dan. Nevertheless, his business was losing customers and money. Another month like the last two weeks and Recamier and his partners would be in trouble.

As he stood there in the archway, Dan felt the heat of the pretty, little Mexican girl's eyes on him. She was standing behind the long counter in the entranceway taking the arriving customers' hats and canes. Little Yolanda most assuredly did not like him, he decided. He assumed that since she'd arrived in El Paso with her mistress her evening duties had been either Sally's

400

O'Neal's idea or Kristina's. But he'd noticed she had a lovely smile on that tawny-skinned face of hers for almost everyone but him.

Her greetings to him were always sharp, and she seemed to begrudge them. Even when he'd complimented her tonight on how lovely she looked with the pretty posy in her black hair, she'd mumbled begrudgingly, *"Gracias, Señor Recamier."*

He was sorely tempted to inquire just why she didn't approve of him, but he didn't.

He was right about Yolanda's not liking him, and she would not try to mask her feelings even though she knew the man was trying to win her favor only because of his interest in Kristina. She was aware that Kristina was planning to dine with him this evening.

She stole glances at him as he stood only a few feet away from her little booth gazing over the room and surveying the crowd already gathered at the faro and monte table. One of the new roulette croupiers caught her dark intense eyes and thought she was staring at him, so he gave her a wink of his eye. Yolanda could not suppress the smile that came to her red lips.

Across the room Sally O'Neal happened to witness the scene and grinned. Little Yolanda was a cute mite, and she was worth her weight in gold. With all the energy and vigor she had, she was proving to be an asset in the evening, and she certainly did her share upstairs, helping the ladies dress and style their hair. The cleaning woman no longer tended to Florine's old living quarters for Yolanda kept it spotless. Sally considered that Kristina had found herself a rare jewel in the girl.

Sally stared across the room at the devilishly handsome Recamier, who'd just arrived. Dear God, he was enough to devastate a woman. Animal magnetism oozed out of him.

401

Many good-looking dudes had come and gone during her time at the Crystal Castle, but few had measured up to this one's standards. He darn well made her tingle with excitement.

That made it hard to believe the rumor she'd heard the other night, that he was in league with that bunch of rowdies over at the Bird Cage. He presented such a fine image she found herself persuaded to turn her back on the gossip. A gentleman like Dan Recamier would surely feel it below his dignity to live off the earnings of the whores who'd been shipped into El Paso by the owners of the Bird Cage.

But could she ignore the talk now that Florine's daughter had apparently begun an association with the man? Shouldn't she tell Kristina and let the young woman judge the situation? If she did, Florine couldn't fault her later, Sally reasoned. For everyone's sake, she decided that tonight she would tell Kristina what she'd heard about Dan Recamier.

Then she turned her attention to a party of arriving customers, delighted to see they were a group of wealthy Mexicans from El Paso. Juan Ortega was one of the group, she recognized him immediately, and the son of Lorenzo Garcia was among them. He was one of the devilishly handsome Latins Sally found so attractive, as she did the Frenchman, Recamier.

She was preparing to move across the room to give these affluent patrons her personal welcome, but when the lights suddenly dimmed Sally remained where she stood.

It was the appointed time in the evening when Kristina Whelan sauntered down the long winding stairway. Like everyone else in the place, Sally turned to watch her descend with catlike grace, slowly and sensuously. The worldly-wise Sally wondered if the little vixen was aware of the flaming, sultry air she projected. Having known her share of men, Sally wondered if it was a man Kristina thought about as she ambled down to greet the sea of admiring men who stared so lustily up at her.

The shimmering silky softness of her black gown quivered with each step she took, and Kristina smiled sweetly, moving her head first in one direction, then the other. Midway down the stairs, she purred softly, "Good evening gentlemen! Welcome to the Crystal Castle!"

Her lustrous hair fell over one shoulder, and as she turned to face the other side of the room, the long tresses cascaded down over her other shoulder. The aigrette's black plumes swayed back and forth in a gentle motion.

Wild, boisterous applause resounded throughout the gambling hall, and the music began to play signaling that Kristina was going to perform.

When she took her seat on the little velvet-covered stool, she announced, "Tonight, I will sing a beautiful Spanish melody I've never sung before. It is a special song I love very much, and I hope you will enjoy it too."

Another rumble of applause arose from the enthusiastic crowd, and of course, she could not have delighted Juan Ortega and Lorenzo Garcia more. Both arrogantly thought that she was paying tribute to them, but Kristina was not even aware that the two men were present. She simply had an urge to sing the lovely melody she'd heard back at Silvercreek at Lucía's fiesta. The strolling caballeros had sung it as they'd played their guitars, and Danton had taken her into his arms to dance to it that night so long ago. That was the only dance they'd had on that night which had started out so wonderfully and had ended on such a bitter note.

Perhaps, it was Kristina's secret musings that made her face reflect such depths of emotion. She wasn't aware of the bewitching aura she projected, those watching her perform were entranced. A glowing radiance was hers as she sang, and as the music led her, she moved with the Spanish beat. Kristina was certainly the most tempting enchantress any of the gentlemen surrounding her had ever seen.

Ortega gave a low sigh. *"Ohhh, bonita! Magnífico!"*

His friend, Garcia, chimed in, "She's breath-taking, Juan. *Madre de Dios!* Such a woman!"

"Sssh, Lorenzo!" Young Ortega admonished his friend, not wanting any distractions right then.

Across the way, Dan Recamier shared the same feelings as the exuberant Mexicans, but he wasted no time in just staring at Kristina. Instead, he slowly began to work his way to a position in which he could take her dainty hand as she moved off her stool and prepared to leave the small platform stage.

Dan wanted to be the one to gather her exclusively to his side and hopefully keep her with him the rest of the evening. He weaved in and out through the crowd without calling notice to himself or what he was about as Kristina was singing a second song. By the time she was concluding that number, he had managed to achieve the vantage point he'd sought.

As she acknowledged her applause and gracefully began to rise from the stool, Dan's eyes flashed bright with a surge of desire. The bustle of her gown had made her movement to rise so sensuous it had fired a wave of instant desire in him. She turned back to look in his direction and smiled, and he moved to give her his hand as she came to the edge of the stage.

"Good evening, Dan."

. As she addressed him, he noticed for the first time that she wore the pearl choker he'd given her. It encouraged him to hope his task was going to be simple. Secretly, he knew most women proved to be an easy mark for his charm.

Dan gave her a handsome smile and offered his arm. "The beautiful queen of the castle," he dramatically declared.

"You're too generous, Dan," she laughed light-heartedly . "That title could go to only one lady and that would be my mother."

"Oh, I've heard of the legendary Madame Florine Whelan. One must spend only a brief time in El Paso to learn about your mother. To correct myself, Florine Whelan and her Crystal Castle are known across the country. I first heard the name back in New Orleans and Natchez."

They were ready to enter the velvet-curtained alcove Dan had reserved for their private dinner, but his words had sparked instant excitement in Kristina. She paused to exclaim, "Really? That far away?"

"Absolutely, *ma petite.*" He gallantly gestured her to a seat inside the lavishly decorated alcove where they would dine.

"My goodness, Dan, you've traveled all over, haven't you? You must tell me about these cities. I've never been out of Texas."

"It will be my pleasure, Kristina." He seated her on the velvet settee and chose to sit beside her instead of on the plush velvet chair placed across the table.

"Am I to assume you were born in the South, Dan?"

"Yes, I was. Don't you think I present the perfect image of the genteel Southern gentleman?" he teased.

Kristina tilted her head to the side and gave him a skeptical, scrutinizing look. Her green eyes danced over his face as she teased him in return. "Well . . . I don't know. Perhaps."

By now, the waiter was serving the champagne Dan had ordered. Kristina took a sip of the sparkling beverage and confessed to him, "Truth is, Dan—I've never met a man from the deep South so I could hardly make a judgment."

There was a casual air about him as he responded to her remark, but Kristina thought she noted a tinge of conceit in his tone. "Well, they are a different breed of men than these Texans."

She got the impression he looked down at the men of Texas, and she resented his attitude. But it would hardly have been fair to spoil the dinner they were about to enjoy over such a minor statement. How was she to know that his comment was not true?

Dan seemed to sense that his remark had irritated her, and quickly sought to change her mood by telling her how much he'd enjoyed her singing. "I told you that first time we met on the stage to El Paso that you reminded me of an actress I'd seen back east. I think you could perform on any stage, Kristina. You are a most talented lady . . . in case you don't know it."

"Thank you, Dan. You're sweet."

"I've been trying desperately to prove that to you, Kristina." He made his first gesture by taking her hand in his and bringing it to his lips to plant a light kiss on it. Kristina allowed him that liberty without flinching, and as he continued to praise her voice and style of performing, he continued to hold her hand in his. Kristina felt the strength in his grip. Dan was once again pleased and encouraged by her response.

If Kristina had tried to find fault with anything in Dan Recamier's behavior as they dined on the delectable dinner brought to them, she could not have for he was the perfect gentleman.

The sounds of laughter and talking outside the draped alcove had heightened during the last hour, and as the crowd gathered Sally O'Neal had smiled with delight. She was too busy to ponder on the two sequestered in the private dining room, but Yolanda and Sid Layman huddled together, sharing their feelings about the dude with Kristina.

Later, when Sid's services were needed elsewhere, Yolanda paced like a predatory feline, staying as close to the alcove as she could. When she heard Kristina's lilting laughter ring out from inside, she grimaced with disapproval. After listening only a short time she knew Kristina was enjoying the company of Dan Recamier. Yolanda's volatile temper was ready to explode as she stomped her feet and marched away, mumbling angrily, "It should be Señor Danton with her. That's who it should be. Not . . . not that gigolo! He's not good for the little *señorita.*"

But Kristina did not seem to share her little friend's sentiments. By the time she had finished dining and Dan was pouring another serving of champagne into the cut-crystal glasses, she was enjoying his entertaining company more than she'd anticipated. By the time she'd finished her champagne, she felt very relaxed and thought nothing about Dan's arm resting around her shoulders or the closeness of him. Maybe she could forget Danton Navarro!

Dan Recamier was a clever manipulator, a man who had spent a lifetime using his wiles on young ladies just like Kristina. His calculating mind measured every little pulse beat, weighing it carefully before initiating his next move. This was what he was doing with the divine Miss Whelan. He was at the point of attempting to kiss her sweet, sweet lips. Like nectar, they would be, he was sure!

When Dan's sensuous lips slowly came to meet with hers, Kristina gave into a reckless whim and she met them. She felt the pressure of his hands on her back, and Dan flamed with a passion as Kristina's supple body pressed against his chest. But when he was about to urge his hand upward to cover her jutting breast, she broke the intimate embrace and gasped, "No, Dan! No. We must not!"

Her green eyes flashed like bolts of lightning and her thick, dark lashes fluttered. Her rosy lips were set with such firm determination Dan knew no urging would gain him more than he'd already gotten from Kristina Whelan.

With such a startling abruptness that Recamier was stunned Kristina then rose and graciously excused herself.

She walked through the gambling hall, seeing no one she passed on the way to the winding stairway. As good-looking and charming as Dan Recamier was, there was no sweet persuasion in his kisses and where his hands had caressed her there was no fire.

By the time she'd mounted the stairs and walked down the hallway, it dawned on her that she'd never been kissed by any other man but Danton Navarro until tonight!

By the time she went through the door of her quarters, anger fired her eyes. That devil, Navarro, had surely branded her for life. That was the problem when Recamier was kissing her, and she disgustedly admitted to it. There'd been no ecstatic magic as there was when Danton Navarro kissed her, held her in his arms, made rapturous love to her.

Danton Navarro! Dear God, she knew she'd never be free of him!

Chapter 47

In Kristina's white and pink boudoir, Yolanda moved around the bed, folding back the pink satin coverlet. She fussed and fumed still, mumbling to the emptiness of the room. While she couldn't boss the little *señorita* she loved so dearly, she could certainly let off her steam here alone. The man was just no good, she felt it so strongly!

If she possessed those powers that the hired hands around Silvercreek swore she had, then she wished she could cast her spell on Dan Recamier and make him disappear. Oh, if only she could! Next, she'd cast a spell on Señor Navarro and make him come to El Paso like a knight in shining armor to rescue Señorita Kristina. Finally, she'd slip Kristina a love potion to soften the hardness in her heart.

Yolanda could not believe that Danton Navarro did not love Kristina. He had worshipped her with his eyes, Yolanda had seen it. That was undying love, she would have sworn it was.

The clicking heels of Kristina's satin slippers announced that she was outside the bedroom. These were welcome sounds to Yolanda, and her face lit up with delight for her mistress was no longer in the company of Recamier.

She flung down the pale pink gown she was preparing to lay across the bed, and she scurried out of the room to greet Kristina. *"Señorita?"*

Kristina answered her, "It's me, Yolanda." The Mexican girl noticed her preoccupied manner as she carelessly tossed the exquisite lace-edged fan on the rose brocade settee.

The fan had been a gift from Recamier. He'd presented it to her just before their dinner was served. He'd made a point of telling her it was a French import, and she knew he could hardly have found something like it in El Paso.

"I . . . I was just turning your bed down, *señorita.* You look tired." Yolanda spoke in a hesitating voice, not quite certain about Kristina's mood. She wondered if that Recamier had made some improper advances toward her in the secluded draped alcove, but that hardly seemed likely since she'd heard Kristina's amused laughter more than once.

"No, Yolanda. I'm not tired, but I'm weary—if that makes sense."

"Sit down and let me take the aigrette out of your hair so I can give it a brushing."

Kristina obeyed her as she had when Solitaire had told her she must have her hair brushed before bedtime. But Kristina was certainly not sleepy.

As Yolanda began to stroke Kristina's long auburn tresses, she inquired, "Was your dinner with Señor Recamier pleasant?" The man's name left a foul taste in her mouth, and she asked more out of curiosity than interest.

"I guess so, Yolanda." Kristina shrugged her shoulders in an offhanded manner.

The wide-eyed Yolanda was most curious now, and she asked, "You don't— He is not attractive to you, *señorita?* He doesn't appeal to you, maybe?" She held her breath, waiting to hear Kristina's reply.

"Oh, he is all charm and I certainly can't say he isn't handsome. Maybe, there's something wrong with me, Yolanda," she sighed. "Sally and Marge make no bones about his effect on them."

A smug, impish smile brightened Yolanda's face, which Kristina couldn't see. Kristina's words made Yolanda's brushing more vigorous, and her voice was more chipper as she retorted, "Oh, there is nothing wrong with you, *señorita.* He is just not the right man for you." Under her breath, she said to herself, "Señor Danton Navarro is that one!"

"You think Dan isn't right for me?" Kristina turned to look up at her little friend.

"If he were, you would know it—*sí?*"

"*Sí,* Yolanda, I would know it!" Under her breath Kristina told herself, "Just as I knew it with Danton. Even now, I know it."

"It is really very simple, *señorita.* A woman knows when she is in love. If she has to question it then it is not love," Yolanda declared with such casualness Kristina turned once again to give the Mexican girl a quizzical look.

With Jason away on a business trip and her daughter stubbornly vowing to go through with the crazy venture she didn't wholeheartedly approve of, Florine Whelan gave way to a sudden impulse to go into town. She might even spend a night or two at the Crystal Castle while Jason was out of town.

The fine Hamilton gig pulled up to the side entrance of the two-story brick building at ten-thirty that September morn. Her driver assisted her out of the buggy and she walked with aid of her gold-etched cane

411

toward the doorway. Rollo brightened with delight at seeing her come up the walkway.

As magnificent-looking as she'd always been, Florine gave him a warm smile, which made Rollo swell with affection.

Her trim, curvaceous figure was clad in an expensive morning suit with a short jacket of black and gold striped taffeta. The gold of the sheer ruffled blouse she wore was a perfect match to the band of gold veiling around the crown of Florine's wide-brimmed hat.

Old Rollo extended his two wrinkled hands to her. "Ah, Madame Whelan! Good to see you as always. You sure look fine—fine!" This is Florine Whelan, the old black man thought. She has a touch of class.

"You too, Rollo. You don't look too bad yourself." As they walked through the hallway together she could not resist teasing her old friend because he still called her Whelan.

"Yes, ma'am. It's hard to change old habits." He chuckled.

"Between you and me, Rollo, I don't mind. A part of me shall forever be just Florine Whelan."

"I know, ma'am. I know. And it rightly should."

Sally O'Neal called to them as they slowly walked along. "Flo, what a hell of a surprise! Come on to my rooms before you go to see Kristina and share some coffee, all right?"

"Sounds good to me," Florine replied, turning to Rollo to bid him goodbye. "I'll see you again, Rollo. I may spend the night here with Kristina."

"Oh, that's nice, Madame Florine. It will be real fine to have you here for a spell," Rollo told her as he turned to go his own way.

Florine smiled, watching him go before turning her attention to Sally. "Well, Sally, how is it going?"

"God, Florine, better than it's been since you had to

412

take off. Guess I should have found out about that certain Whelan flair before I tried to step into your shoes." She laughed good-naturedly. "Damned if I've got it, but Kristina has. She seems to captivate the men, Flo. Honest to God, you'll see if you watch her tonight—heard you say that you were spending the night."

"Thought I might as well with Jason gone for two or three days. Anyway, I have to tell you I've had some misgivings about giving in to Kristina's whims and I like to see how things are going."

The two entered Sally's rooms, and a carafe of coffee was immediately brought in. "Make yourself comfortable, Florine. I'm glad we're having this chance to talk anyway before you get with Kristina." Sally pulled her floral wrapper around her well-shaped body before she sat down in the overstuffed chair and lit one of the little Mexican *cigarrillos* she enjoyed. "Want one?" she asked Florine.

Florine accepted one, and Sally lit hers too.

"Your daughter is fantastic up there on that stage, Flo. I think every one of those dudes thinks she's singing especially to him." The two women broke into laughter.

"She's that good, eh, Sally?" Florine asked her old friend.

"Oh, she's more than good. She's sensational, Flo. There's a new dandy in El Paso and he's very enamored of your daughter, and that's something I want to talk to you about. You see, I've heard some rumors, Flo, that he's a partner of the guys across the street who run the Bird Cage. I don't know whether there's any truth to it or not, but he's sure giving Kristina the rush—if you know what I mean."

"I know exactly what you mean, Sally. He must be the one she was having a late dinner with. She told me

413

about that before she came back into town last evening, but I didn't get to ask her his name." There was a thoughtful look on Florine's face for a moment before she inquired of Sally, "Have you told Kristina this?"

"I was going to last night but the place got so busy I never had a chance to get her alone."

"Leave it to me, Sally. I'll warn her. If there's the slightest possibility of that rumor being true, then he has no business sniffing around my daughter. I'll talk to her. What would you say her feelings are for this man, Sally?"

"God, Flo, all I can say is he put butterflies in my stomach! I've got the feeling Kristina is a passionate young lady, if you don't mind me saying so, and this man is so damned good-looking he puts your eyes out. He dresses like a million dollars. The charm just oozes out. You know the kind—smooth talking, silver tongued."

Florine laughed. "He sounds too good to be true. Seems to me you wouldn't mind being in my Kristina's slippers?"

Sally smiled and winked a bright blue eye wickedly, "Can't lie to you, Florine. We go back too far with one another. But there's a lot of mileage on me. I've been down that road a time or two. I don't know about Kristina. Just don't want her to get hurt if I can help it. I guess I can't help thinking she's still Florine's little kid." Sally and Florine exchanged a look of understanding.

"Nor do I, Sally. God knows, we've both had our share of that kind of heartache." Florine secretly recalled that the same kind of man long ago had bilked her out of a tremendous amount of money and had then left her expecting a baby—Kristina.

After sharing two cups of coffee with Sally, Florine reached for her cane. "Think I'll go check on that daughter of mine, Sally. Thanks, honey, for everything. I'll see you later." Florine walked off with that measured gait required of her, and Sally knew how that must gall her old boss who used to bustle around the Crystal Castle.

Just as she was about to move out of the doorway, Florine paused to ask Sally, "By the way what is this dashing dandy's name, Sally?"

"Dan Recamier."

Sally did not see the cane and Florine Whelan wobble for Florine shut the door hastily. For a moment the courageous, strong-willed woman thought she was going to faint. But she didn't! She did stand frozen to the spot for a few moments before she heaved a deep sigh.

As she marched on down the carpeted hallway the name echoed over and over again. She detested that name and the man who bore it. Long ago, she'd buried that name in the deep abyss of her mind along with the man, Dion Recamier.

Now a man by the name of Dan Recamier had come into her daughter's life!

Chapter 48

The fiery, auburn-haired matron marched down the hall toward the quarters she'd once called her home, determined that she would put an immediate stop to any association between her daughter and a man with Recamier blood flowing in his veins. Never would she tolerate that. Florine's only hope was she wouldn't be met with Kristina's wall of stubbornness. Already, she'd had a taste of the young lady's iron will! It was as strong as her own.

How familiar it seemed to her to turn the double knobs of the heavy carved-oak doors and to enter the suite she'd taken so much joy in decorating with expensive furnishings. Each lavish piece had cost her many long hours of work.

As she recalled the precious moments associated with the individual articles placed in her old parlor, Florine knew Jason's fine ranch would never hold such dear, wonderful memories for her.

Dear as Jason Hamilton was to her, Florine could not deny that what had happened between Kristina and herself had urged her into marriage. Then she guiltily wondered if she'd cheated her wonderful Jason.

She had already entered the parlor and was making

her way toward the center of the room when the wide-eyed, curious Yolanda came bouncing out of the bedroom, imploring, "Oh, you back already, Señorita Krist—"

Blushing with embarrassment and giving Florine a curtsy, she greeted Kristina's mother. Florine had liked her daughter's little Mexican friend at their first meeting when Kristina had brought her out to Jason's ranch.

"Good day, Yolanda. Don't tell me my daughter is still lolling in bed, the lazybones."

"Oh, no . . . no. She went out just a minute ago. I would have imagined that you two would have met in the hall."

"I probably missed her since I went to Sally's rooms for coffee." Florine casually strolled over to one of her comfortable chairs and sank slowly down onto it, placing her cane to the side. Slipping the gold ornamental hatpin out of her wide-brimmed hat, she took it off her head.

"Can I get you something, *señora?*" Yolanda smiled eagerly at Florine.

"No, dear. I don't need a thing. Come . . . sit and talk with me a minute. Tell me how it is all going for you and Kristina."

"Oh, I could not ask for a nicer life than I've had with your Kristina. She . . . she is so good to me."

When Florine gave her a slow, easy smile, Yolanda thought mother and daughter looked so alike. "Tell me, Yolanda, where was she going? Rollo would surely have informed her that I was here if she asked him to drive her somewhere."

"She didn't mention that and I wondered, *señora,* about that myself. She didn't take her parasol either as though she was going to be driving out in the sun. So I'm afraid I can't help you."

"H'm, that leaves us to just wait and see, I guess. Perhaps, a gentleman was picking her up outside?"

Without thinking that this was Kristina's mother and because her protective attitude gave vent to her impulsive nature, Yolanda blurted out her innermost feelings. "Well, I hope she didn't go with that . . . that Dan Recamier." Suddenly, her eyes flashed blacker as she realized what she'd said. But she didn't have to fret too long because Florine quickly replied that she hoped not either.

"Am I to gather you don't care for Mister Recamier, Yolanda?" Florine queried.

"*Sí,* that is right. I do not like him at all—not for our Kristina."

"You appear to be very firm about that so I must conclude that you have observed the man. I must make a point of doing the same tonight. Oh, I will be spending the night here tonight, Yolanda."

"That will be very nice, *señora. Sí,* I have made observations of the man, as you say, and I do not like. Besides, I cannot see any man worthy of Señorita Kristina, except one. That man, I believe, loves her devotedly."

"Am I to assume she does not feel the same way about him then?"

Gesturing dramatically with her hands, Yolanda remarked, "The heart is crazy sometimes. People in love are so stupid. But I will never be convinced that Señorita Kristina and the Señor Danton were not in love. Whatever happened at Silvercreek it is not for me to say, but something went wrong. This I do know, *señora,"*—she came close to confiding to Florine—"it had to do with that evil brother of Señor Danton—that Damien and his usual devilment."

Florine saw the sure look on the girl's pretty face, and she could certainly not doubt the girl's sincerity about what she was saying. Yolanda's devotion to Kristina was obvious to Florine.

"This is all very interesting, Yolanda. I would wager that you are probably right. I think you are a very smart girl." Florine patted the girl's hand affectionately, and she was rewarded with a broad smile.

"About Señor Damien Navarro, I know I am right. Ah, *sí,* I am very smart," Yolanda declared cockily.

Florine didn't seek to prod her any further, but she had some very definite ideas after observing the girl's open, honest face.

"Well, I have a suspicion that if you and I work together, Yolanda, we'll rid ourselves and Kristina of one Mr. Dan Recamier, eh?"

Yolanda was overcome by giggles. "Ah, that we will do, *señora.*" Then in her direct, straightforward way, Yolanda declared, "I like you, *señora.* I like you very much!"

"Well, the feeling is mutual, Yolanda. My daughter is very lucky to have you for a friend. I've been very lucky too, to have such a dear friend as Solitaire." The startling similarity of her daughter's circumstances suddenly slapped Florine square in the face. She could not dismiss the parallels lightly: Florine and her Solitaire, Kristina and little Yolanda. But the other parallel was one Florine would never have conceived could happen. Never had she imagined Kristina meeting up with any of the Recamier family. While she was not a woman given to panic, this unlikely happening sent a wave of fear through this indomitable lady.

She knew one thing: if she saw in this young man any resemblance to Dion Recamier, then she would tell Kristina who her father was. Obviously, this man had a penchant for gambling like another Recamier she knew, so there was a very grave possibility that Dan

419

Recamier could be Dion's son. If that were the case then he was Kristina's half brother!

Kristina had missed meeting Rollo in the hallway as she'd left the building, and she knew when she announced that she was going out for a little while it had put Yolanda in a bit of a quandary. Her little Mexican friend had an insatiable curiosity, but Kristina could not be troubled about it this particular morning. She just felt the need to be alone and away from the Crystal Castle.

When she'd emerged onto the fairly quiet El Paso street—it was not yet bustling with the day's activity—she thought about how nice it would have been to have gone to the Navarro stables, to have picked out one of their fine thoroughbreds, and to have galloped over the open countryside.

As she walked she found herself engulfed in thoughts and memories of the beautiful ranch in the picturesque countryside. Dear God, she was yearning to be back there!

She was oblivious to the few people she passed, and she was unaware that three men were watching her morning promenade. In her mind, Kristina was not strolling down the street in El Paso, she was back at the Navarro ranch. Once again the attractive young woman was going back in time, and this time her memory was very clear. Oh, yes, she could recall every little insignificant incident.

As she paid no heed to the other people on the street, she had no inkling of the intense resentment she was igniting in the men watching her.

Dan Recamier was not present when his three partners gathered at the Bird Cage. One of the trio had spotted Kristina as she'd left the Crystal Castle, and he

420

watched her for a while before he pointed her out to the others.

"There's the little bitch that's robbing our pockets raw, boys. Can't speak for you two, but I'm sure as hell not waiting for Dan to clear up this little problem."

Lucky Lee Thorton, as he was called by the gambling fraternity, chewed on the stub of his cigar and played with the fob of his pocket watch. "What you got in mind, Peel?" he asked. While he spoke he stared out the window of the saloon ogling the tantalizing wiggle of Kristina's bustle. He could hardly fault Dan for wanting to avail himself of the pleasure Kristina Whelan could provide. He wouldn't mind a share in them himself.

"I'll tell you exactly what I got in mind, Lucky. It'll take care of the whole damned shooting match with one fast shot."

The big, quiet-natured Charlie Bedlow shot up from his wooden chair, and his face was ruddier than usual as he snapped, "Holy Christ, Peel, are you saying what I think you are? We barely escaped from Kansas City, and now you— Just hold it a damn minute! A little scaring is one thing or even a little blackmail, but I'm not for torching the place."

Bill Peel grimaced, and a sneer came to his tight-lipped mouth. "I suppose you want to leave here without a cent in your pockets and lose all you've got invested in this place? Well, not me. Not because of some feisty little filly like the one twisting down the street."

Lucky Lee Thornton, who was the sharpest and most intelligent of the three, sought to calm the others. He agreed with Charlie that he wanted no part in the drastic process of elimination Bill proposed. "After all, we've got to give Dan a chance. Hell, one night can't accomplish it. I say we just be patient and keep our

421

tempers for a couple of days."

"I agree, Lucky. Old Dan's never failed us in the past."

"Well, thank you, old boy," Dan Recamier's voice announced his arrival. He had come through the back entrance of the saloon, and hearing Bedlow's remark he'd cockily sauntered forth. "What's your problem Peel, being your usual impetuous self?"

Bill Peel was the one partner Recamier wished they'd not taken in on this venture. He was crude and hot tempered, and to Dan's thinking, he had the intelligence of a donkey. Recamier, with his flamboyant style and manner, was completely repulsed by the shoddy way Peel acted and dressed.

Dan had only allowed Peel to be included in the Bird Cage deal to be sure the man departed from Kansas City with them so he'd keep his stupid mouth shut and not jeopardize the rest of them.

"Yeah, Recamier, but I ain't going to cool my heels while you woo the lady a month."

"One night is hardly a month, Bill. Trust me and you'll see," Recamier casually replied. He noticed Bedlow's eyes staring at the window, and he instantly saw what had him so engrossed. He nudged Bedlow and winked a gray eye wickedly, saying, "Not bad, eh Charlie?"

Bedlow and Recamier laughed, and Thornton joined in. Everyone's mood mellowed, except for the sour Peel's.

Dan Recamier's buoyant, happy-go-lucky air was assumed only for the benefit of his partners, however. He was feeling anything but assured after last night. Kristina had been as remote during most of the evening she'd spent with him as she was with the other gentlemen. Oh, a couple of times he'd felt he was breaking ground with her, but then, so abruptly she'd taken him by surprise, she'd become untouchable—a lovely auburn-haired ice maiden.

His ego was not yet ready to admit to defeat, but he was not foolish enough to lie to himself. Still, the mere fact that she'd arrogantly dismissed his amorous moves challenged him.

His conceit urged him to go to the Crystal Castle again tonight. With that old Recamier flair on his side, he knew in the end he'd win his way with her.

That gorgeous lady would see a different Dan Recamier tonight, one she couldn't resist!

He'd win this high-stakes prize, he vowed fervently!

Chapter 49

When Kristina came through the double doors, clutching a fluff ball of a kitten in her arms, she found her mother and Yolanda in the sitting room. Florine stared at her daughter, an amused look in her eyes.

"Well, there you are, my little wanderer! And just what have you picked up along the way, sugar?"

"Mother. I . . . I didn't know you were coming in. How nice! Did Jason come too?" She flopped down on the carpet at Florine's feet, still holding the adorable kitten which nestled cozily in the circle of her arms.

Florine gave the top of Kristina's head an affectionate pat as she inquired, "Who is your friend?" Kristina had never looked more adorable, her mother thought. Soft wavy tresses cascaded over her shoulder as she looked down at the little kitten who'd followed her down the street until Kristina had been unable to resist bringing him home.

"Oh, you mean *Amigo* here. Yes, we met by chance on the street, and it was love at first sight. Isn't he a darling?" Kristina's green eyes gleamed brightly as she glanced up at her mother, and Florine felt an overwhelming urge to protect her from the likes of Recamier and his kind, men who spent their lives preying on the hearts of women.

"You named him already? *Amigo,* is it?" Florine asked her daughter.

"Yes," Kristina chuckled. "Do you like it?"

"It seems to be a perfect name for him. It is a him, isn't it?"

"Yes, Mother." She patted the top of the kitten's silvery gray head. "What do you think about him, Yolanda?"

"*Sí, Señorita Kristina,* I think he is precious. He sleeps so soundly there in your lap. Poor little *poco!*"

Kristina asked Yolanda to fetch a wicker basket from her bedroom. "The white one and put one of the little pink pillows in it for me, Yolanda. That might just make little Amigo here a cozy bed."

As Yolanda scurried out of the parlor to get the basket for the kitten, Kristina turned to her mother. "Do you remember when you bought that for me to pick the wildflowers when Solitaire and I went for our drives out in the countryside?"

"I sure do, darling," Florine replied. "Dear Lord, you were so young—and now look at you. I find it hard to believe how grown-up you are, Kristina. I've got to give Solitaire credit. She was far smarter than I was. She said you'd suddenly blossom overnight. I didn't believe her at the time."

"Solitaire is very perceptive. I don't think there's another person in the whole wide world like her." Kristina smiled, and then she added, "Unless it might be the one in there." She pointed toward the bedroom, referring to little Yolanda. Then she proceeded to tell Florine about her friend's vast knowledge of herbs and potions.

As she did so, Yolanda returned with the white wicker basket padded with one of the fancy pink pillows. "You wish him in there now, Señorita?"

425

Kristina nodded her head as she slowly placed the tiny kitten onto the softness of the pillow. He was so content he never knew he was being switched from Kristina's lap to the basket. The two girls exchanged grins, then Yolanda carefully carried the basket from the room, intending to place it in a quiet corner.

When she returned, Kristina and her mother were chatting about times of the past, so Yolanda discreetly excused herself and then went to seek out Sally or Margie, as she did often in the midafternoon. By now, Yolanda's friendly warmth had endeared her to all those at the Crystal Castle. So it was not unusual for her to trot around the establishment in the quiet of the afternoon visiting with the other employees of the gambling hall or pitching in to finish some chore.

For all of Sid Layman's grumbling that she was a nosy little pest after she'd first arrived in El Paso with Kristina, he, too, adored the little Mexican girl now. As young as she was, Sid found her to be amazingly smart and wise. She had impressed him.

He was certainly in accord with her impression of Dan Recamier. He didn't care for the man at all!

When Danton Navarro had set out from Silvercreek to journey to El Paso, he was seeking one certain lady, Kristina Whelan, and he would have preferred not to meet with Vincente Ortega. An old friend of the Navarro family, Vincente had been the one to send word to Silvercreek over a year ago when Damien had been playing the hellion in his hometown of El Paso. It had also been Vincente who'd been Danton's host when he'd come to El Paso to fetch his twin brother away from the gambling tables and to drag him back home before he got himself into serious trouble.

While Danton had not succeeded in finding Damien

after he'd journeyed so far at his mother's insistence, he had enjoyed the Ortegas' gracious hospitality. The Ortegas had an elegant home just outside El Paso, where they bred and raised fine thoroughbreds and cattle.

Consequently, when the two men had met on the street and Vincente had discovered that Danton was headed for El Paso, it was difficult for Danton to refuse Vincente's invitation to stay at his home. Vincente finally relented when Danton said the business he must attend to necessitated staying at a local hotel. However, Vincente adamantly insisted Danton check in and then go on out to his home to see his dear wife and children. Danton's good manners did not allow him to refuse, but he resented the delay in his search for Kristina.

Danton did not want to discuss his "business" with the good-natured, jovial Ortega, so when they were met by the Ortega carriage, he allowed Vincente to order his driver to take them to Danton's hotel first. With his luggage deposited and his room engaged, Danton boarded the carriage in which Vincente waited. Forcing a broad grin, he tried to restrain his impatience for just a few more hours.

"Ah, my Nita will be so happy to see the son of Lucía and Victor. You know how we always laughed about our families and the coincidence that we both had twins; Victor with his twin sons and me with my twin daughters."

"How are Juana and Juanita?" Danton asked out of courtesy.

"Ah, fine. More beautiful every day. I know it is boasting but I am weak where my two beautiful roses are concerned. My son is always telling me this." Vincente laughed. He made a point of adding that Juan was becoming a fine young man and a good son.

427

Señor Ortega knew he could not be too obvious for he would look very foolish, but it would be more than pleasing to him if Danton Navarro would take an interest in one of his daughters. That would be a perfect match between two prominent Latin families!

Vincente knew of the promising political career that lay ahead for Lucía's and Victor's son. What a feather in the hat it would be for Hispanic people to have a senator or even a governor of the great state of Texas! He firmly believed Danton could be that man. Seeing him again after almost a year had gone by since they'd last encountered, Vincente was more impressed.

Danton had no inkling about the secret appraisal Vincente was making as the carriage proceeded down the streets of El Paso. Actually, Danton's attention, directed out of the carriage window, was distracted by something he'd seen on a side street. One fleeting glance was all he had, but he'd seen a plaid frock with a profusion of pink ruffles. The woman in it was bending down to pick up something on the street. Danton's heart was pounding. Could it have been Kristina? he kept asking himself as the carriage rolled on. Or was it just a mirage because he yearned to see her so damned badly? He'd dreamed of her nightly for weeks now, and when he was home at Silvercreek she'd haunted every corner of the house and garden.

As they covered the few miles to reach Ortega's ranch, Danton did not absorb any of Vincente's lively conversation. While the elderly *señor* sensed his companion's distraction, he shrugged it aside, deciding that Danton was weary from his long trip from Silvercreek.

A refreshingly cool drink and some delicious little pecan cakes their cook always prepared would liven him up, Vincente thought to himself. The sight of his two lovely daughters certainly should bring some life to him if the refreshments didn't. A man would have to be dead not to be effected by their dark, sultry loveliness, Vincente mused.

Danton came back to the real world around him, leaving his memories behind as the carriage slowed to turn off the main road into a driveway. Situated a short distance away and almost hidden from sight by a multitude of thick-branched trees sat the stone two-story house with its red-tiled roof. Iron railings bordered the overhanging balconies on the second floor of the spacious house, and the lush greenery on the grounds was reminiscent of an exotic, tropical garden. Huge statues stood on either side of the stone walkway, along with large pottery urns overflowing with bright red flowers.

The jolly Vincente Ortega ushered his young friend along the flagstone walk, declaring his joy at being home. "I find no place like my home. A man should feel so, don't you think, Danton?"

Danton smiled, "What is it they say about a man's home being his castle? I guess that's the way it should be."

"That is so. As you well know, I'm sure Victor felt as I do."

"Oh yes, Señor Ortega . . . he felt that way."

"Good women like your mother and my Nita are the ones who turn houses into homes though. I tell my son, Juan, to pick himself a lady half as nice as his mother and he will be fine," Vincente chuckled.

"Quite so. It can't be a castle without a beautiful queen," Danton replied. Once again, he was impelled to get the visit at the Ortega ranch over so he could go in search of his queen, for he had a castle awaiting her at Whispering Willows.

All the Ortega family were gathered in the huge *sala.* It, too, was filled with exotic plants and it gave off

429

an aura of cool, comfortable serenity. The room was so vast that a large crowd of people could have been sitting around in uncrowded comfort. The Ortega offspring were there. Vincente's twin daughters, Juanita and Juana, were alike in looks and temperament, Danton observed. They seemed to be parrots echoing each other—constantly.

He found Vincente's son, Juan, a far more interesting individual than the twittering, blushing twins, so he engaged him in some casual conversation after the greetings were over and Nita had ordered some refreshments sent to the *sala*.

But much to Danton's dismay, he began to sense after the first half-hour of socializing that Vincente appeared to be playing the matchmaker. Danton felt a different anxiety now. Old family friend or not, he wasn't about to be cornered by either of these pretty Latin misses.

The next half-hour was tedious because Danton had to be very guarded, but gracious. When he finally felt he could take his leave, he sighed with relief when Juan escorted him to the waiting carriage.

At the door of the *sala,* Danton said farewell to the older Ortegas. "It was a pleasure, *señor* and *señora.* Nice to see you, Juana, and you too, Juanita. I've enjoyed this brief visit despite my pressing business."

"You're a very busy young man, I know, Danton." Vincente smiled, but he was not exactly pleased that his expectations were proving futile.

As Juan strolled out to the veranda and down the walk, Danton did not look back as he walked beside the tall, lean man who was slightly younger than he was. An amused grin broke out on Juan's good-looking face as he declared to Danton, "My father was rather obvious, I think. Hope you'll overlook it, Danton. I guess that you go through similar situations

430

with your sister, Delores. She's of courting age, isn't she?"

Danton laughed. "Yes, she's of courting age. I don't think the mothers of daughters and the fathers of daughters deal with it in the same way, however. But think nothing about it, Juan." Danton extended his hand for a farewell shake. "I hope to see you again soon, Juan. Please thank your folks again for me."

"I will, Danton, and incidentally if you have a chance to get away from your business appointments while you are here in El Paso, go to the Crystal Castle if you want to see the most beautiful woman in the whole state of Texas." Juan blew a light kiss from his fingertips and exclaimed, *"Magnífico!"*

"And what is this beauty's name, Juan?" Danton leaped into the carriage and slammed the door.

"Ah, the ravishing Kristina! The most beautiful of women!"

It was probably a fortunate thing for Juan Ortega that the carriage was already in motion for Danton's hot-blooded Latin temper was fired by the flames of jealousy. He clenched his fists, yearning to sock the grinning face of Juan Ortega.

Then he recalled how she'd affected the males around Silvercreek when she'd sung. Every gent in El Paso was probably lusting after the woman who belonged to him!

By the time he got back to his hotel he was so riled he was ready to explode!

Chapter 50

Kristina figured that she and her mother were now being rewarded bountifully for the time they'd suffered at the cruel hand of fate. She was enjoying to the fullest the special moments like the one they were sharing this evening as she sat primping at her dressing table while Florine engaged her in pleasant conversation.

The atmosphere in Florine's former living quarters was cheerful. Yolanda's spirits were carefree and happy as she changed from her day frock into the sheer pink blouse and the matching pink floral skirt she wore in the evening. Before she rushed downstairs to begin checking the customers' hats and canes, she tucked a huge pink flower in her black hair. Sid had told her she should always wear a pretty blossom in her hair, and she enjoyed his constant praise about how pretty she was.

Before she went downstairs, she stopped to tell Kristina and the *señora* she was going to work. Tonight, Yolanda knew she would not have to fret about Dan Recamier because she was certain Señora Florine was going to take charge. She liked that lady very much, especially after the time they'd spent together alone. Now, she knew where all the good in

Señorita Kristina had come from—her mother. That was where her spellbinding beauty came from too.

Yolanda jauntily bounced down the steps. She hadn't a care in the world.

At Florine's suggestion Kristina had worn the exquisite white satin broché gown. It was quite a drastic contrast from the elegant black one she'd worn the night before, but Florine was right about the white one. It shimmered under the lights, which picked up the golden threads woven through the satin.

With gold combs in her hair and sparkling little diamonds on her ears, Kristina had completed her toilette. Now, it was Florine's turn to sit at the dressing table to put what she called the finishing touches to a couple wisps straying from her upswept hairdo.

"Now, Mother, I don't want you hidden in that alcove all night. Everyone will be thrilled to see you again," Kristina insisted after Florine had told her that she wanted to remain in the seclusion of one of the little alcoves until Kristina had finished her songs.

Florine threw back her pretty head and laughed. "Oh, darling, I plan to come out and have a nightcap with some of my old friends. Doc and the good Judge Dalton will most likely be in the crowd. I just want to be able to listen to your pretty songs without someone chattering in my ears and distracting my attention while my daughter is performing." Although she didn't say it, she didn't want the sight of her to distract the crowd while Kristina was performing, and she wanted very much to be free to observe Dan Recamier's entrance into her establishment. One glance at that man's face would satisfy Florine Whelan, but at that moment she might need to be alone.

The blue-green shade of Florine's gown turned her eyes into the same hue, Kristina noticed as she surveyed her mother admiringly. "You should wear that color

433

more often," she declared. "I don't recall seeing you ever wear it before."

"I haven't, but I shall—just for you." Florine reached over to give Kristina a light kiss on the cheek. "Now, I'm going to slip on down so I can get settled and have some wine. Come and join me after your performance, my pet."

"Oh, I will. But how will you manage to get through the crowd without being seen?"

Florine gave her daughter a knowing wink. "That's why I picked that particular alcove, my love. It is the only one which has an exit at the back and front."

"Oh, Mother, you are a sly fox."

"Had to be, sweetie, or I would never have made it this far. I'll see you later."

As Kristina watched Florine go, she realized that she was just beginning to know the amazing essence of this woman, her mother—Florine Whelan.

None of the crowd gathered in the Crystal Castle appeared to be curious about the occupied alcove with the plush red velvet drape drawn. A couple of times, Sally O'Neal had slipped in to chat with her old friend or take a quick sip of Florine's chilled vintage wine.

On one of her forays, with a happy, pleased look on her fair face, Sally declared, "It's building up pretty good, Flo. Same as it was last night when it was about time for Kristina to sing. Just thought I'd let you know Recamier hasn't arrived yet, but if he's coming he'll be here soon now."

Florine thanked her and Sally quickly disappeared. She didn't have to peep through the drapes to know more people were milling around the huge room just outside her booth. The voices and the laughter told her that.

When Florine heard the music playing what she recognized as Kristina's cue to come floating down the steps she suddenly became all mother, all nerves. Kristina could have been a young miss preparing to play her first piano recital. There was only one thing Florine wanted to see from her hidden vantage point and that was the striking descent Sally had told her about. Already an awesome quiet was settling over the room, and a few seconds later, Florine heard a soft, very seductive voice say, "Good evening, gentlemen. Welcome to the Crystal Castle."

After a brief, startling moment in which she found it hard to believe that her "little"daughter was purring so teasingly, Florine smiled. The minx!

Dear God, pandemonium was breaking loose. Florine realized what a sensation her little Kristina was with these randy gentlemen! She laughed at herself for thinking her appearance would have distracted any of them from Kristina's performance. Then she ventured to open the drape another inch. By now, Kristina sat on her stool with the light centered at a certain angle. She did look like a glorious angel in her shimmering white gown laced with the gleaming gold threads.

As Kristina began to sing she became a sensuous siren beckoning every man to come to her, and it was at this moment that Florine's green eyes saw a man with the same haunting gray eyes she'd known so long ago. He was built just like Dion and he had the same jet-black hair.

She could not restrain a gasp as she watched him move closer and closer. She felt as though she could not breathe, and her hands went limp. Dear Lord, she'd closed that book of heartbreaking chapters and she'd never intended to open it again. Now here was the past, staring her in the face. Torment stabbed her anew.

This man had to be the spawn of Dion Recamier for

he was the exact image of the Frenchman she'd given her reckless heart to some twenty years ago.

She watched him so intently that later she could not have told anyone what Kristina was singing if she'd have been asked. He elbowed his way through the crowd and made his way toward Kristina.

Another impressive figure stood at the entrance of the establishment, but Florine Whelan Hamilton did not know of his arrival. This towering, strikingly handsome man was consumed by his intense feelings. He had been since he'd parted company with Juan Ortega. He was a man not to be crossed on this night, for his fuse was short and his mood was black.

His finely tailored black broadcloth jacket and trousers had an austere air, and two gentlemen, seeming to sense the danger in Danton Navarro, moved cautiously around him as he lingered in the center of the archway. He'd chosen not to wear a hat when he'd left the hotel so he'd not stopped at the counter near the main entrance.

He'd not gone unnoticed by Sally O'Neal though; her big blue eyes couldn't leave his face. There were men and then there were men, but this handsome brute had her entranced. He had such magnificent, broad shoulders beneath his black coat that it seemed about to rip at the seams. Sally decided that Kristina could have Recamier, but she'd take this one any night of the week. Those highly polished black leather boots of his would be quite welcome at her bedside.

Danton didn't notice the bright blue eyes that ogled him so eagerly. All he could see was a golden goddess across the room—a vast distance away. All he heard was her soft nightingale's song echoing back to where he stood.

Yolanda's big black eyes saw him but they didn't believe Señor Danton could be standing there. Her

436

rose-bud lips parted, but she couldn't make a sound. She was completely stunned. *Madre de Dios!* She finally willed her tiny feet to move, yet they, too, seemed frozen.

Annoyed and angry, Danton turned to see who or what tugged at his arm. As their eyes locked in recognition, Yolanda greeted him in a hesitating voice. "Señor Danton. Señor Danton, how good that you finally came. I prayed you would."

He gazed at her, a skeptical look on his face, and his black eyebrows arched sharply. "Now, Yolanda, am I to believe that? After all, you fled with Kit—or should I say Kristina? Which do you now call her?"

His sardonic tone hurt Yolanda. She questioned what he was going to do next. She tilted her head slightly, and her face was etched with despair when she replied, "I call her Señorita Kristina, Señor Danton. I'm sorry to see you are so bitter toward me." Taking a deep breath, she suddenly stood straight and as tall as her height would allow; then she informed him defiantly, "I am not sorry for leaving Silvercreek with your lady, *señor.* I am her friend. Friends help one another."

How those black eyes of hers flashed and how sincere was her declaration! Danton's mood mellowed somewhat. Such a little spitfire she was! God help the poor soul those two might have encountered along the way if he dared to think these were two helpless young misses, Danton thought with amusement. On a few occasions his auburn-haired Kit had been a firebrand too.

Danton felt he had been a bit of a cad so he sought to make amends. "Your *señorita* is lucky to have you for a friend." His eyes turned from Yolanda in the direction of the small, raised stage. He let his eyes savor the glorious sight of Kristina for a moment before remarking to the girl at his side, "She's even more beautiful than I remembered!"

Yolanda smiled, pleased to hear him say that. Quietly, she lingered by his side, listening to Kristina sing, but her big doelike eyes darted over once or twice to study Danton Navarro. He turned to catch her staring at him. "I've missed her terribly, Yolanda," he confessed. His sincerity was so evident that Yolanda was convinced she must do whatever she could to help him get Kristina back if she proved to be stubborn.

"I think she's missed you too, Señor Danton." She almost had to bite her tongue for she was about to add that Kristina never spoke about him anymore. Yolanda had been so overjoyed by the sight of Danton that she'd forgotten that Recamier might be there again this evening. She thought about it now. That could prove to be a dangerous situation.

Yolanda had realized too late. In the very next minute, when Kristina's song was finished, Dan Recamier's tall figure took precedence over the rest of the crowd which stood applauding. It was Recamier who rushed to Kristina's side, a bouquet of white roses in his hand. It was Recamier who planted a kiss on Kristina's cheek, exuding an air of possessiveness. At least, that was what Danton Navarro thought!

Kristina was not aware that his lips brushed her cheek with his featherlike kiss. She stood immobile, her green eyes straining to see across the vastness of the crowded room.

When the lights had been raised and her songs were finished, Kristina had risen from her stool. At that moment some compelling force—a giant magnet—made her look to the entrance of the gambling establishment. Then her heart had started to pound wildly, for the man she saw could only be Danton Navarro. It wasn't a dream this time; she was wide awake. She would swear to it!

Although Yolanda's diminutive figure was not to be seen, Kristina did not need the sight of her to confirm her certainty that Danton was here in the Crystal Castle.

Like one hypnotized she was drawn to a pair of black-fire eyes that seared her from across the room. The overwhelming essence of him traveled through the crowd to her. Dear God, she felt it!

More than anything in the world, she yearned for this man to be Danton Navarro!

Chapter 51

Yolanda felt the muscles ripple in Danton's arm as she tried to restrain him. It was useless, but she cried out anyway as she rushed after him, "Oh, Señor Danton! Señor Danton . . . please listen to me . . . I beg of you!"

Crazed by jealousy at the sight of that dandy kissing Kristina, Danton whirled around to angrily inquire of the determined little Yolanda, "What? You can't tell me a damned thing. I saw all I needed to see."

Neither Yolanda's beseeching voice nor Danton's roaring growl were heeded by the crowd. The applauding and the shouting drowned them out. Yolanda could not allow the *señor* to approach Recamier when he was in such a fury, not after what Sid Layman had told her about the little concealed pistols Recamier carried. She must warn Señor Danton before he plowed through that noisy crowd.

"I—I only wanted to warn you that the man is armed, Señor Danton. I—I don't wish you harmed." Yolanda had to shout to be heard. "He carries them in his pockets, *señor*. Tiny little things, but deadly all the same."

Danton lingered only long enough to tell her he was

sorry he'd barked at her. Then he patted her shoulder and turned to move on through the crowd. "Never fear that something is going to happen to me—only him," he called back.

While Yolanda couldn't push her way through the group as Danton did, she followed determinedly right behind him.

If there were those who found his shoving offensive, they made no protest, and he got closer and closer to his goal. Kristina had lost sight of him once he'd left the doorway and she didn't see his approach. Beside her, Dan Recamier was completely unaware of the fury that was about to strike. If he had been forewarned, he would not have had a smile on his face as he slowly guided Kristina away from the stage, his arm at her back.

Like a snapping bolt of lightning Danton's forceful hands yanked Recamier free of Kristina, and before Dan could get an inkling of the stormy waters he was treading in, a clenched fist dealt him a mighty blow. The gambler whirled as if caught in the vortex of a hurricane.

Gasps resounded all over the room, but there was no great love or admiration for this newcomer to the town of El Paso so none of the men felt obliged to go to Recamier's rescue, nor were they eager to tackle the imposing figure of Navarro.

Things happened furiously and fast for Kristina. At one moment she was at Dan's side; the next, she was being yanked roughly through the crowd by Danton Navarro. When she finally got her wits about her they had crossed the room and were at the back of the establishment. She made a weak protest, but Danton paid her no mind.

As she stumbled along in her satin slippers and swishing gown, her eyes noted the questioning stares of the employees of her mother's establishment, but Danton ignored them. He rushed her toward the back door leading into the alleyway.

"Are you absolutely crazy, Danton Navarro?"

"Perhaps, that is the malady I have."

"Or am I wrong? Are you Damien?" Kristina smirked, knowing full well this was Danton. Despite the melee, she'd seen the telltale scar on the side of his devilishly handsome face. Yes, he is devilishly handsome, she admitted to herself, and his fierceness filled her with strange excitement.

"You know exactly who I am and if you don't, you will before this night is over, little kitten! This night, if never again, this night, you'll be Kit Winters not Kristina Whelan!"

The way he let his black eyes devour her stirred Kristina. To deny it would have been useless.

A fancy gig stood at the back of the building. Kristina recognized it as her mother's, but she didn't see Rollo. At that point, Danton didn't know or care who owned the carriage, he only knew he was going to borrow it to get her away from the Crystal Castle. He did just that, snapping the bay into a trot.

Kristina said nothing for a moment, and Danton seemed not to have noticed that she hadn't balked when he'd lifted her onto the seat or tried to leap off as he'd moved around the buggy to get up on the other side.

Finally, she dared to taunt him by inquiring, "Am I being abducted, Señor Navarro?"

"I haven't decided yet!"

"May I ask where we're going then?" She jerked irately on her long flowing skirt, which apparently had gotten caught on the edge of the buggy's seat.

"You'll see. A very short distance away so I won't be in too much trouble with the gent who owns this very nice buggy. I understand you know all about borrowing buggies, my little Kit?"

She jerked her head to look away from his grinning face. Now he was taunting her.

"Yes, I guess you could say I learned a lot about many things the last year."

"Ah, that is good!" As if he wished to goad her more, he added, "We'll have to see if you remember some of the things you learned. It would pain me to think you'd forgotten some of the most important things in such a short time."

Kristina's anger was building now. Of all the conceit! She knew exactly what he was hinting at, and if he thought for a minute that she'd yield to him the minute his arms held her, he was crazy. She'd show Danton Navarro. He'd not have his way with her.

"Oh, some things are best forgotten, Danton," she purred softly and sweetly, suddenly changing her manner. "New things come along to take the place of old things. New places and people . . . you know."

This made him flinch. The tantalizing little witch was deliberately trying to stab at him with her caustic little remarks.

His expressionless face and his silence perplexed her more than a curt retort. Danton's reaction was to turn his fathomless black eyes on her and to let them linger for a moment.

When the buggy halted suddenly, Kristina recognized the side entrance of the hotel. Florine had taken her to the tearoom many times in the past.

As he lifted her out of the buggy her body pressed against his, and both were aware of the current of desire that flowed between them.

As firm and stern as Danton's voice sounded when he spoke, Kristina detected a tender gentleness in it. "Don't try to push your luck, Kit—nor my temper—

when we go inside. There's talking to be done between us, and in private. That is why you were brought here."

"All right, Danton. I guess I owe you that much."

He pulled her along with a renewed roughness in his touch, and as they went through the door, he grumbled like a bear. "God damn it, Kit, you owe me nothing nor I you, except what we wish to give willingly. Is that understood?"

She gave him a nod of her head as they went to the wide stairway. The desk clerk slept but Danton had his key so they climbed the steps, sinking into silence as they did so. But his strong hand held her arm, and it suddenly reminded Kristina that Dan Recamier was holding her arm or her waist when Danton had come forth like a marauder.

For the first time since all this had happened, she thought of poor Dan lying back there on the floor. However, only moments before Danton had rushed through the crowd like a knight rescuing the fair damsel in distress, she had spied Recamier at the front of the crowd and it displeased her.

By now, Danton had ushered her through the door of his suite and he'd noticed how quiet and thoughtful she'd become as they'd moved up the steps and down the carpeted hotel hallway. Dear God, she was so beautiful the sight of her took his breath away! Smiling, pouting, or angry, it mattered not what her mood was; her loveliness affected him so! His feeling for her went beyond the limits of anything he'd ever known before. Kit Winters!

He found himself overcome by a kind of awkwardness so he tried to sound casual. "I was not prepared for this occasion, so I've nothing to offer you—no chilled champagne or wine." But he was sorely in need of a drink so he walked over to get his flask out of the drawer of the chest.

"Your usual brandy?" she asked him.

"Yes . . . my brandy." He continued to remove the top.

"May I join you?" She seemed suddenly changed. Danton remembered the occasions when this had happened at Silvercreek. One moment she was that sweet innocent waif he wanted to protect, and the next she was the most seductive little vixen he'd ever seen. He was aware of her air of sophistication and of the wicked, daring twinkle in her emerald eyes. God, he wanted her with such an urgency he ached. But he damned sure wasn't going to let her know that!

"Of course. I didn't think you cared for brandy." He got an extra glass. "Please . . . sit down, Kit."

He gave her the glass and took a sip out of his. Kristina cautiously sipped the brandy, recalling her first time she'd drunk brandy back at Silvercreek.

He took her by utter surprise after he'd taken a generous second gulp of his brandy, for he blurted out his secret thoughts as if he were not in control of his speech. "I—I want you," he murmured softly, his deep voice warm with passion. "Damn, I want you so much!"

The look on his dark, handsome face devastated her. She could no longer hold her own emotions in check, but she made a feeble attempt by remarking, "Wanting a woman is not loving her, Danton." Her eyes tried to boldly challenge him to deny it, even though, like Danton, she was unable to conceal her desire.

Without hesitation, Danton responded, "But loving a woman is certainly wanting her, *querida!*" There was no argument she could possibly give him about that.

As it was and always had been with Danton Navarro, Kristina found herself in his powerful arms

445

and his sensuous lips were kissing her. That was enough to tell her why she'd been lonely and restless. His masterful magic had left her discontent with other men.

She had no desire to move away from the wonderful feel of his strong body. No, she wanted to press closer to him. She arched her body to do so.

"Mine! Always mine, my beautiful little Kit! Try to tell me it isn't so," his lips whispered, remaining close to her face. His hands sought the soft, satiny flesh he'd yearned so to caress, and when he did touch her she made those soft, kittenlike sounds he remembered so vividly. He was delighted.

It seemed forever since Kristina had felt the exhilarating, exciting sensations coursing through her. Her hands encircled Danton's neck, drawing him closer, and Danton knew that she was as hungry for his love as he had been for hers.

Her undulating body was feeding his craving for her, and he moved her bodice to release her full, ripe breasts which tantalized him so. His lips seized one rosy tip, and Kristina cried out, "Oh God, Danton!"

"Querida . . . mia querida!"

He hastily removed the barriers of clothing that separated her silky skin from his own pulsing body, and when he moved back to her side, she opened her arms so he could come into them and love her as she wanted him to. The sweet flush of passion lit her face with radiant loveliness only Danton's dark eyes could see. For a moment, he looked down at her glowing beauty before his strong-muscled thighs straddled her.

Kristina felt his heat as he slowly sank down to meet her, and she knew he was a fever in her blood she'd never be rid of. She knew her life would have no meaning without Danton Navarro.

As his firm, forceful body lowered down on her, she pressed upward like a flower leaning toward the sun's glowing heat. As Danton's lips sought hers in a long, lingering kiss, his tongue prodded for entry, encircling and teasing hers. The kiss deepened for he was determined she would never forget this night. Tonight, she would be his adorable Kit, wild and wonderful. Tomorrow, she might be Kristina Whelan but she would remember this night of love. By heaven or hell, he'd see to that.

He let his hand roam to and fro over her soft body, feeling the exciting little quivers of her hips and hearing her soft moans.

The heat of his eyes danced over her as his passionate caress made liquid fire invade Kristina's body. She writhed wildly and cried out his name.

"Oh, yes, *chiquita,*" Danton moaned, feeling his own passion mounting and swelling.

Kristina was gasping now, breathlessly from the rushing, raging current of the rapture Danton was stirring in her.

Her fingers felt the muscles of his back ripple as she clung to him when his strong hands slipped beneath her hips to press her closer as he buried himself deep within her. She knew he was confirming what she already knew: no other man could give her such ecstatic joy.

She made no effort to hold back a shriek of elation as he filled her with the essence of his maleness. Then, as powerful and masterful as he was, Danton was swept into a frenzy of desire he could no longer control. Kristina soared with him, eager and untamed. Together, they shared those moments of breathtaking pleasure where no one existed except the two of them. It was rare and wonderful. They were united in soul, as well as body. They knew it.

They remained encircled in one another's arms, their languorous state sublime. Both felt dazed by the incredible impact of their lovemaking.

Serenely sated, they were still joined, one to the other, as they lay side by side. For them, time stood still. . . .

Chapter 52

Florine Whelan Hamilton was privy to the whole fiasco, and no one was more stunned than the gaping redhead. The incident had happened so quickly. Instantly she had flung the red velvet drapes aside, and she stepped out of the alcove just as little Yolanda rushed up in wild pursuit of Danton Navarro.

They were together by the time Danton had jerked Kristina away from Recamier and then slammed a fierce blow to the gambler's handsome face. As Florine and Yolanda exchanged glances, slow pleased smiles began to etch their faces, but neither said anything.

However, when Florine watched her lovely daughter being dragged out the back of the gambling hall, the smile left her face and a look of disturbed concern replaced it. Yolanda sensed that Florine was going to try to stop Danton Navarro, and she hastily caught Florine's arm, urging, "Please, *señora* . . . please, let it be. She will be all right. You have no reason to fear anything. Señor Danton loves her. He would not harm her."

"You'd better be right, Yolanda. Dear God, you'd better be!" Florine muttered. "I've got to admit he did me a favor by socking that dude on the floor."

When all the hubbub of the incident had died down and Yolanda accompanied Florine up the stairs, Kristina's mother had some time to think about all that had happened that evening. She turned to little Yolanda and laughed. "Lord, I'm glad I was here tonight. I wouldn't have missed this for anything. Think I could use a drink, dear, and suppose you have something yourself, eh?"

While the happy little Mexican girl served Florine her drink and poured herself a glass of the red wine she enjoyed so much, Florine's thoughts lingered on the forceful man who'd taken her daughter and run off. She liked the masterful way he'd rescued Kristina from the clutches of Dan Recamier.

"He is a magnificent specimen of a man, this Danton Navarro, isn't he, Yolanda?" There was a sparkle in her green eyes for she wasn't so old that she couldn't appreciate to the fullest a good-looking man.

"Oh, *sí*. He is some man, *señora.*"

Florine could certainly understand why her daughter had lost her heart to such a man. How could she resist him?

The earthy, passionate lady Florine doubted that she could have. As she thought about all that had occurred, she could not honestly say she'd seen Kristina struggle to be free. The truth was the little imp probably didn't want to be free, Florine mused thoughtfully.

While the late night and early morning hours were natural for Florine, she noticed her little companion, Yolanda was sleepy. "Go to bed, dear. From what you've told me about this Señor Danton Navarro the hour may be late when our little señorita gets home. I, for one, am not waiting up. Neither should you."

Florine wasn't exactly being truthful with her, but a half-asleep Yolanda toddled on to her quarters without

450

anymore coaxing. The wine had added to her drowsiness.

When Yolanda had left and Florine was alone she sank into more thoughtful reflections. This handsome stranger may have done her another favor this night. Maybe now, Dan Recamier would leave El Paso, and she would have no reason to voice her fears to her daughter.

She felt a debt of gratitude to Danton Navarro for that. It was abhorrent to her that she'd be forced to alert Kristina to the distasteful possibility that Dan Recamier was her half brother and that they shared the same father, Dion Recamier. What a bitter thought that was!

Oh, she'd found out that Dion was a married man with a family somewhere in the south when it was already too late and after she'd lost her heart to him. That startling fact he'd conveniently concealed until he'd gotten roaring drunk one night after Florine had decided she'd had enough of his shenanigans. Oh, yes, what delight it had given him to fling that little surprise her way. She hated him as much as ever, and she found herself sharing little Yolanda's happiness about Danton Navarro's arrival in town for several reasons.

Only a short distance separated the two ladies, whose thoughts seemed to be on one another in the wee hours of the morning. Florine's auburn-haired head now rested on the back of the comfortable rose velvet chair, but she did not sleep yet. Kristina's auburn hair was rumpled from her short spell of sleep, and she had suddenly flung herself onto her side, freeing herself of Danton's muscled arm which had rested around her waist.

Danton slept deeply and contentedly, but Kristina suddenly lay awake. Although, her body was fulfilled by the feast of love they'd both so ravenously shared her thoughts were now troubled and tormented by the scandal she'd been responsible for tonight at the Crystal Castle. She shuddered to think what her mother must be going through at this very minute while she lay here in bed with a man.

Florine had surely seen everything. She must know Danton had left with her daughter in tow. Kristina wondered how many hours had passed since then. Her poor mother was probably worried about her. Suddenly, only one thing became important to her and that was to get out of this hotel and back to the Crystal Castle to make amends for the scandal she'd created.

Because she was now upset the romantic glow was fading under the glare of stark reality. Kristina put the blame on the sleeping Danton. Had he given any thought to how he'd degraded her in her own hometown and in front of so many people? Maybe he didn't even care!

As she slipped out of the bed as cautiously as she could, she reflected that if he expected to find her here when he woke up he'd be rudely surprised.

It wasn't easy to find her articles of clothing in the dark room, and the task seemed to take forever. Possibly because she was impatient to be gone she seemed all fingers and thumbs when she tried to dress.

Disgusted and discouraged when she couldn't manage to fasten the back of the bodice of her gown without some assistance, she decided to forget it and leave anyway.

Danton had not moved a muscle, it seemed, as she slipped across the room and out the door. She trotted down the thick carpeted hall in her stocking feet. When she reached the stairs, she slipped her feet into her satin slippers. Only when she was going out the side door of the hotel lobby did she allow herself to take a deep breath.

The sight of the gig and the poor horse, waiting in the same spot where Danton had left them hours ago, was a welcome one. It was a wonder it hadn't been stolen, for Florine's gig was a fancy one.

By the time Kristina reined the horse into action, her resentment was steadily mounting. Danton Navarro had put her in such an embarrassing and humiliating situation. By tomorrow, the tale would be spread all over town. Christ, she felt like wringing his neck!

There he was back at the hotel, sleeping like a baby, while she had to go back to the Crystal Castle to face her mother, who might even have summoned the sheriff by now. Obviously, Danton didn't care about anything but his own selfish desires, and now she was sorry she'd given in to them.

Couldn't she defy him? Was she so damned weak that all he had to do was touch her to make her do anything he wanted her to? Well, the answer seems to be yes, she told herself sharply as the bay trotted along.

At least, the street was deserted. Not one soul was to be seen, and the streets and buildings were dark. She didn't think much about the buildings she passed by until she came to the side entrance of the Crystal Castle, and that did puzzle her because it was shrouded in darkness. More perplexing was the quiet inside the place. Obviously, no one seemed to be the least bit concerned about her whereabouts.

"H'm, fine kettle of fish, I must say," she mumbled as she turned the knob to let herself into the quarters. As she stepped through the double doors, she reasoned that she might just come upon Florine sitting in the dark, keeping a vigil alone like the proud, independent lady she was.

But Kristina was in for another surprise. There was no sign of Florine in the parlor, and when Kristina peered into her mother's bedroom, she was stunned to see that Florine appeared to be sleeping as soundly as Danton Navarro had been when she'd left his side. Swishing her skirts sharply, she whirled around and went to her own bedroom, in a quandary about this whole insane evening. Madness—sheer madness was what it was!

Florine Whelan was hardly asleep, but she was a pretty fair actress. She'd observed her daughter coming down the street in the gig, and she'd decided that it was best for both of them not to meet face to face at this early morning hour. The night had been long and too much had happened, so her mother wisely decided to get into bed and to pretend to be asleep.

After she heard Kristina go into her own room, Florine could not help wondering why she'd returned alone. Where was this Danton Navarro whose virtues little Yolanda had raved about earlier this evening? Why had he not escorted her daughter back?

Had they had a lovers' quarrel? Florine wondered. If so, Kristina would have been in no mood to talk. Florine told herself she'd played her cards right by pretending to be asleep. Most assuredly, Kristina would not have wished to face her mother if she'd just come from her lover's arms as Yolanda hinted he was.

Within moments, Florine did give way to her need for sleep. Tomorrow it would be up to Kristina to tell her just what had happened between her and Danton Navarro. But would she? That was not a bet Florine would want to lay money on.

Most of the occupants of the Crystal Castle slept late—all but little Yolanda. She required very little sleep to retain her lively, vivacious disposition. When she went to check on the *señora* and Señorita Kristina, she found them both sleeping so she quickly and quietly slipped out of the quarters to go on downstairs and have her breakfast. It was nice to see that Sid Layman was there having his usual ham and eggs.

"Got some coffee brewed too. Get some and come join me, Yolanda. I'm all lonely by myself. A bunch of lazybones around here this morning."

She smiled and did as he suggested, helping herself to Sid's pot of brewed coffee. "They're all sleeping upstairs too. It was a rather hectic night, wouldn't you say, Sid?"

"More than that, honey. Much more than that. I'd say we'd best be on our toes for the next week or so. That bunch over at the Bird Cage ain't going to take too kindly to what happened to their man, Recamier."

"Are you sure about Recamier, Sid? Are you sure he's one of the owners of the place?" Yolanda asked.

"Know where he was taken last night after all that fracas?"

"To the Bird Cage?"

"That's right and he was making some pretty wild threats when he was being helped out of here by dudes who offered him their support."

"I'm glad Señor Danton knocked him down. He deserved it," Yolanda declared smugly.

"This Señor Danton is the one you've mentioned to me before, isn't he? He's the big hombre you think our little Miss Tina is in love with?"

Self-assured and almost haughty, Yolanda replied, "I know it! After last night, I cannot believe otherwise. You will see, Sid. You will see, I am sure."

Sid chuckled, "I believe you, Yolanda. Just tell me how come you are so smart about love and romance?"

Yolanda loved to tease the good-natured Layman, and she knew he was as fond of her as she was about him so she winked at him and boasted, "Why do you think? I've been in love too!"

Sid responded with a weak grin, but he said nothing. Oh, he thought a lot of things—things which would have surprised and shocked the sultry little Yolanda. He'd like to be the *hombre* she was in love with, but he was no fool. He realized he wouldn't stand a chance with a pretty young thing like her.

He could not stop himself from wishing though.

Chapter 53

A maelstrom of emotions whirled in Kristina's pretty head when she'd finally gotten into her own bed. She could not dismiss so lightly the other bed she'd lain in this night—and loved in—with the man she was as mixed up about now as she'd been when she'd left Silvercreek.

Now that he was no longer by her side and his nearness no longer made sanity leave her, she realized nothing whatsoever was settled. She had not even had the good grace to inquire after dear Señora Lucía or Delores. Regardless of her feeling for Danton, Delores and her mother would always remain very dear to her.

There had been no conversation actually—only Danton's sensuous lovemaking which made everything else seem insignificant and of no consequence.

Kristina asked herself if it made her a wanton to feel so reckless and shameless when she was with Danton. She'd never felt that way about any other man in her life. What spellbinding magic did Danton Navarro weave? He affected her like those love potions Solitaire was always talking about. Was it his fine-chiseled, handsome face . . . his dark Latin good looks? Was it his magnificent muscled body, his broad shoulders and trim waist? Other men she'd been around were good-looking and had fine physical attributes.

No, that wasn't it at all. It was a million and one little things, Kristina told herself. It was the twinkle in his dark eyes and the way they could dance, slowly or busily, over her face or body, making her feel the wildest sensations. It was the special way his hands could run over her, the special touch with which he caressed her breasts. There was an excited urgency in his hands. It made her want to arch, made her just as eager as he seemed to be when he pulled her to him.

His sensuous lips and mouth could demand or persuade in such a way that she was always willing to obey or anxiously respond. If this was love or a sickness then she was afflicted, for the man was a fever in her blood, as sure as she breathed.

When she woke, she felt the same mixed emotions she had felt when she'd fallen asleep the night before. But now her conflicting thoughts were not only about Danton. Why hadn't her mother been concerned last night? she wondered. She was glad she didn't have to explain what had happened, and yes, that she was spared facing Florine, who was so sharp.

Maybe, it was the quandary Kristina found herself floundering in upon arising that made her seek out her old confidante, Solitaire. She'd go out to the ranch, she decided, without saying anything to her mother or the busy bee, Yolanda.

She dressed quietly so no one would know she was up and about, and when she had put on the black riding skirt and a soft batiste blouse, she tiptoed out of her room and through the parlor, not making a sound. Only as she was moving down the hall did she realize what she'd chosen to wear this morning—the old riding ensemble Lucía had bought for her back at Silvercreek.

Lord, she could not deny it! She'd missed it—all of

it—since coming home to El Paso. More than she'd realized at the time, Silvercreek had become a part of her, and in a way it seemed as much like home to her as the Crystal Castle here in El Paso.

Perhaps it shouldn't be so, she chided herself. But things had happened in her life that she couldn't change. There was no going back.

As Kristina made her way to the entrance, she was grateful she'd run into no one along the way, especially Yolanda. This morning she felt such utter confusion, as though she was being pulled by strong, conflicting forces. Aside from talking to Solitaire, she wanted to be alone, completely.

But when that familiar voice called out to her, Kristina stopped short and whirled around on a booted heel, snapping out an abrupt retort, "What, Yolanda?"

"Where are you going, Señorita Kristina? I've been waiting to serve you your breakfast," Yolanda said, in a hesitant voice, not understanding the frown on her mistress' face. She was naturally bursting at the seams to know all about the *señorita* and Señor Danton, and it was utterly disappointing that Kristina was not of a mind to confide in her.

"I want no breakfast, Yolanda. I'm going out to see Solitaire."

"Now?" Yolanda didn't understand Kristina's manner.

"Right now," Kristina said, turning to leave.

"But—but your mother is still here," a perplexed Yolanda pointed out. What was the matter with her friend?

"But it is not my mother I wish to speak to, Yolanda. Dear God!" Kristina said, her vexation mounting at the girl's persistence.

For once in her life, Yolanda said nothing. She was too befuddled by Kristina's chilling aloofness. As

Kristina again turned to leave, she did not miss the hurt in her little friend's dark brooding eyes, and she realized she'd been abrupt and harsh with her devoted servant. Yolanda was always saying, "We're friends," and it was true. Kristina understood that she wanted to know about her reunion with Danton, but at the moment Kristina had other things on her mind. God knows, she needed the wise counsel of someone she'd always depended upon. That was why she was seeking out the sage wisdom of the dependable Solitaire.

But as she traveled through the outskirts of El Paso, she vowed to make amends to little Yolanda when she returned to the Crystal Castle.

It was a short journey out to the Hamilton ranch, and the ride alone had been good for Kristina's frayed nerves. It had not helped her mood that she'd acted as she had with Yolanda. Her little Mexican friend didn't deserve that.

The first sight that caught Kristina's green eyes as she galloped up the drive to the long veranda of the ranch house was her beloved Solitaire in her usual colorful frock, a matching kerchief tied around her head.

She'd always thought the tall, willowy mulatto was a striking-looking woman, and age had only seemed to enhance her tawny loveliness.

It didn't seem fair, Kristina thought as she rode up, that Solitaire had never had any life of her own. Her years had been spent in total devotion to her mother, Florine. Kristina determined that this would not be the case with Yolanda. She would not wish it for her little Mexican friend.

As Solitaire saw her "little Miss Tina" astraddle the big roan mare, her first thought was that something was wrong with Florine. When Kristina dismounted Solitaire's first words were, "Is *mam'selle* all right?"

Kristina broke into a soft laugh. "Most likely she's

still in bed asleep. I came to see you, Solitaire. It's been a long, long time since we've had a visit without others around."

Solitaire's dark eyes warmed with the tender love she'd always felt for this precious girl. Many times, she'd pretended that Kristina was her own child, and she loved her as though she was. "Been a very long time, child."

"Lord, Solitaire, at times, I wish I was a child again and we were roaming those fields of wildflowers and going for those wonderful buggy rides in the country. Those were nice and carefree days."

"Wonderful days, Miss Tina. Guess they were the most wonderful days of my life." Solitaire smiled.

Kristina patted her shoulder and smiled in return. "Can you imagine how many skinned knees and elbows you patched up and doctored for me?"

"Never kept count, Miss Tina, but it was surely a bunch."

Solitaire suggested they have themselves a nice cup of coffee right there on the comfortable veranda, and Kristina was quick to agree for it was a pleasant morning with a gentle, light breeze blowing from the west.

Funny how Miss Tina seemed to be reminiscing a lot this morning, like she had when she'd arrived from town. Life here at the Hamilton Ranch was just not the same for her and the *mam'selle* as it had been at the Crystal Castle, and Solitaire had found it lonely and lacking. It was not that Jason Hamilton was not a fine, good man. Solitaire was the first to admit that he'd been like a gift from heaven when Florine needed him and his support after her accident. But those knowing eyes of hers knew Florine Whelan too well and too long pondered not to wonder if she, too, did not get lonely many times.

461

As they sat together and drank their coffee, it was a tonic Kristina needed badly. She talked with her beloved Solitaire without restraint, and Solitaire listened. Kristina even confessed her qualms about missing Silvercreek.

"But why shouldn't you be, child? It is not your destiny to be what you're trying to make yourself be, Miss Tina. Can't change what's written in stars for you, honey. You weren't meant to be any gambling queen—not you!"

"What was meant for me then, Solitaire? Lord, I wish I knew!"

"You know—deep in your heart you know. You found it when you were gone all those months from El Paso."

"How can you be so sure, Solitaire? How can you be that certain about my destiny?"

"'Cause you aren't at peace here. You haven't been since you arrived. It shows, Miss Tina, in that faraway look in those pretty green eyes." Solitaire gave her that know-it-all look she'd seen so many times in her life.

Somehow, it gave her the courage to tell Solitaire all about Danton Navarro. She left nothing untold—even the truth about last night in the hotel.

When Kristina had finished her revelation, she waited for Solitaire to say something but the mulatto woman didn't. Impatient for her response, Kristina prodded, "Well, aren't you going to say anything? Have I shocked you, Solitaire?"

"I've already said it, don't you remember? I told you, honey, you found it while you were gone. You found your Danton Navarro, or shall we say, he found you."

When it was time for her to ride back into town, Kristina knew she'd been right to seek out Solitaire. No longer was her soul tormented, and her heart did not ache as it had when she'd woken up this morning. When she gave Solitaire a hug and bid her farewell, Solitaire saw the mist in her eyes and she knew she'd helped her little Tina by the words she'd spoken.

Perhaps, Tina wasn't her own daughter, and now she knew that no children would ever be born to her, but Solitaire had enjoyed rearing Florine's daughter. There had been compensations, she told herself.

Despite the devotion and undying gratitude Solitaire felt from Florine, she did not always agree with her. Kristina had the right to know who her father was, and Solitaire felt that it was long past the time when the young lady should be told. Mercy, she'd been sorely tempted to tell her this morning!

But after their talk together, when Kristina mounted up on the roan to gallop down the drive, Solitaire watched her until she was out of sight. She felt strongly that she knew who the auburn-haired beauty would go in search of, and it wasn't Dan Recamier.

Solitaire ambled slowly into the house. Maybe it was better this way, for Kristina's sake. What a devastating blow it would have been if she'd found out at this late stage of her life that the man was most likely her half brother! If she had felt the slightest attraction for him, she might have lived with the scars of remorse the rest of her life.

Solitaire shook her kerchiefed head once again, vowing that it had to be destiny that brought Danton Navarro to El Paso at this particular time.

To herself, she mumbled, "It was meant to be! *Mam'selle* won't have to worry now."

Chapter 54

Unceremoniously and raging like a bull, Danton Navarro invaded the lower level of the Crystal Castle. His black eyes flashed and his black hair had not been combed or brushed with care. Actually, he'd leaped out of the bed upon finding Kristina gone and he'd quickly slipped into his pants and then yanked on his shirt. The minute he'd had both boots on, he angrily bolted from the room without brushing his hair. He'd merely run his fingers through the unruly mop.

Bound and determined to get to the Crystal Castle as quickly as his long legs would carry him, he didn't even finish buttoning up the front of his shirt.

After he'd slammed the front door, almost knocking the unsteady Rollo off his feet, Danton marched on into the saloon area of the quiet gambling hall.

When Sid Layman's head popped up from under the counter, Danton's angry voice demanded, "Where is she?"

It took a second for Sid to place the dark, surly Latin before he asked, "Who are you talking about, Mister?"

Danton reached over the counter bar and his hands struck as swiftly as an adder, grabbing Sid's shirt collar. "You know who I mean—damn it!"

A more fierce, dangerous-looking dude Sid had never seen, and he wasn't about to press his luck at this point. "You mean Miss Kristina?"

Danton's hold eased somewhat and he barked, "You bet your sweet life I mean Miss Kristina. If you lie to me, it could cost you your life."

Standing on the second floor-landing and watching the scene below, Florine decided it was time she took charge, but she had to confess it had been wildly exciting to watch the handsome devil come at Sid like a tiger, his fine male body all rippling muscles. That face was something to behold, and his deep powerful voice roared like a lion.

In her own indomitable manner, with her hands placed firmly at her waist, Florine called down to Danton Navarro, "Young man, I think it is my daughter you're seeking. I'm Florine Whelan, Kristina's mother. Now, if you'd be so kind as to release my employee's neck, I'll speak with you up here."

Danton stared up at a most attractive lady with the same shade of hair as his darling Kit, a lady whom he wasn't feeling too pleased with at the moment. He did not reply to her request that he join her, but he did release Sid Layman as she demanded.

This was a very impressive lady, Danton had to admit as he surveyed her. Her flawless fair skin was much lighter than her daughter's, and though they did look alike, each was individually lovely.

In that brief space of time, he saw many little things which told him where Kit had inherited her spirit and fire. There was a flash of emerald green in Kit's eyes just like her mother's.

She stood there towering over him, and the sheerness of her morning gown revealed her most alluring curves and full breasts. In fact, she was a truly magnificent-looking lady for her age.

Danton darted one quick glance back at Sid and remarked, "Sorry, if I hurt you. Nothing against you, you understand?"

"Forget it!" Sid mumbled, then he turned to go about his chore as Danton went up the stairs as Florine had suggested.

Florine tucked the deep blue gown more securely around her for she'd rushed from her room hastily when she'd heard the commotion below. She watched Danton's tall figure mount the stairs. Now that she was about to meet this man her daughter had been linked with, she was feeling some qualms of her own. For weeks, she'd harbored these thoughts and had confided in no one. Jason had not been told, not even Solitaire had shared her feelings. Only she knew.

When he stood before her, Florine extended her hand to him in greeting as she declared, "Well, Señor Navarro . . . we meet at last."

"Señora Whelan," Danton said, taking her hand in his. "Forgive me, I should have said Señora Hamilton, should I not?"

"It doesn't matter. I'm addressed both ways. I've put in more years as Whelan than I have as Hamilton. Jason and I have only been married for a year."

"I've heard of him through mutual friends. Fine man, I understand," Danton told her. "The Ortega family have been acquaintances of my family for many years."

"Ah, yes, I know them. Now, come with me and we will get to the point of this . . . uh, visit. You, Señor Navarro, are a very dynamic person." She took the lead as Danton followed her down the hallway.

"Oh?"

"Oh, yes . . . I would say so. My Crystal Castle seems to bring out the worst of your hot temper. I

466

speak of last night and again just now. Twice in twenty-four hours you've stormed in here."

Danton frowned. He knew where Kit got her temper, and this lady was a little riled. Her voice was snapping and she was finding it hard to be gracious.

"I can't deny what you say, but I won't apologize for my actions. They were justified!"

When Florine turned to look at the young man standing directly behind her, his dark eyes met hers in a daring challenge. Florine saw his unwavering attitude etched clearly on his face.

"Come in, Señor Navarro."

When they were in the parlor, Danton refused her offer of refreshments. "I want only to speak with Kit—Kristina!"

"She is not here at the moment. I have no way of knowing when she'll be back."

She watched his reaction and saw him tense with impatience. "I want to talk to you though, since the opportunity has come my way. I owe you in a way. You did me a big favor last night by what you did to Recamier. He deserved it."

At her words Danton relaxed a bit. At least, she did not approve of Recamier as her daughter's suitor. But in the next breath, she startled him by bluntly declaring, "You might as well know, Danton Navarro, that the name Navarro leaves a bitter taste in my mouth. Maybe I should say bittersweet. Oh, I am eternally grateful for what your mother and sister did for Kristina, and I am told that you were the one who found her alone in the mountains when she had lost her memory so that makes me grateful to you."

In a hesitating deep voice and with a look of utter dismay on his face, Danton said, "I did find her and I cared for her. I took her to our ranch so she would be under the care of my mother and my sister, Delores.

She . . . she was treated like family. My mother became very fond of her as I would have thought Kit—I mean Kristina—would have told you." Now, Danton was feeling the need to defend his family, especially when he recalled Lucía's devotion to the little waif he'd brought home unannounced that day so long ago.

"She told me. But there is something she could not know, Señor Navarro. The night I was robbed and shot in the melee, the leader of that bunch of hoodlums was a Navarro."

Florine made a dramatic gesture with her cane and rose from her chair to display to the young man sitting before her how much effort it required for that very simple motion. "A Navarro did this to me—robbed me of a life I loved and robbed me of a daughter for months. Bitter? Dear God, I am the most bitter woman I know, more than anyone has ever imagined, Señor Navarro."

In a soft murmur almost like a whisper, Danton told her, "I know how you must feel, *señora.*"

"Oh, do you now?" Florine hissed and her green eyes flamed. "No, young man, you could not possibly know. Even my devoted husband does not know the depth of my pain, nor does my trusted servant whose time with me goes back before my Kristina was born."

"Are you possibly laboring under the wrong impression that I am the guilty Navarro? If you are, I assure you I am not the one."

"I saw the man, remember?"

"Am I to assume that Kit has not told you I have a twin brother, *señora?*"

"She mentioned it, but words are easily said. Who is to prove it? Can you?"

This lady gives no quarter, Danton thought. She is a hard-nosed one and bullishly stubborn. Florine glared at him.

"I can't undo what was done to you. I wish I could. I can tell you the truth though, and the truth is, Señora Whelan, I was in El Paso only once before this trip I made in search of your daughter. The other time I came at my mother's request, after she'd received word from her friend, Vincente Ortega, that my twin brother, Damien was playing his usual game of hell-raising here in El Paso—and throwing away his money on a bunch of hoodlums, as you called them. Ortega's loyalty to our family prompted him to let my mother know, and she sent me here. My trip was futile. I spent one night combing the town and left. Yes, I did come to the Crystal Castle briefly on that particular night. As a matter of fact, I saw you that evening, and I recall you gave me a look of disapproval, which I found a little disconcerting."

He was either telling the absolute truth or he was the most cunning liar she'd ever heard.

"Let me say one other thing for whatever satisfaction you may get from it, *señora*. My brother's punishment for what he did to you has been harsh and just. He is now confined to a wheelchair with no hope of ever walking again. Perhaps, the name of Navarro will not forever be so bitter if your daughter loves me half as much as I adore her."

This complicated lady was to perplex Danton as much as her daughter had in the past. Suddenly without any warning, Florine Whelan dissolved into a flood of tears. Before this handsome stranger, she dropped the restraint she'd exercised in front of Jason and Solitaire.

Danton took her in his arms as he would have Lucía, and he held her tenderly, urging her to let it out. Florine did just that. She felt no shame in being a helpless, weeping female, and that was a strange experience for Florine Whelan. The strength in Danton Navarro's arms was so comforting that Florine gave way to the urge to stay there.

When she was drained and no more tears would flow, she released herself from Danton Navarro's arms and looked up at his face. "I was wrong about you, young man—terribly, terribly wrong. I hope you'll forgive me."

Danton grinned, and there was a glint of boyish mischief in his black eyes as he told her, "It's the least I could do for the lady who's going to be my mother-in-law, and it is what Mother would expect of me."

Florine sat up straight, a questioning look on her face. "Why would your mother demand that you do anything for me, Danton Navarro?"

"Because, my dear lady, you were a very good friend of hers once upon a time." Danton was truly enjoying himself as he watched the expression on Florine's face, which was so like Kit's.

With a deep frown on her face, Florine almost gasped, "Your mother and I?"

"Yes, ma'am. I bring you greetings from the former Queen of the Palace—the famous Lolita—the greatly admired faro and Spanish Monte dealer. Remember?" His eyes sparked and twinkled with amusement as he watched Florine Whelan's mouth open to speak. No words came out.

"You don't—you can't—oh, good God!" Florine smiled and shook her head, finding it hard to believe. Her face still reflecting her amazement, she finally asked, "You're telling me that Lucía—Lucía Navarro was my idol—Lolita. Dear God!"

"One and the same," Danton laughed.

"So that is why she disappeared that night never to appear again at the old Palace. Lord, there was a wave of speculation about her whereabouts for months. She became the mystery lady around San Antonio."

"Yes, I can imagine how her sudden disappearance would have set up a furor of rumors and gossip." Danton laughed, "I'm given to understand that my father was a very headstrong gentleman when he wanted something. Mother tells me they both fell in love the minute he walked into the Palace that first night."

"Well, it sounds like your mother has had a very happy life, Danton, and I'm happy to hear it. I thought there was no one—absolutely no one—like the beautiful Lolita."

Danton patted her hand. "She would be most happy to hear you say that, *señora.*"

"Perhaps, she will sometime in the future. I have the feeling that Lolita's son is as stubborn and headstrong as his father, eh?" she said teasingly.

"I confess I am. I am damned determined that your daughter will be mine—my wife."

Florine reached up and planted a kiss on his tanned cheek. "Then, young man, you have my permission to get going. Time's wasting."

Chapter 55

A short distance away from the Crystal Castle where Danton and Florine Whelan were getting to know each other, an unpleasant atmosphere prevailed. At the Bird Cage the owners were arguing.

Lucky Thorton with all his silver-tongued words and cunning ways could not mollify the angry Bill Peel. Because of the incident involving their partner, Dan Recamier, Bill had stomped out of the room, refusing to agree to go along with more of Recamier's schemes.

"I'll handle it my way. You do as you want!" he'd barked back at the others as he'd marched through the door to leave Charlie Bedlow and Lucky Thorton sitting in the back room of the Bird Cage.

Charlie's quiet nature liked a neutral situation and all this dissension was playing havoc with his stomach. He wasn't a cool, calm individual like Lucky or Recamier. But he liked the flashy Recamier's happy-go-lucky personality, and he didn't trust Peel for a minute.

Charlie was frightened, and like a scared rabbit he was going to run before another night descended on El Paso. This venture had been ill fated from the beginning, and now he was engulfed in bad premonitions. Charlie felt if he didn't get the hell out of El Paso before this day was over, he might never leave this town. He wasn't a bold, daring man, nor was he seeking adventure, but he did feel compelled to go upstairs to warn Dan about Peel before he left.

With this in mind, he excused himself from Lucky. "See if I can do anything for Dan, Lucky. He had a pretty ugly cut on his lip, and I suspect that one side of his face is a size bigger if that floozy hasn't been keeping those cold cloths on it like I told her to after I tended to him last night."

He moved his paunchy body out of the chair and crossed the room, leaving Lucky leaning back in his chair and puffing on his cheroot.

By the time he'd climbed the stairs and shooed away the girl sitting by the side of Recamier's bed, Charlie's ruddy face was redder and he puffed to get his breath. He sat for a minute before trying to talk to Dan. Dan didn't try to talk either for his swollen lip urged him not to.

"Dan, I gotta talk to you. You listening?"

Dan nodded his head. Then he grunted and waved his hand as a signal for Charlie to talk.

"All right. I got up here as soon as Peel left the rest of us. He's mad as a hornet and he's not going to listen to you, Lucky, or me. That ignoramus is going to do what he damned well set that crazy mind of his to do. And he is crazy, Dan, crazy as a loon."

Recamier agreed with another nod of his head and another mumble. Charlie bent low as if he didn't dare chance being overheard as he whispered in Dan's ear, "Ain't told Lucky yet and sure as the devil ain't going to tell Peel, but I'm telling you—I'm hightailing it out of here today."

A door slammed downstairs and the jumpy Charlie went to peer out the window of Recamier's room. "Oh,

473

it's just Lucky leaving."

Suddenly, Dan Recamier was making himself talk, painful or not. He ordered Charlie to lock the door and help him dress. Charlie stumbled around the room, fetching his fancy clothes, and then he watched Dan slowly push himself up from the bed. Tediously, the usually suave gambler began to get himself dressed.

"I'm weak as the devil. Would you reach under that feather mattress and get that pouch, Charlie?" Charlie obliged him. By this time, Dan was placing his fancy gold studs in his shirt sleeves. "Like company along the way, Charlie?"

Charlie was stunned for a minute, but he quickly replied, "Sure—sure, I guess so. You want to leave too?"

"As you said, Charlie, Peel is an ignoramus. Dan Recamier didn't strike out with all the ladies. My love life hasn't suffered a bit and the coffer is hardly empty. Since I appreciate what you did for me, I've got more than enough for a high-stakes game in Santa Fe. What do you say, Charlie old boy?"

"I say let's don't let no grass grow under our feet with old Lucky and Peel both gone," Charlie nervously chuckled.

The dapper Dan Recamier and the apple-cheeked Charlie Bedlow hastily made their exit down the back steps of the Bird Cage. They never looked back as they jauntily strode down the alley to the livery.

As the sun was sinking in the western sky, the two men rode in the same direction. Charlie Bedlow's belly had ceased churning, and he was anticipating the big, thick beef steak he was going to enjoy when he stopped for the night. Dan Recamier was anticipating a cute little *señorita* who could ease his pain. They both spurred their horses faster! The sight of La Mesa over in the distance was what they both wanted to see.

El Paso lay back behind them, and they were both happy to be gone from there.

It was not her intentions to stop on the way back into town after she left the Hamilton ranch, but Kristina gave way to the sudden impulse to pause by the rippling little creek where she and Solitaire had lingered so many times when she'd been a child. Some said the little creek was a tributary of the Rio Grande River, but Solitaire had told her about the Indian legend that swore it came from a huge underground lake whose waters were pure and crystal clear. She'd believed Solitaire's tale as a child and she did now.

Maybe, she was overcome with moody reminiscing about the little magical creek back at Silvercreek and the beautiful romantic story Danton had told her about his mother and father and how they'd come to name their ranch. Whatever it was, she stopped to linger awhile, and such a serene peace surrounded her that she laid down on the ground. No longer was her heart or soul tormented and pulled two ways. Now, she knew what she wanted—thanks to Solitaire!

The quiet solitude induced a languorous state, and she fell asleep. When she woke, she was startled to see that the sun was sinking. It amazed her that she'd slept so long. Almost four hours had gone by since she'd left Solitaire, and more than six hours had passed since she'd left the Crystal Castle.

Frantic, she jumped up from the ground, calling herself all kinds of a fool. Her stupidity might cost her dearly, she chided herself as she mounted the roan mare. What if Danton had already left El Paso? He couldn't have been pleased at finding her gone when he'd woken up at the hotel.

If only she'd just kept riding on into town and gone

directly to the hotel instead of making this impulsive stop by the creek, his arms might be holding her right now, she fumed dejectedly.

She pushed the roan to the limit to get to the hotel as soon as possible, but by the time she raced down the street where the hotel was situated, darkness had settled over the town.

But Danton was not in, the clerk informed her, as she rushed to the desk in the lobby. She immediately asked if he'd checked out.

"No, miss, he hasn't. Could be he's visiting his friends, the Ortega family. Know them?"

Kristina mumbled something, but she wasn't quite sure just what it was. She stumbled wearily out of the lobby and headed back to the hitching post, deciding that she might as well go to the Crystal Castle for she had no idea in which direction the Ortega ranch lay although she'd heard of the family for the name was well known in El Paso.

When she entered the side door of the Crystal Castle she was neither prepared nor ready to be bombarded by the inquiries of Sally O'Neal and Yolanda, who'd rushed through the door after hearing her mistress' voice.

She did not know of the furor brewing for the last two hours, but she didn't have to wait long for the chatterbox, Yolanda, to fill her in. "Señor Danton was here and he left to go back to his hotel after he talked to your mother for a while. He returned an hour later, expecting you'd surely be back by then, and they both left to go to the ranch to see if harm had come your way after so much time had passed. Where were you, Señorita Kristina?"

"It's a long story, Yolanda."

"But it was late morning when you left for the ranch, and I told your mother and Señor Danton that was where you had gone." Yolanda was bewildered as well

476

as perplexed.

"And I did and I visited with Solitaire."

"But I do not understand how you missed them if you've just come from there?" Yolanda's dark eyes and face reflected her complete confusion.

"Lord, Yolanda, it isn't any big mystery. I simply stopped to sit alongside the creek and I fell asleep for longer than I realized. All right? I am fine. Now, come upstairs with me and help me get a bath before they return."

The girl tagged along, chattering all the way about how glad she was that no harm had come to Kristina.

"I'm glad too, Yolanda." She flung open the oak doors to enter the suite, and as she passed by the large gilt mirror hanging on the parlor wall she realized what a disheveled mess she was. Her hair was all tousled from her nap on the ground and her furious ride back into town. What a miserable sight she must have presented walking into the hotel lobby!

At least, she'd arrived here before the early arrivals had been downstairs. She needed no more little incidents to add fuel to the scandalous behavior of Florine Whelan's daughter. Now that Florine had become Mrs. Jason Hamilton, a daughter of hers was even a more prime potential target for gossip. Right now though Kristina couldn't have cared less about that.

As Yolanda hustled around, preparing her mistress' bath, Kristina listened to nothing she was saying. She searched the room for her fluffy little kitten who'd failed to run out from where he might be hiding and greet her as eagerly as he usually did.

"Yolanda?"

"*Si?*"

"Where is Amigo?" she called out from the next room.

"You cannot find him?"

"I cannot! He always comes out but he's in none of his usual places. Oh, if he's slipped out there's no telling where the little monkey could be."

Seeing her mistress' partial state of undress, Yolanda urged her to go ahead with her bath, saying she would search every corner of the room. She started to look under and behind each piece of furniture in the suite. She had last seen the silvery gray kitten when Señor Danton was here visiting with the señora.

After he'd left, no one had entered the suite of rooms to see Florine. When the *señor* had returned, the two of them had left together, but Yolanda had been there. She knew the kitten had not slipped out. She'd have sworn it hadn't.

"Have you found him yet, Yolanda?" Kristina's voice mingled with the splashing bath water.

"No, *señorita*. It seems Amigo has pulled a disappearing act like you." By this time Yolanda was deciding that the kitten had slipped out of the doors. "Do not concern yourself, *señorita!* I'll find the little rascal!"

Chapter 56

The silvery fluff ball slept contentedly in much the same fashion that his auburn-haired mistress had chosen only a few hours earlier, but he was beside Danton. Little Amigo found Danton's hotel bed an ideal spot for his nap.

When Danton had left the Crystal Castle after his long visit with Florine Whelan to return to his hotel and change his attire, he'd had no idea that the kitten had slipped out of the room and had followed him outside. Only when he'd walked a distance from the gambling hall, did he happen to turn and spot his new friend. So he'd picked the kitten up and taken it to the hotel with him, deciding that he'd take the little rascal back after he'd shaved and changed his clothes.

He figured by the time he did all that and got back to the Crystal Castle his wandering lady would surely have returned from her jaunt to the Hamilton ranch where Yolanda had said she'd gone.

But in his haste to get back to the Crystal Castle, the kitten was forgotten so here he stayed, content in his sleep.

However, Danton Navarro's patience could take no more idle waiting. When Kristina still had not shown up, he told Florine exactly what he was going to do. She agreed completely. "Let's waste no more time," she said. She summoned Rollo to bring around her gig, and Danton suggested that he do the driving. That, too, Florine agreed with.

But ironically, they'd traveled to the ranch and were standing waiting for Solitaire to open the door at the exact moment Kristina was frantically leaping on her horse to go back into town. But for a hair's breath their paths did not cross.

As the pair faced Solitaire, no one had to tell the mulatto that this was the man Miss Tina had spoken to her about a few short hours ago. Ah, he was a lot of man! But when they told her why they were there Solitaire was consumed with fear.

"She should have been back into town two hours ago, *mam'selle*." Her doelike eyes darted from Florine to the tall man whose eyes were as black as her own. "She was coming to you, *Monsieur*. I know this for almost certain. We have a talk—me and Miss Tina."

In that masterful way of his, Danton didn't ask Florine Whelan, he told her. "Stay here with Solitaire. I'm going to help myself to one of your horses. I can cover ground faster that way."

Florine had no chance to give him any argument if she dared to try. He had already vanished back into the night, and soon Solitaire and Florine heard the galloping hooves of the horse pounding down the drive of the Hamilton ranch.

Solitaire soothed Florine, a ring of confidence in her voice, as she assured her, "Miss Tina will be all right, *mam'selle*. He'll find her. Nothing would stop him."

Florine managed a weak smile and thoughtfully replied, "I think you're right, Solitaire."

* * *

Lucky Thorton was conceited enough to know without a shadow of doubt that he was much smarter than his three partners and when he saw that all the talking in the world was not going to change Bill Peel's mind, Lucky made his decision. He didn't give Charlie Bedlow any hint of his plans, but when Charlie went upstairs to see about Recamier, Lucky began to pick up what spoils he could around the Bird Cage. When Charlie glanced out Dan's window to see Lucky leaving the Bird Cage, he was watching Lucky's departure for Mexico.

Lucky traveled south, while Bedlow and Recamier went to the west. Peel found himself deserted by his three partners when he returned to the Bird Cage by midafternoon. His fury and his drinking mounted as the afternoon wore on. He was obsessed by an urgent, devastating need to vent his anger on a troublesome female by the name of Kristina Whelan. He damned her and cursed her, and he became fixed with a crazed determination to destroy her before the night was over.

He sought out two shiftless drifters who were willing to do his dirty work for a fee. For three hours, he stalked the Crystal Castle to see Kristina return and go inside. Nothing moved yet outside the front of the building for the doors didn't open for business for an hour yet. Only a passerby walked along the street occasionally, but darkness shrouded the back area to aid Peel's plans.

Peel knew Sid Layman's usual arrival time—the piano player walked from his boardinghouse a few blocks away—and he also knew the only obstacle at the rear of the alleyway would be old Rollo. He'd be napping on the little porch at the back entrance.

When he figured the time was just right, Peel gave the two hired hoodlums the nod to go about their torching job. He stood at the back entrance where poor

Rollo now lay in a pool of his own blood. One of the men had whacked him a stunning blow on the head.

When his nose smelled the first hint of the scorching flames burning paper and cloth, an evil smile broke out on Peel's ugly face. He envisioned all those plush, lavish furnishings being reduced to cinders and ashes, and that made him chuckle. If it just happened to do the same thing to that fancy, young lady, that made no difference to Peel.

Sid Layman was about a block away when his nose picked up the strange, pungent odor in the air, and he began to walk faster as if instinct told him there was danger in the air he was sniffing.

As he moved to go in the side entrance, he paused. Something was amiss! For some reason, he went to check out the back of the building. As he stepped into the alleyway, he knew it was old Rollo who was missing. He'd been there to greet him every night.

The sight of Bill Peel made Sid walk faster and reach inside his coat to clasp the short-barreled pocket pistol he carried. He saw his old friend, Rollo, lying by the back door, a bloody gash on the side of his head, and then a sudden scream—a woman's—echoed from the building. Sid asked no question. He aimed the derringer and pulled the trigger.

The shot was deadly and Peel fell forward on the ground, letting out one final groan. Sid did not take the time to linger with Rollo, for the scream had to be Sally's or Yolanda's. As he surged through the door, the overpowering odor of burning rags told him what was going on and who was responsible. But Sid slowed his pace and moved with more caution, not knowing how many adversaries he faced with his one little pistol.

A hissing sound beckoned to him and he turned in its direction to see a scared, trembling Sally O'Neal. She was hiding behind some crates near the back door.

"Sid! Oh, God!"

"It's all right, Sally, baby. Come on," he urged.

Cowering, she came out and told Sid in a faltering whisper, "Two idiots are burning everything in sight, Sid. Yolanda is somewhere in there hunting that damned lost kitten and Kristina is upstairs. Oh, God, Sid!"

"Go outside, honey. Rollo's hurt and I didn't even see how bad. I heard you scream, or Yolanda. Will you do that for Sid? I've taken care of one of them, so you'll find him quite helpless. Go on."

Like a docile, obedient child, Sally did Sid's bidding, and Sid went slowly around the corner to find the bastards doing Bill Peel's dirty work.

As Sid had picked up the scent of a foreboding danger, Danton had too. When he came out of the hotel and checked with the desk clerk to see if Kristina had been there, he smelled the smoke before he spotted it billowing up into the dark night sky. He leaped atop the huge black horse he'd borrowed from the Hamilton stables and rode like a madman the short distance to the Crystal Castle.

No crowd had begun to gather yet so Danton reined the gelding into the alleyway.

Sally O'Neal sat with old Rollo cradled in her arms like a baby, and Danton saw the sprawled figure of the fatally wounded man, who, Sally quickly informed him, was a rascal named Peel. She told him that Sid was inside stalking two more men.

"Is Kit—Kristina—in there?" Danton barked.

About that time, Sid came out the door with a weeping, hysterical Yolanda in his arms. "She is, and this little wildcat was ready to run up those stairs to try to rescue her. It's a goddamn raging inferno all the way up those steps, mister. Hell, I couldn't make it!"

"I can! Is there a rope?" Danton asked.

Sid told him to look in the little store room just inside the back door. Danton dashed to get it while the trio waiting outside the back door wondered how a rope was going to help get him to the second landing.

"Is there anything I can do to help?" Sid wanted to know.

"You get Rollo and the girls out of here and I'll get Kristina," Danton told him. The look in his fathomless black eyes told them all that he'd get her or he'd die with her.

He saw immediately what Sid was talking about when he got inside the archway. He prayed that his skills as a roper wouldn't fail him for it was the massive round-headed post he intended to lasso so he could climb up the rope to get to the second floor. His only hope was that the column was strong enough to hold his weight.

He wasted not a minute, whirling the rope above his head and making a powerful flinging motion to hit the target he aimed for.

Leaving the rope hugging the post, he dashed down the hallway and slammed through the double heavy oak doors. He heard her coughing and rushed in that direction.

He found her crumpled on the thick, lush carpet, looking very much like the same little waif he'd found that day in the mountains. This time her lovely well-formed body was completely naked. It was obvious she'd attempted to get out of her tub and find a towel to cover herself. Her skin was damp as were the edges of her hair, but her eyes looked up at him, dazed and frightened. "Danton? Danton?"

Her voice was weak and cracking and she couldn't seem to tell him everything she wanted to say. Danton was consumed by panic that he'd got to her too late. He gathered her up in his arms and murmured softly, "Yes, *querida*. It's Danton and I'm getting you out of here."

He flung the towel aside which half-draped her naked body and bent to yank furiously at the bed sheet. With her cradled protectively in his arms, he awkwardly tried to drape her with the sheet and rush for the door.

He carried her until they reached the far side of the landing, which was situated at the farthest point from the burning, flaming stairway. But the lapping flames moved closer with each fleeting second. He set her on her feet to secure the loop of the rope around the adjacent posts. He was going down that rope with precious cargo and he wanted to take every precaution possible.

"Now, *querida,* I want you to take a piggyback ride with me down this rope and I want you to hold tight. It's the only way we can get out of here, honey. You understand what I'm saying?"

Her eyes were excitedly bright, and she merely nodded her head as she positioned herself next to his back and clasped her arms around his neck. He took her clenched hands up to his lips and murmured softly, *Mi vida, Kristina mía."*

He straddled the railing, holding fast and firm to the rope. She was nothing on his back. Her petite figure was as light as a feather, but he held his breath that the posts would hold. Halfway down he heard her gasp and tense as she moaned, "Oh, I've got to get my kitten."

"The hell you say! I wouldn't go back up there for anything or anyone but you. Darling, we're going one way—down!"

Now, he felt her sobbing against his back, heard little sniffling sounds. "I loved Amigo, Danton."

He was about to jump the remaining distance, and his taut hands released the rope. They landed with a jarring thud, but his booted feet were safely on the

floor. Swiftly, he turned her around to face him, an
without hesitating he swooped her up and rushed ou
into the night.

Only when they were breathing air free of smoke, di
he tell her, "I admit I like old Amigo myself. He's m
amigo too, from the way he was sleeping in my bed th
last time I saw him." He had a crooked grin on hi
smudged face. His hands tenderly draped the shee
more securely around her, and then he swept away th
rumpled curls from her face.

"Sleeping . . . in your bed? I . . . I . . ."

He gave out a deep, husky laugh as he swung her u
onto the black gelding and mounted behind her. "I
you're a real good girl, you'll see for yourself and I'll te
you how it happened."

They rode the black gelding down the El Paso stree
now coming alive with the curiosity seekers gatherin
from all directions.

She snuggled against him, and in his firm, muscle
arms she felt safe. Not only was Amigo in his room, sh
would soon be there too. Nothing else mattered to her
she realized. How she could ever have doubted Danto
Navarro's love, she'd never know. After tonight, i
would never happen again.

When he reined up on the gelding at the side entranc
of his hotel and leaped down to the ground, his hand
reached up to her. She took them, glancing bac
toward the Crystal Castle to see the fire glowing now i
the sky.

That didn't matter to her now, and she stared dow
at Danton for a minute before acceding to his urging t
dismount. Love was the fire in her eyes, and Danto
saw it there. But nothing could have made him happie
than when she said so convincingly, "I love you
Danton Navarro. I love you with all my heart."

"I've known that for a long, long time, my little Kit,

e told her with a warm mellow look on his face.

Suddenly, he realized that passers-by were ogling the ight of a sheet-draped lady standing in the street, and e light-heartedly suggested that they get to his room. We don't want to be arrested for indecent exposure. esides, old Amigo might be getting lonely."

When he had her safely secured in the stairway, he xcused himself so he could speak to the desk clerk efore joining Kristina on the steps.

When they were in Danton's room and she saw the ilvery fluffy kitten on Danton's bed, Kristina laughed. He obviously does like your bed."

Danton had waited as long as he could to really hold er in his arms and kiss her sweet lips as he ached to do. A wicked gleam came into his black eyes as he strode lowly toward her. "So will you, *chiquita*."

She sought to taunt him just a little by turning from Amigo with the sheet tucked alluringly around her. Are you sure, Danton?" she remarked. Swiftly, she urned her back to him and added, "Tell me, Danton vhen I said I loved you down there in the street a noment ago you said you'd known it a long, long time. When?"

An amused smile played on Danton's face and with n easy, swift move of his hand, he turned her to face iim. His finger gave a simple flick, freeing her of the heet and tossing it onto the floor. "When those green yes of yours peered through the railing we escaped by onight, when you saw me below with a blonde and you vished it was you in her place. When I looked up and aw you, I thought to myself you were the loveliest ingel I'd ever seen. A little young for me, I thought, so 'll let her grow up. Now, *chiquita*—now you're all grown-up." His mouth captured hers in a kiss that :onfirmed his statement. Kristina arched her naked 100dy against his in a way that left no doubt she was all

487

woman. Danton's hands touched and caressed th
pulsing mounds of her breasts which pressed agains
his chest and she moaned softly.

"Oh, Danton . . . Danton, it is true. I did fall in lov
with you that night."

"I know. I felt the same way, *querida*," he huskil
told her as he drew away just enough to rid himself o
his clothes. His hunger for her was now unbearable

This night was going to be theirs, he'd seen to it b
giving the desk clerk a hefty sum to carry the message
to all who might attempt to disturb them. Sid and th
girls were to be informed of their safe escape, and wor
was to be taken to Florine, who was awaiting news o
Kristina at the ranch.

He stood now as bare as she, and he let her eyes savo
the sight of him. After a moment or two, he enticed he
to him. "Come to me, little kitten. See if you like m
bed." She smiled and sauntered over to join him there
He did not hesitate to show her the pleasure he coul
give her, his strong will exerting restraint so she migh
know his touch completely. His lips made her feel tha
a giant flame was devouring her flesh as her swaying
undulating body responded to the wild sensations h
stirred.

Danton felt like a man intoxicated as his nose nestle
in the softness of Kit's thick, long hair and he smelle
the sweet fragrance of her. The nearness of her was
divine madness, and he wondered privately if she wa
aware of that as she swayed so invitingly against him
tempting him with that silken flesh of hers. But then, h
knew this petite woman could change quickly befor
his very eyes from a helpless, innocent into a mos
ravishing seductress.

Which was she right now? he wondered. His blac
eyes glinted as his hand snaked out to enclose her wais
and she giggled. But Danton was not to be denied an

he commanded, "Come here, you little devil!"

She could have been a feather blowing in the night breeze as Danton effortlessly pulled her atop him. He felt himself swelling as her smooth, satinlike thighs enclosed the sides of his firm ones. "I want you to love me, *chiquita*. I want that something fierce," he murmured huskily.

Feeling so happy just to be with him, she dared to tease the man lying beneath her by swaying suggestively and raising a skeptical eyebrow as she asked, "Something fierce, eh?"

But Danton ached too harshly for any foolhardy delay; his two hands lifted her just so to impale her on his throbbing manhood and she gasped with abandoned delight.

"Is it not fierce?" he laughed, undulating sensuously and raising his head up just enough to tease the pulsing tip of one of her breasts. She moved to the beat he set, in perfect harmony with him. Her lips caressed his cheek and she whispered softly in his ear, "You make me feel so very wicked, Danton."

"I certainly try, because you are so very exciting when you're wicked," he declared. The liquid fire of their bodies mounted, becoming a blaze as raging as the roaring fire that devoured the Crystal Castle.

Their passion mounted steadily and each felt the throbbing of their hearts and the jagged intakes of breath as their wild excitement reached the point of ultimate fulfillment. Nothing could delay it any longer, but Danton muttered a curse word for he wanted to linger in their private paradise longer when he felt himself give forth with a mighty quake. In the same instant, Kit shuddered and collapsed exhaustedly on his broad chest.

Such fierce ecstasy was theirs! But they lay now, contented and still. They saw the glowing sky in the black of the night outside the window. The smoldering embers of the Crystal Castle kept it alight.

Kristina was the first one to break the sublime quietness of the room. "You'll have to marry me now, Danton Navarro, or I'll be labeled a shameless hussy."

Danton gave a deep, throaty laugh, "I've already asked your mother's permission to marry you this very afternoon, *querida mia.*"

"You . . . you did, Danton?" she stammered, slowly raising up in the bed with a pleased smile coming on her lovely face.

"Oh, yes. It seems our families both approve very much of you and me getting married. But then, my little kitten, it is very easy to understand why two mothers who were very good friends a long time ago before you or I were born would be elated about their two offspring marrying."

"Our mothers? Friends, Danton?"

"That's right! They both worked at the Palace Gambling Hall in San Antonio when they were young women."

Kristina gasped with disbelief, "You're telling me that Señora Lucía worked in a gambling hall, Danton Navarro?"

"My mother was the famous Lolita, the best damned faro dealer the Palace ever had and your mother was taught faro by my mother."

Kristina threw her pretty head back and broke into a frenzy of giggling. "Guess that makes us two of a kind, doesn't it Danton?"

"That makes us *perfecto, chiquita!*" he declared, pulling her into his arms and drawing her close to his chest.

Passion's flames fired anew.

Epilogue

The devastating tragedy of the fire which left the Crystal Castle in ashes had an astonishing effect on Florine Whelan Hamilton; it forced her to break with the past. When she did so, Jason Hamilton was granted his fervent desire that she be completely content just to be his wife.

The most enjoyable compensations for Florine were the visits of Danton's and Kristina's twin boys to the Hamilton ranch. Little Vincent and Victor proved to be challenging, cunning little imps, as clever as their father and as determined as their mother.

Another wonderful compensation was her reunion with Lucía Navarro. The two old friends shared endless hours of conversation, singing the praises for their two grandsons.

When the very respected, popular senator from Texas and his beautiful auburn-haired lady, Kristina, made their regular trips to the capital and stayed for weeks, they had no problem about where to leave their sons. When they were in Washington, the young couple was always on guest lists and their presence was requested constantly. No lady received more raves than the ravishingly beautiful Kristina Navarro. The other senators' wives could not resist admiringly staring at the tall, dark handsome Texan with his Latin good looks and charming personality.

When Lucía or Florine weren't vying for little Vincent and Victor, there were always the devoted Yolanda and Abeja, who resided at Whispering Willows with their own brood of three little daughters.

Kristina could not have been happier than when her little friend, Yolanda, and Danton's devoted Abeja had first laid eyes on one another and it was love at first sight. Kristina was grateful that Yolanda's nights were not spent in solitude like her beloved Solitaire. She never wanted that for the little Mexican. Yolanda's marriage to Abeja was a happy one.

Life had been good to her, Kristina had to admit—and to those she loved so dearly. She loved the exhilarating excitement and social flurry their life took on when they were in the capital, but she anticipated those times when they were to leave for that serenity of the Texas countryside and their haven beside the Pedernales River, for their meadows of wildflowers and live oaks.

She enjoyed the best of her two worlds. Now, she suspected a new little Texan might be coming. When she told her delighted husband about the possibility, her green eyes prodded his as she questioned him, "It—it couldn't happen twice, could it, Danton?"

"What, *chiquita?* What happen twice?"

"Twins, Danton! Another set of twins! I was told they happen every other generation, but Victor and Vincent are proof that's not true."

Danton exploded with laughter, "My little kitten, I told you a long time ago that we were *perfecto!*" He lifted her petite body up so his lips could capture hers in a long lingering kiss.

And the flame still glowed as bright as ever!

492

If you enjoyed this book we have a special offer for you. Become a charter member of the ZEBRA HISTORICAL ROMANCE HOME SUBSCRIPTION SERVICE and…

Get a
FREE
Zebra Historical Romance
(A $3.95 value) No Obligation

Now that you have read a Zebra Historical Romance we're sure you'll want more of the passion and sensuality, the desire and dreams and fascinating historical settings that make these novels the favorites of so many women. So we have made arrangements for you to receive a *FREE* book ($3.95 value) and preview 4 brand new Zebra Historical Romances each month.

Join the Zebra
Home Subscription Service—
Free Home Delivery

By joining our Home Subscription Service you'll never have to worry about missing a title. You'll automatically get the romance, the allure, the attraction, that make Zebra Historical Romances so special.

Each month you'll receive 4 brand new Zebra Historical Romance novels as soon as they are published. Look them over *Free* for 10 days. If you're not delighted simply return them and owe nothing. But if you enjoy them as much as we think you will, you'll pay *only* $3.50 each and save 45¢ over the cover price. (You save a total of $1.80 each month.) *There is no shipping and handling charge or other hidden charges.*

—— *Fill Out the Coupon* ——

Start your subscription now and start saving. Fill out the coupon and mail it *today*. You'll get your FREE book along with your first month's books to preview.